Her
Man

**He is strong, passionate and *very*
interested in one woman…**

**So how long can Rose and Tess deny
their men *and* their own desires?**

*Two provocative, tempting stories from
Cait London and Fayrene Preston*

Dear Reader,

Here's to a red-hot month with Desire!

This month we have **Her Ideal Man** containing *A Loving Man* by Cait London and *The Barons of Texas: Tess* by Fayrene Preston. The latter is the first story in an inspired trilogy called THE BARONS OF TEXAS by Fayrene Preston which follows the three Baron sisters as they discover how wonderful love can be. Jill's story is available next month.

We all have a few secrets and our **Secret Child** collection demonstrates this. It includes the second story in the intensely popular BACHELOR BATTALION series—*His Baby!* by Maureen Child—and starts a new sheikh trilogy by Alexandra Sellers. *The Sultan's Heir* is the first scorching story of THE SULTANS and the next book, *Undercover Sultan*, is out in July.

Of course, everyone loves reading about those steamy work relationships and in **Business or Pleasure?** two couples show us how much fun it can be to be in love with the boss! That's *The American Earl* by Kathryn Jensen and *Beauty in His Bedroom* by Ashley Summers.

Happy reading!

The Editors

Her Ideal Man

CAIT LONDON
FAYRENE PRESTON

*Silhouette, Silhouette Desire and Colophon
are registered trademarks of Harlequin Books S.A.,
used under licence.*

*First published in Great Britain 2002
Silhouette Books, Eton House, 18-24 Paradise Road,
Richmond, Surrey TW9 1SR*

HER IDEAL MAN © Harlequin Books S.A. 2002

The publisher acknowledges the copyright holders of the
individual works as follows:

A Loving Man © Lois Kleinsasser 2001
The Barons of Texas: Tess © Fayrene Preston 1999

ISBN 0 373 04751 7

51-0602

*Printed and bound in Spain
by Litografia Rosés S.A., Barcelona*

A LOVING MAN

by
Cait London

CAIT LONDON

lives in the Missouri Ozarks but loves to travel the
Northwest's gold rush/cattle drive trails every summer.
She enjoys research trips, meeting people and going to
Native American dances. Cait is an avid reader who
loves to paint, play with computers and grow herbs
(particularly scented geraniums). She's a national best-
selling and award-winning author, and she has also
written historical romances under another pseudonym.
Three is her lucky number; she has three daughters,
and the events in her life have always been in threes. 'I
love writing for Silhouette,' Cait says. 'One of the best
perks about all this hard work is the thrilling reader
response and the warm, snug sense that I have given
readers an enjoyable, entertaining gift.'

One

"**Y**ou're old-fashioned and don't know what it is to be young." His daughter's words raked Stefan Donatien; their argument of the early morning still scalded him. "You can't keep me as a child forever," Estelle had said furiously.

Brooding about her temper, a match to his own, Stefan had escaped the farmhouse he had just purchased. His mission into Waterville, a small Midwestern town, provided a time in which to recover and reshape his defenses. His mother, Yvette, often agreed with Estelle. A man alone against a volatile, twenty-year-old daughter, and his French mother, Stefan often had to find "caves" into which to retreat. They loved him, and he returned that love, but his women could be difficult at times, united against him.

Though he was born in the United States, his daughter and French-born mother, Yvette, often accused him of being "old-world." "Perhaps if you had a lover, you would not be so obsessed with keeping Estelle a child," his mother had stated. "You may have buried your heart with your wife, Claire, but you did not bury your life. At your age, I was already a *grandmère* and I did not stop living when your father passed on. You are only forty-two, and yet you are old before your time. See there? A gray hair."

Stefan inhaled the early May air and tried to settle his raw nerves, raked by the formidable women he loved deeply. They might see him as an overbearing tyrant, but every instinct he possessed told him to protect them.

He listened to the rumbling of the old pickup's engine as he cruised into Waterville. The ancient farm pickup suited the rural Missouri town much better than the luxury car he'd used in Chicago. The small community, wedged amid the surrounding farms and rolling green mountains, was the perfect place in which to protect his daughter from Louie, alias The Freeloader.

Stefan scowled at the truck's rearview mirror and at his right temple; his single gray hair gleamed, mocking him. In many ways, he felt as battered as the pickup that came with the Smith's farm. It was only a matter of time before Louie took Estelle as a lover. To avoid that, Stefan had decided to give his daughter the one thing she'd always wanted—the experience of living in a small, Midwestern American town.

Stefan's old pickup prowled by Waterville's vegetable gardens lined with new green plants. Heavy with morning dew, pink and white peonies leaned against the picket fences and shade trees bordered the streets. A yellow school bus stopped to pick up children clustered on the sidewalk. Seated on their porch swings, women with curlers in their gray hair whispered about the new owner of the Smith farm as he passed. A widower with a slight

accent, a beautiful twenty-year-old daughter and an enchanting, happy French mother was certain to be noticed.

It was only the third day since Stefan had moved his
family to the rural community. With the exception of
clashing with him over Estelle's adult status, they seemed
happy. It wasn't easy uprooting his family and moving
them to the safety of the small town. But then Stefan was
a powerful businessman who knew how to make decisions,
especially when his daughter was endangered. As soon as
Estelle's college finals were over, Stefan had put his plan
to protect his daughter into motion. A trusted friend and
employee now managed the restaurant line that Stefan's
father had begun, Donatien's French Cuisine Restaurants.

*His father, Guy, would have dealt harshly with Estelle,
just as he had with his boy, Stefan, demanding perfection
and obedience.*

Stefan smiled tightly, remembering his father and better
understanding the fear that sometimes ruled a parent. Guy
had wanted the best for Stefan, just as Stefan wanted the
best for Estelle.

He inhaled abruptly. *Though he loved his father, he did
not favor Guy's strict parental control and too high standards. Stefan had promised himself not to be so exacting
and controlling with his daughter. He wasn't happy that
his protective-father-mode sometimes erupted into just
that—"I forbid you" sounded exactly like his father.* His
headache started to throb in rhythm to the rumble of the
old vehicle's engine.

A horde of young boys on bicycles soared past him, and
Stefan braked slowly. Beneath the ball caps turned backward on their heads, their expressions were wary and curious of the new stranger. Even the dog, running at their
side, noted Stefan's presence with excited barking.

At least Estelle was safe for the moment, her insolent, lazy boyfriend in Chicago.

Stefan's hands tightened on the old steering wheel as he heard his snarl. With long dirty hair and baggy pants, Louie had already started asking for handouts from Stefan. Louie had made it clear that he would not lower himself to work in the renowned Donatien Restaurants. Estelle was like her mother at that age: innocent and trusting, and she did not notice Louie's gaze stripping other girls, or his flirtation. Stefan recognized the look of lust, though he had been celibate since the death of his wife ten years ago.

Stefan rolled his taut shoulders as he parked in front of Granger's Wallpaper and Paint store. He had the summer until his daughter went back to college; Louie was certain to be unfaithful and Estelle would be protected.

He stepped from the pickup, and glanced down at his unfamiliar clothing—jeans, a T-shirt and worn jogging shoes. At this time of day in Chicago, he would be dressed in a suit, busy in his office. Later on, he would dismiss his jacket and vest and roll up his sleeves, put on an apron and enjoy cooking in a Donatien kitchen. He couldn't wait for the fresh herb starts that he had ordered to arrive; soon only the best fresh farm eggs, milk and butter would go into his omelettes, a dash of chopped chives, a sprinkle of—

Stefan inhaled the fresh morning air, studied the small neat town with its shops opening for customers. His mother and daughter weren't the only ones looking forward to life in Waterville; he planned to enjoy puttering on the farm. He smiled, enjoying the sunshine. His women were happy, nestling into the farmhouse, decorating it, and in his pocket were the paint samples his mother had chosen on her two-mile bicycle ride to town. Busy with the plumbing, Stefan had enjoyed exploring the tools the

Smiths had left behind. A man who had never had a vacation, he intended to relax in this interlude while Estelle came to her senses. Life was good...without Louie.

He entered the busy paint store, prepared to wait his turn as other customers milled around the cash register. A tall woman, wearing a baseball cap with her auburn ponytail thrust through the hole at the back, glanced at him. She hefted a gallon of paint onto the counter, slapped two wooden paint stirrers on it, rang up the bill and chatted with the customer. When the burly farmer, dressed in bib overalls, rambled out of the store, the woman scowled at Stefan. Clearly in charge of the store, the woman behind the counter wore a T-shirt that said Waterville Tigers. She was possibly in her early thirties, with soaring eyebrows, clear blue eyes, a bit of a nose and a generous mouth. Freckles covered every centimeter of her fair skin. She tapped costs into the cash register for more paint and nodded at Stefan, indicating the gallons of paint on the counter. He shook his head, not understanding her needs. With a doomed look up at the ceiling, the woman grabbed one gallon and tucked it under her arm. She eased the other into her free arm and tromped out of the store, following the elderly woman.

Stefan noted and appreciated the length of the younger woman's legs, the cutoff shorts cupping a trim, swaying bottom. The wooden paint stirrer sticks in her back pocket enhanced the movement. He was surprised that he had tilted his head to better appreciate that little feminine jiggle of flesh at her backside. She walked back into the store, strode to him and shook her head as Stefan noted the slant of her eyes, those strong cheekbones gleaming in the overhead light. The drop of cobalt-blue paint on her cheeks matched the color of her eyes as they burned up at him. The shadows beneath her eyes said she had missed sleep

and the area around her mouth was pale, demonstrating
her strain.

She reached to tug away the two bits of toilet paper on
his jaw. He had been unwise to shave after the furious
argument with his daughter; the small cuts marked his broken promise to remain calm. A man who spared little time
on women of moods, except his daughter and his mother,
Stefan firmed his lips. He was determined not to let this
woman ruin his day. Then she said, "I know you can't
talk—you're the cousin that Ned Whitehouse told me
needed work. I told him to have you turn up and work,
helping me. Well, that's what you should be doing—helping. You could have carried out that paint for Mrs. Mariah.
Come on. Follow me."

She moved through the displays of paint and carpeting
toward the back room, behind the checkout counter. Unused to taking orders, Stefan stood still and crossed his
arms.

The woman continued talking—"I want you to clean up
the storeroom and then fix that back door—it's almost
coming off the hinges. One good yank and hell-o—free
paint for everyone. Not that anyone in Waterville steals,
but a good business should have a good back door, don't
you agree?"

Stefan thought of the alarm systems and locks he'd required on all Donatien restaurant back doors, ones made
of sturdy metal, and nodded.

When she noted that he had not followed her, she turned
and those arching fine eyebrows drew into a stern frown.
She walked back to him, her hands on her hips. Stefan
tried not to notice the T-shirt that had tightened across her
breasts. They were just the size of medium cooking apples,
not too big or too small, but just perfect.

Stefan frowned, unprepared for the turn of his thoughts.

He did not usually compare women to his favorite pastimes—choosing fine foods, preparing and enjoying them.

In his mind, he compared her height to his, how she would fit against him. The top of her head would just come to his chin. Those breasts would press against his chest and those long legs would—

She crossed her arms and tapped her running shoe on the floor. "I know you can hear. Ned told me so. He also said that sometimes you can be stubborn as his mules. Well, today isn't one of them, got that? I haven't got time for this, so get your butt in gear and start helping me. Saturdays are usually busy, but nothing like spring and fall. I've been running shorthanded during the busiest season of the year and everyone wants to paint every room in the kingdom. Not that I'm objecting to the sales, which aren't good except for spring and fall, but *I could use some help*," she stated meaningfully.

Then shaking her head, she said very carefully as if to make him understand better, "Okay. I'll up the hourly wage and pay overtime. If you don't help me, I don't know what I'll do."

She placed her hands on her ball cap as if holding her head together. Her hands were feminine, yet strong, with short nails spotted with paint. Stefan tried not to smile; if he were in a business argument with power titans, he would have known that he had the upper hand at her concession. On the other hand, he was enjoying the masquerade—no one had ever mistaken him for a laborer. The scenario into which he had dropped amused him. Clearly this woman was under pressure and it appealed to him to rescue her. He decided not to speak, because his slight accent would surely mark him as the newcomer in Waterville. He wondered what it would be like, not to be Stefan Donatien, powerful restaurateur, rather to be an ordinary workman for a day. He had found his "cave" away from the brooding women he loved.

She looked up at him. "My name is Rose and yours is Bruce, and we'll get along fine, if you just do what I tell you to do. It's Saturday and the whole town is set to buy paint, wallpaper and carpet and I need you. Not that I don't appreciate the business. I'll even buy lunch—hot dogs and potato salad with lemonade from Danny's Café, and all the coffee you can drink... Just don't use my cup. Lyle and Joe are out laying carpet, but you can meet them later. Everyone here works part-time, but me. Did you come to work or not?"

Stefan nodded slowly, though her choice of food turned his stomach, and in seconds they were in the back room where she was pointing and ordering like a general. "Sturdy up those shelves, separate the paints—oil and latex based...interior and exterior—fix the back door, and if I call you, come up front. Ned said you had your own pickup and could deliver and you may have to. I'll draw a map for you, but just don't go anywhere. Don't leave me. I've got enough problems with Dad."

He wondered about "Dad" as she turned and hurried into a small cluttered office. The bell over the store's front door jingled and she hurried to help the customer who had just entered.

Rose plopped into her desk chair, slipped her foot out of her worn running shoe and rubbed it. She was too tired from processing the store invoices until midnight, then going home to heaps of laundry. She'd missed her early-morning run, tossing her pillow over her alarm. But at seven o'clock she was making her father the bacon and egg breakfast he liked and by eight, she had opened the store. Rose frowned slightly; Maury rarely came to work, even on the busiest days. Her father hadn't stopped mourn-ing his runaway wife and now a whiskey bottle came too readily to his hand. He'd taught Rose the business and lately he almost never asked about it. He was slipping away from her and life, spending long hours staring out from the house porch at the rose garden his wife had loved.

Maxine Granger had not loved her family enough to stay and raise her daughter, or to deny the passing trucker. He offered her excitement and in time, the world, and Maxine hadn't hesitated.

When she was ten, Rose had come home from school to find her father crying, Maxine's goodbye note in his hand. For a few years, there were hurried postcards from all over the world and then nothing. It had taken Rose years to understand that she wasn't the reason why her mother left in that big diesel truck and why her father's heart remained broken. As a child, she'd sat for hours at her mother's vanity table, littered with polishes, creams and an expensive brush for her blond hair. Rose had tried to forget the pain, but she couldn't. Instead she pasted that heartbreak into a locked chest marked The Past and threw herself into helping her father at the store and at home. In her young mind, when the ache came upon her, she raised her arms to the moon and asked for faeries to love and cherish her. It eased Rose-the-child to fantasize she was being held and kissed and loved by the whimsical creatures who would never leave her alone. Then, at times, the pain curled around her and sucked her back, but she fought her way out by keeping busy and thinking of the faeries that waited for her.

She was thirty-seven now, and twelve years ago her mother had passed away in a flaming truck wreck on the Interstate. Her trucker-lover had sent Rose what little was left of Maxine Granger's life. The shoe box of trinkets included a picture of six-year-old Rose, just missing her front tooth.

Rose had little illusions about her chances for a one-and-only love. Back in the days when she believed in romance and happily-ever-after, Rose had thought her future husband and children would fill her father's aching heart. But love hadn't come to her, and she'd settled into the routine of living with her father, tending him, in the house she'd grown up in.

She rubbed the bruise on her thigh, the result of swinging a paint can from the counter to the floor. Ned's cousin had been working for an hour in the back room, straightening the gallon and pint cans on the floor. Now he was hefting the odd remnants of carpeting to stand along one side of the wall. He'd towered over her five-foot ten, looking all dark and scowling. There was an arrogance she couldn't place, just that tilt of his head, that black waving hair gleaming and neatly combed. His deep brown eyes were the color of her father's whiskey, narrowing and darkening as she talked to him. That line between his black brows and the grooves beside his mouth had deepened as if he didn't like taking orders—or smiling. His jaw had tensed, the muscle running along it contracting.

She frowned, glancing at him as he easily lifted a box of old carpet samples up to his shoulder—a very broad shoulder. Ned was right; his cousin was "strong as an ox and a bit moody." He seemed to bristle each time she gave him a task, those whiskey-brown eyes narrowing on her, his jaw tensing.

Then Rose saw Henry, who she had held down and kissed when they were both in the fourth grade. When she'd shared her faerie whimsy with him, he'd laughed, later apologized. He understood Rose's pain and through the years had become a good friend.

She hurried toward the adult Henry, stood on tiptoe and kissed his cheek. In turn, he reached to turn her ball cap around, tugging it down on her head. She grinned up at him, a longtime friend and an ex-fiancé, now married to Shirley MacNeil. Rose could always depend on Henry to make her feel better—good old dependable Henry. "New man?" Henry asked as he handed her Shirley's paint list.

"Bruce. Ned's cousin. He's only helping out during the spring decorating season. He's got a surly attitude and if that doesn't stop, he's out of here."

"Maybe he doesn't like bossy women. Try a little patience," Henry offered with a warm, familiar smile.

"No time. Dad didn't place the orders or check the invoices and now I've got to do it."

"Is he feeling poorly?" Henry asked in his kind way. Everyone in Waterville knew that Maury Granger's visits to the liquor store were becoming more frequent.

"Sure," Rose returned curtly. Instead of the usual truck delivery of paints and orders, she'd had to borrow a truck and drive one hundred miles to a manufacturer, pay over price and drive home, unloading the truck herself last Sunday. This Sunday she intended to pamper herself and firmly deal with Maury. He was a good man, but he was sinking deeper into darkness.

By noon, the new handyman had fixed the back door and was straightening the front of the store. He seemed happy until she called him into the back room for lunch, takeout food from Danny's Café, hot dogs and potato salad. With her feet propped up on the gallons of uncolored paint, and balancing her food on her stomach, she frowned as he prodded the wiener with his finger and sniffed at the bun. He scowled at the food, which nettled Rose, but then she badly needed his help and couldn't risk offending him over hot dogs. He frowned when he sipped at the coffee she'd brewed early that morning. Rose inhaled slowly and pushed her temper down; maybe Henry was right, maybe she needed to try a little kindness. "So, Bruce, do you think you might want to move up to mixing paint? It's a matter of checking the color number chart, measuring the pigment and mixing it into the uncolored gallons."

He nodded slowly, considering her with those unreadable brown eyes. Just then Larry Hershall strolled into the store, peered over a carpet display and sighted her in the back room. She waved him toward her. "How's it going, Larry?" she asked her former fiancé.

Larry nodded and grinned. "Mary Lou wants me to see that wallpaper sample she picked out for the nursery."

"Sure. Meet Bruce. He's helping me out today. He's about to move up to mixing paint."

Larry reached to shake the workman's hand and nodded. "Glad to meet you."

Ned's cousin nodded, his dark eyes following Rose and Larry as they moved to the front of the store. As comfortable with Larry as she would be with the brother she never had, Rose showed him the wallpaper sample. Standing beside him, she placed her arm on his shoulder, leaning slightly against his strength for just one moment in a hectic, tiring day.

When she returned to the back room, Ned's cousin was pouring the rest of the coffee down the paint-stained sink. His food remained untouched on the rough plank picnic table. Rose was starved, and disliking waste, asked, "Going to eat this?"

When he shook his head, she slathered mustard, relish and ketchup onto the hot dog. Rose had balanced a household budget from an early age and did not waste food.

"Yummy," she said when he watched her devour the hot dog.

She didn't want to ask about his disdainful expression. He was a good workman and she desperately needed him. If she could manage to establish a basic relationship with him, he might stay to help her. "So, Bruce. Let's put in a hard day here—I'll move you up to mixing paint—and then if you'd like, you can come fishing with my dad and me. Crappie start biting at the lake just after supper. You might even catch a bass. What do you say?"

He nodded slowly just as the bell over the front door jingled. The delightful Frenchwoman who had come in the previous day smiled warmly over the displays. Rose, followed closely by her new handyman, went to help the customer.

"Ma chérie," Yvette Donatien said smoothly with that enticing accent. Her blond-and-gray hair softly framed an exquisite face, shaded by a floppy straw hat. A simple cotton dress swirled around Yvette's rounded body, emphasizing her femininity just like the spring daisies tucked into her hat ribbon. She carried a shopping basket made of oak strips. The basket had been made locally by Linda Brooks and fit perfectly into the metal one on Yvette's bicycle. Rose had instantly liked the charming Frenchwoman with her ready smile and humor.

Yvette smiled warmly at the man behind Rose, and then momentarily a puzzled expression crossed her face. Tracing Yvette's stare, Rose looked up swiftly to see the handyman stroking his index finger across his raised brows. His expression was bland and innocent. "Oh, that's Bruce," Rose said. "He's new. He's a good worker and he's about to graduate to paint mixing."

"I see," Yvette said, glancing at the man again and then back at Rose. Her blue eyes twinkled as she smiled warmly. ''I stopped by to say how much I enjoyed our visit yesterday. My son will be stopping by soon. I hope you like him. He can be very formal and arrogant at times, perhaps a little old-world in his ways—stuffy, if you will. But he is a good boy. He tries very hard to be a good *papa,* though he sometimes does not understand women. I'll be going now. I'm so enjoying your delightful community.''

Yvette frowned slightly at the man behind Rose, who sensed the restlessness in him. She hoped that he wouldn't show his poor manners to a potentially good customer and a woman she liked immediately. After Yvette exited the store, Rose shot an elbow back into her employee's hard stomach. He grunted and when she turned, his scowl was fierce upon her. ''Listen, you,'' she said. ''You're going to have to put on a nice face for customers. It may be hard, but try. I could almost feel you bristling behind me. I've already heard that Stefan Donatien is a hard case, but his mother is very nice and I like her.''

She ignored the flaring of his nostrils, the tightening of his mouth. A woman who related easily to men, she wasn't intimidated. Perhaps the handyman had been bruised by life, or had a serious health problem. She was very good at getting men to relate to her; once she understood his problem, perhaps they could develop a smooth working relationship. She decided to push right past his bad mood before she fired a man she badly needed. ''Are you going fishing with us tonight, or not?''

He nodded grimly, his big body rigid. Waves of temper poured off him, and she had no time for dealing with that. ''Well, let's start you on paint mixing then. It's all done by formula. Here's the chart of the amounts of dry powder that you mix into the basic formula. You use this—'' she held up a rubber mallet ''—to close it and shake—'' She indicated a machine. "Make certain you seal it and clamp it good, because it's a big mess for you to clean up, if you don't. Oh, stop sulking and scowling. You'll scare away my customers. You really need to lighten up, Bruce."

By three o'clock, Rose craved a refreshing nap that she wasn't going to get. Business was really good, and her new handyman was efficient at mixing paint. Though he didn't speak, he seemed to be making an effort to be charming, smiling at the customers. He wasn't that hard looking when he smiled and the women seemed to like him, discussing their decorator plans with him and considering his pointing finger on the samples. In fact, he had made several good sales, selling the carpet remnants from past years. He carried purchases out for customers and Rose decided to trust him with making a delivery to Ella Parsons. "Hey, Bruce. Here's the map to Ella Parsons. She lives a distance out in the country, so try to help her with whatever she needs doing and get back here to help me close up, okay?"

He took the map she had drawn, folded it neatly and slid it into his back pocket. He crossed his arms and considered her intently. His dark gaze roamed her face, her throat and slowly moved down her body. That close examination caused Rose to shiver. Ned's cousin didn't need words to express a male attraction to her. She flipped over the thought; perhaps he was just shy and looking for a friend. She knew how to be a man's friend, if not his love.

In the next minute, a rush of customers consumed her. Her new employee efficiently mixed paint and when the rush slowed, loaded Granger's delivery truck. Alone and tending the customers, Rose worked furiously. During spring and fall seasonal rushes, every minute counted.

Just minutes from closing time, a thin, clean, but poorly dressed young man entered the store. When she went to help him, he signed with his hands. Not understanding his meaning, Rose offered him a pad and pencil.

"I'm Bruce Long, Ned's cousin," he wrote. "Woke up feeling bad. Had car trouble. Sorry to be late."

Rose stood absolutely still, her mind replaying the day's scenarios. Whoever the stranger was who had worked all day, he wasn't Bruce. "Come back early Monday, okay?" she asked, hurriedly pushing him out of the door.

She rushed to the telephone beside the cash register and dialed Ella Parsons. The man she had mistaken for Bruce Long could be a murderer, a thief, and she'd sent him directly to a dear elderly woman. Fear tore through Rose as she worried about Ella's safety. "Ella? Did you get your delivery?"

"I did, dear. Everything is in perfect order, and so is that nice Mr. Donatien. We had the nicest chat. He cooked a lovely dinner for Edward and me, and we dined together. He's coming back with his mother in the morning for fresh eggs and milk. She wants some good cream cows and my Edward is going to help find someone with cows to spare. I love a man who treats his mother well like Mr. Donatien. He clearly loves her and his daughter. Not every man would give up a fancy business office and a secretary waiting on his every command to give his family the country life they want. He's on his way back to your store now, I think. Lovely man, Mr. Donatien."

"Oh, he is, is he?" Rose asked very slowly and gripped the counter until her fingers ached. She had a few things to say to Stefan Donatien, and none of them were sweet.

Two

Stefan parked the delivery truck in the lot beside Granger's store. He carefully retrieved the two pink plastic flamingos from the passenger side of the truck. He held the yard ornaments carefully, a welcome gift from Ella Parsons, who said that everyone who was anyone in Waterville had pink flamingos in their yards. At five o'clock, the store would soon be closing, and he had had an interesting, stress-relieving day. He'd put the blistering argument with Estelle back into perspective—she was becoming her own person and it was normal girl-to-woman development to test herself against life—and her father. He loved her and she loved him, and once they were through this Louie-phase, life would be much simpler.

His mother was delighted with Waterville. The small town reminded her of her youth in France. The farm was as quaint as the town, the milk cows perfect for the cheese and butter Yvette longed to make. She loved feeding her baby chicks and planning her vegetable garden. In the pasture next to his farm, Estelle was already riding horses with a girl her age.

His women also loved the contents of the old farmhouse. It was filled with ordinary, mismatched furniture, far from that of Stefan's penthouse. The Smiths were ready to travel full-time in their camper and didn't want the old furniture that so enchanted Stefan's mother and daughter.

He smiled, cruising along in the mellow and happy lane, certain the Donatiens' lives would settle happily.

Sunlight filtered through the trees lining the street and danced along the flower beds resting on the sidewalk in front of the stores. Next door, the barber was just locking his front door. Waterville was quiet and peaceful and perfect, the spit and whittle men's bench vacated until Monday.

Stefan entered the front of the store with a sense of wellbeing. Around the towering stack of gallon paint cans, he spotted an angry Rose. She stalked right toward him, and on her way, reached for a softball from the counter and hurled it at him. He caught it in one hand, while protectively cradling the pink flamingos with the other arm. She came to stand in front of him, her hands braced on her waist, her legs apart as if readying for a fight. Her blue eyes lasered at him, and her freckles seemed to shift on her face as if waiting to attack him. In his good mood, Stefan smiled slightly at the thought of a "Rose" freckle attack. He realized instantly that humor had not been a part of his life for some time.

"You're grinning. Some big joke, huh? *You are not Bruce Long,*" Rose stated tightly.

Stefan turned the Open sign to Closed. He wanted this conversation to be private. Rose looked as if she might erupt. "I did not say that I was."

"You cooked for Ella...put wine in her spaghetti sauce. You gave her tips on the presentation of green beans, not snapped, but whole.... Everyone here snaps green beans. They usually cook green beans with bacon, and maybe onion instead of steaming them...sometimes with new potatoes. You'll have everyone canning their June beans upright in the jars...and every once in a while, I get to sit on someone's front porch and snap beans. I enjoy that— *and you're messing with Waterville tradition.*"

"The presentation of the meal is ultimate. We dined together. The Parsons are quite charming, and I was quite hungry—my stomach could not bear your infamous hot dogs," Stefan returned, watching in fascination as Rose tore the rubber band confining her ponytail away. A sleek curtain of burnished reddish brown hair fell to her shoulders. He longed to crush it in his hands, to lift it to the sunlight and to study the fascinating color and texture. It would feel like silk, alive with warmth from Rose. He breathed unsteadily as an image flashed through his mind—that of Rose's hair dragging along his bare skin, the sensual sweep of the rich reddish-brown strands across his cheek.

Stefan held still, shocked by the turn of his thoughts; he had not been so susceptible since he was in his teens. Perhaps it was spring, the flowers, the lack of Louie— "Hello, Rose," he said gently, loving the sound on his tongue.

She reminded him of a flower, as fresh as dewdrops glistening in the dawn.

"You've got an accent. That's why you didn't talk. And I fell for it," Rose-the-flower stated darkly. "Very funny."

He looked down at the check she'd thrust into his hand. "Get out," she said tightly. "I know you own a chain of French restaurants and that check isn't even the price of a

meal in one of them. But I owe you for the work and I'm
paying up."

For an instant, Stefan tensed. No one spoke to him in
that tone. He focused on Rose and said slowly, "Does that
mean that the invitation to go fishing with you at the lake
is off?"

"You knew that at the time—" she began hotly.

"So you are a woman who takes back what she has
offered," he said, watching her closely. Ella had briefly
informed him of Rose's unfortunate love life—engaged
three times and never married—and of her dedication to a
father who was slowly drinking more. Stefan wanted to
hold Rose close and protect her, this bit of a woman, all
sleek and soft and exciting. His verbal nudge was intended
to seal his time with her at the lake. He wanted to know
more about her, this woman who fought so valiantly
against odds, who loved so deeply. He wanted to see her
eat one wholesome meal and relax. He wanted to place his
hands on those taut, overworked, feminine muscles and
give them ease. He wanted to capture that capable feminine hand, turn it and press a kiss into her palm. He wanted
to cup that curved bottom in both hands. He wanted to
taste the flavor of her breasts, those perfect, applelike
breasts.

She seemed so natural and totally unaware of her appeal,
unlike the women in his experience. Women who seemed
interested in him usually wanted his checkbook, not himself. He'd watched Rose tend her customers. She did not
hide her emotions. She genuinely liked most of them, that
brilliant smile flashing at them, or she touched them. Once
she'd waited on a customer, her face taut and grim, all her
walls were up and Stefan knew she did not like the man.

Now, the sunlight shafted through the store's windows

and tipped her dark brown eyelashes in fire. An answering flame danced in his heart, in his loins.

Ten years of abstinence was far too long, he decided instantly, and wondered if the flush upon her face would be the same after they made love. He longed to see her soft and drowsy beneath him. Somehow, his instincts told him that he had found a woman to enjoy and treasure; with her, he could find peace.

"I don't like being made a fool of," Rose shot at him angrily, shredding his vision of peace and pleasure.

"Ah, so then, you retreat from the battle," he nudged again. "You fear you might like me. You fear that I might catch more fish than you. You fear that your father will like me, too."

Her lips parted and she blinked up at him, her expression blank. "You haven't talked all day and now you're saying too much. Don't you get it? I'm mad at you."

He shrugged, determined to have his way. "So you do retreat. I have won."

Those blue eyes widened and blinked again. "Won what?"

"The game. You are afraid. You retreat. I win. Simple."

She shook her head and the reddish hues in her hair caught the overhead light. "You wouldn't like fishing at the lake. Chiggers, mosquitoes, every biting insect possible," she explained. "When the flies bite here, it hurts. The johnboat isn't a yacht—it's a chopped-off metal boat—and the crappie are sporting, but they aren't swordfish, Mr. Donatien."

"It sounds delightful," he said, watching that faint sunlight stroke her cheek and wondering if the freckle pattern continued over her body. He went a little light-headed thinking about those long, athletic limbs, those perfect apple-shaped breasts, the way she took fire. Rose Granger

was a passionate woman for certain, and just watching her
move provoked an excitement in his body that he hadn't
expected.

She inhaled slowly, balled her fists at her sides, and
frowned up at him. "Be at the north end of the lake at
six-thirty. You'll have to find the johnboat tied to the dock.
I've got to pick up Dad."

"I must get the paint my mother wishes."

"Take care of your own order. Just leave the cash on
the counter, or leave your check and I'll send the change
to you," Rose said, moving restlessly behind the counter
and avoiding his gaze.

She was sweet and shy of him, Stefan realized as she
hurried out the back door. He enjoyed that little jiggle of
soft flesh below her shorts' ragged hem; he traced her long
legs down to the back of her knees. He closed his eyes,
riveted by the need to kiss her there, where she seemed
most vulnerable and virginal.

In a good mood, because he would spend time with an
enchanting woman later, Stefan kissed one of the flamingos' plastic beaks. He frowned into the bird's vacant yellow eyes. Was he nervous? His first attraction to a woman,
since his wife? But, of course, and he was so hungry for
the taste of that lush, sassy mouth—

Carrying her tackle box and fishing pole, Rose tromped
from her pickup, across the lush grass of the lake's bank.
She'd tried desperately to rouse her sleeping father and
had failed. She'd debated leaving Stefan—the wealthy,
continental businessman she'd ordered around all day—to
the mosquitoes and biting red chiggers. But her competitive streak, which allowed her to be captain of the mixed
softball team, was revved. Nothing could have kept her

from watching him itch—payback for deceiving her all day.

Her thoughts slapped against her in rhythm to the sound of her plastic thongs. She glanced at the slash of scarlet, a male cardinal bird in the oak trees. *If he had only spoken just one word, she would have known who he was—his deep enchanting accent would have marked him as the newcomer…though he didn't seem as cold as Harry at the gas station had inferred.*

She pushed away the memory of Stefan's smile at the pink flamingos. It was excited, almost as if he were a boy, excited at winning trophies.

Stefan was sitting on the dock, his pole already in the water, the shadows and sunlight flowing over his body, the water sparkling beyond him. At around six-feet four inches he could intimidate with that dark scowl, but not her. Her thongs clumped as she walked out onto the dock, studied the metal johnboat and decided she didn't want to baby the worn motor into life. She slung her backpack—filled with cola, a peanut butter sandwich and insect repellent— down to the worn boards of the dock. Out in the glimmering still water, a big mouth bass surged up for a juicy water bug, reminding Rose of how she had taken Stefan's challenge. She glanced at the expert way Stefan cast into the lake's dead timber, the perfect place for a "crappie bed." It was her private place. "Dad couldn't come. We can fish here," she said. "You stay on your side of the dock, and I'll stay on mine. You'd better have your fishing license. I like your mother. I don't like you."

His hair was damp, curling at his nape and that all-man soap smell curled erotically around her. The clean T-shirt tightened across his shoulders as he patted the billfold in his back pocket. "I have a license…. So you have had a bad day, and you wish to take it out on me, right?'' he asked.

Rose slipped off her thongs, plopped down on the dock and dangled her legs over the side as Stefan was doing. She wouldn't be waylaid by that sexy, intimate accent. She opened her tackle box and selected just the right fishing ''jig,'' a plastic lure to entice crappie. Only meeting Stefan's challenge had kept her from falling facedown on her bed and sleeping through Sunday. She was *not* a woman who offered and then took back her invitation. She cast, propped the handle of her pole into the slot between the boards and took out her insect repellent, rubbing it on her arms and legs. She sniffed lightly and recognized the slight tang of citronella, also an insect deterrent, coming from Stefan. He would not be leaving her dock soon. ''Can we just be quiet?'' she asked. ''I've looked forward to this all week.''

For the next half hour, she felt the old dock tremble slightly as Stefan cast into her favorite fishing hole. The crappie responded to his lure, flip-flopping in the water as he reeled them in and released them. She refused to ask what he was using for bait, because nothing was nibbling at her line. He held up one and asked, ''How do you prepare crappie?''

She looked over her shoulder and wished she hadn't. The fish was Old George, a legendary giant of a crappie, who had escaped her hook. ''You wait until you get a 'mess' and then fillet, score, bread in flour and cornmeal and fry. Or you might dip them in egg or beer batter…serve with wilted lettuce… But I'd throw that one back, he's too small,'' she lied, because she wanted Old George on her dinner table. ''Did you enjoy yourself today, your little masquerade?''

He unhooked Old George and tossed him back into the

lake. Stefan dipped his hands in the lake and washed them as would an experienced fisherman. He looked over his shoulder at her and grinned. It was a devastating, boyish grin that took her breath away. "I learned so much."

Rose turned back and promptly missed the dip of her red bobber in the water as a fish nibbled on her lure. It was difficult to concentrate when Stefan spread his blanket, sat upon it and began opening the basket he had brought. "My mother likes you, too. She was excited that I had a date with you and packed this meal for us."

Rose pivoted to him, temper flashing. "This isn't a date, Mr. Donatien." She leveled her words at him, not wanting him to get any flashy, upscale ideas about a country girl.

"But I am with a very fascinating woman and I am enjoying myself. Surely that is a date." He began unpacking, carefully placing a wine bottle that looked very costly, onto the blanket. He opened the bottle with a flourish and poured the wine into two very expensive-looking stemmed glasses. He unwrapped cheese and studied it. "My mother thinks she will make cheese here. She is happy and reliving her young life on a French farm, I think. My daughter is…happy in one way, not so in another."

Rose watched as he sliced the cheese and a very-hard looking sausage, placing crusty bread rolls beside it. She couldn't resist the temptation to ask, "Why isn't your daughter happy?"

He shrugged a broad shoulder and looked out at the peaceful lake. His features were unreadable. "She is happy to be here. She is not happy with me. It is a hard passage from the girl to the woman. A boy I do not like wants her."

Rose stared at him; the unlikely, worldly Donatiens moving to Waterville suddenly made sense. "You maneuvered this whole move to Waterville, didn't you? Just to get her away from—''

Stefan scowled and handed her one filled wineglass. ''From Louie The Freeloader. Estelle wished to live in an average, small town and I merely arranged her wishes. Perhaps I was ready for a change, too. My mother had been speaking of her homeland and selfishly, I wished to keep my family—what there is of it—together. Waterville was selected after very thorough research. We will spend the summer here. The farm was a compromise to make them both happy. It had been up on the market since the Smiths decided to see the West in their camper. There is a college some miles away, which might suit Estelle's needs, if she wishes to transfer.''

''I hate to tell you this, Pops, but there are hot-blooded boys here in Waterville, too.'' Rose sipped the wine and studied him. ''You left everything to prevent Louie and Estelle from—''

His scowl deepened. ''They have not consummated. I would know.''

''Maybe they are in love,'' she suggested, fascinated by his absolute confidence. ''How would you know?''

''I am her father,'' he said roughly with an arrogant tilt to his head, that accent more distinct. ''You think I do not know my own daughter? That I have been so absorbed in business that I would not recognize the change?''

Though she'd been angry with him, and had found his tender spot, Rose recognized the troubled road between father and daughter. She sympathized with both of them. ''I was engaged about that age,'' she said gently.

''But it did not last,'' he prompted as another bass rolled in the lake, turning a silver side in the dark, shadowy water. ''That is why you and I are here together. A good husband would have kept you happy.''

The crickets and frogs chirped as Rose shook her head. She munched on the crusty bread Stefan had torn apart and handed to her and thought about how romance wasn't for her.

"What happened?" Stefan asked softly.

A flat-shelled water turtle crawled up onto a log, half sunken in the still water, and looked at the humans. Stefan was just passing through her life; it was a moment in time that meant nothing, she told herself. There was no reason not to share with him something that happened long ago. "It seemed only natural to marry Henry. We were lifetime friends and everyone else was getting married at the time. It's contagious, you know. He came into the store today and got paint. Henry is like a comfortable old shoe, all broken in and fitting just right. We did the engagement party thing, but as the wedding date came closer, neither one of us wanted to go through with it. Not really. We sort of got caught up in the engagement fun, the party and excitement. But he wasn't happy and I knew it, because I wasn't, either. So I pinned him down one night—sat on him—and we had an honest chat. He married my best friend, Shirley MacNeil. They've got two great kids...boys. They're hoping for a girl next time. I am godmother to their children, and others in Waterville. I guess that's as close as I'm going to get to motherhood."

Stefan's dark brows rose. "The man you hugged so intimately? You remain friends with him?"

"Sure. No hard feelings. It just wasn't right between us. I can always count on Henry to help me in a tight spot." She shrugged and munched on the cheese and meat he handed her.

"Good old Henry, right?" Stefan said tightly as he refilled the wineglass she had just emptied. "Who was the man you leaned against as if you trusted him?"

She eyed Stefan, considering him. They were strangers sharing a quiet moment on a lovely, peaceful evening. The wine was relaxing her after a hard week of work. "I don't know why I shouldn't tell you, everyone else knows. Waterville's quiet country life will bore you soon enough and you'll be back to the city's society set soon. That was Larry. We were engaged for a time. He rented a motel room away from Waterville for our first—" She raised her wineglass, toasting the moment when neither could become aroused enough to make love. "Happening. It didn't happen. End of story. He and Mary Lou are expecting their first baby. Everything turned out fine."

Stefan's dark eyes cruised the body she had just spread full-length upon his blanket. He lay down, sharing the blanket, the food between them. He propped his head in one hand and placed a bit of cheese into her mouth with the other. His eyes darkened as she ate. He asked, "Why didn't it happen?"

"I laughed when I saw him naked for the first time. And my bony mystique seemed pretty funny to him, too. Our batteries just weren't charged. We decided we were better suited to be friends than lovers. We used to come here, my friends and I, when we were young. We used to tell ghost stories and—I don't know why, but the attraction just wasn't there, not enough to…to do it, or to marry. Then there was Mike. He hadn't been in town very long when we started dating. He was a super pitcher on the team. He was a good mechanic—could fix anything. We got engaged and then one night, I caught him tuning someone else's engine and he left town soon after…. I'm sorry about your wife. Your mother said you loved her deeply."

"I still do. Claire will always be a part of my life. She lives in my daughter. She had the same straight black hair."

Rose studied Stefan's broad, blunt cheekbones, that square chin, and wondered about his wife. What kind of woman could take his heart? A gentle woman? Feminine and pretty? A quiet woman, who understood? A fascinating woman, full of life? A corporate wife, all glossy and perfect? Or was she a woman like Rose's mother—who loved and captivated every man and left them mourning her as she moved on? "Estelle will have to make up her own mind, you know. You can't protect her from life forever."

"Who protects you?" he asked softly and ran a finger slowly down her cheek.

Her skin heated at the touch and she shifted away, uneasy with a man who seemed too intimate, too soon, too foreign, too unique, too exciting—and just "too." She looked at the clouds floating gently across the sky, just as her life seemed to be doing. "I'm way, way past that age."

"So old." Humor hovered in Stefan's deep voice.

"Well, let's just say I've settled in for the long run. No surprises, no problems—"

She stared up at the man leaning over her, looking deeply, intimately into her eyes. "What? Is something wrong?"

"You have given up on life as an appealing, vital woman. You are preparing for your rocking chair and shawl. Are you not aware of how enticing you are?"

She sucked in air when she realized she'd stopped breathing. Men usually thought of her as a good friend. Stefan's sultry gaze seemed to devour her mouth as if he wanted to kiss her. The quiver passing through her body, the raised hairs on the back of her neck, startled her.

"Are you making a pass at me, bud?" she asked carefully, because men never flirted with her. She'd added the "bud" to keep him at a distance.

His smile was slow and warming and mind-blowing. It was definitely not a good-buddy smile. "So blunt. I will have to adjust to your frank style of conversation. It has been a while, and perhaps I am out of practice at making my intentions known."

Then he placed his hands on either side of her head, studied the shape of her mouth beneath his and lowered his head. The kiss was that of a man who knew what he wanted and was confident he could obtain it. The kiss felt like a possession, a tantalizing gift and a choice. His lips were firm, yet light against hers, seeking more than demanding, exploring the shape and taste of her as if he had all the time in the world. Rose mentally rummaged for her resistance and failed. She felt herself drift away in the summer evening, tethered only by the temptation of his mouth. The dock shook...or was it her?

When he lifted his head, his eyes were dark and warm and yet tender. Rose slowly pushed away the sensation that she could melt into his arms and forget everything but the steamy pulsing of their bodies— She breathed carefully, studying Stefan's dark, sultry gaze. "If...if you're looking to start something, don't."

He stroked a strand of her hair, studying the reddish shades in the dying light. "Why not?"

She couldn't afford to give herself again. While she had explained her love life to him as though it hadn't affected her, the pain had been terrible. Though the decisions to break the engagements were shared, she'd been left with the sense that others moved on—like her mother—while she was left alone. She did not want to open herself again for a security that wasn't there. Stefan was only passing through her life, testing her and playing his games. "I've never been a one-night stand and I don't intend to be."

That warm, intimate look cooled and sizzled with anger. "You think that is what I offer you?"

Rose pushed herself to her feet, gathered her backpack and tackle box and stood looking down at him. Stefan's arms were behind his head. He took up too much space on the dock, and too much of Rose's air—she was suddenly finding breathing difficult. She forced her gaze away from that wide chest and flat stomach up to his dark, sultry eyes, locking with them as he said, "You are afraid. You like to be in control of the men you take, and yourself. You fear giving away too much."

"I do not," she said harshly. How could he possibly know how she *had* to be in control, to survive, to take care of her father and herself and the business that supported them? How could he know how much she had loved a mother, who had deserted her?

He slanted her a disbelieving look. "You responded. You are a woman. You are alive."

"Oh, I hate it when you shoot out those machine-gun sentences, summing up everything to your reasoning. If you need relief, I'm not your girl." With that she hurried away to safety, to her home. Her hands shook as she shifted her pickup, and the gears protested her careless handling.

Her father continued to sleep and Rose settled in for a restless night. She tossed upon her single bed, the rosebud sheets tangling between her legs. Stefan did not kiss like other men in her experience. He kissed her as if he was imprinting her taste upon his mind, as if he needed the taste of her to carry with him. He spoke very softly, his accent curling intimately around her. She sensed an awakening within herself that wouldn't be quelled. It was a long time before she slept, the taste of Stefan's kiss—firm, sensual, tempting, hungry—dancing through her dreams.

She tried to snuggle down in her bed, and into the safety she had created in her life. But dreams of Stefan, stretched out on the dock and looking sexy, wrapped around her.

On the one morning she could sleep in, Rose smelled coffee. If her father—if Maury was tipsy and cooking, the situation could be dangerous. She pushed herself out of bed, and dressed only in briefs and the T-shirt she used for a nightgown, slowly made her way down the stairs. At the kitchen doorway, she yawned and rubbed her eyes and longed to curl up back in bed, regaining the sleep Stefan Donatien had robbed from her. "Dad? Are you okay?"

Sunlight shafted through the kitchen windows and Rose blinked. Seated at the kitchen table, her father waved an airy greeting. His face was wrapped in a towel. A basin was on the table, and Yvette Donatien was rubbing a shaving brush in Maury's old-fashioned soap mug. She eased off the towel, slathered his jaw with soapy foam and began expertly stroking a straight razor over his jaw. Dressed in another soft flowing, flower-print dress, she looked at home in the kitchen. "'*Al-lo,* Rose. You look so sleepy, *ma chérie,*" she said, her voice soft and musical. "Come, sit down. When Maury is shaved, we will eat. Come. Enjoy this beautiful morning. It will only be a moment before Stefan serves his famous *Piperade* omelet, from the South of France. We have the basket of fresh eggs from the Parsons and a few ingredients from your home, and *voilà,* my beautiful son's omelet. I think we will soon have our own cows and mushrooms from the farm's root cellar. Stefan and I were just passing by and I noticed Maury—looking so alone—in his beautiful rose garden."

"I invited them in for breakfast. I was going to cook some bacon and eggs," Maury murmured in nasal tones, because Yvette was holding his nose to shave beneath it. "I said I'd better shave first, and Yvette offered to give me an old-fashioned one with a straight razor. And sure enough I found mine in the medicine cabinet, still sharp as a knife. Couldn't pass that offer up," he said cheerfully.

Stefan turned slowly from the kitchen stove to look at Rose. She couldn't move, pinned by his narrowed gaze, as it roamed her body. Yvette continued to talk while Rose tried to find reality and slow the racing of her heart. Stefan's look said he wanted to carry her off to bed, to claim her. The stark desire written on his expression terrified Rose...because if his kiss of yesterday was any indication, she didn't stand a chance to resist him.

"Be right back," she said and turned, hurrying upstairs to dress in a short, summer shift. After one look in the mirror, she remembered Stefan's expression as his gaze traced her legs. She quickly changed to jeans and a T-shirt. Instinctively she knew that Stefan was not a man to take a "just friends" attitude with her. He was too intense, and she had to protect herself. She would manage to be civil for their parents' sake and that would be the end of Mr. Stefan Donatien, she decided firmly.

When she returned, Maury was watching Yvette in the laundry room, located just off the kitchen. Laughing gayly, she was filling the clothes washer, and Maury's expression caused Rose to stand still and stare. He seemed younger, more intense, and if Rose didn't know better— She shook her head. Her father couldn't be flirting. She blinked. Yet he was and there was that *hungry male* look at Yvette's hips as she bent over to fill the clothes dryer.

She looked up to see Stefan studying her. "You are worried," he whispered simply, quietly. "She has a good heart and does not hurt."

Then he bent to place his cheek beside hers for just that

fraction of a heartbeat. "Do not worry, your father is safe. There is no need for you to protect him. It is only friendship she offers. She has never been truly involved with another man since my father, though she likes to dance and laugh and enjoy their company."

Rose shivered, uncertain of herself, of her suddenly animated father, and of Stefan, who had just turned that slight little bit to brush his lips across hers. That light touch packed a jolt of electricity and she stepped back, frowning at him. She remembered all the times she'd reached for happiness, only to have it slap her in the face. She'd cling to the safety of approaching spinsterhood, no worrying about engagements, weddings or love that just wasn't there. "I'm just a country girl and I will not be the dessert of the day," she informed him.

But Stefan was wearing that same *hungry* expression she had seen on the face of her father. It was a look that said Stefan wasn't likely to be dismissed easily.

Three

—

"**I** thought you would be here," Stefan said as he walked onto the dock that evening. Rose was sitting in the johnboat, the rope still tied to the dock as she fished. Stefan noted that her line was in the exact place where he had caught the crappie she obviously did not want him to have. He knew the average size of crappie and his catch had been a prize. "If you are not careful, you will catch that small crappie I released last night."

Dressed in cutoffs, a T-shirt and her ball cap, she ignored him as he sat on the dock. With her legs draped over the side of the boat and her bare feet in the water, she was lovely against the evening shadows. She slowly reeled the line, causing her lure to quiver beneath the water. A bullfrog bellowed, cutting coarsely across the gentle evening sounds. Rose continued to ignore Stefan, and he settled his dinner basket on the dock. "You spoke little at breakfast. You ate little."

Rose breathed slowly and the setting sun stroked the rise and fall of her breasts. "Breakfast—that whatever you call it—was good. You were uninvited then and you are uninvited now."

"That was quite by accident. My mother is impulsive and friendly. She also is very soft in her heart. She wanted to stop. When you know her better, you will understand. And your father did look lonely."

Rose turned to look at him fully. "Well, he's not lonely now. He's at your place, painting walls with your mother. It took him an hour to get ready. He pressed a good cotton shirt and asked me how he looked. Dad hasn't cared about his looks since I don't know when. Tomorrow he's coming to work for the first time in months. He said he needed to get back 'in the flow.' He hasn't been 'in the flow' since my mother left."

Stefan shrugged. His mother might appreciate the company and help, but companionship was her limit. His daughter was at the movies with her new girlfriend, swooning over the latest screen hero. It was good for Estelle to be with friends of her own age and for Louie to be far, far away. For the first time in ages, Stefan felt at peace. "This is good," he said, meaning it as he inhaled the sweet evening air. "And I am not playing a game, by the way."

"Hey, guy. You're here for the summer as I understand, and you're messing in my life. You're temporary. I'm permanent. There's a difference. What do you want from me?" Rose asked, her voice carrying huskily across the lake's distance, her expression shadowed.

Stefan reached to grip the rope tethering her boat and gently pulled her closer until he could see those magnificent blue eyes and those wonderful freckles. He wrapped his hand around her ankle and stroked it with his thumb, enjoying the feel of her flesh. "I find you attractive and enchanting and magnificently delicious."

"That's quite the line," she tossed back at him after a moment's hesitation in which she was obviously picking her way to safety. She pulled her leg away from his touch.

Stefan smiled, pushing aside the way she could nettle him, dismissing his good intentions. "You just missed a nibble."

She frowned at him and reeled in her line. Stefan appreciated the graceful cast into the crappie bed, the way her slender arms held power and confidence and beauty. He wished they were holding him tightly, that her skin was damp and soft and sweet against his own. The fading sunlight gleamed on her long, bare legs and he wished those, too, were wrapped around him. It was not easy to wait for her when his body had just awakened to his needs. "How long will it take for you to trust me?"

"You haven't got that long. I know exactly what you want and then when you have it, you'll move on. I don't intend to be one of the local delicacies you choose to sample. And if you knew me better—which you aren't going to—you'd know that I'm not delicate."

"I would guess that Mike is the reason for your opinion. You said he came into town and left. The other two fiancés were lifelong friends. Since I am new here, I am to pay for Mike and his defection, is that it?" Despite his intention to gain her trust, his anger was simmering now. He was an honest, honorable man seeking a woman he found desirable. Rose pushed at the dock and her boat floated back out onto the water, a distance away from him. Without weighing her disfavor, Stefan reached to grip the rope mooring her boat to the dock. He pulled it, bringing her back to him. She stuck out her foot, bracing it on the dock and keeping the distance between them.

"Would you care to have dinner with me?" he asked, perhaps a bit too forcefully, nettled that she could draw his anger from him. Only his daughter and his mother were allowed to see beneath the rigid control he had inherited from his father.

"What do I owe you for it?" she asked, watching him. Her tone was too cautious, as if some terrible game had been played on her, and she wasn't paying that penalty again.

The innuendo that he would expect payment for a meal he had prepared for her slapped him. When he was a child, his father had hammered into him that a man's honor and pride were everything. Stefan would not humble himself before Rose, telling her how his heart leaped when he saw her, how much he needed her warmth—how much he needed to give *her* warmth…and safety. Those wary blue eyes told him she had been badly hurt, and every step would be carefully weighed. That she did not trust him— a man who tried his best to be right and good—hurt. "Forget it," he said, stood and walked off before he said too much.

An hour later, Stefan gripped the farmhouse board and tugged it free, the extra force supplied by his temper. His mother had left a note that Maury had taken her for a private tour of the store, so that she could select her bathroom wallpaper undisturbed. Estelle was still out with her girlfriend. Left alone with his hunger for Rose—to hear her voice, to dream of her—Stefan concentrated on taking down the wall between the kitchen and the back porch. At least that wall was solid and could be dealt with, whereas Rose's walls were intangible but just as effective.

Stefan shook his head and tore away an old board, discarding it to the growing pile. In business, he knew how to act. But personal relationships had never come easily to him. His lack of experience with flirtation clearly was a disadvantage now.

Headlights lasered through the windows on the back porch and at a glance, Stefan recognized Rose's pickup. He had been wounded enough for one night, his attempt at friendship with her slapped in his face. He did not like the simmering anger, that of the man placing his honest intentions in front of the woman who enchanted *and* rejected him. He glanced at the woman coming up the stone walkway to the house, and with a shake of his head, opened the door.

She held up the picnic basket, her face pale in the light shafting from his home. "You forgot this."

He felt too vulnerable, an emotion denied the young son of steely Guy Donatien and firmly embedded in the man. He reached to take the handle of the basket. "Yes, of course. Thank you."

"You're lonely, aren't you?" she asked quietly above the chirp of the crickets. She did not release the basket to him.

Was he to be denied his pride? Did he have to explain the emptiness he felt in the odd hours when work did not fill his life and his family was not near? Who did this woman think she was, to pry so deeply into his life? "Are *you?*" The question was a reflex, a defense.

She shook her head and that fabulous mane of reddish-brown hair seemed to catch fire in the light. "You could get a carpenter team to help you with the house," she said, changing the subject.

Stefan did not want to admit how much he was looking forward to his new role away from business and the kitchen. He, too, wanted to enjoy average American rural life, a vacation away from stress and the city. "I do not need them."

"Larry could help. He and his brother and a few others—"

Stefan breathed deeply. Did she think he was incapable of simple tasks? He had helped remodelers and his father and knew basic carpentry. Did she think him incapable of everything? "I do not wish your ex-fiancé to be of assistance to me."

"You don't have to be so rigid about someone helping you. It's a neighborly thing to do. I've got time. We got off to a bad start, but I'll help you tonight and we'll be friends. I'll introduce you to Waterville's single women looking for a man. Just remember to keep it light, because you're only here for the summer, and some of them might want to get serious. I don't want to be held responsible for anyone's heartache."

Stefan clamped his lips closed. He refused to debate his choice of women, or to have her select them for him. He tugged the basket from her and turned, walking up the steps into the back porch. He placed the basket on a table, flipped open the top, gripped the Beaujolais wine he had selected especially to go with the *poulet en cocote*. He poured the wine into a glass, swirled it and downed it quickly. He eyed Rose, who was studying the stack of old boards and broken plasterboard. "You are a frustrating woman. Do you think me incapable of the smallest task? The smallest sense of responsibility? Do you think I ask every woman I see to have dinner with me?"

"Yes," she answered truthfully. "You're probably pretty available... I mean, a man who looks like you, who is very smooth and who is obviously wealthy."

She hadn't spared him, and Stefan reluctantly admitted

that certain women did want him. So far none of them had appealed. "'Very smooth,'" he repeated darkly.

"I've never trusted men who know how to look sexy and appealing, and how to touch a woman. And you're one of them."

Her words were both a compliment and a put-down. "Thank you for your honesty. So, I am not to be trusted."

"It's like the major leagues and minor leagues. You probably play in the majors, while I just don't want to get in the ball game at all."

He had finally found a woman who aroused and satisfied him intellectually and visually, and she did not want him. Stefan ripped open the zippered thermal pouch containing the chicken and vegetables, then tugged off a drumstick. He ate it without prowling through its taste as he usually did. Rose sniffed delicately, coming to peer down into the basket. "Eat," Stefan ordered, unconcerned with manners or presentation of the meal at the moment.

Rose studied his expression, then reached to pat his cheek. He gripped her wrist and eased it away from him. He could not bear to have her sympathy. "Don't."

She watched him carve the chicken and ladle the vegetables onto the plates, handing one to her. "Do you have to bristle?" she asked as she probed an artichoke heart with her fingertip.

When she reached for the wine, pouring it into a glass, her breast brushed Stefan's bare arm, electrifying his senses. He tensed and held his breath until the initial sensual jolt passed. "That's why I 'bristle,'" he said coarsely as she suddenly stepped back, a blush rising up her cheeks.

He took the finger she had used to test the food and brought it to his mouth, sucking it. Then his teeth closed around the tip, nipping gently. "I want you."

Rose stiffened and jerked her hand away. "I don't know

anything about you, except you just may have an evil temper. Your eyes flash and I hear thunder in your voice. I'm not intimidated, of course, but nothing happens this fast. Not in Waterville, Missouri, U.S.A. Life sort of meanders into the right course, without pushing it before its time. You're a person who likes to arrange things on your schedule.''

"Why are you here?'' he asked abruptly, dismissing pleasantries. He rubbed his free hand across his bare chest and noted Rose's blue eyes following the movement. She was aware of him as a man, he decided, and yet she complicated the attraction between them. Women could be confusing. "You aren't here to return the basket. You could have sent that with my mother or Estelle later on.''

"I didn't want the food to go to waste.''

Her answer was too petulant, too quick, and Stefan circled it. She was too wary of him and yet he admired her bravery for confronting her fears—for wanting to face down and file away any question she might have about an attraction to him. "Yes, I am lonely,'' he said finally. "It has been a long time since I have wanted the company of a woman. To feel a woman's skin against my own. To say these things aloud is difficult. I have had only one woman—my wife—and so it is that I am not so competent at this.''

Those blue eyes blinked and Rose looked down at the bowl she held, studying it intently. "Don't kiss me anymore, bud,'' she whispered.

The air had stilled and warmed and trembled as Stefan studied her. "You don't like it?''

"I think I'll be going now. Nice knowing you,'' she whispered before hurrying out the door. Stefan noted that she had not lied or attempted to disprove that she'd enjoyed that kiss on the dock and the one in her kitchen.

After her pickup skidded out of the farm's driveway, Stefan slapped his open hand against the wall. He had always considered himself to be a patient man and now he knew that with Rose, he was not.

The telephone rang; Louie had chosen the wrong moment to call. "Estelle?" he asked sharply when Stefan did not respond to his greeting.

"Louie, I think you should come here," Stefan said, after the brief pause. "There is much work to do. The chicken house needs to be cleaned and the refuse scattered on my mother's garden. You could milk the cows she is getting and help me move the outhouse. I will not offer to pay you, of course, because I know you would not accept. But you will see my daughter at odd moments—when you are not shingling the roof, or crawling beneath the house to help with the bug problem. When can we expect you?"

Louie stuttered an excuse and quickly hung up. Stefan smiled briefly. At least he had accomplished one feat— discouraging Louie from visiting Estelle. But Stefan still longed to hold Rose warm and close against him. He rubbed his bare chest, just over his heart and the ache in it. The pursuit and capture of Rose Granger would not be easy.

He heard the roaring of an engine and glanced outside to see Rose's pickup soaring into the farm driveway. It skidded to a stop and Stefan smiled. He suspected Rose's style of meeting problems was either head-on, or repeat attacks until she resolved the matter to her satisfaction. Apparently Stefan was worth a repeat attack; he took that as a good sign. He watched her hurry along the walkway and jog up the steps.

She jerked open the door, pinned him in the bald light and said, "Look. I've been attracted to guys before, okay? You're not the first."

"Okay," he answered slowly as she began to pace across the worn linoleum. Rose was struggling with her past and fear of the future. The war fascinated Stefan.

"You need new linoleum. We can make you a deal on floor coverings since you're going to need so much. Our paint sale is still on, too. This whole place could use two coats of outside paint. We give discounts when you buy twenty gallons or more at the same time. This old place will soak up the first coat. You'll need plenty of caulking, too."

"Yes, of course. Thank you for the suggestion." Stefan tried not to smile. He enjoyed watching her, this tall, lithe woman whose loyalty to her father and friends ran deep.

She placed her hands on her hips and studied him. "If you haven't been with a woman in a long time, how can you kiss like that?"

Stefan pushed away from the wall and moved toward her. He placed his hands on either side of the kitchen counter, bracketing Rose's hips. He couldn't resist stroking that soft curve of her hips with his thumbs. She was so perfect, so feminine, a delicate flower and quite possibly a very passionate woman. If she made love with the vitality she applied to everything else, he might not recover. "Like what?"

The little quiver passing through her body pleased him. She was fearless, though, eyeing him defiantly. "You're too close and you know it. You're sucking up all my air."

"You can suck up mine," he returned, enjoying the warmth of her body close to his, the fragrance of her skin, her hair.

"I know a woman who would be perfect for you," Rose whispered shakily. "Sophisticated, feminine, very good conversationalist. Maggie White is not married, her children are grown and she's a marvelous cook. She's very attractive and always wears dresses—sometimes long, flowing ones—with just the right jewelry—sometimes dangling earrings, and men seem to love being with her. She's very trendy and worldly. You might want to meet her. I can fix you up.... What's so funny?''

He ran a fingertip over the freckles on her cheek. ''Do you always talk so much when you are nervous with a man?''

She shivered again, but refused to look away. ''You're standing too close and you're not wearing a shirt.''

Stefan pressed his case; Rose needed to admit to herself that she was a very sensual woman—attractive, desirable—and that she, too, was simmering. He wanted to remove himself from the ''bud'' bin, where she tossed the other males in her life. ''You have seen men without shirts before, surely.''

''I've got a hard day tomorrow. Big paint sale and sure to have plenty of customers. I'm leaving,'' she said unevenly after a long pause. She swallowed and locked her gaze with his.

Stefan sensed that she was forcing herself not to look at his body. He nodded and stepped away from her. ''As you wish.''

She did not move. ''I feel... I feel as if you could devour me.''

''I could,'' he answered curtly, truthfully. ''But I would expect you to do a certain amount of devouring on your own.''

''I'm athletic. I run every morning that I can. I play ball. Men usually think of me as a tomboy,'' she whispered, trembling now, her hands gripping the counter behind her.

''I don't. I think of you as a desirable woman.''

She took an unsteady step away from him, then another,

and at the door she turned to stare at him. "You'll get over this. Most men do. I've been referred to as 'macho-woman.' Summer will end, and you'll be gone."

When Stefan continued to look at her, she shook her head and closed the door behind her. After her headlights faded into the night, Stefan stood a long time, alone with his thoughts and his hunger for Rose.

In the morning, his mother patted his cheek. "You had a restless night. And up so early, hammering away downstairs. It has been a long time since you have wanted to be near a woman."

"We only have a short time before my stove arrives." Stefan picked up boards and hurled them out of the open back door. "She calls me 'bud.' Like I am a brother. She wants to introduce me to a woman more suitable. Am I a man, or an old cooking pot to be passed around?"

"Some old cooking pots can be quite in demand." Yvette tossed an apple to him. "I wondered when you would come to life, and it appears that now you have."

He studied the perfect apple, which reminded him of Rose's breasts and the taste he had not managed. "Stop scowling, Stefan," his mother said. "You move too fast and you frighten her. Have patience. Let the pot simmer a while. At breakfast, it was easy to see how wary she is of you. Your arm brushed hers and she jumped. A woman likes to choose her own course. Especially a woman like Rose, who has managed by herself for quite some time. Patience, Stefan."

By noon, Estelle had complained of his bad mood and had left to pick up cleaning supplies in Waterville. While Stefan cooked on the simple farm stove, he longed for his own stainless steel range with ovens and warming shelf.

Remodeling the house, making it livable, kept his body tired, but his mind still prowled through his images of Rose.

By early afternoon, his mother was cheerfully doing laundry in the new washer and dryer, which had just arrived. Stefan made his daily call to check on the restaurants and was a little disappointed that business was running smoothly without him. Yvette peered around the corner and folded a towel as she smiled at him. "So much like your father. He couldn't believe his business could do without him."

Stefan remembered all the times he'd wanted his father to be at home. "Have I missed so much of my daughter's life?"

"No, but you have missed much of your own. You are only coming awake now, with this girl, Rose. You are only now realizing how lonely you've been. This summer will be good not only for Estelle, but for you, too, I think. You have not played since you were a very small boy. Perhaps it is time."

Stefan considered the raw blisters on his hands, the ache of his muscles and the hunger of his body. "Perhaps. Do you think Estelle misses Louie?"

Yvette laughed gaily. "No. But she doesn't want you to think that you have had your way. She wishes you to know it is her choice. You cannot keep Estelle from becoming a woman. Look outside."

Stefan frowned at the teenage girls and boys who were talking with Estelle. She looked like any country girl, healthy and laughing and flirting a bit, too. Stefan's head began to hurt. Memories of his daughter circled him—first a tiny baby, then a toddler and now she was a woman. "Since she was twelve, boys seem to be all around her. I'm losing her."

His mother shrugged. "It is life. It is not something you can stop. You did the right thing to try Estelle's dream for the summer, Stefan. You always do the right thing for your family. Perhaps it is time you started thinking of doing what is best for you. You sacrificed much too early for your father's demands, and for that I am sad. I tried, but Guy feared failure so much, and he did want the best for you. He loved you."

"Yes. And you." He had often wondered how his mother could bear such a cold man, but then bits of tenderness that he had seen filtered back to him. A woman could change a man, but could a man change a woman?

Four

"**Y**ou should see what the house looks like now. I didn't know Daddy was a carpenter. We've only lived there two weeks and, already, he's got the kitchen the way he wants it, and the house is perfect. Grandma and I had the best time at a farm auction, bidding on furniture and household things. We went to the church bazaar and to yard sales for the rest. We bargained—can you imagine that? And we traded things. Just like Grandma used to do in her village. Grandma says the best things are those that have been well-loved and she's right. They're all just great—homey and worn and soft. I've got a kitten, Jenny Linn bed and a homemade quilt just like any other country girl," Estelle said as Yvette and Rose knelt, digging carefully to uproot starts from around the abandoned log cabin.

The old cabin was falling apart, the barn no more than rusted sheet metal and broken, weathered gray boards. But some long forgotten homestead woman had loved plants and Rose enjoyed Yvette's delight when showing the rustic cabin, overgrown with scarlet climbing roses and circled by peonies and violets. The lavender bed had started most of the herb gardens in and around Waterville. The overgrown azalea bushes hid rabbits, and the field of daffodils and tiger lilies had long lost their blooms. After a hard day at the store, Rose hoped that "flower rustling" in the evening with her new friends would relax her. She'd lost too much sleep and it was Stefan Donatien's fault. *He had set her sensors humming and she felt as taut as a bowstring. If she were a paint can and he touched her, she'd explode.*

Yvette carefully dug the daffodil bulbs and placed them within the dampened newspaper for the trip home. "Stefan appears to have a certain amount of excess energy. He works long into the night and he is up before my chickens."

Rose carefully slipped her trowel beneath a cluster of lavender, gently easing the roots from their rich earth mooring. Stefan Donatien had cost her sleep. She didn't want the warmth his touch had brought. She didn't want that throbbing deep inside, aroused by the memory of his kiss. Though Yvette and Estelle were regular customers at the paint store, he hadn't appeared; he just might have taken her suggestion about Maggie, a woman more suitable than Rose. Exactly why would a man like Stefan Donatien take a second look at her?

Why would he move so fast and so certain?

How could he look so warm and simmering, so intimate as he stood near her?

Stefan's trial separation of Estelle and Louie seemed a good game plan for Rose to employ, too. Stefan would get over any notions he had after a time and everything would settle down into the comfortable zone she preferred. She knew she couldn't afford any unexpected sexual developments, not when she was just sliding safely into midlife's home plate. She'd already paid high prices for believing in love and romance. Whatever Stefan was offering, she couldn't afford to take. She didn't trust him, rather she didn't trust her startling reaction to him—as if she wanted to grab those wide shoulders and hold tight to see where the ride would take her.

Well, she had tried that with Mike, in a desperate effort to find romance. She'd had all the heartbreak she wanted in this lifetime. She tried to change the topic from Stefan, because he occupied enough of her thoughts already and her senses started jumping just at the mention of his name. "Dad and I are going to start shingling the roof next week. He is feeling better."

Her father seemed almost boyish when he talked about Yvette; he no longer seemed to mull the past. Yvette fascinated most of the men in Waterville and the barbershop gossip had changed from crops and machines to current feminine fashions. In the grocery store, older women were humming and bright and cheerful, the result of more attentive husbands. In the post office, the scramble for new catalogs was fierce, the demand for soft flowing dresses increased. The local dry goods store started ordering more dress fabric and sewing machines were whirring. Yvette and Estelle fitted easily into the community. Stefan seemed apart and distant; his tense argument with the cook at Danny's Café about the correct cooking of pasta had started an immediate scandal. The cook went on strike during dinner hour, and as a result, Stefan was immediately banned from Danny's, which had already excluded him from the men's morning coffee group.

"My dad is grumpy," Estelle noted as Yvette was silent, her floppy straw hat hiding her expression. "It can't be Louie, because he hasn't called for some reason. It can't be business, because according to the office secretary everything is just fine. He works late every night to keep the business running smoothly, and on top of problems. I don't know what his problem is apart from that, but he's not talking. Sometimes he just sits on the front porch and stares into the night. He looks so lonesome, sitting there alone. Sometimes I think that if he didn't have us to cook for, he'd just sit there forever.''

Rose stilled; ''alone'' meant Stefan hadn't taken up with Maggie, because she never let a man be alone until he was wrung-out and used up. Rose inhaled and her hand trembled on her trowel—but then there was plenty of Stefan to use up.

''Some things are private, *ma chérie*,'' Yvette returned gently. ''I'm so happy our new friend is helping us. This flower rustling is so much fun. Your *papa* is also having fun, I think, on that old tractor, plowing that field so early this morning. And he adores that old pickup. It's really his first chance to enjoy something he should have been allowed to do as a teenager.''

Estelle stood and shaded her eyes against the mid-May sunlight, staring toward the farm road. ''What's going on?''

Rose pushed herself upright, then reached to help Yvette rise to her feet. They watched a flood of piglets tear across the field; Zeb Black, a burly farmer, hurried behind them, panting and trying to catch his breath. Rose rubbed her hands together. ''This calls for action.''

''Count me in.'' Estelle grinned. With her black, gleaming hair in a ponytail and wearing a T-shirt and shorts and joggers, she looked like any farm girl. ''Let's go!''

''Thanks, Rose,'' Zeb called as the two women ran after the five squealing piglets. ''Old Mary, the sow, broke through the fence again, and those rascals just decided to take off…chased 'em a fair piece with the pickup. Bring 'em back to me and I'll put those little rascals in it.''

Rose caught three squirming piglets, and Estelle caught one, and Zeb seemed flustered when Yvette came to the pickup, admiring his stock. He said he didn't want her to stand too close for fear some of the mud that encrusted them—and him—might soil her ''pretty dress.''

A long-married man, Zeb flushed when Rose stared at him, disbelieving his gallant behavior when he barely noticed his tiny, silent wife. Rose was dripping in mud and so was Estelle. He smiled feebly at them, before they ran off after the last piglet who was headed for the farm pond. Estelle was shouting, obviously enjoying herself as they trapped the piglet, who ran back and forth between them. ''Gotcha!'' Rose yelled and dived for the squealing animal.

Victorious at last, she hugged the squirming prize to her, tripped and fell into the pond. Sloshing in the muddy depths and trying to regain her balance wasn't easy, but she laughed, enjoying the cheers from the bank. Then something gripped the front of her sleeveless blouse and hauled her out of the muddy water. ''I got him,'' she exclaimed happily, hugging her squirming piglet until Zeb took him.

''Yes, you did,'' Stefan said, his deep voice threaded with humor.

Riding high on her victory, Rose grinned up at him. He grinned back, looking not as foreign and stern, but with a stubble covering his jaw and wearing a dirty, grease-stained T-shirt, he looked like any farmhand, just in from spring baling. He smelled like freshly cut alfalfa, a scent that she'd always enjoyed. ''This is farm life, bud. I was the best greased pig catcher at the fair in my time.''

''I can see that—'' Stefan tensed as Rose threw her arms

around him and kissed him just as she would any good
"bud."

This "bud" wrapped his arms around her quickly,
tugged her close and changed the kiss into a sensuous,
stormy heat. She dived into the enticing, mysterious taste
and the feel of his body close to hers, and tossed away
everything but the sense that the inevitable had come calling. His hands trembled on her as he lifted her off her feet
and continued kissing her, his mouth slanted, fused to hers
as lightning danced around them and thunder roared and
her senses began an unfamiliar beat.

His lips lifted slowly from hers and she shocked herself
by taking one last quick kiss, then met that dark, intense
gaze with her own. "I can't breathe," she whispered.

"I'm holding you too tight?" he whispered back unevenly, his accent more pronounced.

"Not that. You're just sucking up all my air again. And
you've got a definite problem," she whispered shakily.
Stefan's hard thighs were pressed against her damp ones,
his body taut and humming as he held her.

"You think I am happy about this?" he asked harshly.
"That I act like a boy around you? That thoughts of you
keep me awake?"

Somewhere in the distance, Zeb cleared his throat. "I'll
just be getting these little ones back to their mama."

Stefan placed Rose back on her feet and his hot, intimate
look raked down her muddy body, where her wet blouse
clung to her breasts and her nipples peaked. His swallow
was rough as he smoothed her damp hair from her face.
"Rose," he whispered so softly, wrapping her name in the
taste of midnight rendezvous, sensual touches and heart-
stopping intimacy.

When Rose pulled herself out of the daze she had just
slid into, she looked to find Estelle and Yvette. She hoped

to use them to put distance between Stefan and herself, but they were walking across the field toward the plant starts. Clearly Stefan's family had left her to fend for herself.

"What are you doing here?" she asked him.

He motioned to his pickup on the farm road. "I needed a part for the tractor and was going into town. I could not resist stopping when I saw you and Estelle acting like happy children in the field, chasing those pigs. Estelle has never looked so young and free. It was a beautiful thing to see, and to hear your laughter. You've become friends with my mother and my daughter. It seems that is more than I can do."

"We were flower rustling," Rose explained shakily, as Stefan carefully took a clean white handkerchief and began methodically wiping her face, holding it gently with one hand. She heard herself talking and knew it was because she was so nervous, her skin heating as he touched her. "It's an old custom here for new homemakers in Waterville to take a piece of this beautiful old home-place to theirs…an inheritance, so to speak. Taking those starts thins out the bulbs and lets the plants grow better. Sometimes people come out here to separate the plants and start them at another place on the farm, like those willows over there. It's a family sort of thing to do. You know, like Grandma Granger did when she was a girl, and like Mom and Dad did when they were dating, and like— Lily of the Valleys are pretty down in that hollow…little white bells on dark broad leaves—"

"Why did you kiss me?" Stefan asked softly. His intimate study of her face, her eyes, her cheeks and mouth took away her breath.

"You were there," she answered truthfully. "It seemed right after catching the pig. I had to celebrate somehow."

"I would like to carry you off and feast upon you," Stefan said raggedly. "Do you not know how seductive you are—part girl, so innocent, and all woman?"

"'Seductive?'" Rose circled the thought. "You're mistaken. Not one of my—"

"They were blind fools," Stefan said passionately. "I do not want to hear about them."

His command shifted Rose's unsteady emotions into simmering anger. In her lifetime, no one had spoken sharply to her, or ordered her. "Oh, you don't? And I don't like your tone. Take it back."

Stefan blinked as if she had reached out and struck him. "Take what back?"

"That high-handed order, like you were a general or something."

He was silent for a moment, his expression darkening. "Perhaps I speak too formally to you. I was born in this country, but sometimes my upbringing—some schooling in France—emerges when I am…emotional. My father spoke thus—very proper—when he was…emotional."

Stefan shook his head as if a new thought had entered it and he wasn't certain of it or himself. He started again. "You arouse me. I do not like that I am so susceptible to your touch, but I am. You think I like to think of you with other men?"

Rose held up her hands. Stefan was volatile and cruising off into areas of her life that even she didn't want to examine too closely. "Let's get back on course. There's nothing between us. There isn't going to be."

"Is that so?" Then Stefan reached out one hand, curled it around the back of her neck and tugged her close. She pushed at his chest and then, failing to dislodge herself, stood staring defiantly up at him. "So you decide what is to be, do you not? You open yourself to no one, especially me. I am too old, you think? I am not suitable? You wound me, *ma chérie*,'' he said in a scathing tone, his accent more pronounced.

''Do you have to be so darned open about what you're thinking?'' she demanded and realized that Stefan's other hand had settled firmly on her bottom, caressing it, as if her curves pleased him. Stefan was the first man to look at her like that, to touch her as if he had all the time in the world to enjoy her. She began to shiver, her nerves dancing as if they needed to lock on to an anchor—

Suddenly Stefan bent, picked her up on his shoulder and carried her to the pond. When he tossed her into the water, it was cold, and mud sucked at her feet as she struggled free. Rose didn't think; anger pushed her out of the pond. She ran at Stefan, who was walking back to his pickup, and hit him with a linebacker's tackle.

He went down in the field grass, turned, grabbed her and pinned her beneath him. Rose frowned up at him, her wrists clasped by his hands. Stefan's grin flashed; he lowered his head and took her mouth in a devastating kiss. It was a rough, hungry kiss, and not the kind that she could stop—if she'd wanted to, if she weren't grabbing him with her arms and legs and wrestling him beneath her to have more of that fiery, wide-open hunger. She raised up once to look at him, to stop the whirling furnace, and Stefan stared back at her, his dark expression just as wild and fierce as she felt. Then he looked down at her breasts, to the buttons that had opened to reveal her lacy bra. His body hardened beneath hers, and in the next second that dark, heated gaze was slowly easing away from her face, from her lips, and rising to Yvette and Estelle who were standing near them. Yvette was trying to hide a grin and Estelle was staring down at them, her expression shocked.

Her mouth moved once and no sound came, and then, *"Daddy! Just what are you doing?"*

"Playing. Rose likes to play. I think she wants me," he said unevenly, though his expression would have been sheepish, if he weren't Stefan Donatien, power business-man. "Go away."

"Stay," Rose ordered and couldn't seem to push herself upright, away from Stefan's big, aroused body...or the se-ductive stroking of his hands on her back. She blinked when she saw her fingers pressed deep into his strong shoulders.

"That's the first time Daddy has ever—" Estelle mur-mured in a disbelieving tone.

"I know, dear," Yvette said cheerfully. She tugged on Estelle's arm and began walking toward the old cabin. "Let's go take my new plants home. It will be a nice little walk. Coming, Rose? Stefan?"

"Not me," Rose stated firmly as she eased herself to her feet. She was headed for safety—anywhere away from Stefan. "I'm going home."

Standing beside her now, Stefan lightly tugged her wet hair and Rose swatted at him. Estelle and Yvette were having an animated conversation as they walked, which became more energetic each time Estelle looked back at her father. With as much dignity as Rose could manage, she marched off across the field toward town, her shoes filled and squishing with mud.

She couldn't resist turning, just that once, to see Stefan standing in the lush green field, his arms crossed over his chest. His boyish, devastating grin shot straight across the dying sunlight and hit her with the force of a thunderbolt. She turned to stare at him and his expression changed into a darker, sensual one that caused every molecule in her body to vibrate and heat.

She couldn't—Rose swallowed the tight emotion in her throat. She'd been through enough pain and she couldn't expose herself again. She forced herself to turn and walk away, and then she began to run. She ran until she thought her heart would burst—just like it did when her mother left her.

At her house, a cold shower did not erase Stefan's arousing touch, the intimate way he looked at her. Rose shook her head beneath the spray. "I can't help it if I'm a physical woman. I feel like all my senses have been sleeping, just waiting to leap on Stefan. I didn't feel like this with Larry or Henry or Mike, no matter how much I tried. This is just *not* fair. I've just now got my life under control. *I was safe.* I will not get involved with Stefan. He'll get tired of dull rural life in Waterville and he'll move on. And he's just too—just too unsafe," she finished saying.

She blew the water from her bottom lip, the lip that Stefan had gently suckled. Still sensitive and tasting him, Rose Granger decided that in the ball game of life, she wasn't meant to have fair and just umpire calls. Dressed in a long emerald caftan, with her damp hair propped high on her head, she went out on the porch to curl up in the white wicker chair, to sip lemonade and to contemplate while she painted her toenails. She always fought life better with scarlet toe nails and with Stefan, she was certain there would be a battle.

In the evening hours, Henry and Shirley strolled by. They stopped at Rose's front white picket fence. "Heard you were rolling in the mud with Stefan Donatien," Henry called. "Heard you pinned him in five seconds flat."

"Hi, Shirley. Keep on moving, Henry. No offense," Rose answered and frowned as they moved off and Henry's guffaws carried back on the sweet May air.

From the other side of the hedge that Mrs. Wilkins was shearing, she called merrily, "I heard that, too, Rose. Zeb was thankful you're such a good pig catcher, though."

"Next time he can catch them himself," Rose muttered.

"What was that you said? Yes, that Donatien man would be a good catch," Mrs. Wilkins agreed. "But he's not apt to let you roam free like those other boys. He's the man-kind that would want a ring on your finger to brand you as his. He's the real up-close-and-personal type."

"I'm going in the house, Mrs. Wilkins. Have a nice night." Rose closed her eyes and tried not to think of Stefan, which was difficult since he was opening her front picket gate and walking through it. He had showered, shaved and she resented how delicious he looked—coming up the steps with that wildflower bouquet in one hand and a picnic basket in the other.

"No more picnics with you," she said bluntly and wished she were wearing underwear. When she shifted restlessly, Stefan's dark eyes immediately locked on to her breasts; he had that hot, steaming look that both terrified and excited her. The evening air carried the scent of the flowers, the good food and Stefan, a heady combination. "I'm all done with erotic stuff and I'm on a diet," she added, so that he wouldn't mistake the way she couldn't breathe or take her eyes off him.

"Tell me about your mother, Rose," Stefan said quietly as he began to unpack the picnic basket, in quick efficient motions.

"You do that like you were a waiter," she said, as he whipped out a linen tablecloth and smoothed it over the small, round table between the wicker chairs. She didn't want to reveal her deeply hoarded feelings about her mother, the terrible pain of abandonment, the decline of her father. She suspected that Stefan was very thorough and she didn't want him prowling so close to pain she'd stuffed away for years.

In a short time, she'd learned that Stefan was very likely to be efficient at everything he did—including kissing. She didn't want to think about his lovemaking techniques.

"I started waiting tables when I was very young. Before that, my father would tutor me as to the right wines, the right glasses, the right breads, cheeses and sauces. Your mother?" he repeated, as he poured red wine into a glass and handed it to her. He settled into the other wicker chair and spread paté on crackers, artistically arranging them on the plate before taking his own wineglass.

"Your wife?" she countered, reaching for her second cracker and paté. She didn't want him to know about the dark corners of her life; he knew enough already.

"I loved her. Not a passionate love, but it was warm and soft and good. It was more than I had hoped for in a girl matching my background—"

"Matching your money?" she asked, anxious to point out the differences between them.

"Our families knew each other," he returned quietly with a nod.

"An arranged marriage?"

Stefan looked out into the evening, as though settling into the past. "It happens, and I did love her. When she gave me Estelle, I thought we were complete. But Claire's heart was delicate, and childbirth weakened her. Estelle was only ten when her mother gave up the struggle. I will always regret the time I spent away from them both, building the restaurant business. For a long time, Estelle blamed herself for her mother's death—she may still—and I didn't suspect until much later...I was too busy, you see."

Rose knew exactly how a child could blame herself for

circumstances she couldn't control. On the porch, Stefan's shadows surrounded him and Rose didn't think—she acted. She patted his jeaned knee and asked, "Hey, bud. Are these crackers all there is to eat?"

Stefan smiled gently. "You always give to others, don't you? Trying to help them? You have a soft heart, *ma chérie.*"

"I'm just hungry, bud. Don't read more into it than that," she lied lightly and tried to let the shadows hide her blush. Stefan looked as if he needed a friend—or a lover. She didn't want to be his lover, but she knew how to be a good friend. "You know what this looks like, don't you? People are already gossiping about us. I don't want to get them all stirred up and expecting more than they're going to get."

"Well, getting stirred up can be quite—exciting," Stefan murmured, humor threaded through his deep voice. "When you are ready, I would like you to tell me about your mother, but for now, let us eat."

Rose wished she could have refused his meal, but her stomach clenched at the sight of the light dinner, a lovely dome of spaghetti noodles, artichokes, eggs and cooked ham. "Yum," she said, before diving into the plate Stefan handed to her.

He ate more slowly, serving her a second helping. "You eat without stopping. Do you ever relax fully without charging into your next project?"

"This is good, but I would really like to top it off with a hot dog and plenty of mustard," she managed to say around the salad she was eating. She stared meaningfully at Larry and Mary Lou who were trying not to be too obvious. They slowly cruised by her house, taking stealthy looks.

Stefan breathed deeply, but did not respond to her hot

dog comment. Instead he began methodically, grimly packing the food and plates back into his basket. "I can see your breasts through that material," he said finally, pinning her with his dark, intimate look. "And I want you. But I want to be your friend, too. You give, but you do not accept the same in return. Your defenses are high, Rose Granger. You fear a broken heart and you trust little. This makes the journey to your heart and hopefully to your bed, a difficult one."

"Do you always have to come straight to the point?" she asked, crossing her arms in front of her. Stefan could jar every cell in her body with that look. Now, standing and leaning against the front porch post, his cotton shirt unbuttoned above his crossed arms and wearing jeans like any other Waterville male, Stefan took her breath away.

She could have leaped upon him and dragged him up to her bed. Rose forced herself back to the garden of reason, picking out the weeds of temptation. She'd only known him for over two weeks; he came from a different world. He would be leaving, once boredom hit him—or the summer ended—and she'd be left in a dark, depressing hole.

"Yes, I do always come to the point," he said unevenly. As he spoke quietly, he smiled at Mrs. Wilkins, who was peering over the hedge.

"You know," Mrs. Wilkins said, "the last time Rose had man-trouble, she painted that whole big two-story house by herself, then redid every room in it. In the summer, I had my windows open and I could hear her crying over that no-good who dumped her. I'm getting old and I'm not in the mood to hear that poor girl cry again. You'd just better have good intentions."

"Mrs. Wilkins, thank you—but I can handle this," Rose

said, loving the woman who had tried to ease her mother's desertion. "I'm thirty-seven now, you know."

"I changed your diapers, Miss Sass. Don't think the whole town isn't buzzing about this man paying so much attention to you."

"I assure you, Mrs. Wilkins, my intentions are purely—" Stefan shot Rose a sultry look, then murmured, "honorable."

"Here in Waterville, people take their time courting and when they do, there's usually a wedding ring at the end of it," Mrs. Wilkins persisted staunchly, unswayed by Stefan's deep, seductive voice. "Rose ought to have a flock of children around her by now, but since she doesn't, I'd guess you'd better leave well enough alone. She's pretty well over the hill for that game."

"Thank you, Mrs. Wilkins. I think you've pretty well said all there is to be said." Rose's life had always been an open book to the people of Waterville. When she was growing up, most of them had either fed her or patched her scraped knees. As they aged, she'd started taking care of some of them—not because she felt an obligation, but because she loved them. Their lives fitted together like one of the old pioneer quilts, worn and soft and comfortable. She knew they meant well, and she tried not to show her heartbreak because they worried for her.

She stared meaningfully at Stefan. Stefan looked more like lover material, than like that of a husband. Rose didn't want to dip into dreams safely tucked away. Just looking at him caused her body to hum and she didn't want to get started all over again—she suspected that Stefan could leave even more scars than Mike. "One of you has to leave. I'd prefer it was you."

"Very well. But I want you to think about this—we started off wrong, but I have waited too long for a woman like you. According to what your father told my mother, you fixed up Henry with Shirley and Larry with Mary Lou. Maggie White has started hunting me and I want you to call her off. I cannot oblige Maggie's not-so subtle invitation to her bed, because I intend to be in yours."

With that, he lifted her palm up to his lips and pressed a kiss into the center.

"You know how you are, dear," Mrs. Wilkins called while Rose tried to slow her heart. "Too sweet and soft and naive for big-city men. Better shoo him away before you get all tangled up again."

Stefan's sultry look took in Rose's blush. "Yes," he said very quietly. "I would like to be tangled up with you."

The first of June marked the Donatiens' one-month anniversary on their Waterville farm. For Stefan, it marked two long weeks without that enjoyable sparring with Rose. He sat on the porch he had just repaired, tipped back his chair against the side of the house, propped his bare feet up on the railing and gave himself to the sweet early-summer night.

A reasonable man, he told himself as he ran his hand across his chest, would give a woman time. When his daughter spoke of her friend, Rose, his heart shouldn't stop, his mind sliding back to how she looked, dressed in that emerald lounging gown and curled upon the wicker chair. He'd been too blatant, telling her of his need for her. With the fireflies blinking in the June night, the scent of his mother's garden wrapped around him, Stefan tried not to think of Rose. He tried not to think of how she looked when he'd come into town that early morning. She'd been jogging, her damp T-shirt plastered to her breasts, which bobbed gently. Her shorts had fluttered around her smooth bottom, those long legs eating up the road.

He'd give her time to think, Stefan promised himself as the vision of Rose, all hot and sweaty and sexy raced through his mind. Then he stopped thinking and breathing as Rose's pickup pulled in front of the house. Dressed in her usual T-shirt and cutoff shorts, Rose stalked up the walkway, her thongs slapping against her soles. "I want to talk with you," she said bluntly, tapping her hand against her bare thigh. "I see no point in beating around the bush, while you're the cause of all my problems. So I've come right to grab the bull by the horns as we say hereabouts."

She blinked, hesitated as though she were replaying her own words and pushed on. "I wanted to talk with you privately…Estelle is at my house watching a video with her friends. I know your mother is with my dad—and I'm not certain I like how he's acting lately, all sappy and happy—enough to make Maggie White take notice. She called to see what was making him seem so frisky. He bought new aftershave and new undershorts, all by himself, a sure sign that he's up to something."

Stefan removed his feet from the railing and stood abruptly. "We have a television. Why is Estelle not here, in my house? She refuses to bring her friends—"

Rose stared off into the night. "Would you put on a shirt? Just as mosquito protection?" she added, and in the slight glow of the citronella candle, her face seemed rosy.

Five

Maybe this wasn't such a good idea, Rose thought as she tried to avoid looking at Stefan. He stood on his front porch, watching her approach on the stone walkway to the Donatien farmhouse. She picked her way through the scent of the insect-repelling citronella candle to the one of a freshly showered man. Stefan's chest gleamed in the candlelight, that wedge of dark hair still beaded with water. His jeans were opened at the top snap and the worn places in them evidenced the all-male package beneath. She tried to swallow and failed, because she'd never seen a man's feet look so—big and bold and strong. When he locked them in that wide-legged stance, he looked as if nothing could move him. He looked as dependable as a mountain, as hot as July and as tasty as Mrs. Wilkins's strawberry jam on buttered, freshly baked bread. Rose fought the ripple of desire within her and damned it for taking a sweeter course.

Stefan's black hair was still damp and curling. Rose thought of how a sweet little baby would look with those curls—the idea caused her hands to grip the railing as an anchor…because her knees were giving way at the thought. Long ago, she'd forced the door closed on dreams of her own children and settled into the safe lane of god-mothering.

Pain shot through her and she regretted the soft cry that escaped her keeping. Instantly Stefan reached for her hands, turning them upward for his inspection. The raw blisters left by removing shingling nails mocked her. Stefan's grim silence demanded an explanation. "I've been shingling," she said. "I had to put it off because business was so good at the store and I pulled off a good quarter of the roof today. I didn't want Dad up on our two-story roof and I was really feeling up to tearing something apart."

"You will wait here while I get the antibacterial cream and gauze to wrap your hands," Stefan ordered as he placed his hand on her shoulder and firmly pushed her down onto a chair. In a heartbeat, the front storm door closed behind him.

Rose sat in the quiet night, the fireflies blinking in their mating patterns, and wondered how Stefan could take the breath right from her with one look.

"I should be going," she whispered as he came back to the porch, kneeled at her side and began intently applying the cream. She felt a little light-headed with all the intoxicating scents of man and soap and Stefan and summer night curling around her.

Stefan closed the tube, placed it aside and gently wrapped the gauze around her hands. Then, in one swift motion, he scooped her up. Still holding her, he eased into the big old rocking chair.

"Now, this is silly," she whispered, trying to sit upright and away from all that darkly tanned chest, and the enticing wedge of hair. He'd shocked her, treating her as if she weren't a tomboy and muscle-packed and independent and unavailable.

Stefan eased her head upon his shoulder and began rocking her slowly.

"I want to cry, and I don't know why," she whispered as her throat thickened with emotions she didn't understand. Stefan's lips brushed lightly across her forehead, her brows, her lashes. His kisses weren't helping her unstable condition. She thought that she could stay here forever, with his big, safe body beneath her, his skin against her cheek. His thumb caressed her wrist, just there, where she was too vulnerable. He made her feel unique, delicate and feminine. Unable to resist, she rubbed her cheek against him.

Stefan stilled, then his hand cupped her chin, lifting her face to his. "How have I caused you trouble?" he asked gently.

Looking up into that rugged face and dark, seductive gaze, Rose tried to focus. "I can't think just now. Things are just too complicated. Give me a minute."

"Okay." Stefan smiled tenderly, then brushed his lips against hers. Lightning went zigzagging through her veins, struck her heart and made it race. Thunder rumbled in her blood and her skin suddenly felt too tight.

"You didn't make a bet, did you?" she heard herself ask. Her heart would never recover if Stefan had acted like Mike.

He frowned slightly. "Bet?"

"That you could get to me."

The seductive smile returned and Stefan kissed her again, lightly and gently, as if he were seeking something precious from her. "I didn't make a bet, but am I getting to you?"

"I'd be foolish—with my background in men—to give in to this." Rose trembled as Stefan's sizzling-hot look swept over her face and her body.

He urged her hips toward him, his hand smoothing her bottom and up her back, across her shoulders. Everything inside Rose seemed to clench, despite her restraining order on her body. He looked down to where her breasts nestled against his bare chest, closed his eyes and groaned shakily. He leaned his head back against the rocker and through his lashes, studied her. "Why have you come?" he asked huskily.

Sitting on a man's lap—which she hadn't done in her lifetime, with the exception of her father—gave a woman certain rights, Rose decided. She lifted her wrapped hand and extended a fingertip to smooth the line between his brows. "For Estelle. And for you," she added, letting that fingertip roam across his thick, fascinating brows. Stefan was a man of textures, of passion and of control. She wondered just how controlled; what she could do to tempt him— He held very still beneath her touch, but the jerk of muscle beneath his jaw said he wasn't exactly calm. Rose smoothed that taut muscle, wanting to ease his trouble. That was what she did best—understand pain. "You're too controlled for your own good, Stefan. You've got to lighten up. Estelle has some idea that you're keeping Louie away from her on purpose, which you have admitted to me. She's invited him to come, but Louie always has an excuse. And you glare at the boys in her new crowd, especially when one of them gets too close."

"They are too easy and too quick to touch her, to put their arms around her," Stefan stated roughly.

"You're touching me," Rose reminded him as she

looked pointedly to where his hand was stroking her thigh. Rose decided to put that action into the erotic bin, especially the movement of his thumb, just there on the inside of her thigh.

"Do not be foolish. You are a woman. I am a man. I care for you. You entice me. Fascinate me. Excite me. I am not a man who relates easily to anyone, but in you, I find…contentment."

Rose tried to recover from his rapid statements, her emotions buffeting her. She smoothed his jaw again and realized that he had eased his taut defense slightly. She ran her fingertips across those blunt, wide cheekbones and had the sense she was easing all the brooding storms within him. "You're a good father, Stefan. Estelle will make the right choices. You have to give her a chance to explore them first, though. You've got to stop being so bossy. And never, ever say 'I forbid you.'"

He exhaled as though he had been holding his breath. "In this case, I know what is best for my daughter. Louie undoubtedly has fast-moving sperm. She will not have a chance to know herself until years have passed. He will keep her pregnant and waiting on him to insure his grasp on what our family has worked so hard to keep. I would love grandchildren, but without Louie's inherited fish-mouth. Yes, it's true. He has a mouth like a fish and a mind that serves his own purposes. He would not, for one moment, consider my daughter's welfare or happiness. I caught him in my office copy room with one of the temporary help. They were not studying the menus. I could not bring myself to tell Estelle. And I could not hit him, as much as I wanted to—he is small and slight and wears dark glasses all the time."

Rose studied him, seeing all the stormy passages inside and knowing without explanation that Stefan wanted the best for his family. "It's been hard on you, hasn't it? Trying to take your father's place in business and then playing the role of both parents for Estelle?"

"You feel so much. You know so much." He kissed the gauze covering her palm and held it gently to his cheek. "I wasn't a good parent to Estelle." The admission came raggedly, as though it was the first time he had dragged it into the air. "I worked long hours. Too long and suddenly she wasn't a baby anymore. I didn't even spend the time with Claire that I should have—and she was so fragile. It was as if Estelle was a baby, and then suddenly she is a woman, and I don't understand anything—except that I am making the same mistakes as my father made with me. I am too harsh with her. I am used to managing business, not a family. The ease between your father and you does not flow between Estelle and myself. In business, I am not…sweet. I come home tired and too quick to snap at her about Louie, or her hair or that blue nail polish she used to wear. I work for hours after dinner. It's different here. It's good. She is very happy here. She has a glow about her. I never realized how much she really wanted this life. I was too involved with business. Perhaps here, she can find some small bit of what she's wanted."

Stefan frowned and held her slightly away. "Why am I causing you trouble?" he asked again.

"Everyone is talking about how you kissed me…that unbrotherly way, and then how you dropped me. They're feeling sorry for me again and I don't like it. You're not staying here any longer than it takes and I'll be left to deal with the pitiful looks of people I've known all my life. The tuna casseroles will start to arrive with the poor-old-maid looks, and then people will invite me to visit for Sunday dinner to meet their unmarried cousin, what's-his-name. He'll either be a total zero, or he'll have a houseful of children who won't want a stepmother.''

"What about your own children?" Stefan asked softly as he studied his fingertip, which had just come to gently circle Rose's breast. Her nipple peaked beneath her T-shirt and bra. She shivered and stared at him, trying to fight the raging storm within her. Stefan stared back, and the inches between their faces seemed charged with electricity looking for a place to zap. She couldn't move as his hand slowly enclosed her breast, so gently, as if it were petals. She tried to breathe, to focus, as he caressed her and slowly moved his hand lower to find the hem of her T-shirt.

Rose hadn't been touched so carefully, so lightly and gently, and Stefan's dark gaze burned at her as though he were waiting for her reaction, and giving her a choice to reject or welcome him. By the time his hand slid upward, she was certain her heart would race away from her keeping into the night. Stefan bent his head to kiss her throat, behind her ear, her cheek, and the warm beat of his heart seemed to wait for her answer. She feared answering the needs of her body, to take the invitation of the hardened body beneath her. "My batting average isn't good in this department," she managed to say finally. "I have three ex-fiancés."

"You seem to do exceedingly well, *ma chérie,*" Stefan murmured as he nuzzled her throat and trailed kisses to her breast. Once there, he gently suckled in a rhythm that caused Rose to cry out and to lock her arms around him, holding him close.

Just there, on the edge, with Stefan's breath uneven against her skin, the night soft and sweet around her, she sensed him withdrawing and rearranging her clothing. When she finally opened her eyes, it was to the blinding light of head beams and the reality that Stefan was thoroughly aroused beneath her. His hands pressed her close against him and a telling shudder racked his big body. "It appears that privacy is a problem," he stated grimly as two women moved up the walkway to the house. "Hello, Mother. Hello, Estelle."

"I was just leaving," Rose said as she pushed free of Stefan, stood shakily and hurried past his mother and daughter. "Good night."

She hadn't intended to nick the Donatien's gate with her pickup's fender. The post had seemed to leap out at her while she was thinking of Stefan holding her, that big body taut against her and the pulsing, wild rhythm surging between them. *"I cannot go through this again,"* she muttered.

Stefan crouched on Rose's roof, studying the delicate bare feet, which were resting on her windowsill, the lace curtain fluttering over her ankles. At five-thirty in the morning, Waterville was quiet, dawn pushing away the night—a restless night for Stefan, with desire pounding at him, his body awakening after years. Rose's soft cries of pleasure had curled through his night, the taste of her body feeding his desire.

He had already been working for an hour, tearing off the old shingles and removing the nails. Rose's abused hands were a reflection of her emotions, of her fear of loving and being deserted. Stefan scowled at those slender, curved feet, fighting the anger within him. *To think that a man would make bets on such a loving woman, who cared for all those around her.*

The lace curtains fluttered delicately around her ankles and Stefan couldn't resist stroking the vulnerable curve of her insole. Her toes wiggled and he smiled at the red polish, a contrast to the natural woman.

Suddenly the curtains were ripped aside. Rose stared blankly at him, shrieked and grabbed the curtains. A clump sounded behind them as the curtain rod tore free and slanted out of the window. Worried for Rose, Stefan grimly wrapped the yards of white froth in his fists and pushed it through the window. He glimpsed Rose, struggling to her feet, her rocking chair upended on the floor. She grabbed the lace, hurled it aside and peered through the open window at Stefan. *"What are you doing here?"*

If he hadn't been staring at her breasts through the thin material of her shortie nightgown, he might have been able to speak. "Never have I wanted to tear a woman's clothing away," he heard himself whisper raggedly. "But I want to see all of you."

She grabbed the lace curtain and held it up to her, a blush warming her cheeks. She blinked rapidly and said, "You're wearing a tool belt and knee pads and *you're on my roof.*"

"I'm finishing the roofing. You are not to come out here."

"Stefan, people will talk. They know that I do most of the home repairs. They're still talking about my attempt at plumbing. 'Rose's great plumbing episode,' that's what they call it."

"Well, then. They'll know that I haven't dropped you as you said last night. They'll know that the romance continues with Rose Granger. Did you sleep well last night?" he asked and heard his own uncertainty.

"My feet got too hot—that's all. I stick them out the window sometimes. I like the drift of the lace across my skin. Last night—you kissing me—had nothing to do with my...um, inability to sleep," she added firmly.

Stefan studied her flushed face and couldn't resist the laughter and happiness bubbling within him. "You're fibbing, Rose. You are a very sensual woman. You kissed me back. Would you like me to come in there and prove it?''

He was enjoying her sweet, wide-eyed look when a boy called up to him, "Hey, Mr. Donatien. You want me to put you on my paper route? After I finish my bike route, my dad takes me out in the country.''

Stefan glanced down at the boy, and at Mrs. Wilkins, and at several other townspeople, including Rose's two ex-fiancés who were scowling up at him. Those dressed in jogging gear had apparently spread the word that he was on Rose's roof. On their way to work, others had pulled their vehicles against the curb. The early morning fishermen sat in their lawn chairs on the back of pickups, sipping coffee. Rose was beloved by Waterville's residents, and her roof visitor was clearly under suspicion and surveillance by the curious crowd. "Get in here," she said grimly behind him, and tugged on his T-shirt.

"She needs her roof reshingled," he called to the small crowd below. He couldn't resist, "She needs me—"

"Get in here," Rose ordered more firmly and with both hands pulled his shirt. Stefan had the heady notion that she was claiming him for her own, protecting him. He eased his tall body through her open window and hung the curtain rod that Rose pushed into his hands. He'd never felt so good, so free and happy and couldn't help his grin as Rose frowned at him, pushing her hair back from her face. She jammed a tattered old flannel robe over her short nightgown and glared at him. Her father's snore sounded through the rose-spattered wallpaper. Stefan watched, fascinated by Rose's stormy, frustrated expression, as she stalked the length of the room, her long legs flashing beneath the folds of the robe. He righted the small rocking chair, perfect for a woman, and studied her feminine bed-

room—the mussed bed, the pillows on the floor, the family pictures on the wall and the cotton summer dress hanging on the closet door.

"Well, what's next?" she demanded. "You can't go out the window—"

"Breakfast is next," Stefan answered, before drawing her into his arms. This time she came more easily, he noted, all fresh and warm and fragrant from sleep. Her lips gave him more than he'd ever known, her arms locked tightly around his neck, her body arching to his. He caught her closer, wanting more of her, of that natural sweetness that was Rose's alone. When her fingers caught his hair, her lips parting beneath his, Stefan fought his need to lay her on the bed, and eased her away. "Breakfast in twenty minutes," he whispered against her lips. "Then I'm finishing the roof."

There were other things he wanted to finish, Stefan thought grimly as he whipped eggs for an omelet. The image of Rose in her little nightie caught him and he swallowed—very little kept him from going upstairs to... It was a good thing his mother sent a good supply, he decided, as he opened the back door and called to the small crowd staring up at Rose's window— "Breakfast!"

Late that night, in the bedroom that served as his office, Stefan replaced the business telephone he used to communicate with his main office. He sat back from his desk, rubbed his hands over his face and groaned when his aching muscles protested. The price for showing off for Rose had settled into his body and he resented the long night without her in his bed. He turned to his mother and daughter who had just entered the room, their expressions a mix of humor and love. "Rose called you, no doubt. I cooked breakfast for half the town this morning and then her two ex-fiancés helped me finish the roof, so that I could be gone from her. They suspect I will hurt her, you see. In the middle of the pregnant one's logical argument about why I should leave Rose alone, she came up to the roof and started some nonsense about reclaiming her life and territory. She waves her hands when she is emotional. The one who admits to sharing his pregnant wife's symptoms had to lie on the roof for a time because of his morning sickness. Rose went immediately to his side, cradling his head and stroking his brow. The sheriff's loudspeaker asked if Rose needed help, and if the pregnant one was lying so still because I'd hit him. Then the sheriff came up to help finish the Grangers' roof. There is no privacy in this entire town…and I am sore from muscles I have not used. It does not help to know that I am old and out of shape.''

Yvette shook her head. ''Poor Stefan. Brooding about how he is to come back into life.''

''Daddy, you can't just take control of her. You act as if she were a business you were planning to take over— or a kitchen that you needed rearranged. Rose has managed her life and her father's for the most part. She's run her own business, and she's had terrible heartbreak. She's very independent and you're pushing too hard.''

Stefan bit into the apple that Yvette had just handed him with a plate of cheese and crusty bread. He studied the apple and placed it aside as he remembered the shape of Rose's two perfect breasts. ''Women,'' he finally muttered as his daughter came to kiss his cheek and his mother kissed the other side.

''It's because you are so protective, Stefan,'' Yvette stated gently. ''You feared that something would happen if you did not control everything, make us safe. When your father suddenly died of a heart attack, you tried so hard. Rose is not a woman to have her life controlled.''

"I am frustrated," Stefan admitted unevenly. He was unused to spreading his needs before his family; for years he had tried not to worry them. "I want the best for her. She is angry at me."

"Poor Daddy," Estelle murmured with humor.

"You think this is funny," he said, studying her. *When had she become so lovely, so caring? How much of her life had he missed?*

"Very." This time, she was grinning at him. "Daddy, if you're worried about that one gray hair, there are dyes for men now, though I can't see you using them…so far as I know, you have never dated, even when women pursued you. I bet you don't know how."

The truth, spoken by his daughter, nettled Stefan. "Of course, I do. What could there be to dating? Dinner, dancing and—"

Estelle crossed her arms and shook her head. "Not very inventive."

A mouthwatering vision of how he'd want a date with Rose to end, danced through his head. Stefan wondered what to do with this girl, his daughter—the woman. On impulse, he reached for her and tickled her until she squealed and squirmed. "You think you are too old for that, huh?" he asked as she giggled.

The family telephone rang and she ran out of the room. Yvette lifted her eyebrows. "My, my. You're changing, Stefan. Not so grim. This move—or someone—has also been good for you."

"And you. I saw several men around you in the hardware store. You seem to enjoy country life."

"I like men, you know that. I like the look of them, the fresh-shaved smell, the way they talk. I always have. But you know that I have never given my heart, or my body to any man but your father. By the way, do you need anything at the lumberyard? Oh, and we didn't know what had happened at Rose's until you told us. Stop pushing her so hard and let her make up her own mind and come to you.''

"It seems to be my nature to push. I have to go back to Chicago. Another restaurant is courting our chefs and business manager. Will you be all right here?''

"Stefan, I am at my happiest. I feel so good. My first batch of cheese is in the wooden rounds and aging. The mushrooms are growing in the root cellar, I'm preserving jams and the pleasure I have from feeding my chickens and gardening has added even more joy. I love milking cows, the daily routine with animals who return the love you give to them. With your father, it was necessary to live in the city, but I am most at home in the country. Will you bring Louie back with you? Or will you take Rose with you?''

"A definite no to the first part, and the second thought is a good idea.''

Estelle ran back into the room, her face alight. "Daddy, it's Rose on the telephone, and she's really mad. I think she wants a showdown, like in the Western movies. She wants to pay you for the roofing job and she said that check for your day's work at the store hasn't cleared her bank account. She wants to know if you want her to write another one, adding on the roofing job.''

Stefan listened to the crickets in the June night. He wanted privacy for the discussion he wanted with Rose, away from interruptions. He wanted her for himself. Rose wasn't a woman to wait, once she'd made up her mind. If his plan worked, she would come to him. "Tell Rose that

I'm busy and I'm leaving for Chicago in the morning. I'll talk to her when I get back in a month or so.''

"It's been two weeks since I tried to talk with you and you wouldn't answer,'' Rose began as she sat facing Stefan, across his massive office desk. She was glad she had chosen the black business suit, despite the mid-June heat in Chicago. She wanted to present a picture of an independent, knowledgeable woman who knew exactly what she was doing at all times. She'd never traveled and the safety of Waterville was far away. Despite the strange hurried ways of the city, she was determined; she wanted her discussion with Stefan to be businesslike and effective.

She tried to focus on her mission. Stefan had to see how unsuitable they were for each other; she wanted to pay her roofing debt to him. She did not want to owe Stefan anything. Just moments before, she'd been stunned by the expensively groomed power-businessman who had her ushered into his meeting with associates. His answer to the competing company who wanted his chefs was to buy them out. He wasted no time in itemizing details, or arranging dismissal of the top executives who had tried to undermine Donatien's operation. With the exception of a few tender moments in which he recognized her presence, Stefan was curt and to the point. He had finalized the meeting with a cold nod.

His associates had slanted Rose curious looks, her inexpensive black suit, blue blouse and practical walking shoes at odds with the sleek interior of the office. Stefan had briefly introduced her, had given her a light kiss as though greeting an old friend and then had asked her to stay while business was concluded.

The man facing her across the desk did not look like the man who had kissed her after the piglet-episode. His expression was grim and taut as if he'd lost too much sleep. She ached for the shadows beneath his eyes and the lines between his brows and bracketing his mouth.

"It's pretty dramatic, isn't it? Coming all this way to set me straight?" Stefan stated quietly, looking too powerful in his expensive gray business suit. His whiskey-brown eyes drifted warmly over her and his grim expression seemed to ease. "Come here."

The anger that had simmered since the night she'd tried to set the rules between them came to a boil. Stefan was the only man who could nick her temper. "Oh, no. I came here to say my piece—to set the rules between us." She hitched up the large traveling tote in front of her, propping it on her lap for protection. With Stefan, she always felt very unsafe, and she didn't trust her reaction to him. He had an easy way of moving around her, as if his body recognized hers, and all his antennae were focused on her. "If you're going to stay in Waterville, you'll live by the rules. You worked on my house and my store, therefore, you get paid. You can't just run off with me owing you wages. With that kiss in the field and the town talking, it will look like I'm paying you with something other than money."

"I'm staying." Stefan turned a very expensive-looking pen between his fingers and studied her. "Come here," he repeated too softly. Then he dropped the pen to the desk and the metallic click mirrored the warmer one in her body.

That familiar quiver started deep in Rose's belly, but she tried to push it away. She glanced at the elegantly furnished office, the walnut paneling, the leather couches and chairs, the lush silver carpeting and the skyscraper view of Chicago burning in the early-afternoon heat. Stefan was a part of all this, not a part of her life. "I can't play games," she whispered, her throat drying as Stefan stood and moved around the desk. "You belong here, not in Waterville. You'll get bored soon enough, and I can't afford all that sympathy again. I've already gotten one sympathy tuna casserole for losing another chance at marriage. You can't just stir up a town, Stefan. There are consequences."

Stefan leaned down to pick her up. He carried her to the couch and sat with her in his arms.

"I'm dressed for business," Rose said shakily, when she could speak. "I *mean* business," she said in an effort to sound more firm. She sat very straight, her mind blanking as she saw Stefan's dark gaze roaming her body. His finger prowled down her buttoned blouse. "People will think we're doing something here that we shouldn't be."

Stefan stroked the side of her throat with his finger and then eased her hair away to nuzzle her skin. "Shall we?"

"You know that I'm out of that game," Rose whispered unevenly as his lips warmed the sensitive skin at the corner of her lips and his fingers began unbuttoning the blouse she wore beneath her jacket.

"I've never been in it—until now," Stefan murmured against her throat as his hand slid inside to cup her breast. "I've missed you."

Rose tried not to sigh in pleasure, for her body had just remembered everything her mind was telling her not to do. "If you're trying to soften me up, it's not working."

"Isn't it?" Stefan eased away her jacket and her blouse and settled her on the leather couch. She knew she should be saying "no," but her body ached for his touch. His hands trembled as he tore off his own jacket, tie and shirt. That slow, flickering look down her body caught Rose, pinning her.

"It is hot outside," she whispered as Stefan slowly lowered himself full-length upon her. He closed his eyes as if drawing pleasure into himself and Rose watched, fascinated. "I've made love before," she said. "It wasn't that good. You wouldn't like it with me. It leaves me all—restless."

Stefan made a growling noise and seemed to shiver. He closed his eyes, groaned and pushed himself upright. He glanced at her, then ran his fingers through his hair. "I promised myself this wouldn't happen. But one look at you and—"

He stared grimly out of the window as if he couldn't bear to look at her. "It's true, then, just like Estelle says. I do not know how to play or to romance. All I want is to be in you, against you, breathing the air you breathe, holding you tight. I sense that if we made love, I would only want you more."

Rose tried to catch her breath. Stefan seemed so vulnerable, so frustrated, and her senses told her to comfort him. She had always been very good at comforting men. She patted his bare, taut shoulder. "You're worried about performing, aren't you? About that too-soon release? You said you hadn't loved anyone since your wife and people say that men lose their edge when they don't keep in practice. It's like any other sport, I suppose. Practice counts."

He glared darkly at her. His words were stiff and grim. "I would hope that I do not have that 'too-soon' problem, and I do not wish to discuss it with you."

She buttoned her blouse and briskly patted his knee. "Well, then. We have other things to discuss, don't we? Before I leave? Like exactly how are we going to deal with the gossip about us? And another thing, I don't like having to run you down to have a conversation about setting the rules between us. Your mother didn't know when you'd be back and she suggested it could be months. *I will not owe you for all that time.* I had to close the store for one whole day to make this trip. I'm going to probably make mistakes on the cash register tomorrow because I'll be tired. Dad and the other men in town are too busy riding their bicycles with your mother. So let's just clean up all the muck and I'll be on my way."

Stefan's large hand encircled her wrist. "You're not going anywhere. Do you think I like this…this lack of control with you? With you, it is natural to love. With me, it is difficult to show those feelings and yet, when I see you—touch you—"

"Well," Rose said, trying to help Stefan deal with his emotions, "there are some people who are talkers, and there are others who show their feelings by actions—take for example, how you moved your life to Waterville, to keep your mother and daughter happy."

She patted his knee again. "You're a man of action, Stefan, and that might be more important than words. You express yourself in cooking, putting all those tender little touches to the basil leaves and the patés. I'm a fried chicken and potato salad girl and sugar-in-iced-tea myself, but I see how much of yourself you invest in cooking and the presentation. There's always that little flourish, as if you can't resist leaving your work."

"Always so kind," he murmured darkly as he studied her hand on his knee, taking it into his own and placing it over his heart.

The hard beat jarred Rose, traveled straight up her arm and into her body. She stared at him, her senses humming, echoing the heat between them. "Come up to my apartment, Rose," he whispered unevenly. "We can discuss all this there."

"Just us?"

He brought her hand up to his lips and sucked her fingers gently. Over their hands, his eyes were dark and soft and warm. "Just us," he repeated huskily.

Six

Stefan watched Rose roam through the modern apartment living room, used for private meetings. He stayed in the corporate building, rather than reopen the Donatien home, because he had every intention of returning to Waterville as soon as his business was finished. In the short time he'd been there, he'd never known such peace, and then there was Rose.

She softened the apartment's sterile decor, her shoulder-length hair catching reddish lights from the sunlight passing through the ceiling-high windows. Always in motion, she touched the sprawling leather couch, skimming her hand over the smooth surface. Everything about her was feminine and graceful and soft. She took in the chrome-framed abstract paintings, and studied the gleaming ultra-modern kitchen. Rose glanced at her wristwatch. "Let's get this over with. I've got a plane to catch and just enough time to tell you off. *Do not come near me with those lips.*"

His lips still tasted of her, his body hardened and ached to hold her long, lithe one close. She'd taken the bait and had come to him. Now he was angry with himself for trying to control her and their relationship. He'd been selfish in his needs, and he didn't like that image of himself; he usually placed his needs after his family's and the business's. "You look tired. Would you like to have a nap before dinner?"

She shook her head. "You're very busy. I won't keep you. And you don't look so hot yourself."

"I have had difficulty sleeping. I missed you. I need you in my bed." He regretted rapping out his emotions as though they were corporate plans. His uncertainty weighed heavily upon him, while his senses told him to go to her, hold her and tell her more gently of the rigid man losing control. Stefan closed his eyes momentarily—*he was feeling delicate, a man awash with frustration, desire and much softer emotions.*

For just a heartbeat, Rose met his intent gaze and then looked away to the city below, a blush quickly rising on her cheeks. "This won't do, Stefan. You can't just tell me things like that."

Of course not. I should have— But in the land of uncertainty, Stefan opted for a direct approach. He had to tell her what he'd done without her leave, and take the consequences. Avenging his lady love's honor was important. "Then you tell me. My daughter tells me that when you were little, you believed in faeries and elves. Think of me as a large elf, happy in my work. But then your ex-fiancés were there, too, weren't they? And the sheriff. Did you offer to pay them?"

"No." Rose turned to him. "Henry and Larry always help. And I help them. That's the way it works. I baby-sit for the sheriff sometimes when he wants a romantic evening with his wife. Most people won't baby-sit for them because their children are pretty inventive. They once handcuffed Mrs. O'Reilly to a rocking chair while she slept...and you're too big to be an elf.''

Stefan took off his suit jacket, placed it over a chair and slid off his tie. He flipped open the top buttons of his shirt and watched Rose. He had to tell her. He took an envelope from the table. "This is for you. It's the money you paid Mike to start his business.''

Rose blinked and stared blankly at him. "What?''

"He asked you for money and you gave it to him. Now he has returned it to you.''

Rose sat slowly onto a chair. She gripped her large black tote tightly. "You saw Mike? Why?''

Once Stefan understood the basics of the encroaching restaurant company, he'd taken a day to deal with Mike. The image of a big man in the greasy, cluttered Ohio garage lined with girlie pictures swept by Stefan. Mike was blond, less than intelligent and far too sure of himself. "I thought it was best to have a discussion with him.''

"You just went out and found him? *Just like that?*''

Her disbelieving tone deepened Stefan's guilt. He was uncomfortable in relationships and Rose was definitely volatile. He lacked experience in pacifying a woman like Rose. He wanted to sweep her into his arms and take his fill—also, he wanted her to take her fill, as in equal opportunity. He ran his hand through his hair and realized that facing Rose was much more daunting than facing a horde of argumentative business associates. "I merely visited him. A research agency found him—''

"You hired a private detective?"

Off balance and uncertain now as her eyebrows raised and she placed aside the tote, Stefan nodded grimly. Rose stood and walked across the lush silver carpet to him. She kicked off her shoes and looked up at him. "I said 'why?'"

Stefan looked down at the feminine fist clutching the front of his shirt. He had other intentions for the evening, and at the moment, the path looked rocky. He wasn't backing up— "We had a discussion. He agreed that he had made certain bets about you. He took money from you. I thought your honor needed defending—"

Rose's other fist latched on to Stefan's shirt. She scowled up at him. "I gave him that money to get him out of town. You just take it right back and you apologize."

Stefan shook his head, trying to clear it. "Why would you want him out of town? You were engaged when he left. He ran off with your money."

Rose tried to shake him and failed. "I didn't want to marry him, get it? I just couldn't imagine marriage to Mike. Eventually I saw what he was. He was lazy and he talked too much, and he didn't get along with Dad. In the end, it was just easier giving him money and the idea that Waterville already had too many mechanics. He left because *I* wanted him to. So you've got to apologize and give it back. And what makes you think you've got any right to settle my honor, anyway? I've never been a damsel in distress. I've always managed my own life quite well, without your help."

"You rejected him?" Stefan's mind was whirling. Rose hadn't wanted to marry Mike. "You paid him to leave town?"

Rose tried again to shake Stefan; he stood like a granite boulder. "Even when I caught him with another woman, he still told me he loved me. He was determined to marry me, probably just to prove that he could. I took the easy way out and bribed him with the money I'd saved for that super-duper wedding I'm never going to have. *You have to return it and you have to apologize.* Mike wasn't a bad guy, but he wasn't for me. He's had a hard life and he was sorry about the bet. I think he would have tried to be faithful, even though he might not have been successful. So you just go to him and tell him how sorry you are and give him back the money I gave him.''

Stefan thought of how badly he'd wanted to brawl with Mike after he'd insinuated that Rose was under par as a lover. But Mike hadn't taken Stefan's too quiet invitation. He'd backed off and had taken an hour to get the cash amount. Stefan met Rose's narrowed eyes. ''I do not like orders.''

''You give enough of them. I just watched you course through a meeting like a human shark, tearing apart anything you didn't like. You can't manage lives like you do business, bud.''

Stefan's headache began to throb. He should have known that nothing about Rose was as simple as it seemed. The tag ''bud'' nettled him. He'd wanted her alone, away from interruptions, and he'd maneuvered her into coming to see him. His pride needed one bit of encouragement that she could care for him as he cared for her. Now she was glaring up at him and, once more, he had offended a woman dear to him.

When Rose picked up her tote, preparing to leave, Stefan had to act. He rubbed his chest and wondered how she could have surrendered to him so sweetly just a moment ago and how his plans could go so wrong. It seemed that from the first day he met her, he was making mistakes. He should have known from his experience with his mother and daughter and wife that simplicity wasn't the nature of a woman. He was a man alone, unsteady at the helm of a relationship he wanted very much. He was vulnerable and

that made him uneasy. He sorted through his options—
what would make Rose want to kiss him again? After a
long, deep breath, he reluctantly said, "Very well. If it
means so much to you, I will apologize to Mike and give
him back the money."

"Thank you," Rose said tightly.

Stefan studied her, the tote gripped tightly in her hands.
"Where are you going?"

"Home." The single word sounded like the falling of a
tombstone on his plans for a romantic evening with Rose.

"Fine," he said, not wanting to humiliate himself further with her. He'd draw back, consider another approach
and wait until she was more receptive to logic.

"Fine," she echoed, meeting his gaze.

The air stilled, quivered and heated between them and
each stood perfectly still, Rose clutching her tote. "I'm
hungry," she said suddenly and dug inside her bag to re-
trieve a large homemade cookie. "Granola. Nuts. Raisins.
Courtesy of Mrs. Wilkins. She's already warming her oven
up for the sympathy dishes. Want one?"

He wanted Rose. "Thanks," he said, his senses heating
when her tongue crept out to claim a crumb.

His secretary chose that unfortunate time to put through
a call from an irate chef, unhappy with Stefan's decision
to revamp the new restaurant's kitchen. The intrusion reminded Stefan that he had little time alone with Rose.
"Quit then, if that is what you want. All your specialty
dishes are the property of Donatien Restaurants—I taught
them to you—they are recipes that have been in my family
for generations. You will have to develop complete new
ones, if you work elsewhere."

Stefan punched the intercom button to Megan, his secretary. "I told you to hold all calls. One more and there
goes your Christmas bonus."

Megan was silent in the way that meant she was not pleased. He regretted speaking sharply to a woman he respected. He trusted her logical decisions as to the importance of calls. An irate chef could cause bad publicity for Donatien's and she had been right to put through the call. Ordinarily Stefan would have called her back and thanked her. Business and his relationship with Rose were not compatible ingredients. "I apologize, Megan. I am under stress," he admitted. "You are very efficient and I am grateful for your help. Your bonus is intact. You were right to put through this call. Thank you."

Tonight, however, he wanted no interruptions. Rose eyed him as he took the cookie, automatically assessing the ingredients. "You're having a bad day, aren't you?"

He'd had a bad two weeks without her, but a man's pride would only let him say so much. "Yes."

He caught Rose's soft, motherly look and tossed it away. He wanted her all-woman look, the one that said he wasn't a "bud." "But spare me the sympathy."

They ate the cookies and Rose studied him. "You've got that little-boy look again. If you're doing it on purpose, it's a killer. You're pouting, aren't you?"

"Mike is a lowlife," Stefan muttered. "I do not pout."

"You didn't hurt him, did you?" she asked worriedly. "He talks like he's tough, but he's really not in shape. Even I could take him in a wrestling match. In fact I did. He's big and slow. I pinned him in ten seconds."

Stefan did not like the low growl that was his own. In his mind he was tearing Mike from Rose and challenging him to a duel at dawn, in the fog-draped trees. "When are you returning?"

She glanced at the big chrome clock on the wall. "In about five hours."

Five hours alone with Rose could be heaven. Stefan's

hopes lifted. Perhaps he could correct the errors he had
made with her. "Have dinner with me?"

She shrugged. "Okay, but if it's too much trouble, the
sandwiches at the vending machines in the airport are
fine." She smiled at his grimace.

Later, after a fried chicken and potato salad meal, she
sipped her iced tea—just perfect, the way she liked it, with
sugar added to the pitcher. "I didn't know dinner was
going to be here, in your apartment. You're pretty good at
home cooking. This is quite a meal for late afternoon."

"Nothing to it. A simple meal." Stefan did not want to
tell her that he'd salvaged time from his tightly packed
days to prepare the same dinner for his staff. He'd kept
chicken and potatoes on hand every day, just waiting for
Rose to appear. He'd noted the staff's comments and adjusted from his first failures. He also noted that Rose was
in a better mood, because she had a loving heart and once
she'd said her piece, she was ready to move on.

Stefan was also ready to move on—straight into making
love with her. His body told him that lovemaking would
seal and settle their future, that all else would fall into
place after the event. His logic told him to move slowly,
carefully with Rose, to obtain her in the most gentlest of
ways, to make certain that she received her due as a well-
loved woman. "Let's move to the couch," he suggested.
"You must have had a long day. Let me rub your feet."

The road to desire started with her toes and insoles, Rose
decided twenty minutes later as she lay on the couch—and
the path wound upward. With soft music playing, Stefan's
big, warm hands on her feet, and the good meal filling her,
she was ready for more dessert than the rest of the cookies.
Sitting on the couch, Stefan had that appealing, male-at-
home look, his shirt opened to show that fascinating wedge

of hair on his chest. She studied his expression, that infinite concentration as his hands moved carefully over her, massaging her feet in his lap. She'd seen him in action, laying out the foundation for acquiring a new company, curtly itemizing the changes that needed to be made, the contract clauses that needed defining. He'd methodically ripped through a mountain of decisions, slashing his signature on paperwork at the same time. Rose had listened to his voice very carefully; not once did his voice lower and that seductive accent appear.

Yet she had known that every moment, he was aware of her. Those darkened eyes had periodically pinned her. His smile was brief and pleased, before he cruised into the business meeting like a warlord moving through battle. The intensity of that knowledge had shocked her. Once, while he was pacing, wrapped in the business takeover and staff changes, he had stopped those curt, one-two-three sentences and touched her hair. He had lifted it to the light and smiled tenderly at her. "Catch any pigs lately?" he'd asked huskily as his accent curled intimately around her.

Everyone in the room had studied her critically, the woman who had Stefan Donatien's attention. "One or two," she'd answered, because she'd been in charge of the children's greased pig contest at the town fair.

He'd run a fingertip across her cheeks and the bridge of her nose, and smiled softly at the other businesspeople in the room. "She has freckles. I think they are kisses from faeries. Isn't Rose beautiful?" he'd noted softly, in the slight accent that said his emotions were touched. Then he had stroked her hair once and turned back to business as if it were never interrupted…as if she weren't blushing and everyone in the room smiling knowingly at her. They had been good, warm, honest smiles, as if they were pleased that Stefan was pleased.

She frowned now, listening to Stefan's low, rumbling voice. "I will apologize. I will apologize. I will be sweet."

"I do appreciate you trying," she said, smiling at him and realizing how difficult the apology would be for him. It seemed very natural to sit up and tug his head closer to kiss his cheek. "I forgive you for not answering my telephone call, and you'll take the wages, of course. I know they are only a pittance compared to what you earn, but my pride is important to me."

Stefan nodded, and watched her in that dark, smoldering way. "I have not entertained another woman in this apartment," he stated quietly. "In many ways, you are the first for me."

"I think—" Rose inhaled and closed her eyes, because Stefan's soft, tempting kiss had stopped all her thoughts. She jerked back the hand she had just slid inside his shirt to smooth that wonderful chest.

He turned slightly, kissed the side of her mouth and then the other. He pressed her hand over his heart. "Did you miss me?"

"Yes," she whispered against his lips, mentally scolding herself for dropping into the danger zone with him. The taste of him filled her, throbbed low in her body, rocketed through her like a heat-seeking missile. She realized dimly that she was bending over him, and Stefan was really only responding to *her* kisses—she was seeking him, her arms around him. His head lay back on the cushion, and she was definitely making all the moves.

Rose, the adventuress, wanted him. Rose, the woman who had been hurt, feared coming too close—and then Stefan's hands began to smooth her body and with a sigh, she gave herself to the pleasure. She feared the tenderness she felt for Stefan, more than a physical need.

She feared trusting him, and yet she sensed that Stefan

wouldn't hurt her, that he would be very protective and safe.

She feared "safe."

"I'm not too certain about this," she said in an attempt to be logical. Despite her will, her body was coming to life, pounding with the need to make up for all those lonely, restless nights.

"Well, then," he murmured against her throat. "I am. Continue, please…if you wish, that is."

The formal phrase pleased her because Stefan was very affected by her. Men normally weren't; excitement brewed within her. Was it possible that she could seduce Stefan? Heat shimmered through him, she could feel his heart racing against her hand. The hard texture of a male nipple etched her palm. And yet, Stefan held very still, a vein in his temple throbbing. She kissed his temple, wanting to soothe him. In the taste of Stefan's skin, in the beat of his heart, she found pleasure she had never experienced. When she'd made love with Mike, it was an experiment with a novelty—to test herself and see if she were still "womanly," and it was over very quickly. She sensed that Stefan would linger and savor and pleasure and be very thorough.

"I regret—" Stefan tensed as she kissed his throat. "I regret that I am sometimes grim and formal. It is not because I do not feel, it is because—"

"I know," she whispered softly, allowing her tongue to flick that dark, wonderful texture of his jaw. She shook when she saw his hand enclose her breast and cuddle it gently. He eased the fabric aside and studied the creamy mound, and his body vibrated with the tension racking hers. His eyes closed momentarily as if he were taking the sight into him to hoard. The sight of him so pleasured, so engrossed in her body, enchanted Rose.

Rose-who-feared knew she should be listening to reason—that Stefan wasn't meant to live in small rural towns like Waterville, and she couldn't think of living anywhere else. She should be thinking about how she'd feel when he left. But she wasn't—because right now, he looked too delicious to resist. Like a great big package that just needed unwrapping to discover the good stuff inside.

"Be careful," he whispered as she moved to sit on his lap and stroke his hair. She'd wanted to do that since that night he held her when she cried. She wanted those strong, safe arms around her. "You think you will have me and fly away home, don't you?" he asked unevenly and eased away from her.

He stood, ran a trembling hand through his hair, and walked to a small cabinet. He opened it and poured a small amount of wine into an elegant glass. He swirled the drink and shook his head. "I have feelings for you. They are deeper than a momentary feeding of needs. I think if I took you quickly, you might excuse that passion as an impulse, some indulgence between flights. I want you to be very certain about me, that it is not only a seduction I wish, but also a relationship. I do not wish to be considered a 'bud.' Therefore, I think it best to adjourn."

Rose's heart flip-flopped and fell into anger. She stood and straightened her clothing, her hands shaking. "You could at least drop the business language at a moment like this."

"It is how I speak when deeply affected. I apologize. How little would it mean, if we were to hurriedly make love. I would feel used, a sexual object, rather than a companion of the heart. You would be able to justify your actions as a weakness you indulged and regretted. You would have to comfort me, because you have a soft heart and do not wish to wound anyone, and then I might misinterpret that kindness and make love to you again, and then our roles would become a habit. Each of us might be uncertain of the whys and hows of the true relationship. I wish no regrets on either of our parts. If you wish to rest in my bed, I will not bother you. But I would like to lie beside you. In bed. With my clothes on. Without touching you.'' Stefan's deep voice was uneven, his body tense as he spoke. ''I would wish to touch you, of course, to hold you close and naked against me—but it is not time yet.''

''You're not in control of this situation, you know,'' she said unevenly, images of Stefan's tall muscled body tangled with hers stunning her. He'd be all rumpled and cuddly and magnificent. ''It's a share-and-share-alike deal. And we're not on a specified schedule.''

He nodded grimly. ''I must make certain that you know my intentions are not frivolous. Base rules are always a necessity. I would not like to immediately hit a home run and then lose the game. It would be like taking a soufflé too soon from the oven.''

Rose threw up her hands. For the first time in her life, she'd wanted to fly from her safe anchors and Stefan had just rejected her attempt at seduction. ''Well, you have me there!''

Because tears were burning her lids, she hurried into the bathroom. She tried for composure and failed. Finally, emotionally drained, she opened the door to find Stefan leaning against the wall. His expression was grim, lines of fatigue showing in his face. ''Rose?''

With as much dignity as she could manage, Rose walked to the bed and lay down stiffly. After a moment, she curled on her side, tears flowing down her cheeks. She was exhausted from nights of wondering about Stefan, if he'd had a lover since they'd kissed, if he'd missed her, if she could trust her heart again. Some hidden place inside her had wanted him to make love to her quickly, to ease that empty, aching void, if only momentarily. *She'd offered herself to him, and he'd refused.* So much for her appeal to men, even ones proclaiming to need her in their bed. Nothing was safe anymore, not with Stefan. She'd rest and then she'd face reality. "I'm just tired. I'll rest a moment and then I'll be on my way."

The large bed sagged slightly and she heard Stefan's deep, ragged sigh behind her. "You're tired, too. It's okay. Lie down. I won't jump you," she murmured.

His big, warm body curled around hers, spoon-fashion. He nuzzled her hair and smoothed it away from her nape. "You're too tired. You could stay. You could fly back later," he whispered against her throat.

"Is that an invitation?" she asked, already beginning to slide into sleep. Stefan pulled her back against him, his hand cupping her breast. The gesture seemed so natural that Rose placed her hand over his. "Yes, I missed you," she whispered sleepily, drained by travel and emotion.

"Mmm," Stefan murmured as if deeply pleased. He gathered her closer and gently pulled her hips back against him, his hand sweeping over her stomach and lower on her thighs, then returning upward over her hip to recapture her breast. "That is a good sign. Are you staying?"

"No. I'm going back to Waterville where it's safe and I know the rules. Make certain I don't miss my flight at nine. I've got to open the store in the morning. Dad has taken up a morning exercise routine and it's really good for him." Then Rose gave herself to the gentle caress of his hands. Later, she would remember turning to Stefan. She would remember his indrawn breath when she flung her arms around him, her leg wrapping around his long ones and his body trembling as he drew her against him. She'd hovered there for a heartbeat, thinking of how sweetly he held her when he could have taken her so eas-

ily. The rocking of his body was not that of desire, but
rather of a companion giving comfort. She would remember feeling safe with Stefan.

Hours later, Stefan watched Rose board her plane, the
night wind whipping at her hair, the floodlights outlining
her willowy, tall body. In their goodbye, she'd held him
close and tight, her body shaking. She held him as if he
were an anchor in a changing, dangerous sea. Rose's fatigue had opened an insight to why she feared a relationship. She hadn't wanted marriage, not deep down inside,
where the scars still bled. Rose smiled and laughed and
warmed hearts, but she feared loving too deeply. He wondered if she knew how she had cried out in her sleep,
"Mommy, you said you loved me. Why did you leave?"

The second week of July, Stefan clamped his lips closed
against comments about Estelle's driving. She had picked
him up at the airport in Kansas City, and had driven him
straight to the rolling green hills surrounding Waterville.
The long drive helped him adjust to the change from city
to country, to the slower pace of small, rural towns. Slower
loving, slower kisses with Rose, Stefan thought.

"I've signed up for the fall semester at the local college," Estelle was saying. "If you and Grandmother move
back to Chicago, I can stay in a dorm or rent an apartment.
And Rose said if that is the case, I can always come home
and stay with her when I can. Do you know that as loving
as she is, she doesn't have one pet? Not one. She's got a
houseful of plants and talks to them like they were alive,
but she doesn't want a pet. How do you figure that?"

"I imagine she feels she's too busy at the store," Stefan
said, studying the tall oaks that would turn fiery in the
autumn. He sensed that Rose didn't want the attachment

for fear of losing something…someone that she loved. Her nightmare had been revealing; Rose basically didn't trust life—or Stefan.

He'd worked long hours getting the new restaurant incorporated into Donatien's chain. It was uniquely decorated, while its dishes retained the fine quality of his other restaurants. He had spent a whole day with the disgruntled chef, smoothing his ruffled pride. Rose with her ability to make people comfortable could have done it in ten minutes. Stefan was exhausted, but now he was coming home to his fields and barn and life away from chef-stealing businesses. His daughter was blooming, her tales of country life running from one into another. "I will cook dinner for your friends," he offered. "You can watch movies at our home. I think your grandmother and I will probably stay on the farm. I may have to return to the city, now and then, for business, but from her calls, she is quite happy."

Estelle looked at Stefan, her hair flying away from her face as she gripped the steering wheel of her small red compact truck. "Daddy, you don't need to cook for my friends. Please…I mean, there is no reason to go to so much work. After all, you've got Rose to think of now. You need to cook for her."

Stefan reeled from Estelle's statement. He had called Rose, but the telephone lines between them were frustrating and he regretted sounding so curt. He sensed that if she were in his arms, he could be more relaxed. "What do you mean, I have 'Rose to think of now?' Has she said something?"

Estelle lifted an eyebrow. "She misses you and you know it."

Stefan's exhausted senses awakened, surging to life. He barely noticed Mrs. Wilkins's smiling face and waving hand. He returned the wave automatically. "Glad you're back, sonny!" she called. "Come over to my house anytime. Never seen Rose in such a stew."

But Stefan was too wrapped in Estelle's "Rose-comment" to be stunned by the older woman's sudden enthusiasm for him. *"She said that?"*

"A woman can tell, Daddy. It's how she looked after her visit with you, as if she wasn't quite certain. Rose is always certain of everything. And the way she talks about you like this—'arrogant, macho, beast, hard-to-get, low-down, hunk, righteous, uptight, crappie-stealing, gorgeous.' When I asked if she'd heard from you, she glared at me. So I know that something is cooking between you two. You know, you could call and talk a little, you know, sexy—if you know how—to her. I hope you didn't talk in that stiff way—that business way that you use when you're deeply touched."

Estelle reached to tug his tie. "I love you, Daddy, but please don't try to cook for my friends."

The third week of July, Waterville buzzed about the watermelon-eating and the seed-spitting contests, and about Rose making mistakes at the paint store. She wasn't in a good mood, the gossips said, and Stefan Donatien was the reason. For his part, Stefan was picking carefully through his decision to wait for Rose's heart. Business at night and day farmwork helped relieve his body's tension, but his mind ran on to sweeter things—like how she lay beside him, all fragrant and soft and cuddly. Like how, in her sleep, she'd turned to him, thrown her arms around him, snuggled her face against his throat and had latched one long leg over his as if preventing him from escaping. The incredible tenderness he'd felt for her at that moment had stunned him. He'd lain very still for a moment, her easy breath sweeping across his throat and then it was only natural for him to give her comfort, to rock her. The pleasure was in giving to Rose when she needed him.

Stefan cherished that memory while he considered how to make his next move. He wanted it to be well-planned, so that his words flowed smoothly for her.

He didn't have to make that move, because the next day he was alone, on top of the barn. He worked to straighten the old copper rooster weather vane. Below him, Rose's pickup shot like a bullet over the curved road shaded with oaks. She had given him just one week before she came calling. It had taken all of his strength not to see her, to touch her, to call her, but Rose didn't trust him now—not enough to openly share her nightmares with him. That slight bruise had hurt—that she didn't trust him. With trust as a missing ingredient in their relationship, the future would always be threatened.

Now, with Rose's pickup skidding to a stop in his driveway, Stefan shook his head. Behind the windshield, her expression was similar to his mother's, when she decided to clean house and let nothing stop her. He was without the protection of his mother's smoothing grace and his daughter's lighthearted conversation. Estelle was at work at the hamburger drive-in and Yvette was at a church social. Later, she would stay with the widow Harris for "girl talk" and Estelle would stay overnight with her friends. Everyone in his home had a social life but himself, Stefan brooded, and admitted that his body was already humming at the sight of Rose.

He studied the way she slammed her pickup door and headed for the house, before she saw him up on the old barn's roof. "I want to talk with you," she called as she started toward him. Her tone said she was not happy; her frown said lightning bolts were about to strike. Stefan could almost hear the rumble of thunder. He could feel the excitement that Rose always created, simmering inside him.

He descended the ladder and Rose stopped in front of him. Her eyes widened as she looked at him, her gaze tracing his hair, his cheeks and lips and throat and bare chest and all the way down his legs. "You're all sweaty," she whispered in a husky, sensual way that dried his throat.

Stefan couldn't move. Every part of him wanted to snare her close and feed upon her, to carry her into the barn and— But that was not his intention on his way to understand Rose's needs. "Of course. If you wish, you may wait while I shower. Then we can talk."

He added a shrug to appear casual, when his senses were racing. "Then perhaps I could cook for you. It is almost time for dinner and my family will be away for the night. It would be very nice to talk with you."

"A shower?" she repeated in a tone that unnerved him. "Yes, I think I'd like that."

In the shower, working hurriedly, Stefan reconsidered her words. Of course, she meant that he needed a shower; he had obviously misinterpreted her statement. He quickly ran through his planned talk with her—about how he knew that trust was difficult for her, but that he would cherish her and never do anything to make her feel less than safe. He would tell her he understood about her fears and how she had talked in her sleep; he would tell how he knew that her pain from her mother's desertion was unresolved and sometimes pain had no easy closure.

Then he weighed not discussing her mother and Rose's fears of safety and stepped from the shower, drying and wrapping a towel around his waist. How could he explain to her that on a primitive level, he sensed she was the other part of his heart, his body? If she was wary of a deep relationship, a commitment to a love, that might frighten her even more.

Crossing the hallway from the bathroom to his bedroom, he saw Rose standing in the living room. And then she turned to find him in the hallway and he stopped, pinned by Rose's sultry expression, the way she seemed to soften as she studied him through the shadows. He made no effort to hide the hardening of his body, though he feared the obvious beneath his towel might shock her. In that moment, as natural as sunrise and spring rain and the dark secret night, they were nothing but a man and a woman, without the years of complications between them.

"I hadn't planned on you, or feeling like this," Rose whispered so quietly it rocked his soul. "I'm terrified, but I want you."

"I do not see this as a problem, because I want you, too," he answered slowly, but with all his heart.

"What shall we do?"

"I think we should explore all possibilities, *ma chérie.*"

Seven

Rose's heart pounded as Stefan walked down the hallway to her, a tall man whose shoulders filled the narrow space. He moved sleekly, gracefully toward her, the dim light skimming over his powerful body. In a suit, he looked hard and chiseled and cold, but with only a towel around his narrow hips, he bore a primitive warrior look as if his time had come to take what he wanted.

Rose couldn't move, pinned by the sight, his muscles flowing beneath that dark skin, that wedge of hair on his chest, droplets gleaming there. He came to stand near her, framing her face with his large, rough hands. In his eyes, she saw a reflection of her desire; it sparkled in the beads of water on his shoulders, in his waving hair. He lowered his head to hers, placing his lips exactly so on hers. Then he studied her so closely she thought he could see the fears and shadows she didn't want exposed. ''I didn't expect you in my life, either," he whispered. "Are you certain you want to make love with me?"

"If you're feeling up to it," she returned unevenly, shivering as she controlled her need to wrap her arms around him.

His smile was soft and tender, his gaze searching her face. "It has been so long since I've first wanted you. That first need to make love to you has grown with each day. In my lifetime, I have never wanted another woman like I want you."

She hovered between the fear and the need for Stefan. "No inconvenience then?"

"None at all. In fact, it will be a pleasure," he returned softly. With that, Stefan gently lifted her in his arms. It seemed so natural to settle against him, to place her head on his shoulder. His heart pounded heavily, safely, as he carried her up the stairs. She hadn't realized how powerful he was, how hot his skin was beneath her lips, how strong that vein in his throat pounded as he carried her into a large room, starkly masculine and uncluttered.

The setting sun slid through the windows, laying gentle stripes across the heavy wooden furniture, books stacked on the night table beside the sturdy, big bed. Browns and tans mixed with the sheen of the wooden floor, broken only by a rectangular cream rug. On the tall, old dresser, bold with its antique metal knobs and pulls, lay his trappings for business—his expensive gold watch, a flat wallet, his compact cellular phone. Framed pictures of his family stood nearby. On the outside door of the closet hung two suits, a gray and a black, a tie hung round the hanger of a pristine white shirt. Nearby were his dress shoes, the Italian leather polished, almost mirrorlike. His work books, with leather lace, stood by worn running shoes. Jeans, pressed with a crease were folded over the back of a big chair, and a stack of folded T-shirts rested neatly on the seat.

Holding her, Stefan breathed quietly, his body tense. She sensed that this was important to him, bringing her to his bed, a ritual that was both beautiful and terrifying. There in the dark planes of his face, he shielded his emotions, as though giving her time to deny what had begun.

Rose closed her eyes, taking in the moment, dissecting it. Long ago, she dreamed of a man carrying her just like this, of making her feel feminine and desired. She smoothed his damp shoulder, admiring the beauty of the powerful planes, the tense cords and muscles shifting beneath that wonderful tanned skin. The soft light of evening spread gently into the room, filling her heart with peace. Somehow, a part of her always knew that Stefan would be very courtly, very gentle with her.

He placed her on her feet and traced her flushed face with his fingertip, tilting her chin up for another intense study as he waited for her to tell him this was what she wanted, to let her decide. Rose stood very still, then let her hands speak for her, smoothing his shoulders, his throat and latching in his hair. "Yes," she whispered, drawing him down for her kiss.

She hadn't expected the heat, the sudden storm as Stefan trembled and opened her lips with his, his intimate kiss searching and pleasuring. She heard the tear of cloth and knew that he was as eager as she, and that pleasured her more. The seductress rose in her, slipping from her lifetime hiding place, as she skimmed his body with her hands, over that flat stomach and lower and up to flatten on those sliding muscles of his back. They quivered to her caress, exciting her because she knew that his body was susceptible to her touch, reacting almost as if the leashes of his control were slipping. The temptation to tear away those tethers circled her, for she had never played at lovemaking, and in comparison, her one experience had seemed sterile and without emotion, a mechanical disaster that left her unsatisfied.

She sensed deep inside, where all her fears lay quivering, that Stefan would not use her quickly and for his pleasure alone. He was too thorough, too thoughtful and considerate. She gently nipped his lip and enjoyed his suddenly indrawn breath, the shock and the surprise heightening the passion between them. Her blouse and bra came away, carelessly tossed by Stefan onto a chair. He eased her body against his, looking down to where her breasts nestled against his chest. He had that same fierce look she remembered, as if he would struggle against his own primitive desires to please her, yet the sight of her breasts, small and pale against him, seemed to intensify his need.

His hands were at her stomach now, shaking, hurrying to unbutton the snaps of her denim shorts. They slid from her and Stefan's touch roamed her bottom, before sliding inside, tugging away her briefs. And there in the cool, dark room, he held her away from him as he roughly stripped the towel between them, and slowly, so slowly fitted her body to his. The brand of his desire nudged her, and Rose stood still as the shocking warmth spread within her, the softening and opening.

"Rose...." he whispered unevenly as his hands caressed and seduced and prowled intimately lower. The clean sheets on his bed smelled like sunshine and wind as he settled her upon it. Lying beside her, Stefan tugged her against him, and Rose quickly caught him with her arms and legs.

He momentarily stiffened with the gentle attack, then began to smile. It was a confident, devastating, tender smile that warmed and softened his face. "That's it. Hold me, Rose."

For an instant, she regretted her action, a strong athlete claiming a prize, rather than a woman softly welcoming a man to her. But Stefan's smile said he was pleased.

It would be no gentle journey, she knew, for the need to devour him, to pleasure him rose too sharply within her. He came slowly upon her, pushed back a bit to study her in the shadows, his expression honed and tense before he kissed her throat, her breasts. She cried out, vibrating with excitement and pleasure, as he suckled gently there, pleasuring her. She couldn't lie still, her body undulating, aching. Then, after reaching for protection, Stefan settled firmly over her with the caress of his hand sweeping her body, her thigh.

The nudge of his desire caused her to tense and Stefan paused as she adjusted, waiting for her. Their gazes locked, he began the sensual journey, entering her so gently that she cried out at the beauty.

She shivered and gripped his arms, her fingers digging in to hold him as the sensations of fullness riveted her.

He lay quietly, locked inside her, watching her, holding himself slightly away. He studied her flushed face, her shielded eyes, the lips that had opened for his. "I dreamed of you like this—warm and soft and fragrant, tight and damp and—"

Rose shook beneath him, her hips arching, her body taut and she closed her eyes as she sealed in the first rippling pleasure. When she opened her eyes, Stefan had begun to move gently, the rhythm so timeless she met and drifted in it, locking her gaze with his. Then suddenly, deep inside, the pounding, flashing heat would not be denied and she tightened around Stefan, meeting his feverish kisses, digging her fingers in to hold him just there. The riveting flash and thunder struck within her, she realized slowly as Stefan's body stiffened, and there on that silvery, glittering plane, time waited and yet ran on in waves of pleasure.

He breathed unevenly, coming slowly down to settle against her, to hold her tight in the aftermath of that heat as her racing heart slowed, her breast against him quivering. His hands skimmed over her, defining the softness and the curves, caressing them lazily.

She wanted to talk, to tell him that now she knew—that now she knew what? How wonderful a caring man could be, a tender man? That she was woman and soft and melting and happy and…in the end, Rose settled against Stefan, wrapping her arm and leg around his so he couldn't leave her. She drifted in the peace running through her, one she'd never enjoyed. Peace…whatever had been wrong in her life was now right, at least for the moment.

Then Stefan was kissing her again, his warm body seeking hers, filling her and suddenly she was flying and happy and hungry for him….

Rose awoke in the morning, her arms and legs tangled with Stefan's heavily muscled ones, his heart beating slowly beneath her cheek. She breathed quietly, adjusting to the bold light skimming into the window and the icy slash of fear, the past churned and stormed and caught her.

She could ruin both of their lives, the dark shadows chasing her.

Her muscles ached slightly, her body tingling now, and she fought the tears behind her lids. He was already too close, and he wouldn't be sent away so easily.

That afternoon, while repairing the barn's stall, Stefan damned himself for his hunger, for his need of Rose. He'd taken her twice in the night and once almost before she awoke. No considerate lover would initiate his sweetheart

so quickly—in one night—especially when she was so
tight and new— Stefan held very still in the silence of the
barn, the kittens mewing in their mother's nest. His mind
flashed back to that tightness, to Rose's surprise, and he
damned himself again. Whatever sex Rose may have had,
it wasn't with a demanding lover who also gave her pleasure. Her blush this morning, her hurried, flustered exit
from his bed, leaving her bra and briefs behind, wasn't
that of an experienced woman. Stefan scrubbed his hands
over his face, and shook his head. He'd wanted to say so
much, but his body and heart had taken control. So much
for a man, powerful in business and helpless in love—
love?

Of course he loved her. Who wouldn't? The whole town
loved Rose Granger, a tall, fresh-faced woman with a
beautiful, caring heart and a dazzling smile. They were a
part of her life, just as she was of theirs. She was probably
having a difficult time this morning, and seeing him might
only disturb her. Stefan decided that the next time he saw
Rose, he was going to draw upon whatever charm he could
manage and tell her—what? In his stiff, rigid way when
he was affected by his emotions, he could hurt her. But
the next time, Stefan promised himself, he would not make
love to her until she knew how much he cared. He should
try that sexy telephone talk Estelle recommended. He
should call Rose—it was almost quitting time and only
hours since she'd awakened in a tangle of sheets and had
blown the strand of hair from her face.

Stefan smiled wistfully. She'd looked like a faerie, all
rosy and warm and tousled in his bed, bewildered as she
slowly awoke to him. He frowned then, remembering her
sharp knee as she quickly crossed him, scrambling on her
way to the floor on the other side. Just awakened and
rudely so, he wasn't exactly happy, his unique ache not

the one he had planned, as she hurriedly tugged on her clothing and muttered about being late to open the store. Stefan was still recovering when the front door had slammed behind her. Her pickup had skidded out of his driveway, hitting the already crooked post once more. Rose's expression had been that of fear and shock and because of that, he'd decided to give her time to resolve what had happened between them.

She wasn't afraid of him; she'd come too freely to him, opened for him. Yet another fear held her, that of loving and losing.

He watched his mother in her vegetable garden, the sound of her happy humming carried to him by the gentle summer breeze. Yvette snipped her roses and began filling her basket. When Stefan finished hammering the last board into the repaired stall, he had sorted his priorities for dealing with his long-term Rose-relationship. He would make her comfortable with him—how could he do that when his body ached for hers so passionately? Would she ever trust him enough to share her heartbreak?

He rubbed his forehead. If he were better at relationships, his words more smoothly crafted, he might be able to open the shadows she guarded so fiercely. They slithered between a complete relationship and full trust. Rose's pain wasn't something he could lay out as he might a problem on the business table.

Last night, one look from Rose and he had been stirred into desire that he couldn't waylay. He looked at the bouquet of summer flowers his mother had stuck in front of his face. "Go to her," Yvette ordered softly, an understanding, tender smile upon her face.

"Everybody knows," Rose whispered urgently as she sat across the café booth from Stefan. She held the bouquet tightly against her, not yielding it to Peggy the waitress to place in water. "Don't ask me how, they just know you and I...*you know*."

Stefan smiled as he studied the café's menu. He didn't want to tell Rose that her expression hid little, that she glowed. Everyone in Waterville knew Rose's very open expressions and when she was distracted and by what— rather, by whom. He was quite happy with that rosy glow, because it meant he had succeeded in giving her pleasure that wasn't easily forgotten. Rose's flustered expression when seeing him at the store's closing time had shifted into a sensually hungry look. Stefan inhaled slowly; life was good. With Rose as a dinner enchantress, all rosy and warm and flustered and nervous of him, he could tolerate whatever the cook could serve.

"You're not picking at the food," Rose noted as they ate.

"It's good," Stefan returned lightly. "Filling, nutritious, fresh vegetables—a bit overcooked, but good."

"Doesn't it bother you?" she asked, leaning across the booth's table to whisper to him. She glanced at Danny, whose hands were on his generous hips, his eyes narrowed on Stefan.

"Mmm." Stefan scanned the small, comfortable café. He smiled at Danny and gave him a thumbs-up sign. After a warning frown, Danny shifted his three-hundred-pound bulk back into the shadows of the kitchen. Locals were enjoying familiar fare, dining and talking and sliding searching glances at Rose and himself.

Rose's foot came up to nudge him. "Stefan. Doesn't it bother you that they're looking at us, and what they must be thinking?"

He captured that slender foot, and surprised himself by grinning and slipping off her shoe. Her eyes darkened immediately when he caressed her foot, bringing it to his lap. Her eyes widened, her hand trembled and her water glass spilled. She hurriedly plucked napkins and covered the ice. Her smile at the waitress who came to clean away the mess was shaky. "Nice touch, Donatien," sixty-year-old Suzie murmured with a wink. "You can do my feet anytime."

"I am certain they are quite lovely."

"Stefan!" Rose said in a hushed tone after Suzie left with a knowing giggle. "You can't just do things like that."

He released her foot and took her hand, toying with it. "I would like to have you for dessert," he said quietly and enjoyed her rising blush. "No one eats pie like you, sliding it from the tip of your fork into your mouth. Closing your eyes as you take the pleasure into you—"

Rose blinked and her mouth parted and moved as if she were trying to speak and couldn't. She swallowed finally and managed unevenly, "I've got plans for tonight. And you're not them. I'm going to take a long bath and read updates on the paint catalogs and—"

"I held a faerie in my arms last night," Stefan heard himself say quietly. "I would very much like to hold her now and taste the unique flavor of her desire—"

Rose's delicate shudder said his statement had had the impact he'd sought and meant. "I think we should leave," she said breathlessly. "People are staring and you can't talk like that here."

"So proper," he teased, enjoying himself, feeling very young and carefree and reckless. "What did you come to see me about last night? Before we were…distracted?"

"I forget. But I remember it wasn't good. You've got to go home now, and I've got to go to my house, before…you know," she said urgently as she watched him bring her palm to his lips to kiss the center.

"Why?"

"You know," she said more urgently.

"Can't you be trusted?" He almost released his laughter, the joy warming him. He wondered when he had enjoyed life so freely and the answer came back—never.

"Not with you," she answered as if the words were dragged out of her. The admission was enough to soothe whatever doubts Stefan had about her attraction to him. Flirtation was new to him and he reveled in his success.

"You're leering. Men do not leer or look steamy and all revved up at me. It has to do with my low sexuality," Rose said darkly as she stood, holding her bouquet close to her.

"That has been disproved quite efficiently, I believe," Stefan returned and watched her rising blush. Then because nothing else would do, and because Stefan had definite delicious proof that he wasn't in Rose's "bud bin," he swept her into his arms. He bent her back, crushing the flowers between them and kissed her as his hunger demanded.

A half hour later, Rose broke her silence with a curt, "When they started cheering, you didn't have to take a bow. Arrogant, full of yourself, crappie-catching, lip nibbling— The next thing you know, they'll be watching *us* instead of television soaps."

He studied how sweet she looked, framed in the cab of his old beloved pickup. "You're quite enchanting when you're in a snit."

"I don't do 'snits.'" She bashed him with the bouquet and petals flew fragrantly into the air, reminding him of the scent of her body.

She studied him, silence within his pickup quivering louder than the evening crickets and frogs along the lake. "You're all warmed up right now, aren't you?"

"Did you think last night was all there was between us?" He carefully took the battered bouquet from her and placed it on his dashboard. Rose inhaled sharply, and his gaze jerked down to the nipples pushed against her T-shirt. "Yes, I want you," he admitted, his mouth aching to taste her.

"Men don't usually come back for a second helping."

Stefan brought her hand to his lips, kissing her fingers. He studied her before stating gently, "You are not an experienced woman. Your body says more than your words."

She shivered, closing her eyes. "Just once. I gave myself to that stupid idiot because I thought that would make everything right. It didn't. It hurt and he fell asleep right away."

Stefan wished he could see Mike once more—the mechanic needed lessons in consideration. Stefan had little time for anger in his life, plowing through it with schedules and demands, but now it flamed inside him. "You're right. He was an idiot. Not worth a moment's thought. Discard the incident. It never happened."

"You think so?"

"Erase it. You should know how attractive and desirable you are. How natural and sweet and feminine. You're a perfect jewel, a dewdrop on the soft petal of a rose. Only a fool would let you slip away." Stefan wanted to give her more than the truth in his words, but they were the best he could manage without getting into his rigid-emotional mode. He put his arm around her and drew her close to him, nuzzling her hair. He smiled softly into it— he felt as if all the pieces in his life were placed together at the moment—a man, his beloved pickup, his love sitting close to him in the night while the moon rose over the lake. Its silvery trail slid amid the lilies where the faeries slept curled and safe.

Then Rose lifted her face, studied him and placed her hand along his cheek to draw him down for a short, light kiss. "You're basically a nice man, Stefan. I don't regret making love with you."

"No?" he managed to say as he reveled in the sense that Rose thought well of him. "I thought it was an especially nice occurrence."

She laughed knowingly then, an enchanting, husky laughter that was more like music. The next thing Stefan realized after a clumsy scuffle on the front seat, in which his tall body demanded that the door be opened, while his hand found Rose's breast, was that he was lying beneath her. "You're an unusual man, Stefan Donatien. You try very hard to smooth the rough edges of life. I heard how you donated money for the school's playground and for the town library, and how you've been helping the elderly whose pensions don't meet their medical expenses. Yvette asked me to suggest names and said that she was acting on your orders, paying bills they couldn't. You've got a good heart, too," she noted raggedly before she came down upon him in a storm of quick, hungry kisses.

Dazed and floating in pleasure, Stefan forgot notions of a proper bed and how respectable lovers acted who were his age. His hands roamed up her shorts and found the petals of Rose's desire. It was some time later, while Rose lay draped and soft upon him that Stefan looked up into the blinding flashlight beam. His daughter's shocked voice came from above him. "Daddy!"

"Turn it off, Estelle," he said as quietly as he could manage. When the night was black and safe again, Rose pushed herself from him, and he grunted as her knee hit him again. She hurried to straighten her clothing, bumped her head on the ceiling as she buttoned her shorts, and her elbow hit Stefan's eye as he was sitting up. He rubbed his eye, and to protect Rose at her vulnerable moment, got out of the pickup and faced his daughter. "What are you doing here?"

"What are you? Daddy, did you know this is the local lover's lane? I hope you know about protection and that—"

"Stop. Be quiet." Stefan ran his hands through his hair and stuffed his cotton shirt back into his jeans.

"You could at least take Rose someplace nice, Daddy. Wherever old—I mean, older people go to be alone," Estelle continued in a hushed voice.

Stefan inhaled deeply, wondering why privacy was so difficult to find in Waterville. With Rose in his arms, he had not felt old at all. "I repeat—what are you doing here?"

"Louie came to visit. We were…ah, checking out the local flora and fauna. Grandma is staying with her friends again tonight."

Louie appeared behind her and placed a possessive arm around her shoulders. He smirked at Stefan. "Hi, Pops. You look like you've been steamed, rolled and pressed. Next time you try reverse psychology, like telling me how much work there is here and how much you'd like me to visit, remember that you're dealing with Louie-the-dude."

Before he could stop, Stefan's hand shot out to grasp the front of Louie's shirt. He hauled the youth up close to him. "Listen, you—"

"Daddy…don't you dare!" Estelle cried.

Rose moved from the shadows and stood by Stefan. "Louie, I've heard so much about you," she said in a delighted tone while she pinched Stefan's butt. Stunned, he held very still. The next movement against his bottom was an affectionate pat.

Rose's warning look at him was too deadly to mistake. Stefan released Louie and smiled tightly. After loving Rose, he didn't want an all-out yelling match with his daughter. Donatien tempers, when aroused, weren't sweet. "I'll take Rose home now and see you later."

"You do that, Pops. Rose is hot stuff with all her motors humming, a real biobabe," Louie said with a knowing wink and as Stefan tensed, Rose gave him another warning pinch.

Later, while walking her to her front porch, Stefan finally managed to speak. "I dislike that boy intensely. I do not understand what Estelle sees in him."

"Mmm. Are we having a bad day?" Rose asked in a teasing, cooing tone. "Estelle will handle him." Then, just before she disappeared into her house, she took his face in her hands and pressed tiny kisses all over it. Stefan forgot about Louie and found himself humming as he drove home.

Back home, his head filled with delicious thoughts of Rose, he forced himself to settle Louie comfortably on the downstairs couch; he made certain that Estelle was in her upstairs room. Then he lay down on his bed, still sweetly scented of Rose, and shook his head. *Life used to be uncomplicated. Why wasn't Rose in his arms now, breathing that soft, panting way, her muted cries curling around him?*

When sleep eluded him and he could wait no longer, Stefan knocked lightly on his daughter's bedroom door; he entered after her "I'm awake, Daddy. Come in."

He feared discussing the delicate subject of sex with Estelle; she looked so young and sweet. He paced the room, placing his thoughts in order so that his words would not be so curt. He promised himself he would not say, "I forbid it."

"Daddy, stop thinking so hard," his daughter said quietly. "Don't worry about me having sex with Louie. I think he's disgusting—now since I've had time away from him—now I'm into the clean country boys, with all those muscles and tans and tight buns. And no, I don't have sex. I'm saving myself for the man I really love enough to marry. Louie was just a phase. I've changed so much. I guess it was a rebellion or something, because I'm twenty now and not a silly teenager anymore. Every time you objected to him, I wanted to prove that I could make my own choices, so I kept dating him, even though I knew he is a louse. Rose and I had this discussion a long time ago, and you don't need to worry…but you do need to know about protection. Keep it in your wallet. You never know, and by the way, I think Rose's biological clock has started ticking. She said something about how beautiful you must have been as a little boy. That's stuff a woman says when she's in the mother mode. Wouldn't it be great if it worked out between you and we'd have a big family?"

Stefan stared at her, this girl-woman who was his daughter. Thoughts of babies with Rose danced around his head and he felt himself go all soft and vulnerable inside. "It's been a long day. I'm exhausted," he admitted finally. "And I love you, very, very much. I want only the best for you."

"I know. That's the good part. I know how much you love me, how deeply you care and how hard you've tried to make up for being a single parent. Not every dad would rearrange his work and life, and relocate to make his daughter's dream come true."

His heart filling, Stefan nodded curtly. He rubbed his

eyes, tears burning there. "I think I have a little something in my eyes," he lied. "Sleep tight."

In the shadows of her mother's rose garden, Rose lifted her arms to the moon. Long ago, as a girl, she'd asked the moon to send her faeries for comfort, to hug her and love her as her mother couldn't do.

She dropped her arms and her hands became fists. Why did making love to Stefan open the past? *It had been silent so long, and she had been safe.*

Her father watched her from the back porch and she knew he worried. "He's not like the others, Rose," Maury said gently. "You're going to have to deal with this and what you want. Stefan is a good man, and he hasn't had that many easy times. He's rock-solid. He'll understand, if you tell him. This is something you can't control or shove away. From the looks of things it's time you faced this— you didn't come home last night and Sylvester Frank said that he saw your pickup at the Donatiens' this morning. Come here, and sit by me."

When Rose settled on the steps beside him, Maury took her hand. "I should have been there for you, Rose, but I wasn't. You shouldn't have had to take care of the house— or me and the business, not at such an early age. You went to school some days in the clothes you wore the day before—a pitiful, scraggly little girl with toothpicks for legs."

"We did okay, Dad."

He patted her hand. "You did fine. Not me. I was selfish and the bottle offered me escape from guilt. I knew your mother wanted to travel, but I'd never taken the time to indulge her. I moved in my own world, worked more hours than a happily married man should. Yvette has told me a lot about Stefan and he's succeeded where I failed. He's a man you can trust, Rose. Maybe it's time you thought about making a home of your own, and starting that family. Don't worry about me, I've got plans.''

She looked at him and smiled. ''Want to tell me what they are?''

''Nope, but I can tell you that it's not that easy to find privacy in this town to get to know a woman.''

''Yvette?''

Maury avoided the direct question. ''She's sure opened up my eyes to all the living that is to be done. The thing is, Rose, life moves on. I'll bet that ringing telephone in the house is for you. Better answer it.''

Eight

Stefan's voice coursed low and sexy across the telephone lines. "I'm in our bed."

"Our bed." Rose shivered, though her bedroom wasn't cold. Flashes of the previous night went skimming through her as she settled upon her single bed. She saw Stefan, poised over her, his hair mussed and warm in her fingers, his chest wide and gleaming, his throat taut and a cord pulsing there as he held himself for her greatest pleasure. "I'm sorry about tonight," he said. "I had plans to kiss every beautiful freckle on your body. Why did you come to see me last night?"

Rose was lifting up the neckline of her blouse to see how far her freckles extended downward. "Mmm, what?"

"Why did you come to see me last night? You said you wanted to talk."

She had a few freckles low on her breasts and a dot or two on her stomach, and just a few on her thighs. She

remembered how Stefan's big hands had dug in slightly,
possessively, and her body started to soften, her hips lifted
just slightly— ''Hmm? Oh, I wanted to know how it went
with Mike and I wanted to give you that check for the
roof.''

The silence on the other end of the telephone wasn't
friendly. ''Stefan?'' she asked.

''I returned the money as you requested. The matter of
the roof isn't up for discussion. I merely wanted to tell
you that the morning didn't end as I had planned. I should
have brought you breakfast in bed. Crepes, perhaps, with
strawberries.''

''Stop saying 'bed.' ''

After another silence, Stefan murmured, ''What's the
matter, Rose?''

Her body was humming, aching and Stefan was too far
away. ''I had a nice time. I meant to tell you so, but I
got—mmm—I don't just wake up in bed beside a man
every day, you know.''

''I know. Perhaps we should do that again sometime.
Good night, my darling.''

When the line clicked off, Rose held the telephone receiver and stared at it. *''My darling.''* Stefan's endearment
was her first. She was usually just plain ''Rose.'' She liked
being just plain Rose—no fear of being hurt, just one day
after another, no more emotional bruises. Rose scooted under her sheets and watched the night wind play with the
curtain's lacy ruffles. She couldn't erase Stefan's gentle
lovemaking—she'd seen him in action…Stefan would
want everything.

She called him back, on the private number he'd given
her earlier. ''No. Just no. I've tried all this before, and it
didn't work. I got all closed-in feeling and sweaty and
panicked and we've got to stop right here, Stefan. You

saw how I ran out this morning. I didn't mean to, I just did."

"I thought you said this was a 'share-and-share-alike deal.' That we would make decisions together."

She recognized that hard, determined voice without the beautiful accent. "You'll be sorry."

He chuckled. "I don't think so."

"I'm not dependable in the stretch."

"I know you are...quite dependable and efficient."

Rose clenched the telephone. Stefan wasn't backing off. "Are you trying to start an argument, because if you are—"

"You were very soft and tight, my darling. If I hurt you, I'm sorry."

Rose swallowed, her throat constricting as she remembered how gently Stefan had taken her. "Could we...um, say good-night?"

Stefan began talking softly in French, and though Rose didn't know what he was saying, the rhythm and the deep roll of his voice told her that Stefan was telling her how he wanted to make love to her. When the call ended, Rose lay flat on her bed and shook, her body tensing, remembering every caress the night before, how he had filled her gently.

She swung quickly off the bed and raced for the cold shower. She passed the room her mother had used, now redecorated by Rose. The shadows were still there, the blond woman combing her hair in front of her vanity. Maxine Granger had told her daughter she loved her and then she'd left her.

Rose stepped into the icy water, letting it sluice over her face and tried to forget everything, to wrap herself away from the past—and from Stefan.

* * *

In the morning, Rose flopped over her tangled sheets and turned off her alarm. She just had time for a good, hard run and a nice shower before opening the store. A night of dreaming about Stefan's lovemaking, those soft, sweet kisses, the way he handled her so gently, reverently, didn't allow a deep, restful sleep. At six o'clock in the morning, she stepped out onto her front porch and noted her father coming in the back way, looking very pleased with himself. "Be down to the store later, Rosie," he called. "Need a little shut-eye first and my exercise program for vim and vigor."

She stretched, listened to the birds singing, and jogged down the front steps. She opened the front gate and sailed out onto the street. If she tried hard enough, she could trim away the need to see Stefan, to know if those warm dark eyes really looked at her so intimately.

Just as she sailed around the corner of the street, she noticed Stefan, running toward her. His hair caught the dawn, tousled and gleaming, and his bare chest glistened with sweat. The muscles in his legs bunched and contracted, his stride even, that of an athlete. He looked all warmed up and just right for—Rose's instincts told her to push him down into the lawn behind Mrs. Black's bushes and have him.

But that wouldn't do. She'd get used to having him on a regular basis and the next thing she knew, it would be the end of summer and she'd be looking at heartbreak trail. She turned, heading the other direction, and picked up speed. He quickly closed the distance. "Louie is gone. Estelle took him for a walk last night in the pasture. He stepped in a fresh cowpile. Then later, at the lake, he experienced his first authentic chiggers, which seemed to have caused him discomfort during the night. It appears that my mother and daughter forgot to tell him of the dan-

gers of walking through brush without insect repellent,"
Stefan said, running easily beside her. "My mother came
in too happy this morning. Do you know anything about
that?"

Rose kept running. She had an idea why Yvette's happiness might match Maury's smile. "No. But this is my
street. Not yours. I run here every morning. Well, except
for yesterday."

Running beside her, their strides matching, Stefan
was...delectable. They ran side by side beneath the shady
oak trees, with the dawn skipping through the leaves and
the mockingbirds singing, just as they did every morning.
For a while, the paper boy pedaled his bicycle beside them
and chatted with Stefan about prime fishing worms called
"nightcrawlers" and where to dig for them.

When they were alone—the boy riding ahead and sailing
his papers onto front porches or on top of shrubs—Stefan
shot Rose one of those intimate, dark glances that ripped
down her body, heating it more. "You have sweat between
your breasts. They are bobbing gently and I remember the
taste of them, the shape in my hand, how readily your body
opens to mine," he stated unevenly. "I would like to kiss
you, just there, where the sweat makes your shirt cling to
you. How long do you think you can keep your secrets,
Rose?"

"What secrets?" A wave of panic slammed into her.
Stefan was definitely too close for comfort.

Stefan reached for her arm and slowed her to a stop. He
wrapped his arms around her and drew her close, studying
her as they tried to catch their breaths. "When you tell
me, I'll know that you trust me. Trust is important for you
and for me. But you are my lover and I am yours and you
have my heart. I do not give it lightly, but I cherish you
as you are, a delight and a beautiful, loving, exciting

woman. You can call me, if you wish—at night, when you think of me.''

''I've never done that in my life, Stefan. I can't imagine talking to a man like that.''

''And I've never spoken so to a woman. But isn't it a wonderful time to start, just after making love?'' With that, he tugged her closer and gave her a kiss that tore through her like wildfire.

Stefan reached low to cup her bottom and lift her against him, her arms encircling him. ''I could pin you in two seconds flat,'' she whispered, when she could speak. She pulled his damp hair back, easing his face up to hers, and looked down at him. ''If I wanted to.''

''You want to seduce me. I see it in your lovely sky-blue eyes. I see it in your freckles. They want to attack me. To rub themselves all over my naked body until I melt into a mindless pool of gelatin.''

''That's not possible,'' Rose whispered raggedly because Stefan was already hard against her.

Stefan lowered her to the ground and his hungry look at her breasts started them peaking. Then he smiled tightly, turned and set off jogging on the road toward his house.

When Rose stared after him, thinking how nice and tight his backside was, Mrs. Wilkins called, ''You'll have to run faster than that, Rose. He's a mover. And he's the kind that will want to marry you. Not just waltz up to the altar and bolt. Sonny is out for the whole tamale. That's why he's taking his time.''

By the first of August, Rose was having difficulty concentrating on paint and wallpaper samples, and on ordering fall carpet samples. Business was slow, though she expected the usual fall rush—when Estelle went to college and the Donatiens packed up and left Waterville. Maury was looking better every day, losing weight, his color returning. He began puttering around the house and would often go home in the middle of the day to fix the plumbing. He usually returned near to closing time with quite a cheery look. Rose could only hope that Maury would enjoy his life as much when the Donatiens left. He would miss— Rose didn't want to think about what Maury might miss with Yvette, other than her friendship. "Don't worry about me," he'd told her frequently when she worried. "I've got plans."

With his help, Rose had more time to run in the morning and Stefan usually met her. It was comfortable with him, running through the dawn, forgetting everything and settling into the routine. She liked routines; they were safe.

She loved to sit with him at sunset. Stefan's childhood hadn't been wild and free like her own; he'd led a structured life, pushed by a demanding father, and made bearable by a loving mother. Stefan seemed to enjoy listening to stories of young Rose's escapades, such as rescuing kittens from the tops of trees. When she described going into a narrow cave to rescue puppies, he became very quiet. "Where were your parents?"

She had shaken her head. They'd both been occupied— her mother with her lover and her father with his broken heart.

Stefan's evening calls were not routine in Rose Granger's life, because whatever he was saying in French, so dark and sweet, caused her to tremble and tighten and dream of him. Their lovemaking seemed too delicious to be real now, because Stefan appeared to have withdrawn slightly, which was what Rose usually expected of the men who were briefly interested in her. He seemed less interested about wanting her. When they had met, he felt like more of a companion, a bud, a friend, than the man who called her every night and turned her to one big, molten shivering ache.

Well, then, Rose thought as their paths met or they jogged together and Stefan bent to kiss her cheek, or touch her hair. His expression was warm and tender, when she really wanted that sexy, smoldering sensual look. *She had another bud, when she wanted a lover.*

And then, the whole town was gossiping about Maggie White and how she seemed to be purring and content— her usual when she was being satisfied on a regular basis.

Rose looked out of the store's windows and sighted Stefan's truck at Danny's Café. She'd worried enough about Stefan rolling in Maggie's experienced arms, a known man-zapper. After a full fifteen minutes of walking back and forth in the store and trying to concentrate on an attractive display of brushes, Rose had had enough. It was only two o'clock in the afternoon and her father would be back soon. She flipped over the Open sign to Closed and locked the door as she crossed the street to the café. If Stefan was enjoying Maggie's charms, Rose wanted to know.

When she entered, she saw Stefan back in the kitchen; Danny's bulk was threatening a bar stool. He was discussing summer heat and slow business with the spit and whittle bench-men, who had moved inside Danny's to take advantage of the air conditioning. Rose nodded to Danny and the elderly men and walked back into the kitchen, taking in Stefan's chest-to-thigh cook's apron over his white T-shirt and jeans. Despite her dark mood, it struck her how comfortable the scene was—Danny taking a break and Stefan cooking.

He looked nothing like the stiletto-lean man in his Chicago office; he looked nothing like the lover who had betrayed her with Maggie White.

He smiled briefly at her and then gave his attention to braising the slices of a large pot roast and placing them in a Dutch oven. "Beef *Arlesienne,*" he explained and with a flourish, added fresh, peeled country tomatoes, mushrooms and olives. If she hadn't been worried about Maggie zapping Stefan, Rose might have enjoyed the artistry of his movements, the little experienced flourishes. She wanted his full concentration when she asked him the vital question and decided to wait. Stefan deftly smashed garlic cloves with the flat of a chef's knife and tossed them into the mixture. Fresh, chopped basil was next, followed by bay leaves, and then Stefan covered the heavy pot and placed it on the back of the big cookstove. "There," he said, as he washed his hands in the big kitchen sink. "Now I can talk. Danny wanted something different for tonight. He doesn't feel like cooking, so I made a little coq au vin—chicken with wine—a little braised cabbage, a little dressing for his usual salad, and he will provide the required mashed potatoes."

He studied her. "You look hot. Let me get you a glass of ice water."

While he went to the fountain area in the front of the café, Rose tapped her toe and thought of how she would ask him about Maggie. When he admitted seeing Maggie, Rose would be calm, unaffected and simply go back to her life without him.

Stefan returned and handed her the large glass of ice water—which Rose promptly threw at him. Water hissed and beaded on the large grill and Stefan shook the droplets from his face, then wiped his hand across it. "And what, may I ask, is the problem?"

"Maggie. You've been seeing her." She'd never been jealous and hated the fiery cords running through her now.

Stefan frowned, then slowly took the mop and wiped up the floor. "And you don't like it?" he asked thoughtfully.

"You can't just call me every night and say whatever you're saying, and run with me every morning, and then—there was that time about two weeks ago—and then *take up with Maggie.*"

"You want me? Alone? For yourself? Why?" Stefan asked very carefully, as he studied her. A drop of water fell from the shelf over the grill and sizzled on it, mimicking Rose's temper. She did not have a nasty temper, and yet, here it was.

Rose threw up her hands. "Hey, I don't have a problem. No, I don't want you. Not me, no way. Stop rapping questions at me."

Stefan began to smile slowly and then he wrapped his arms around her and walked back into the storeroom, closing them in the darkness with the canned goods. He pulled on a cord and the bald light trapped her. She wanted to shield her expression, to prevent Stefan from seeing how angry and hurt she was, but instead she glared at him, her emotions too stormy for her to speak.

Stefan studied her closely, tugged the cord again and the room was dark and scented of him. He pulled her into his arms, not tenderly, but with just the edge of possession, and his mouth fused to hers. Not gently, or persuasively, but with the stamp of a man who desired her without caution. She heard a click and knew her control had snapped.

The wild, sweet taste shot through her like a rocket and she locked her arms around him, meeting that desire with her own. His hands were on her breasts, shaping them, tormenting her gently, and then her bra came free and his mouth scorched her skin, his suckling tearing away all the frustration she'd had every night and day. She ran her hands under his shirt and he quickly stripped it away, pull-

ing her tightly against him, his mouth hot and open on
hers.

"Stefan. Now," she whispered raggedly as he un-
snapped her shorts, they fell to her ankles, and his caresses
began that fiery journey. Riveted there, held by her own
desire for him, Rose cried out, holding him tightly. His
voice rushed to curl around her, driving her pleasure higher
as she dug her fingers into his hair, locking his lips to hers,
taking and giving. Then the rush of pleasure shot over her
and she sagged with the force, her knees unable to hold
her. His kisses slowed and sweetened and soothed.
"*Chérie,* for me, there is no other woman. I live for the
taste of you, the feel of you."

"Mmm," she managed to say when a "Likewise" was
churning in her mind.

Stefan rocked her gently against him until she managed
to catch her breath. "Better now?" he asked gently as she
felt his smile curling against her temple.

She could only nod and meet the sweet, tender, searching, reassuring kiss he gave her. "I cannot leave now.
There are the last-minute sauces…the eggplant meunière.
Sit and talk with me," he asked, his hands caressing. "It's
good to talk with you. It gives me ease. Your voice is like
music, but your body—"

Stefan's telling muscles tightened and quivered around
her and his hands swept downward to cup her bottom,
drawing her tightly against him.

That was all the reassurance she needed to know that
Stefan had not adjourned with Maggie. Rose reached to
smooth his hair; she stood on tiptoe and kissed him because he deserved kissing and tenderness. Their kisses
were brief and meaningful, giving her a peace she hadn't
known.

Because Danny's "French Night" was crowded, Rose

stayed to help Suzie serve the people. Danny and Stefan made an odd pair and everyone barely noticed the yelling in the kitchen. First Danny quit, surging his bulk out of the kitchen, and tearing off his apron and sitting to glower at the remaining contender. Then regrouping, he put on his apron again and pushed his bulk back into the kitchen. Stefan was next, stalking out of the kitchen, muttering darkly in French, and tearing off his apron. He stood, seemingly transfixed as Rose looked at him. Then he walked to her and asked her, "If I get through this night, I will be nothing but shreds of my former self. You know that, don't you?"

Rose may not have been experienced in lovemaking, or handling a too-interested male, but she did understand how to make peace. She wanted Stefan to fit into the difficult situation, while Danny wasn't ready to admit the new-comer in the cooking ring. Timing was everything; if this conflict weren't resolved now, Stefan would lose kitchen rights and possibly his temper, and Danny's would be off limits. "I know. But you're always so wonderful in diffi-cult situations. You run Donatien's Restaurants, an entire chain. I've seen you in action. You know exactly when to be firm and when to relent."

Stefan considered that thought. "Yes, I do, don't I?"

"Danny has always been a little touchy about his weight." She wanted Stefan to avoid that pitfall.

"It is difficult to fit into that small space with him," Stefan muttered. "But I have not said anything."

"Of course you wouldn't, because you're considerate of other people. Think of how you're helping him and think of how difficult it would be for you to give up the helm of Donatien's. Give Danny time to think about all the won-derful things you're doing for him. He just needs time to adjust. Just compliment him on his dishes and he'll be more acceptable of yours. He loves to cook, so you share a common interest, if not the exact recipes. And he is very, very careful about food preparation. Every vegetable is washed thoroughly, and his kitchen has always been very clean. In that, he's just like you, very neat and clean. You're like generals in the same army, but with individual styles that work well together. You'll see.''

Stefan scowled at the kitchen, clearly considering Rose's thoughts. ''Yes, perhaps that is true. He is very good about washing vegetables and cleanliness. Not every chef—cook—is so cautious and I admire his slicing and dicing techniques... I merely added a little wine to his tasteless chicken and he exploded.''

''Think of Danny's dishes as ethnic food—Italian, French or soul. But instead it's good old Missourian. It has a right to distinct flavor and presentation, too. The point is, people around here like it. You're wonderful at give-and-take relationships. Look how you're coping with your life here. Your family worked together to redo that old house. Danny really likes you, you know.'' She patted his cheek with her free hand while balancing Mr. Peterson's berry pie with the other.

Leroy Evans popped in and asked if Stefan was cooking tonight. When Stefan frowned at him, Leroy quickly exited the café. Rose wondered about his boyish grin, because Leroy, a dairy farmer usually kept to himself. His wife had passed away years ago, and the usually solemn man quietly tended his land.

In Stefan's frustration, his hands running through his hair and that dark scowl on his face, he looked hot and sweet and delicious, just perfect for—but then she remembered that Stefan had pleasured her and asked nothing in return. She didn't want to be the cause of him losing the

kitchen battle. "You're not going to give up, are you?"
she asked sweetly. "Not when there are people to be fed?"

"You think I would give up? *Me, Stefan Donatien, master chef, give up?*" With a grim expression, Stefan
whipped on his apron and returned to the kitchen. After a
few more moments of the two men arguing loudly, they
settled into a low rumble. Later, after the crowd cleared,
Danny and Stefan sat in a booth, discussing the fresh farm
vegetables and "Italian Night." Stefan reached to tug Rose
down by his side, holding her hand. It all seemed very
natural and good and safe, Rose thought, looking at Stefan's big hand laced with hers. *But summer was ending….*

Summer was ending too soon, Stefan thought as he sat
in his home office, the second week of August. In another
three weeks, Estelle would be away at school, and her
giggling and racing through the house to meet friends
would stop. Stefan frowned slightly—he still hadn't convinced Estelle to bring her friends home for dinner and a
movie, which was a test he just couldn't pass as a rural
parent.

At night, he'd finished studying the figures that his Donatien's Restaurant account firm had given him. Business
was good, but there was another problem, according to his
manager—a known restaurant pest was circling each one
of the restaurants. This woman and her husband were
known for suing—falling on flooring that wasn't slick,
finding insects in food that they planted there, feigning
sickness from food.

Stefan tossed his pen to the table and listened to the
window air conditioner hum. He knew that there would
always be a business problem that would require his personal attention—grand openings, celebrity dinners, pro-
motional events that marked Donatien's presence in the

Chicago restaurant scene. The expansion plan he'd put into effect the previous year was requiring decisions and meetings, and his top man was going through a divorce—his torn emotions were affecting his work. His errors would take time and patience to unravel and they were costly.

Stefan's father would have never allowed Tim Place to continue working after his first error, let alone his others. But Stefan thought the investment in Tim, letting him take time to resolve his life, was a good one. The Donatiens had always made the important decisions and Stefan would eventually have to go back to the city. He was determined to see the summer through, until Estelle returned to college. An absence from Rose would diminish any delicate relationship they had established. He would not push and she would not surrender—

Rose still didn't trust him. He could taste it in her goodnight kisses—the desire and the reluctance to fully trust him. He ran with her every morning, watched her determination to withhold herself from him, never giving over freely. They walked and talked and ate ice-cream cones, but Rose seemed to be drawing away from him. *She was sealing herself from him, protecting herself against pain.*

While they ran, a greyhound named Walt sometimes joined them. They slowed their pace for the old dog, and Rose explained how Walt sometimes slept on her front porch when his master was in the hospital. In winter, she kept him in the warm back porch. But she couldn't bear to take Walt, when his master passed away, and so he had become everyone's pet, and loved by all. That example told Stefan how carefully she guarded her heart.

She ran gently through the lives in Waterville, resolving differences just as she had with Stefan's Danny incident. But Rose never came too close to love's commitment.

His fatigue was telling, and he thought it wisest not to

bother Rose with his problems. She would only interpret
that to mean he would be leaving her life and returning to
business. Stefan ran his hand over his jaw, the sound of
stubble there scraping in the quiet room. He was tired, and
one glance in the mirror told him of the shadows his face
wore, the lines more distinct. Balancing a large scale, fast-
paced business from a distance wasn't easy, and he'd been
too abrupt with the office manager.

He wasn't pushing Rose, Stefan promised himself,
though every instinct he possessed told him to claim her.
More than once, after an evening walk, they had kissed
and Rose had ignited, the sounds coming low and deep
inside of her triggering his own desire. He would not push
her to give him something so precious as her trust; yet it
wounded him that her shadows were stronger than the love
they could have. Rose needed to make her own decisions
and the tension ran through them like the hot, muggy air
after a summer rain.

The humming tension in his body nudged Stefan. There
was no escaping the fact that they should be making love
each night and weren't.

*Rose had protected herself all of her life and she wasn't
committing to a relationship she feared might hurt her. If
he told her of his love, and the marriage he wanted, he
could frighten her badly.*

Rose needed time to adjust to the change in her life.
And time was running short for Stefan. He eventually
would have to return to Chicago, and the gap between
Rose and him might widen, because Rose had said many
times that Waterville was her life. He couldn't imagine
plucking her from it. He couldn't imagine her being happy
anywhere else. *What kind of a marriage could he offer
her—flying back and forth on business, the late nights and
the dilemmas? Rose deserved those children she had*

*wanted, and they deserved a full-time father...if Estelle
were right and Rose's biological clock was ticking, Stefan
preferred that he be the father of her children.*

He smiled at the thought of blue-eyed, freckle-faced
girls in braids—long-legged, beguiling faerie imps, climbing up trees to rescue kittens and taking time to ease
wounded hearts.

Stefan listened to the creak of his mother's bedroom,
her footsteps down the hallway and onto the stairs. Soon
the back door opened and closed and he knew she would
not return until morning.

A fax listing the new employee benefits package purred
out of the machine. He firmed his lips, disliking the idea
that his mother would meet a man in secret. And no righteous man would make her do so—Maury needed to have
his daughter's inner strength.

Rose was very close to her father. If Stefan accused
Maury of being less than honorable, he would have to deal
with Rose. Stefan shook his head and then he called Larry
and Henry. Much as he resented asking for Rose's ex-
fiancés' help, he would need them in the next few days.

Nine

Rose listened carefully to Estelle's hushed whisper over the telephone. "It's Daddy. I told him that my friends were coming over for a little party. We've only got a week until September comes and everyone takes off to their different colleges. We were just going to watch movies and have some hot dogs and potato chips and sit around and talk. *You've got to come.* Daddy is all set to cook a full meal and he'll be hurt if we don't eat it. But the kids won't like tournedos with cream, and crepes for dessert. Jason is a botany major. He's bound to say that mushrooms are spores, and he won't eat them. There isn't anything else they'd like, and if we leave, he'll really be hurt. *You've got to come. You always know the right thing to say and do,*" she repeated desperately.

Rose frowned slightly as she replaced the telephone. Stefan had seemed distracted for the past week, and shadows brewed beneath his eyes. He seemed to be a man caught in a dilemma, and he wasn't sharing it with her. People usually shared their problems with Rose, and she didn't like being unable to help Stefan when he needed her. At times, while they were walking, she sensed he was about to say something serious, and then he shifted the conversation to the ordinary. Stefan was always a man in control—what could worry him so?

The answer came back—business. Stefan was leaving and he was debating how to tell her. She had to make certain that he knew one night of loving was not a commitment for life, though she would hold it dear forever.

He'd called at night, that deep, husky voice coursing over the lines in beautiful language she didn't understand. But in the distance, another telephone rang and faxes whirred, and Stefan's curse came short and dark. He'd apologized, but she sensed his great strain and impatience.

She sniffed delicately, trying to minimize the slight bruise. She had handled her problems and most of the town's for years and she was a known "soft heart."

At eight o'clock in the evening, Eb's Grocery had closed for his birthday. Rose dialed Danny and a half hour later, she pulled into the Donatiens' driveway. Estelle rushed out to meet her and Rose handed her boxes of buns and chips from the back of her pickup. When Rose turned to lift the box of hamburger patties and wieners, Stefan loomed over her. "Oh, hi, Stefan."

"I will cook these," he said very formally. "*This* is why I trained in France," he muttered darkly. "To be a fry cook in my own home. No, wait. I've graduated to the barbecue grill."

Estelle's eyes widened at his sarcasm as Rose gave her the bucket container of potato salad. "Daddy—"

Yvette took the sack of lettuce, tomatoes and pickles.

"He is in a bad mood. At times he is like his father, too stiff to bend."

Stefan seemed to growl at her. "Was I wrong to want to know the name of the man you are seeing? Am I not your son? Do I not have that right?"

The clash between son and mother was easy to see, and Rose ached for both of them as Yvette's accent deepened. "I am tired of men's rights. I have my own as a woman who has lived and loved, and wants to love even more."

In an uncustomary show of anger, Yvette glared at him. "You are up all night, calling and faxing and punching your money keys. You will work yourself into an early grave, just like him. Always the restaurant business when life waited. It was Guy's dream and his fear of failure. His life. You should have your own dreams and your own life. When you return to Chicago, you will once again slide into that cold grave your father prepared you for. Oh, I fought, but I lost. Failure does not only apply to business, it applies to life. Take life, Stefan, embrace and enjoy it. Rose has been good for you, and we are all much better for her in our lives— Tend to your own romance, Stefan, and do not make the mistakes that your father did. If he had said, 'I forbid' one more time—"

With that, she walked back into the house, and with a worried, helpless look, Estelle followed her.

Clearly at odds with the women in his family, Stefan looked frustrated and nettled. "I have the grill ready," he said, in a doomed tone. "For hamburgers and hot dogs."

Because he looked so disturbed, slapping the hamburger patties onto the grill and standing with his spatula like a spear at the ready, Rose wanted to ease him. She placed the flat of her hand on his back, felt that powerful ripple of tension. "I love tournedos with cream," she said in her best I'm-really-starved voice.

She wasn't certain exactly what Stefan's dish was, but she wanted to help as the hamburgers sizzled on the grill. Yvette set the picnic table, clearly ignoring Stefan, before returning to the house. "She has a lover," Stefan brooded. "They are all growing up and leaving me. No one needs me."

Rose didn't know what to do except to lean against Stefan's back. He seemed so alone and brooding and she wanted to help. She knew the comfort in being needed. "I do. I need you. I haven't eaten tonight and I'm dying for your tournedos."

His "Hmm" sounded disbelieving. She placed her cheek against his back, smoothing the strength of it. She realized how much she liked holding him, comforting him and sharing. The hours were flying by now, when Estelle would go to college, and Stefan would eventually return to his business. "Are you back in control now?"

"No, stay there. It is the only good thing that has happened all day—your breasts against my back, your hands on me."

Yvette walked to them and smiled tightly at Rose. Clearly her anger at Stefan was still brewing. "I have not finished. He thinks Maury and I are having an affair. That is not so. Maury and Leroy and Maggie White and I were going to double date tonight, but since Stefan is no fit company to chaperon, I invited them over to show these young people how to swing dance."

"My father? Dancing?" Rose asked and rummaged through her memory. Not a trace of Maury's dancing appeared. *But Maggie White was an excellent swing dancer.*

Yvette faced Stefan, a woman determined to make her point. "I think I will marry Leroy, Stefan. He loves cows and good cheese as much as I do, and we have much in common. I have been lonely for years, despite my social life, and it is time I had a man in my bed. You see, passion is not only for the young, and Leroy seems to be getting more so all the time. He is a gentle man, if not the first love of my life. If you have objections, they will wait until we are alone.''

''*Maggie White*,'' Rose murmured and walked to sit on the picnic bench. She rubbed the ache in her temple. It all made sense now. No wonder her father was trying so desperately to get in better shape. No wonder he needed rest. No wonder he took lengthy noon breaks. No wonder Maggie had been so friendly lately. ''I always thought I'd lose him to poor health, not to a woman,'' she said as the summer night swirled around her.

''Rose...'' Stefan's tone was concerned.

''Huh? I don't want to be here when Maggie and Dad arrive. When he's ready, he'll tell me. I'm going home.''

Stefan ran his hand through his hair, studying her closely as if he feared for her. ''You haven't eaten.''

Then because he looked just as uncertain as she, Rose said, ''Bring carry-in. Those tournedos things.''

Rose hurried to find that special dress in the back of her closet. Stefan had looked so stricken at his mother's announcement, and nettled by his daughter's food preferences, that Rose wanted to dress especially for his tournedos with cream or whatever else he wanted to cook. Cooking provided Stefan with a release, she'd discovered, and while he would be polite to his guests, he would be brooding about his empty nest.

She was used to empty nests, and when her father told her of Maggie, she would be prepared to be happy for him, if not for herself. Was it so selfish to want to keep him with her? To know that he was always there—snoring and safe—in the next room?

What kind of a woman was she anyway, to want to keep her father from love? Just because she'd had heartbreak as a child, didn't mean that others should give up their lives for her. Rose blinked, shocked by the idea flashing in her mind—maybe Maury had drives she hadn't thought of— maybe he had needed alcohol to get a reprieve. After that night of lovemaking with Stefan, Rose better understood the result of denying the body's and the heart's needs.

Rose eased herself into the dress then shivered delicately as she stared at her freckles rising on her breasts in their too-tight confinement. She could almost feel his mouth against her—a tingling shot down to her lower body as she remembered his lovemaking.

Rose closed her eyes, remembering what Stefan had said—he'd only made love to his wife and then no one else until Rose. He wasn't a man to take lovemaking lightly, rather he gave it the same intensity as he did everything else. Stefan was not a hit-and-miss guy; once started on a course, he usually followed it until the end.

The preparation and serving of food would soothe Stefan and she would share how she felt, and she would listen, and perhaps he wouldn't feel so alone.

Rose frowned. Alone was not a good feeling. She didn't want Stefan to feel alone. She wanted to give him something, and because she was just a bit selfish—she wanted to take something, too. She added a little shade of smoke to her lids, to darken her eyes. A little lip gloss and a few pins to lift her hair off her shoulders in an attempt at sophistication, and she was ready for Stefan's dinner. She studied the tight black dress, which emphasized her long legs. She turned, viewing her backside in the mirror, then inhaled whatever courage she could rummage. Stefan came from a sophisticated world, and she didn't even have perfume to go with the outfit. Rose thought about cooking vanilla and dismissed the idea—Stefan would recognize the sweet scent immediately.

She turned to face the mirror. "This is it—all I've got for a fancy dinner. Just a plain old dress that I've really grown out of, and some Christmas candles on the table. So much for giving Stefan something else to think about."

Maybe it was wrong, but she was just selfish enough to want one more night in Stefan's arms. She wanted to hoard the taste of him, the feel of his body against hers, that rush of his breath across her cheek.

She heard the doorbell and smiled briefly—Stefan was always so proper. She looked in the mirror once more, noting the flush on her cheeks, the excitement dancing around her. She almost felt sorry for Stefan, because he was coming for consolation and dinner and she intended to zap him. They'd grown to be friends, running together each day, and walking together in the evening. He would be unsuspecting....

She tossed away her guilt on the way downstairs. Summer was coming to an end and Stefan would be gone soon. She cared for him, trusted him with her body, and he had not disappointed her with his gentleness. A woman had few chances in life to experience a man like Stefan before she settled down again into the comfort of spinsterhood and godmothering. Rose smoothed her dress and breathed deeply and opened the door to Stefan.

His gaze ran down her body, touching on the bodice that was too tight and pushed her breasts upward. His eyes darkened as he studied the tight fit covering her hips and the hem that just barely touched her midthighs. When he placed the basket on the floor, just inside the door, she thought she'd lost him. Then his darkened gaze ran back up her body to her lips, which she moistened because she was terribly nervous. He didn't speak, but his body tensed—she could feel the impact upon hers as Stefan stood, considering every feature of her face and those slow looks down her body caused her to shake.

"The dress is old, but I thought it might suit your fancy dinner." Rose Granger didn't like uncertainty, and now she knew that she'd lost trying to seduce the man who had become her "bud." In fishing terms, she'd just lost the nibble. The bait wasn't right; the hook wasn't set.

"The dress is fine. I like it very much. I like the way the light dances over the freckles on your breasts. They are creamy and soft and quivery every time you breathe…. Take it off," Stefan said huskily as he stepped inside her house and closed the door behind him.

Rose had just time to blink in disbelief and then Stefan's arms were around her, his mouth on hers and that wild, sweet hunger shot through her like a lightning bolt. His hand tugged down the zipper, flattened to her back and searched. "No bra," he whispered unevenly as if he had discovered the ultimate delight. He seemed to vibrate, held still by the thought before diving into the kiss.

She was certain a volcano had struck Waterville; she could almost feel the ground rumbling, if Stefan hadn't lifted her off her feet. The dress slid from her and she arched into the kisses that ran from her lips to her throat and downward. Stefan was hot and hard and shaking against her, and she needed him to be complete, the ache growing almost painfully.

"Rose," he whispered roughly, swinging her up into his arms. Once again, he carried her upstairs, to the small feminine room that was hers. But Rose stopped him, nodding to another room. There in the shadows, with the window air conditioner humming and the world shut outside, Rose watched Stefan's tight expression as he lowered her to the double bed and quickly stripped off his clothes. The

dim light outlined his tall body, those shoulders, that ta-
pering waist and narrow hips and long, powerful legs. Just
the sight of him eased Rose's tension, because she knew
he wanted her as desperately as she wanted him. That
knowledge wiped away any idea that she wasn't appealing,
or feminine and nestled within her like a warm, sweet
flower bud. She reached out to touch him, needing no gentle time between them, only the doing, and the pleasure.

When he came down on her gently, his body shook, and
all the heat and lightning of a summer storm enclosed her.
The bed was old and creaked with his weight as he braced
himself over her. He smoothed her hair over the pillow,
kissed the slender hand that tenderly stroked his warm
cheek, comforting even as she aroused.

Stefan's hand slid down the sweep and dip and softness
of the woman he loved. Just there was her soft hip—he
dug his fingers in slightly, possessively, wildfire raging
within him. Her thighs were smooth and quivering, desire
dancing between them. He tensed as she found his nipple,
gently biting it, and then Stefan touched her intimately,
and the jolt flattened her to the sheets. He whispered to
her quickly now, the rush of sweet, dark words careening
around her, sweeping up inside, heated by his lips on her
body.

She opened to him, the blunt pressure filling her, com-
pleting her, Stefan holding her so closely they were one.
The storm came quickly, flashing and pulsing and still he
wanted more, and she gave more, gathering him close to
her, stroking his back, nipping his shoulder as the world
whirled and caught fire and blazed, her muscles straining
for release that seemed so close.

Stefan's body flowed with hers, familiar and bold and
hungry. His lips and tongue battled gently with hers for
she would have the taste of him, the desire that sparkled

and tormented and pleased. His hands ran over her, caressing, cupping, touching. She dug her fingertips into his
upper arms, caught the power there and took it into her,
hoarding it. Within the pounding rhythm came a bloodred
heat and she clung to Stefan, matching him until the world
quivered and stood still and released its warm flood.

She rested her cheek on his chest as he came to lie close
and snug against her, their passion still joined as each was
reluctant to leave what had passed. She stroked his taut
body, his heartbeat slowing its race, and enjoyed the soothing of him, this man she had taken. He kissed her forehead
and smoothed back her hair. "I missed you."

Rose moved to lie over him, her lover, pinning him to
the bed. She looked down into his face, those blunt cheekbones, those dark brown eyes, and traced a thick eyebrow.
"I missed you," she returned, praying that he wouldn't
leave her too soon.

The admission startled her, for she was not one to give
it lightly, intimately. Stefan smoothed her cheek, studying
her. "It's not good away from you, Rose," he said too
quietly.

"I know." She waited for the panic that came when
people got too close and it didn't come. She knew how
much she missed him, how she dreamed of him holding
her warm and safe. This time their kisses were more gentle,
the first fiery hunger fed. Slowly, carefully, their lips fitted
and brushed and lifted and Stefan's caresses treasured her
breasts, her back, her bottom. He stroked her intimately
then, and the motion became a soft desire and then Stefan's
body completed them as they rocked gently, savoring the
intimacy, the pleasure, the completion. In the creaking of
the old bed, she found comfort and safety. In Stefan, she
found answers that both frightened and pleased her.

Later, she lay quietly in his arms, listening to the old

house settle. The branches of the old oak tree scraped gently against the rain gutter she needed to clean. But all she wanted to do now was rest in Stefan's arms. She realized that peace wasn't a commodity she'd experienced very much in her life; she'd had to battle too hard to keep her walls up.

"This isn't your room," Stefan noted softly as the shadows quivered around them.

"No. It's hers. I redid it years ago. I scrubbed away everything that was hers and still she stayed in me. If she would have lived until I was grown up, I'd have told her how awful she was—to tell a child she loved her and then to run away on a cheap thrill and never come back. I spent hours up in that tree, watching the road for the first sight of her coming home. Before I gave up hope of becoming a mother, I feared how awful I would be, and would I have enough love for a child. And then after telling me she loved me she would tell me the truth—that I was unwanted and an 'accident' that trapped her. Would I want to abandon my own child?" Rose wished the bitterness weren't there, but it was. She'd released it to no one else, but Stefan.

"You would love your child," Stefan said firmly and his hand flattened low on her stomach. He caressed it gently, thoughtfully. "And I do not think that you should completely give up that idea. You would make a wonderful mother."

She struggled against the tears that burned her lids and slid, one by one, onto Stefan's bare chest. "It's silly, I know. I never cry. Never. I haven't told anyone else, and now I have someone else to remember in this room."

She lifted suddenly, feeling very vulnerable and feminine. "Stefan, I planned to seduce you tonight. You just wouldn't fit into my bed, so—"

"I am honored. I very much enjoyed the pleasure and it's a lovely room. Thank you for sharing it with me."

"I'm not done with you yet." She looked down to where Stefan had placed his mouth—on the tender skin between her thumb and her index finger. He gently nibbled and sucked and she realized she couldn't breathe. Sensations were already purring and revved, simmering and hungry. "That's nice. Keep it up."

"Oh, I intend to."

Later, Stefan spread his reheated dinner on the kitchen table. He mourned the sauce's texture and lit the Christmas candles. He wanted a life with Rose, a wedding and a family. He would have to move very carefully so as not to frighten her while she dealt with her ghosts. He knew that she had shared more with him than with anyone else, and that they were cruising into trouble—abstaining for a takeover had been difficult and he'd almost asked her to marry him. He would have to make the right decision for Rose and for his family. Yvette and Estelle and he had worked together as a team on the old house and were growing closer every day. But he needed Rose. Was it asking too much to marry the woman he loved? *He wanted to wake up every morning in their marriage bed.*

The telephone rang, and Rose answered. She frowned slightly as if puzzled. "Yes, that's Stefan's pickup outside. You want to speak with him? Henry has plans for tonight? What do you mean, Henry haš plans?"

Stefan hurried to take the telephone from her. He spoke in a hushed, firm tone, similar to those in spy movies. "Not tonight. I will contact you."

Rose studied him as he disconnected the line. Stefan had sounded very determined. "What's up?"

"I'm trying to bond with your ex-fiancés. We're having an all-men's night soon. I apologize, but I will be unavailable to you at that time,'' Stefan said very carefully as he admired the long, curved line of her body beneath his T-shirt. It all seemed too good to be true, cooking in a home kitchen, wearing his boxer shorts while his love hungrily eyed dinner.

''Henry and Larry used to invite me along for those late-night fishing trips. When we were younger, I had to dig and provide worms. They're older, and they left me alone in a cemetery while we were snipe hunting. Dad made them apologize and explain to me that there weren't any such creatures—you're getting ready to leave Waterville, aren't you? You're bored and ready to get back into the swing of things. That's what your mother was talking about, wasn't it? That you miss the city and the action?''

Stefan turned to face her. He placed aside the plate he had just filled. He concentrated on finding the right words and not frightening Rose. ''Surely you know that I have found enough 'action' here, with you.''

''I can't imagine you staying here permanently.'' Rose's bald statement hit the room. She gripped the back of a chair for an anchor. She would miss him all her life, but she'd had this unique time to remember and cherish.

''My mother is happy here, so is my daughter. They are already planning holidays. There is no reason I could not be happy here, too. I am considering making arrangements to remain here—with you.''

The kitchen was suddenly too quiet and tense, waves of emotion hitting Rose. ''I've seen you in a business meeting. You're tough and there's an excitement dancing around you, like a warrior going into battle. Estelle and Yvette may stay, but you need that edge, that challenge. It's as if you're pitting yourself against all odds and enjoying it. There's nothing to fight in Waterville, Stefan. If you came back at times—that's visiting, not living day-today, watching the gardens and the children grow and the elderly age."

"True, and those are good battles, ones to fill the heart. Do you think so little of me, that I have no heart?"

She couldn't bear to hurt Stefan's feelings and returned quickly, "You've got a marvelous, generous, loving heart. Look what you've done—no easy matter to take time away from your company to live here. But that other part of you needs something else."

"Yes, it does need something else—you."

Rose placed her hand on her throat, which had just tightened as she panicked. "Did you think, my darling," Stefan said too softly, with an edge of temper brewing in his words, "that I would want your body and not your heart?"

"That last faerie is a little slanted, old buddy. If her tutu tips any more, I'll see up her skirt," Larry noted as he sipped his beer, then placed the bottle on the sundial held by a faerie statue. "Better prop that wooden one up straight before it falls on that fern."

Henry held up his beer and used it to sight the upright faerie, with wings glistening in the September 1 moonlight. The leaves rattled gently overhead, the oaks preparing for fiery autumn color. The roses in the Granger garden were still lush and huge, but soon they would fall on the faeries that now stood in various poses in the garden. The largest ones were concrete and gleamed in the moonlight; the more delicately fashioned polyresins seemed lighter, their gauzelike clothing almost floating in the slight breeze. The artist had given the wings special care, embellishing the individual parts with ferns and flowers and lace. Their faces seemed almost childlike, waving hair decked with daisies and ribbons.

Stefan held the petals of a rose in his palm, the wind

fluttering them gently, stirring their scent, which reminded him of Rose. He had to leave, and Rose's expression the night of their dinner haunted him. She'd hurt him—thinking that her body was only for his play, his enjoyment, and that his heart didn't come with the mix. In French, he'd told her of his love many times during those evening calls; he'd told her of how he felt holding her close, their skin hot with desire, their bodies shaking, and yet his heart had ruled him—for Stefan had found that he was a man who could only make love when he cared deeply.

"The girls should keep Rose long enough for us to get the job done, Stefan. We've got plenty of time. After Mary Lou's baby shower, a bunch of the girls will go down to the Lizard Lounge to top off the night. Rose usually goes with them. So what's to eat, Stefan? Nothing fancy, I hope, maybe just some cold cut sandwiches? These statues are heavy things," Henry said as he put his shoulder against a four-foot faerie holding a wand and muscled it upright.

"Rose will love them," Larry said as he sat down on the ground to study the statues in the rose garden. "Faeries were all she had to comfort her years ago. She gave me a black eye for laughing at her, and she was right to do it. I'm teaching my boys to be more sensitive. Glad you asked us to help, Stefan. Rose deserves nice things."

Stefan prayed he wasn't adding to Rose's fear by placing the statues in her garden, just as he wanted to place his love in her heart. He hadn't meant to sound so cold and hard—*Did you think, my darling, that I would want your body and not your heart?*

He'd sounded as if he were making a business acquisition, but the sting went deep—that Rose would think so little of him. The panic in her wide blue eyes had told him not to push the matter, and he'd hoped that the rose garden faeries would add a gentler persuasion to his case for romance. He'd been very careful not to give Rose gifts because she was still simmering over his refusal to accept payment for roofing her house. He'd torn up the check she'd written for his day of work at the store. He discovered that she was very determined to give an "equalizing" gift when one was given, but the several hundred pound statues weren't easily returned. They were set in concrete, a permanent fixture as was his love. He wanted her to think of him when he was away—and he would have to leave soon.

The men settled down to drink beer and eat bratwursts on buns, slathered with good mustard. Larry and Henry, old friends who had grown up with Rose, cared very deeply for her, and Stefan enjoyed listening to their Rose-stories.

Around midnight, when they were all lying flat on the lawn, studying the moon above, Mrs. Wilkins called, "If you boys don't hurry up and leave, Rose will be home soon and find you snockered in her garden. You're a nice man, Stefan Donatien."

"He sure is," Larry said very slowly and distinctly.

"Sure is," Henry added, seemingly pleased with his loud belch.

"I love Rose, and I love you guys, too," Stefan returned, feeling very mellow as he lay on the ground with his friends. He balanced his bottle of beer on his stomach and studied the faeries surrounding them. They were in different poses, their wings arching, almost fluttering, holding gifts of flowers and birdbaths and sundials, and love. He could almost see them kissing freckles all over Rose's long, delectable body. He wanted her to have something to remember him by when he left on his business trip. "Good job, men," he said.

"She'll love them, but she gets uppity sometimes when

people give her things...because she doesn't want anyone feeling sorry for her," Mrs. Wilkins said, coming to settle on the old wooden bench. "I think you're feeling some-thing other than that and this is a nice way to show her how much you love her. It's unique and sweet, and I'd like to tell you a few stories about Rose, so you'll under-stand her pride better. She's a giver, you see. She's wound through our lives, a beautiful caring girl, who became even more considerate as a woman. You could always count on Rose in a hard spot, like when I had those bouts of pneu-monia. She was right there, taking me to the doctor, taking care of me, like she has other people in Waterville. She spreads kindness like sunshine, and that's why we call her 'The Love Spinner.' But she hasn't learned that in taking gifts, she is also giving."

She took her scissors and snipped lengths of blue ribbon. "There, if we tie these around the faeries, they'll seem more like gifts. This blue is the exact shade of Rose's eyes. Got any more bratwursts?"

Stefan served more bratwurst and more beer and settled down into a mellow expectation of how much Rose would like his surprise. With the air sweet around him, and im-ages of Rose steaming nicely to his caresses, Stefan sighed happily. "I think I love all of you," he stated grandly.

"Uh...you're okay, too," Larry said after a look at Henry.

"And Rose?" Mrs. Wilkins prompted.

"Rose is my delight, my dessert, and my life. She glows when she smiles, and opens the sunshine of my heart. She holds it in the palm of her hand and I can only breathe when I am near her. Like good cheese and wine, she will only grow better with time. I am a happy man. I adore her. Every freckle and every scent and every look and—"

Henry frowned at Stefan. "Say, Steve, could you say

something romantic in French so I could make points with my wife? After watching you with Rose, she thinks I need to study your technique.''

Stefan taught Larry and Henry endearments, and as they curled over his lips and drifted into the night air, he savored the moment when he could whisper them to Rose. He smiled again, and thought of how he would teach Rose and how she would whisper them back to him....

The next morning, Rose stepped out onto her front porch. She did her warm-up stretches for running and sailed out of the front yard. She thought of the tense moments between Yvette and Stefan. Rose decided to call Yvette and Estelle and make certain they knew how much Stefan loved them. He always seemed so strong—Rose wondered if they knew how much he needed them in his life, how he needed to be needed. Rose decided to visit Leroy and explain how important it was for Stefan to help those he loved, and to see that they were treated gently. Rose's needs ran to seeing that Stefan wasn't hurt; she wanted his life to be safe, even though she wouldn't be in it when he returned to the city.

She'd hurt Stefan's feelings that night after they'd made love; she'd seen it in the flash of his eyes, the tilt of his head and the set of his jaw. Two nights ago after their reheated dinner, he'd been very silent as he dressed, gave her a brisk kiss on the cheek and walked out of her home. There had been no evening calls, that beautiful language curling around her, and last night she'd missed him all through the night at the Lizard. She kept wishing for him, wanting him to hold her. It should be so easy to tell him she loved him, but it wasn't. She thought of how she could hurt him when the panic set in—her fear of loving too much.

Stefan surged down the street and soon ran at her side. This morning he wore sunglasses and he hadn't shaved. She remembered the scrape of his beard against her skin, the exotic texture of man. When he didn't speak, Rose asked, "Having a good day?"

"Hmm," he returned darkly, clearly not wanting to indulge in conversation. He glanced down at the blue ribbon trailing out of his pocket and jammed it back in without explanation.

He smiled briefly, as if he were both satisfied and anticipating whatever memories the ribbon stirred. *But he wasn't speaking to her. He was preparing to end their summer. That's all that it was—a summer love…he wasn't a teenager anymore…she could adapt to this…life moved on…* Rose wanted to make ending their affair easy for him, though she would remember him forever. "You'll feel better when you're back at the helm. You know, steady at the rudder, and all that business talk."

The mirrored sunglasses flashed down at her and Stefan's taut mouth did not resemble a happy lover's. Rose decided this wasn't the morning for talk. Then he sailed off and left her with old Walt, who was panting and tired— and Rose ached. "I love him, of course," she whispered to old Walt. "But you see this is for the best, don't you? Stefan deserves someone who isn't going to panic at the thought of commitment. Estelle is in college now and he'll be going back to the city, and I'll be staying here with you, and life will go on the same as always."

Life went on that morning at the paint store, the same as always for Rose Granger. She moved through the sales as if she were a robot, and knew that every day after Stefan left would be the same. He'd become a part of her life— the morning jogging, the late-night calls, those steamy, soul-shattering kisses— Stefan's emotions ran deep, despite his sometimes cool, controlled exterior. She'd hurt him; there had been that tilt of his head, the arrogance and pride in his too soft tone. *Do you think that I would want your body, and not your heart?*

Then at midmorning, Stefan carried a tray into the store and walked back into the storeroom without speaking. She hurried back to see him, to explain how she'd miss him and that things were for the better, and— She looked at the tray filled with crepes and strawberries, coffee and a beautiful rose. "For me?" she asked, delighted that he would think of her.

Then her delight shifted into wary expectation—*the beautiful food was Stefan's way of softening the end of their interlude, and that's all it was,* Rose repeated to herself. *An interlude that both knew would end.*

"Danny let me make crepes this morning. They called them 'Steve's pancakes,' but it is no matter. They were a success with the breakfast crowd, and these are for you for helping me resolve those first yelling matches." His boyish, triumphant smile dazzled her and while she wasn't thinking of the summer ending, filling herself with how beautiful he looked, Stefan closed the storeroom door and locked it.

"I'm really hungry—" Rose began. Her body vibrated at his dark, intense look as he moved toward her, tugging her into his arms.

"I am hungry, too. For you," he whispered huskily as his hands ran over her, and his mouth came down to meet hers. Because she needed the taste of him, because she loved him and knew that time ran short between them, Rose locked her arms around him, pouring herself into the kiss.

Stefan tensed and slowly eased her away, sweeping the tendrils that had escaped her braids back from her face.

He studied her flushed, upturned face, her closed lids and sensitive, well-kissed lips. ''You want me now?''

He always reacted so well, she thought. His tone held surprise, amusement and hunger and anticipation. Rose licked her lips and looked at his body, wondering where to start— ''Start here,'' Stefan whispered and touched his lips.

Ten

The next time Rose saw Stefan, it was at closing time. She looked out of the store's windows to the sidewalk where he had parked the big leased black Town Car he used for traveling to the airport. He wore those mirrored sunglasses, and the wind tugged at his expensive dress shirt and slacks. He looked nothing like Danny's cook or her lover. Stefan had that lean, stiletto look of a fierce, determined knight going off to battle, already leaning into it, his mind preoccupied with specifics. He glanced impatiently at the expensive watch on his wrist, and Rose's heart began to ache. When he looked up to the dark gray clouds as if he couldn't wait to be off, *she knew that it was closing time between them.*

She forced herself to swallow, her throat gone dry and tight. There would be the usual nicey-nicey talk, the explanations that didn't really need to be made. She'd known all the while that he'd be leaving, once business called him back to Chicago. She fought running and hiding, pain streaking through her. She damned herself for wanting him so, for being so selfish as to take some part of life for herself.

He'd called during the afternoon, but she'd been too busy. He'd been hesitant to tell her what bothered him, and she'd said she'd call him back. Rose inhaled and wished she'd closed the store and taken the time, because now she had to paste a smile on her face when her heart was breaking. She smiled brightly as Stefan entered the door and came toward her. He wouldn't see the tears she guarded closely. She would see him off and step back into the dull reality and safety of her life. "Hi, Stefan. How goes it?" she asked cheerfully.

He'd been so passionate this morning, growling playfully and teasing and hungry for her, just as she wanted him. But the hours had shifted and reality had come to call....

He took off the glasses and his eyes were dark and stormy. She could almost feel his touch, his body as it riveted and completed hers this morning. She could almost hear his chuckle as he held her limp body close and safe on the storeroom's picnic table. *You knew this time would come. Be a good sport, and let him go. Don't get mad. Don't cry. Don't make him feel as if he needs to stay because of you. Stefan is doing the best that he can and you're not going to interfere in his life. What were you thinking?*

"I'll be back," he stated firmly.

"Sure," she returned with a smile that didn't show her breaking heart. She started to study the cardboard advertisement that she'd just unbalanced with her elbow, but her hands shook and it tumbled off the counter.

Stefan picked it up and watched her as he replaced it. He ran his hand through his hair and glanced at his watch and studied her. "I would like you to come with me."

Why prolong the ending? Why not make a clean break? "I've got work to do. You know how it is."

She sounded too chirpy, too happy, and she avoided Stefan's study of her expression as she began clearing the cash machine. "It's business. I've just got time to make my flight," he said quietly. "I wanted to tell you this morning, but I was so—"

Hungry for her. But then she wasn't exactly calm, and had torn his T-shirt to kiss that beautiful chest and place her body against his. The old picnic table in the back would always hold a memory of moving over Stefan—

"Sure. See you." Rose couldn't bear any more. "Look, let's just leave it, okay? No long goodbyes, no promises, no future together. I understood from the start what I was getting into—that you would be leaving and that we had just…intersected at a time when we both needed—"

"I love you, Rose," Stefan said quietly. "I'll be back."

The admission broadsided her, hanging in the air between them. "You don't have to say that. There's no price tag on what we've had. I'm a big girl, Stefan. I know when the ball game is over and there is no need to make it easier for me. Go on, take care of business."

Stefan's jaw tensed. "I'll be back," he repeated darkly. "And we'll settle this between us."

"Sure. For holidays and vacations. That will be nice. It's settled. See you." Then because her heart could not bear more, Rose turned and ran out the back door. She ignored Stefan's call and ran as fast as she could into the woods near town. She scrambled up the old tree where she hid from life long ago and let the tears flow.

After a time, just after sunset, her father came to stand below her. He looked up at her and called softly, "Rose? He's gone. You can come down now. There's something you should see."

Rose hesitated; she knew how she looked—torn by emotions, her face streaked with tears, her hands and knees scraped by the climb. Then because she didn't want to worry him more, she made her way down the tree. "I'm just fine, Dad. Honest."

"Sure," he said in a wry, disbelieving tone. He took her hand as they walked back into Waterville on a course they'd walked many times. "You always are, aren't you, kitten?"

"This is silly of me, getting all worked up like I didn't expect him to leave. Is this how it felt? When Mom left?"

Maury shook his head. "No. Your mother left with another man. Stefan left because he holds other peoples' lives in his hands, in his decisions. Families depend on him, and retirees need him to protect their pensions. He's a powerful businessman, Rose, but he's also just a man. He'll be back. Everything will be fine, you'll see."

They walked to their front gate and Maury said, "Let's go around back. It's pretty out there in the rose garden. Your mother named you 'Rose' because it was the flower she loved best. I think she tried to stay, for your sake."

He watched Rose for a moment as she stared at the faeries in the moonlit garden. They would be there when the fiery leaves began to fall and when snow came and when spring came again to the roses. Then Maury left her alone with Stefan's gift. He paused at the back door and watched Rose wander amid the faeries, looking very much like one of them. "He'll come back, Rose," Maury said quietly to the night, because he believed in Stefan.

Rose skimmed her hands over each unique faerie. They were firmly set in concrete, too big to move, too beautiful to dismiss in the moonlight. She wrapped her arms around the largest one and held it close, just as she wished she could hold Stefan now.

She touched a delicately fashioned wing, smoothing it. *What did Stefan's gift mean? Was it a parting gift? Something he thought might ease the break? Dare she believe?*

Then Rose waited for the faeries to answer her questions, but they only smiled softly. "I've got to be careful that I don't interpret this the wrong way, you know," she told them and settled down to discuss her next move, which of course, was to thank Stefan.

He'd said he loved her.... He'd said he loved her. Stefan wasn't a man to say anything he didn't mean.

Rose went into the house and got the old shoe box that was her mother's. It was battered by a young Rose, furious with life. But now it was time to put away the pain and begin living—to be complete as a woman and leave the rest behind. She'd never wanted to get married, despite her engagements, because part of her still mulled the past and feared how she would be as a wife and mother. The memories had dulled, but they remained inside, simmering, until loving Stefan began to open the unresolved past. She had feared commitment, and the pain of losing. She'd wanted to be so strong and independent within her walls that nothing could ever touch her again.

Then Stefan had come into her life—big and bold and sweet—opening and tearing away the past, bit by bit, filling it with beautiful memories. Rose moved carefully through her thoughts, sorting the important from the clutter. It was time to meet life and what it offered, rather than running from it. *I love you,* he'd said and Stefan wasn't a man to toss words easy and free—he always meant what he said. *I love you.*

Rose scrubbed away her tears and leaned against a faerie. If ever she wanted to believe in fairy tales coming true, it was now. "I love you, too," she whispered to her palm and blew the words away into the wind.

The next morning in Chicago, Stefan sat at the Donatien discussion table, his mind on Rose, on her too-bright expression, and on the way she ran from him. Nothing would have been gained by following her and pressing a point she already doubted. And he'd been hurt, too, that her belief in him ran so thin. In the end, he thought it best to give Rose time—one of the hardest decisions of his life.

A hot debate raged between the Donatien businessmen, some of them elderly and steadfast in his father's strict policies. The younger staff presented a new retirement plan and struggled against the "We've always done it this way." The older members had their points and logic, and the two factions weren't agreeing on anything.

Stefan tapped his pen on the table and tried to follow the debate. He was too tired, and not up to the decisions he must make. He'd tried to call Rose until all hours; she wasn't taking his calls, locking herself away in her safe place, away from his love. She'd been stricken when he told her he loved her, and he'd chosen the wrong moment and issued his emotions too hurriedly. But he'd struggled to give her time to adjust, and then there was no time, an elderly retiree calling him with pension problems that affected several hundred other people.

The issues soared back and forth across the table and

Stefan made notes. He found it best to let the tempers rage, clearing the air and getting to the real heart of the issues, rather than the polite cover-ups. He itemized each issue, dissecting it on his yellow pad. He smiled briefly at the small faerie sketches he'd drawn, and picked his way through the latest storm on the discussion table. "Tim isn't going anywhere. He's made his mistakes and learned from them. He has years of service at Donatien's and I stand behind him," he said quietly. "You're not moving me on this issue."

The older businessmen nodded sagely, because when Stefan's father sounded like that, there was no arguing.

Megan, his secretary, moved close to whisper, "Private call. Line one. It's her. A Miss Rose Granger. Shall I say you'll call her back?"

Stefan knew the value of staying with heated debates and not leaving the room at a crucial time—but he wanted to talk with Rose. "I'll take the call here."

"Here?" Megan's tone reflected her astonishment— Donatien business meetings were never to be interrupted with personal calls—Miss Rose Granger must have indicated she had personal business with Stefan.

"Stefan here," he said and waited for Rose to speak. Had she seen the faeries? What would she think? Would she believe his love? Had he terrified her, telling her of his love, giving her gifts of his heart?

"I can't pay for all these," she said finally. She spoke as if she didn't know where to start and that was the top issue on her mind. "Larry and Henry said they were cus- tom made."

"They're a gift from me. To keep you company while I'm away." Her silence said she was weighing his words and that struck Stefan's pride. There was always that doubt in her, that tiny nagging lack of trust.

"I have nothing to give you," Rose said quietly.

"But of course you do, my darling. And this isn't a gift to be equaled, Rose. It's one of the heart and freely given." Stefan ignored the silence around his board table, the downcast faces, the tense poses that said they were listening closely. Stefan studied them, the staunch, elderly peers of his father who wanted to change nothing, and resisted women into the mix. The women at the table had earned their place and the younger men were all part of a family—his family. Estelle had expressed interest in entering the business, in managing it. It would take her years to win over the old guard, but then Estelle had learned a few things from Rose. Simple things, like listening and that gentle persuasion.

He saw no reason not to throw his "Rose" problems on the table with the rest of the current business. "I love this woman. I want to marry her," Stefan told them, making certain that Rose could hear, because he'd punched the loudspeaker button. "I gave her faerie statues for her rose garden and now she wants to know how much to pay me. What do you think of that?"

Stunned silence flattened the room. Stefan Donatien was his father's son, bred to business, not to emotions or romantic gifts. His heritage was grim and weighty. He smiled at Rose's slight gasp at the other end of the line. "I love you, Rose. Get used to it. I'm not going to be an ex-fiancé. I want to be your husband, if you'll have me. I asked your father some time ago, because after all, I am a traditional man. I have his permission to ask you. All we have to do—you and I—is to settle the fine points between—like if you love me and want to màrry me. We'll live in Waterville, of course. We'll take whatever time you need."

He smiled grimly at Rose's next gasp. "Is everyone listening to this?" she asked unevenly.

"I have nothing to hide. You make me very happy." He hadn't meant to hurl his intentions at her that way, but he was still new at separating business and love. "You're very good at relationships, the best at facilitating tense situations. I'm in a discussion now where no one wants to budge. Please help me, Rose."

He smiled and waited, because Rose always knew the right answers when it came to people. She was wandering through his "I love you," and her fears, but she never let anyone down who needed her. He held up his hand when the staunch old guard looked like they might object.

"Well," Rose said softly, thoughtfully. "First of all— I think you should send out for ice-cream cones. They always make things better. And if the weather is beautiful there, as it is here—a bright fall day—open the window to let the wind blow in and clear away the tension. And listen to the life passing through on the sidewalk below. I think by the time you've done all that, and talked about the different flavors of ice cream, everyone might be flowing along in the same track."

"That's a good idea. Thank you, Rose. I miss you." Stefan nodded to his secretary, who blinked and silently mouthed, "Ice-cream cones?" He nodded again and she hurriedly left the room.

"Do you need me for anything else, Stefan?" Rose asked over the loudspeaker in a professional tone.

"Yes," he said huskily and smiled again at the pause.

"Oh. Bye," she returned in that breathless tone he loved. He inhaled briefly when the line clicked off. Then

Stefan started to work, settling the issues, because he wanted to go home to Rose.

When his secretary came into the room again, her expression concerned, Stefan nodded. He picked up the telephone and smiled as he heard Rose's voice. "I'm not happy," she said. "I don't know how to handle all this."

"It won't do for our children to have an unhappy mother," Stefan said, enjoying the play. He listened to Rose's uneven breathing and imagined her steamy, quivery look like just before she tore his T-shirt to have him. "I'll be home soon and we'll fix that."

"Oh. Goodbye," she said airily after a slight hesitation, and the line clicked off.

Stefan looked around the table, at the older, rigid faces, silently admonishing him for his lack of business protocol. The younger ones were softer and Stefan relaxed a bit as the women smiled fondly at him—they'd always been a little uncertain of him and now that gap seemed to be closing. "We'll manage, and we'll succeed," he said firmly. "I forbid anything else."

How could Stefan be so confident of her? Of them? Rose wondered as she spent hours amid the faeries he had given her, each one perfect—except the one with the tutu and that was slanted oddly, her gauzy panties showing. Each day Rose wondered what she could give Stefan, and the leaves of the oaks shading the faeries gave no answers.

The casseroles didn't come to her as they usually did after a breakup. Life was odd and lonely, and she waited for Yvette's tidbits of Stefan. He sent her a tiny, perfect pin, one with diamonds on the fragile faerie wing. It was elegant and contrasted her T-shirt, but she wore it anyway—at night in her rose garden with the faeries. She sent him a thank-you note, because that seemed very proper to do. *What could she give Stefan? Was it possible he really loved her and that he was coming back?*

Another week took Rose into mid-September and Stefan wasn't calling. She knew he was very busy and giving her time to think. Yet all she could think of was needing him close and safe. To show her father that Maggie White was perfectly welcome in their family, Rose threw a swing dance party at the Granger home. Yvette and Leroy attended and moved together as if they had all their lives. Leroy obviously adored Yvette. Maggie had centered on Maury and wasn't looking at other men—a soft, well-loved look replaced her chic, manhunting one.

While the music played loudly and Mrs. Wilkins took care of the refreshment table, it seemed to be a perfect time for Rose to call Stefan—just to hear that deep drawl, his beautiful accent. Instead when he answered, his tone was weary. She wanted to make him feel better and also to relieve the nagging need to— "Oh, hi. Just thought I'd call to tell you that I love you, too.... And your gifts are far too expensive, but I love them anyway. Bye."

There was silence and then the rush of French seemed to be in the swearing mode. "You are there, and I am here, and you would pick such a time to tell me?" he demanded unevenly.

"Tit for tat, equality and all that," she said, defending her right to equal what he had said.

Stefan's voice was uneven and threaded heavily with his accent. "I wanted to propose to you differently—I wanted to see you alone, but in Waterville there seems to be very little 'alone.'"

"It just came to me slowly, no big flashes of thunder

or anything. But it's there, in my heart, and it's good and strong."

Rose listened to the laughter and music coming from the living room. It all seemed very right that she should call Stefan at a time like this—when all the people she loved were enjoying themselves. "Am I on the loud-speaker? I hear other men there. You're probably in a business meeting. It's too late for that, Stefan. You need your rest because when you come home—"

"We speak privately," Stefan stated huskily. "Proceed with your definition of the activity."

"Well, then, I should tell you how much I love you. Maybe a part of me was always waiting for you, my prince. I moved into the bigger bedroom, because I want to remember you with me. How much I want to touch you and feel you close and naked beside me. I want to kiss you—on the lips—have patience with me, because I'm new to this. I want to nibble a bit on your lips and then on your throat and then on your ears—and blow a bit there—"

Rose blew softly into the telephone for effect and she smiled at the slight hissing of Stefan's breath as though he were stunned and inhaling sharply. She liked shocking Stefan; he reacted so beautifully. She was woman, feminine, strong and erotic, and leaned back against the kitchen wall to concentrate on her best effort. Rose smiled as she continued to explain how she wanted to love Stefan. "That's enough," he said roughly after a time and she knew that nothing was more enjoyable than teasing him.

In the background, a man asked, "Stefan, are you feeling all right? You look like you might have a fever."

"Good night, *ma chérie,*" Stefan said softly. "I will think of you in your new environment. I will try to accommodate your specifications to my utmost ability at our next meeting.''

She turned with a smile to replace the telephone and found Mrs. Wilkins fanning herself as she stared at Rose. ''Goodness, Rose. I'll bet you never talked to the other boys like that.''

Rose grinned, her all-woman feeling at sky-high level. Mrs. Wilkins had been a part of her life forever—she was a dear heart whom Rose trusted. ''Nope, never have. I think I might be pretty good at it, too. Stefan had this funny little strangled sound that I've never heard before. Oh, he's so much fun!''

''That's what I've been waiting to hear. You never were really excited about those other boys. You never blossomed and floated on air like you do now. You'll be married and pregnant before you know it.... And now I think I'll put a little gin in the punch, drink it and let myself have an old-fashioned good cry...a happy one.''

''It just came to me so gently, loving Stefan, that I hadn't realized how much I do love him. I love him so much that I fear nothing, that I know he and I will survive—together. I know the weight of responsibility and Stefan carries such a heavy burden, not exactly of his making. He needs me in a soft way, the way a man needs a woman. I've waited all this time for him, just him. He's very emotional, you know, and he worries too much. Stefan is a dynamic man and I know that waiting for me couldn't have been easy. I intend to make that up to him.''

Mrs. Wilkins blinked away the tears in her eyes. ''He's getting a very special person, and he knows it. Um, dear? Does he know you can't cook?''

Waterville had waited for the wedding of Rose Granger, and everyone came to the October event. In her faerie gar-

den, Stefan and Rose took their vows beneath their fiery
oaks. Stefan was very formal, firmly hiding his excitement,
and Rose's flowing, soft gown was designed by Yvette and
Estelle.

Stefan's whiskey-brown eyes were too bright, but his
hands were firm on hers as he slid his wedding band onto
her finger. When her ring was upon his finger, he stared
at it as if he couldn't believe she had placed it there. He
spoke unevenly, huskily telling her of his love, and she
pledged hers to him without hesitation.

Their kiss was soft and told of the years to come, of the
life they would build together.

Then Walt loped into the garden and sat between them,
looking up expectantly as they were pronounced man and
wife. Because Walt knew he had a home with Rose—he
always had.

Black limousines lined the side street, because the front
street and yard around Rose's house was filled with smiling, happy people. They surged toward the bride and
groom and the tables piled high with Stefan's and Danny's
food. Danny's wedding cake towered above the platters of
French cuisine and fried green tomatoes and hamburgers
and French fries. After snapshots, Stefan, Yvette and Estelle moved into action. Stefan rolled up his sleeves and
began serving in his elaborate, flourished waiter-way, and
Rose sat beside Walt, listened to congratulations, and wondered about her wedding night. ''The missing ingredient
in all this, Walt old buddy, is that Stefan hasn't made love
to me for a very, very long time.''

Then Stefan paused in serving his petit fours and met
her eyes across the garden. The riveting shock was enough
to assure her that he wanted her desperately. She decided

that was the time to tug up her beautiful feminine gown and slowly, enticingly remove her lace garter.

While staring hungrily at his new bride, Stefan hadn't realized that the tray had tipped and the desserts were plopping to the ground. Sensing food, Walt hurried to make the best of the day. "We're leaving," Stefan announced curtly, and made his way to her. From the narrowed, hot way he was looking at her, Rose knew there wasn't much time. She threw her bouquet to Maggie, who blushed prettily and leaned against Maury, who tightened his arm around her. As if giving his blessing, Stefan tossed Rose's garter to Leroy, who promptly tugged it onto his upper arm and grinned at her before he stole a kiss from Yvette.

Stefan picked up Rose and strode to his pickup with her. When Rose opened the door, Walt hopped in. He sat between them as they drove off, tin cans rattling as the crowd was silent. Some were thinking that she wouldn't have time for them anymore, not with a new husband and that big new addition he'd just built on to the Smith's farmhouse. Then, from the hot-eyed look of the hungry groom, she'd probably have that flock of children she deserved and even less time.

She'd wound through their lives like the multicolored ribbons tied to the faeries and fluttering in the slight breeze. Rose deserved the best possible, and from the look of her groom, she wouldn't be lacking for love.

On the other hand, Rose wasn't going anywhere, except for business trips Stefan had to make to the city. Eventually his daughter would take over some of his burden, and Waterville would still have Rose. And best of all, she would be happy and they'd get to see her life become even richer. Then Henry let out a cheer, holding his glass of champagne high. "Here's to Rose and her faeries and her prince."

"This is quite elaborate, isn't it?" Rose asked as Stefan closed the wooden barn doors behind them. The huge old barn had sat empty, gray and weathered for years on the far side of the Smith farm. Now it had been cleaned, and in the exact airy center was a very spiffy new camper. Walt trotted around the barn, examining the different smells, while Stefan picked Rose up in his arms and walked determinedly toward the deluxe camper.

"This should take care of the lack of privacy here. I want no interruptions," he said grimly as Rose opened the camper door and he carried her inside. A moment later, he opened the door and with a flourish, placed a rug on the barn floor with dog food and water. "No," he said firmly to Walt, who was hoping for an invitation inside.

Stefan turned and closed the camper door, locking it. The soft light seemed to embrace his bride as she stood still, staring at him. "I love you, Stefan. I didn't think this would ever happen for me, and now it has."

She looked stunned, a reflection of his own emotions, which mixed with his hunger for her now. "Don't be afraid, Rose," he said. "I love you. We're going to have a wonderful life together, and I'll never leave you."

"I know. You love me, and I love you, and dreams come true. It's all pretty amazing how the pieces fit together. Now how do I get out of this dress?" she asked softly.

"I believe I can help you with that, Mrs. Donatien," Stefan offered and moved toward her.

Later, when she was soft and draped over him, her toes playing with his, Rose smoothed his chest and nestled close. "You can tell me now, the gift that you said I gave to you?—other than the obvious."

Stefan was silent so long that Rose thought he might be resting from the event they had just shared. He stroked her hair and spoke softly. "You made me see that my father's dreams and fears aren't mine. That life waits outside business and work, that each breath is rich and full, when you want it to be…. You give me peace and happiness and the joy in living. You make me look forward to each day, and anchor my heart and my soul. You fill me with one look, soothe me with one touch, and you make me feel like I am a better person than I am. You give me courage and strength and wisdom."

"Goodness. How do I do all that?"

"By being just you, Rose."

Stefan looked into Rose's eyes and knew that life with her would be full and rich, buttery and smooth, with a delicate, loving texture that would always be fresh, the spices perfect and exciting.

*   *   *   *   *

THE BARONS OF TEXAS:
TESS

by
Fayrene Preston

FAYRENE PRESTON

published her first book in 1981 and has been publishing steadily ever since. Fayrene lives in north Texas and is the mother of two grown sons. She claims her greatest achievement in life is turning out two wonderful human beings. She is also proud to announce the arrival of her first grandchild: a beautiful baby girl. Now she has even more to be thankful for.

This book is dedicated
with many, many thanks to:

R G Font, PhD, CPG, PG,
EurGeol President, Geoscience Data Management

One

Tall, lean and bronzed, the man stood at the edge of the terrace watching her, just as he had for the last fifteen minutes. Tess Baron tried to ignore him and focus instead on her party guests, but she found it virtually impossible.

Something about his stillness compelled her attention. It was like lightning caught in a bottle, an electric tension that would be safe only as long as it was contained. And he didn't strike her as the type of man to contain his energies for long.

This was her birthday party. She knew everyone here. Everyone, that was, except *him*.

She skimmed the crowd, wondering who had brought him, but everyone was either dancing or mixing. No one looked as if they'd brought a guest, then forgotten him. Besides, she reflected ruefully, it would be impossible to forget him.

Behind him, the sun was slowly setting into the Gulf of

Mexico, its great orange ball searing the water with its heat
as it dipped lower and lower. Silhouetted against the elemental tableau, with the sun surrounding him, the man
looked larger than life—a sun god.

At that moment she wouldn't have bet money against the
possibility that he had lassoed the sun down from the sky.

She exhaled a long breath, reminded herself that she
didn't have a quixotic bone in her body, and forced her
focus elsewhere. At least everything else about her party
was going well.

A warm breeze from off the Gulf waters somehow
matched the band's sensual bossa nova beat. Icy margaritas
and long neck beers were being served, along with mounds
of jumbo Gulf shrimp and oysters harvested fresh that day.
Out on the lawn, barbecued *cabrito* turned on a spit.

He ate or drank nothing, though she'd seen waiters offering him his preference of drinks.

"Happy birthday, Tess."

The voice of a longtime friend snapped her mind back
to her party. "Thanks, Becca." She kissed the cheek of the
pretty young woman, then reached up to hug Becca's college sweetheart and husband, Mel Grant. "I'm so glad you
two could come."

Becca laughed. "Are you kidding? Your birthday parties
are way too much fun to miss. Besides, Corpus Christi is
a pretty cool city."

Mel smiled at her. "It's become a party game to try to
guess where you're going to hold your parties each year.
The year you threw your party in Kuala Lumpur is now
legendary. But last year I felt a little let down."

She grinned. "Oh, yeah?"

"Southfork?" He shook his head. "Not very original,
Tess, and way too close to home."

She laughed. "Sorry, but the location of my parties depends on where I'm working, and last year I was working at home.''

"I know, but personally, I was hoping for an oil rig in the South China Sea."

"An oil rig is no place to throw a party—*which* you very well know. Too much chance for harm on either side."

Mel worked for Coastal Petroleum, one of the world's major oil companies. Nevertheless, he sighed dramatically. "Okay, okay, I'll give you that, plus a big thumbs-up for this year."

"What a relief," she said dryly.

"Yep. This is a great house, right on the beach and with a fabulous view. I'd say you made up the points you lost last year."

"Ignore him, Tess," Becca advised.

"He's much too entertaining to ignore. Besides, he's right. This is a great house. I leased it because my new offshore drilling site is straight out there." She pointed toward the Gulf. "And because there's a great helipad at the side of the house."

Mel nodded. "By the way, congratulations. Word is you think the reservoir you've found out there will be your richest oil discovery yet."

She grimaced, and her hand automatically went to cover her stomach, where a heavy dread appeared every time she thought of what she was gambling on this one site. "Do me a favor and don't congratulate me yet. I'm superstitious. The initial tests were very encouraging, but in the end, we both know that could mean nothing. I won't celebrate until we strike that first oil and the well actually starts to produce."

Becca waved a dismissive hand. "You're like a blood-hound when it comes to oil. I'd back your instincts before I would all those sophisticated tests they do. If you like what you've seen out there, then the oil is as good as in the pipeline.''

Tess gave Becca a quick, grateful hug. ''Thank you.''

Her instincts had always been solid; Becca was right about that. Yet the stakes were so high on this particular venture that she couldn't be sure her instincts hadn't been tainted by her need for this well to come in big, not to mention quick.

''Word is also out that you've been having some problems,'' Mel continued. ''In case you decide you need some help, just remember, my company is always interested.''

Unfortunately, it was very hard to keep secrets in the oil business. ''You know how I feel about my oil ventures, Mel.''

''I know, I know. They're your babies, and you keep them until they're raised and well into old age.''

She nodded. ''It's a family tradition.'' She'd hoped this party would help her relax and have a good time, something she hadn't been able to do in a long time. Unfortunately, though, her nerves were tighter than ever. Between Mel and his well-meaning talk of her problems and the *man*… He hadn't moved, and he was still looking at her with that laser gaze of his. Beneath his stare, her skin felt just like it was being sunburned.

''Listen, do either of you know that man standing over there, leaning against the balustrade?''

Both Becca and Mel glanced over their shoulders. ''No, but if I weren't with Mel tonight, I would *love* to.''

Mel frowned at his wife. ''Excuse me, but I don't think that's funny.''

''No?'' With her eyes twinkling with laughter, she reached for her husband's hand. ''Then how about dancing with me? Maybe it will come back to me why I love you so much.''

"That sounds like a challenge and I'm definitely up for it." With a wink at Tess, he pulled his wife onto the dance floor. "See you later."

"You bet." Surely there was a simple explanation for the man's presence. Tess pondered. One of her guests must have brought him, but if so, why weren't they with him? Why hadn't they introduced him to her? And most of all, why did he keep looking at her?

And, damn it, where was Ron? He might be able to tell her the identity of the man. Ron Hughes was a bright, competent young man in his late twenties. As her assistant, it was his job to know everything and everyone, and he usually did. But he was probably still in the house, working in the two-room suite they'd appropriated as their offices for the time they would be there.

Someone lightly clasped her elbow. "Dance?"

She started, then inwardly laughed at herself. No, she reflected wryly, there was nothing at all wrong with her nerves. She looked around. "Colin! Oh, great, you made it."

"Did you doubt it for a minute?"

She smiled. "No."

Colin Wynne, tanned, suave and incredibly good-looking, was one of Dallas's most eligible bachelors. He was also one of her favorite people, though they'd never dated. She'd never had the desire to go out with him other than in a group, and she knew the feeling was mutual. Over the years, she'd found friendships to be much more satisfying than a love life. He held out his hand to her.

"Thanks," she said, "but not right now. I still have some details to see to. The party's really just beginning."

"Nonsense. I'm here. You're here. The party has officially started."

She grinned. Few people possessed the self-confidence

Colin did. He made everything he did look easy, yet he was one of the hardest-working people she knew. "Who did you bring tonight?"

"I didn't bring a date, if that's what you mean—just a planeload of the usual suspects."

"Oh, that's right. I heard you were going to fly down some of the group in your new jet. Thanks."

"No problem at all."

She leaned closer to him. "Do you know that man standing over there by the edge of the terrace?"

He threw a casual glance over his shoulder. "Nope. Who is he? A party crasher?"

She shook her head. "He must have come with someone. I just can't figure out who yet."

"You want me to go over and check him out?"

"No. I'll do it in a minute."

"Happy birthday, Tess." A cool voice slipped between them and they both turned.

"Jill." She gave her sister a quick, automatic hug. If the hug lacked the spontaneity and ease of the hug she'd given Becca, she prided herself on her belief that no one could tell. No one except maybe Jill. And Colin, who knew them both well.

Just as quickly, she released her middle sister and stepped back. Jill was wearing a short black Armani sheath that emphasized her inherent elegance and sophistication. Until Tess had seen Jill, she'd thought she looked pretty good in her short, ivory silk dress with straps that skimmed over her shoulders and crisscrossed several times in the back until reaching her waist.

But then, it was Jill who had inherited the classical beauty and elegance of their mother, not her nor Kit. Even Jill's dark hair was styled into an elaborate French twist from which no hair would dare escape.

Annoyingly, Tess could feel the wind blowing at the untidy blond tendrils of her hair, which had already managed to elude the containment of the ivory silk scarf she'd tied at the nape of her neck. "You're late. What happened? I expected you earlier."

"My ride took off without me, and I had to make other arrangements to get here." Jill's bourbon-colored gaze flashed at Colin.

The very picture of innocence, he spread out his hands. "I had a schedule to meet."

"You weren't running a bus, Colin." Jill's words dripped with ice. "You were flying your own plane."

"Ever heard of a little thing called a flight plan?"

"Yes, as a matter of fact, I have. And I know they can give you a certain leeway."

He shrugged. "Everyone else was aboard. I didn't see why they should be punished just because you couldn't arrange your day so you could get to the airport on time."

Tess rolled her eyes, though neither Jill nor Colin saw her, so intent were they on squaring off against each other. But she'd grown used to their behavior. For whatever reason, whenever the two of them got together, some type of sparks usually flew, and more often than not, it was sparks of anger.

"I have an idea," she said. "Why don't you two go dance and I'll see you both later?"

Colin looked at her, then at Jill. After a moment, he slowly held out his hand to her. Jill hesitated for several seconds, then glanced at Tess. "Have Uncle William and Des arrived yet?"

"Uncle William isn't feeling well, so he won't be coming."

Jill's perfect forehead creased in a frown. "Is it serious?"

Colin dropped his hand.

"He didn't give me any reason to believe that it was. Besides, you know Des would let us know if something was seriously wrong."

Jill nodded. "What about Des?"

Good question, Tess thought wryly. It was the eternal question that kept her and her sisters occupied. "I have no idea if he's even coming."

"You haven't heard from him?"

"You know he rarely lets us know what he's up to."

"Right." Jill chewed her bottom lip for perhaps three seconds, then stopped. It was a habit left over from her childhood. "Well, let me know if Des arrives, okay?"

Sure she would, Tess thought. When pigs flew.

Jill switched her attention to Colin. "Well?"

"Well, what, Jill?"

"Do you or don't you want to dance?"

This time it was Colin who hesitated. "Maybe later," he finally said and walked off.

Tess hid a smile. If looks could kill, Colin would now be dead. Jill stared after him for a moment longer, then turned and went in the opposite direction.

The Des in whom Jill had been so interested was their uncle William's elusive stepson, a high-powered lawyer. Women flocked to Des like bees to honey, but he was much more than a highly eligible bachelor to her and her two sisters. She, Jill and Kit had each inherited one-sixth of their family's business upon the death of their father, conditional upon each of them meeting a certain criterion. But Des was due to inherit fifty percent of their family company upon Uncle William's death.

That fact put Des smack in the center of the collective crosshairs of her and her sisters. In theory, if one of them married him, they would gain control of the family company. And there wasn't one of them who wasn't hungry for that control and more than willing, able and raring to go after him. Too bad for her sisters that *she* planned to be the one who got him.

However, pursuing Des was frustrating as hell. Though she was no expert on love, it seemed to her that the only way to get Des to fall in love with her was to arrange it so that they could spend time with each other. But time was something Des rarely gave any of them on an individual basis.

Still, she wasn't deterred, nor, she knew, were her sisters. Winning control of the company was too important for each of them. If Des showed up tonight, Jill would go after him like a heat-seeking missile, but she would have to stand in line behind Tess. And then, of course, there was Kit.

The three of them had been competitive with each other since birth, encouraged and egged on by their father, who pounded into each of them the importance of being the best at whatever they did. One of their competitions involved fighting to be the one who, at the end of the company's fiscal year, had made the most money for the company, and there wasn't much they wouldn't do to earn that yearly honor. *Or* to win Des's agreement to marriage.

But this year, she, even more than Kit and Jill, had a tremendous amount to prove.

"Dance with me."

She looked up and took a reflexive step backward. She'd been so lost in the dysfunctional dynamics of her family that she'd momentarily forgotten her unknown guest. Now he was standing in front of her, tall, broad-shouldered and a bit overpowering.

And his eyes, she finally saw, were a startling amber.

"Who are you?"

"Someone who would like very much to dance with you."

His voice reverberated deep inside her, warm and compelling, like a playful silken ribbon that dipped and curved throughout her, making her heart pound like a bass drum.

His amber eyes held her gaze. His name. She didn't know his name.

It didn't matter.

He took her hand, and suddenly she found herself on the dance floor, and she wasn't entirely certain how she'd gotten there. Surely she'd told him no.

Apparently not.

His arms were strong as they held her to his hard body. His dance steps were smooth, so that following him was easy, which allowed her to register other things. Such as the heat his body generated—it had the power to melt an iceberg.

This was a man who was definitely confident with his own sexuality and did nothing to hold it back. In addition, those amber eyes of his held dark, intriguing depths she hadn't expected. And his skin was bronzed to a beautiful golden brown that made her think he must spend a great deal of time outdoors. His dark brown hair was almost outshone by streaks that could only have been put there by the brightness of the sun.

Truly he *could* be a sun god.

If she believed in such things.

Still, all her instincts were shouting at her that she would be safer if she simply walked away from him. There was just one problem. She wasn't certain she could. His body had suddenly become her own private universe's center of gravity.

Thankfully, she could still think, and truthfully, she was

way too curious to attempt to leave him at this point.
"Were you invited to my party?"

"No."

Just the single word. No explanation, as if none was
needed. "Did you come with one of my guests?"

"No."

A shiver raced down her spine. He was studying her as
if she were a book he was trying to learn, yet he wasn't
asking any questions. He was leaving that to her.

"Then why are you here?"

"Because of you." His voice was soft, yet intense and
with a faint trace of some dark emotion. "You're really
quite beautiful, you know. I didn't expect it."

"You didn't...?"

He slowly shook his head, his gaze never once leaving
her.

She found herself speechless. She felt as if he'd isolated
her from the rest of the world, yet she was surrounded by
friends, none of whom seemed the least bit alarmed that
she was dancing with a perfect stranger who radiated a
barely contained electric energy and thus danger.

But then, they couldn't see what she was seeing, nor
could they feel what he was making her feel.

A dark fire simmered in the depths of his remarkable
eyes—eyes, she was convinced, that, if he chose, he could
use like a lethal weapon. With a single glance he would be
able to mow down anyone who got in his way or, con-
versely, reach across the terrace and touch her, making her
aware of him in every part of her body. And that had been
when they were yards from each other.

Now, as she danced with him, he was having an even
greater impact on her. She couldn't have said what the band
was playing. She only knew that the two of them were

moving slowly, sensually and in perfect unison. And, oddly, it seemed very right.

Her reaction didn't make sense.

He didn't make sense.

The sun had almost set, leaving behind fading streaks of red, orange and gold just above the horizon. The lights around the dance floor and in the trees had come on, yet he remained every bit as powerful, as elemental and as comfortable as he had been with the sun behind him.

"Happy birthday, Tess," someone called.

"Thank you," she said, blindly glancing in the direction of the voice, then immediately looked back at him, the man whose heat had melted her and whose strength had molded her against him with ease. Her breasts were pressed against his chest, her legs rubbed against the steel of his thighs. She didn't even know his name, yet the aggressive, masculine force of his body impacted her every cell, bringing out feminine urges and needs so new, she wasn't sure what to do with them.

"You throw a great party," he murmured.

"Thank you. It was so good of you to come."

For the first time he smiled at her—a partial smile, a knowing smile, a completely self-assured smile. And the effect was a shock of electricity that bolted straight through her and made her catch her breath. A full smile from him might stop her heart.

Her hand moved restlessly over his shoulder, the fine cut and expensive cloth of his dark suit adding one more piece to the puzzle of him. Simply by dancing with him, she was coming to know his body well, and she could tell his strength didn't come from bulky muscles but rather the lean, elongated muscles of a natural athlete. Yet another piece. "Do you make it a practice to crash parties?"

"Actually, this is my first."

"And are you having a good time?"

"So far I can't complain."

"If you'll tell me your name, I might put you on the guest list for next year. Or would you just prefer to crash again?"

"Neither. I'm afraid I can't wait a year to see you again."

"Why—" Someone bumped against her back. Protectively, he tightened his hold on her and circled her in another direction.

"Hey, Sis. Happy birthday."

She looked around, then inwardly sighed. She should have known. No one but her youngest sister, Kit, would deliberately bump into her. And no one but Kit would have dressed for what she knew to be a dressy affair in a tight T-shirt, even tighter jeans and a pair of Western boots that Tess knew for a fact were eight years old and looked twelve. "Thank you."

The man didn't relinquish his hold on her, but he did allow room for her to turn toward her sister.

"Is Des coming?" Kit asked, all the while doing some sort of dance that amazingly fit the music.

Kit's red hair was flying; her green eyes were sparkling. Her arms were in the air, and her hips and feet were moving in a way that not only looked incredibly sexy but made Tess feel a tinge of envy that Kit could move so uninhibitedly. Kit's partner was someone she didn't know, but from the looks of his jeans, Western-cut shirt and boots, she guessed he might be a new hire at the family ranch.

"I don't know. Des didn't RSVP."

Kit came to an abrupt stop, though her partner didn't seem to notice and kept on dancing. "Des couldn't be more exasperating if he tried, and I sometimes suspect he does."

"You got it."

Tess knew that Kit's aim in bringing one of the ranch hands to her party and dressing like she had almost every day of her life since she'd gotten out of diapers was to flout tradition and embarrass her sisters. But what Kit didn't realize was that she looked better in her jeans and T-shirt than half the women at the party whose dresses had come from Neiman Marcus. And a cursory glance at the crowd showed her that at least three of her single friends and two of the married ones were openly salivating over Kit's date.

Kit hooked her thumbs in her pockets and flashed Tess's dance partner a smile that revealed a perfect set of dimples. "Who's your date, Sis?"

"I haven't the slightest idea."

Kit's eyebrows rose. "Cool," she said, her tone for once sincere. Then she danced away.

The man laughed, a deep chuckle.

Drawing away from him, she looked at him. "Is there some reason you won't tell me your name? Like maybe you're at the top of the FBI's Most Wanted list?"

"No."

"Then tell me."

He shrugged. "The thing is, I doubt my name will mean anything to you."

She exhaled a long breath, reaching for patience. "Why don't you let me decide that? I'm tired of this little game you're playing. Tell me or I'm going to walk away."

A slow smile spread across his face, this smile even more powerful than his last. "Ah…a threat from the birthday girl."

She refused to be affected by his smile, though she could feel the futility of her resistance as it slipped by the moment. "Are you or are you not going to tell me?"

"Nick Trejo. My name is Nick Trejo."

The name sounded vaguely familiar, but for the life of

her, she couldn't place it. "Okay, you're right. It doesn't mean anything to me."

"I didn't think it would."

"Uh-huh. Okay. Let me try another tack. How did you know about this party tonight?"

"I've made it my business to find out as much as possible about you."

Suddenly cautious, she stared at him, wondering if she could figure him out if she stared at him long enough. But no. He wasn't giving anything away—not by expression, and certainly not by words.

"Don't worry. I'm not a stalker."

"No? Then, Nick Trejo, I think it's past time you told me what you want."

"That's easy," he said, pulling her against him while his amber gaze held steady on her. "I want peace on earth, food and shelter enough for every living being, but right now I'm satisfied just to be dancing with you." His voice turned raspy. "You feel good against me. You *fit* me."

One minute he had her regarding him with caution, the next he had her melting with heat. And she couldn't very well protest or say she didn't understand what he was saying, since from the beginning of their dance, her body had involuntarily molded itself to his and there had been nothing she could do about it.

One song had stopped. Another had begun. An intimate cloud of music settled around the party and mingled with the night's scents to mesmerize, tantalize. But it all paled in comparison to him.

"Did I tell you that you look beautiful?"

She couldn't remember if he had or not. In fact, she was having trouble remembering anything. It was as if he had taken her over, body, mind and soul. She wasn't used to being called beautiful, and she certainly had never thought of herself that way. Not with Jill as a sister.

Abruptly, she tore herself from his arms. "I need something to drink."

"It's your party," he said mildly. "I imagine you can have anything you want."

"You're right." Fully aware that he was following her, she threaded her way through the dancers, a smile pasted on her face for her friends, but barely acknowledging their comments.

"A shot of whiskey with a beer chaser, please," she told the bartender as soon as she reached the bar. It was a unique request for her, but tonight she felt the need for something stronger than her usual beer. She glanced at Nick. "What would you like?"

"Since I'm not an official guest at the party, I wouldn't presume."

She gave a short laugh. "More than you have already, you mean? Give me a break. You've already crashed the party. What's one drink?" She glanced at the bartender. "Give him the same thing, please." She couldn't see a man like Nick Trejo drinking anything else, certainly not the margaritas that were flowing more freely than water tonight.

Nick shook his head at the bartender, then returned his gaze to her. "I hate to tell you this, Tess, but I truly haven't yet started to presume. Believe me when I say you'll know when I do."

Jill walked to the bar. "A margarita, please. Tess, have you heard anything from Des since we last talked?"

"*No.*" She'd been dealing with Nick, trying to retain her mental balance while she played his guessing game. At the same time, she'd been fighting to keep her body from completely betraying how much she had enjoyed being held against him. And it had all taken more out of her than she had realized, leaving her with zero patience for Jill and her preoccupation with landing Des.

"Okay." Jill threw an assessing gaze at Nick, then at her. "I think I'll try to locate him by phone."

"Fine. Do that. And be sure to mention how much I've missed him tonight." Even though she knew Jill would ignore her request, she'd thrown it in to nettle her sister.

For the first time in what seemed hours, she forced herself to draw a deep breath and look away from Nick. A quick assessment of her party showed her that it was going strong, but she caught several surreptitious glances from some of her closer friends, and she knew why. They'd never before seen her allow one man to monopolize her time as she had with Nick. Except there had been no *allowing* on her part. He was like a force that she had no defenses against. It was past time she rectified that.

The bartender placed her requested shot of whiskey and mug of beer in front of her. She picked up the whiskey, but sipped.

"Okay, Nick, I'm ready to admit it. You've got me completely baffled. Why on earth do you want to see me and why here? If it's about business—and it must be, since we haven't met before tonight, and you've assured me you aren't a stalker—why didn't you simply call my office and make an appointment?"

"Let's step away from the bar," Nick murmured, taking the shot glass from her and setting it on the bar. Then, with his hand at her elbow, he led her to a less populated area of the terrace. And she went with him, telling herself it was because she was curious and not because she couldn't refuse him.

When they reached a corner of the terrace where a profusion of sweet-scented Maid of Orleans star-flowered jasmine grew, Nick turned to her. "I tried for weeks to get an appointment with you, Tess, and couldn't get one."

"Who did you talk to?"

"Your assistant, Ron Hughes. Actually, I spoke with him on almost a daily basis, but he would never put me through to you or even give me an appointment. He kept insisting you had no time to see me."

She shrugged. "Well, that's true. My schedule is always packed, especially lately, with the details for my new offshore venture." Normally she wouldn't tell someone who was practically a stranger the reason she was busy, but something told her Nick already knew the reason. Her curiosity grew stronger. "Still, I notice Ron couldn't stop you from getting to me."

"That would have been hard for anyone to do."

She could only stare. If he'd looked amazing with the sun surrounding him, he looked astounding by moonlight. The moon's silver light threaded its way through his sun-streaked hair and touched his bronzed skin, cooling down his coloring—in a way, gentling it. Perhaps someone less suspecting than she would, at first glance, think him tame.

She knew better.

The moon might be offering him camouflage, and at the moment he might be masterfully controlling his innate power, but his amber eyes still held the intensity that earlier that evening had been able to reach across the terrace to her. She had no doubt that, if he chose, he could sear layers from her skin with just a glance.

"What's so important to you? What did you tell Ron you wanted to see me about?"

His gaze was level, his tone assured. "I wanted to ask you to stop your drilling as soon as possible."

She couldn't help it—she laughed. "No *wonder* he turned you down. Such a request is preposterous."

A muscle jumped in his cheek. "From most people, maybe. But then you and I aren't most people, and you haven't heard my reasons yet."

She didn't think she'd ever heard anything as ludicrous as his request. Obviously he knew nothing about the oil business and even less about her business dealings. "It doesn't matter what your reasons are. There's no way I'll stop."

He surprised her then. With another one of his slight smiles, he circled her throat with his fingers and stroked her skin with his thumb in an almost casual manner that completely derailed her thoughts. "You're a very ambitious woman, Tess Baron, but somehow, I think I have a chance to change your mind."

"You're crazy," she whispered, as the heat from his touch backed up in her lungs.

"Maybe, but will you at least give me a chance to explain what my reasons are?"

"I—I can't. The party—"

"Not tonight. Tomorrow. I'll meet you for breakfast, wherever and whenever you say."

She'd known him for only a short time, but she already knew that saying no to him would do no good. If nothing else, his actions tonight had showed her that he was determined to give her an explanation of some sort. *Plus,* there was an annoying feeling of excitement inside her building at the prospect of getting to see him again. "Okay. Tomorrow morning for breakfast. Here at nine."

"Good," he said softly, his hand still at her neck, his long fingers moving up and down her throat. "Very good." Then he bent his head and kissed her, slowly, as if he had all the time in the world, and thoroughly, devouring her taste as if he wanted to make it a part of him so that he could take it with him. By the time he lifted his head, she had to reach out for the terrace balustrade in order not to fall.

"I'll see you tomorrow morning."

She could only nod and watch as he slipped through an opening in the terrace railing and disappeared into the night.

Gradually and with great effort she pulled herself together. Once her breathing had evened and her pulse had steadied, she returned to the bar and downed the rest of her whiskey. Ignoring the beer, she ordered a large margarita. With it firmly in her hand, she rejoined her party.

Around four in the morning, when the last of her guests had either left or gone to their rooms, and she'd had way more margaritas than she should have, she slipped into her bed. And she couldn't help but wonder what would happen in five hours when she saw Nick Trejo again.

Why was he so sure he could convince her to stop drilling? Then again, his reason didn't really matter. He was wrong. There was nothing more important to her than striking oil as soon as possible, then pumping it into the pipeline at a record rate. And she couldn't allow anyone or anything to stop her.

Not even a sun god whose kiss contained fire.

Two

Tess stumbled out to the terrace clutching a bottle of aspirin in one hand and sunglasses in the other. As soon as the daylight hit her eyes, she groaned and carefully eased on her sunglasses.

"Coffee, ma'am?" Guadálupe asked. Guadalupe was one of four people who worked in and around the house and whose salary was included in the price of the lease.

She started to nod, then immediately realized her mistake as pain jolted through her head. "Yes, please," she whispered.

Gratefully she sank into a chair in front of the table, where breakfast had already been laid out. She took a searing gulp of coffee, downed four aspirin, then slumped back against the chair. Damn gulls. They sounded fiendishly cheerful. And...*loud*. Lord help her, were they that loud every morning?

She'd never had a hangover before, and if she lived through this one, she swore she'd never have one again.

"Is there anything else you'd like, ma'am?"

She almost jumped. She'd forgotten Guadalupe's presence. Warily she eyed the table. Orange juice, fruit, sausage, eggs and an assortment of rolls, jellies and breads—enough to feed your basic small army.

"This will do for now, thank you."

The thing was, her intake of alcohol had always been limited to the occasional beer or a glass of wine with dinner. Even in college, when most kids were celebrating their freedom from their parents with copious amounts of drinking, she'd spent her time sating her appetite for learning about business and oil. Succeeding had always been the most important thing for her, and it still was. She was convinced she could overcome this hangover just as she overcame all obstacles—by sheer determination. If she stayed really still…

Tess. Nick paused at the bottom of the terrace steps. She was already at the table, though it didn't look as if she'd eaten anything yet. Her head was resting on the back of the chair, with her loose blond hair hanging down behind it and blowing lightly in the breeze. The hemline of her short, simple blue dress cut across her upper thighs. The morning sun gilded the skin of her bare arms and legs.

How in the hell was he supposed to keep his mind on business when she looked like that?

It was the same problem he'd had last night. Due to his research, he'd thought he was fully prepared for her. But all it had taken was one look and he'd known he wasn't prepared for her.

He hadn't known that one look at her would transfix him. He hadn't anticipated that each time she talked to a friend, her face would light up so entrancingly that it would take his breath away, nor how a fleeting, anxious expression would make him want to be by her side to ward off whatever or whoever was responsible for the look. He hadn't known that when he took her into his arms he would feel a powerful punch in the gut and, lower, a hardening that made him want her to the point of pain.

He'd definitely been thrown off his stride.

Still, he never should have strung her along as he had. He should have told her right up front who he was and what he wanted.

But…her blue eyes had sparkled with such a delightful curiosity as she'd sparred with him that he hadn't been able to resist. And as they'd danced, she'd moved against him with a beguiling, unconscious fluidity that had made him crave her with a strength that had been nearly impossible to ignore.

And her soft, full lips… They'd beckoned him to taste. *Honey.* They'd tasted like honey and whiskey—potent and unforgettable. Still, he never should have kissed her, because with one kiss, he'd known it wouldn't be enough.

Except it *had* to be.

What he wanted from her was far too important for him to let his sexual urges get the best of him. No matter what happened this morning, he had to remember that.

He climbed the steps to the terrace.

"Good morning."

She started at the quiet, deeply masculine voice. Slowly she pushed her sunglasses to the top of her head and squinted up at Nick Trejo. Sunlight radiated around him like a brilliant nimbus. She pulled her sunglasses down to cover her eyes. "Good morning." She straightened.

After last night, she should have known better than to arrange a meeting with him this early *and* outside. She

should have known the sun would be more intense wherever he was. But, unwilling to dredge up the memories of
why she hadn't been thinking straight last night, she decided there was nothing to be done about her decision now.
He was here, and she was just going to have to deal with
it. With *him*. "Have a seat."

He smiled at her, and she shut her eyes. She'd planned
to look not only presentable for their meeting this morning
but businesslike. Unfortunately, she'd barely managed to
slip on a short cotton shift and sandals. And her hair...
Normally she wore it up or secured in some way, but with
some heavy metal rock band's percussion section currently
booming its merry way through her head, she'd barely been
able to run a comb through it.

Opening her eyes and watching as Nick settled himself
into the chair across from her, she considered whether or
not she could blame him for her hangover. No, she decided.
To be fair, she couldn't.

After all, it wasn't his fault that her reaction to him had
unnerved her to the point that she'd ordered the bartender
to keep her glass filled all night. Besides, she seemed to
remember having a really great time.

"Help yourself to anything you like."

"I'll just have coffee." He reached for the carafe, poured
himself a cup, then glanced over the terrace and lawn.
"You must have had a terrific cleanup crew. If I hadn't
been here last night, I wouldn't have known there'd been
a party."

"Really?" She didn't bother to conduct her own survey.
The movement would have hurt. As he had the night before, Nick was holding all her attention. He was casually
dressed in jeans, boots and a rosy beige open-necked shirt
beneath a medium brown sport jacket. And his amber eyes

were even more vivid in his tanned face than they had been last night.

It didn't matter if it was night or day, she reflected ruefully. It didn't matter if he was dressed up or down. His virile masculinity was enough to stop the heart of a healthy woman. Fortunately for her, she wasn't at all well this morning. She reached for her cup and downed more coffee.

He studied her for several moments. "I gather your party lasted well into the night?"

"I must look even worse than I think I do," she murmured, then watched as his lips curved ever so slightly upward into a half smile.

The sight of his lips brought back the weak, heated way she'd felt when he'd kissed her. Funny. She would have thought the impact of his smile and the sight of his lips would affect her less this morning. After all, everything in her body was hurting, right down to her toenails. Plus she was wearing sunglasses with the added precaution of ultraviolet protection. But...

"Actually, you look quite beautiful. And I like your hair loose."

...he affected her more.

A flush rushed to her face, and self-consciously she raised a hand to her hair. Then she realized what she was doing and dropped her hand. "Thank you." The sooner she got this meeting over with, the better. "Are you sure you don't want anything other than coffee?"

Food. That reminded her. If the way her stomach felt was a color, it would be green. For all she knew, she *was* green. Maybe she would feel better if she tried to eat something. One thing was for sure, it couldn't make her feel any worse. At least, she hoped it couldn't.

"I've already had breakfast. The coffee is all I want."

"Okay." She glanced at her watch. A mistake. She

couldn't get the numbers to focus. Then again, he didn't need to know that. "You have fifteen minutes before the world figures out that I'm awake and starts calling and or party stragglers come down in search of breakfast." Cautiously she eyed a wheat roll, then tore a small part of the roll off and carefully ate it. If it stayed down, she would consider herself ahead of the game.

"I realize what an important woman you are, and believe me, I'm very grateful to you for working me into your packed schedule."

He'd said it with a straight face, but a light in his eyes told her that he was mocking her. At any other time she would have called him on it, but not this morning. It would take more effort than she was willing to exert right now. Besides, in the next moment, his expression turned serious.

He leaned back in his chair and fixed his intense amber gaze on her. "There are two things you need to know about me. One, I'm a professor of archaeology at the University of Texas, though currently I'm on sabbatical."

"Archaeology?" Clever cover for a sun god, she thought, and might have laughed at herself if she hadn't been so convinced it would jar loose something in her throbbing head.

She had to get past that sun god analogy, that amazing kiss they'd shared last night and those amber eyes of his that even now were heating her skin. She had to consider him as she would any other business person who was coming to her with a request.

Simple.

She just wished she knew how to do it.

"The other thing you need to know is that in the 1880's my great-grandfather discovered a rich vein of gold in the Sierra Madre mountains in Northern Mexico. It was an enormous find. He literally mined a fortune out of those mountains, and he had great dreams for that gold." Nick's voice was strong, and his gaze never once left her face. "He turned it into bullion and loaded it aboard a ship, the *Águila*, at the port of Tampico. The ship's destination was here." His index finger pointed to the table, indicating Corpus Christi. "That fortune was to be the start of a new life for him here in Texas. His plan was to buy a vast amount of land, found a great ranch and build an empire."

The aspirin seemed to be working a little. It had muffled the acute pounding in her head to a dull pounding. She risked another bite of the roll and washed it down with more coffee. "That's very interesting, but what does your family's history have to do with me and my current drilling site?"

"Just listen. Please."

In many different and unusual ways, the man defined the word power, but he'd said please to her with a sincerity and a supplication she wouldn't have thought him capable of. In that moment she knew she would sit there and listen until he finished his story. "All right."

"The *Águila* had almost reached its destination when it met a hurricane. It was a killer. At a certain point, it turned away from the land and headed back out to sea. It caught the ship up and blew it farther out into the Gulf. The waves were too high, the ship took on too much water, and it sank."

She rubbed her aching forehead and wondered how long hangovers lasted. "What a shame, and after he'd worked so hard."

"The loss of the gold all but killed him. He had what I suppose today we would call a nervous breakdown, but somehow he managed to go back to the Sierra Madre one last time. However, in his absence, other prospectors had descended on the mine, and his heart wasn't in it anymore.

He managed to extract only a meager amount before he left the mountain for good. Back in Texas, he bought a relatively small amount of land outside Uvalde and ran cattle on it until he died.''

''It must have been very hard for him,'' she said, for want of anything better to say. Nick was a compelling man who could affect her with a mere look or touch, and his story was a sad one that moved her. Yet she had a mountain of her own problems waiting for her as soon as she stepped into the house and sat down at her desk, plus she had this damn hangover to deal with.

As if he could sense her mind wandering, Nick eyed her consideringly. ''I don't think you can imagine the full extent of how hard it was for him, because even I can't. I only know that he was a man of great pride and felt humiliated by his failure. To build his self-esteem, he talked incessantly to the people he came to know in and around Uvalde, telling them about the great fortune that he'd wrested from the mountains, then lost. Unfortunately, none of them believed his story of how close he'd come to founding an empire, and they scorned him. He died brokenhearted.''

Through the windows of the house, she could see Ron already handling calls, but she'd committed to hearing Nick out and that was just what she planned to do. ''Your family certainly has an interesting history.''

She'd managed half of the wheat roll, and despite the color and uncertainty of her stomach, she was pleased the roll was staying down. She still didn't have a clue what Nick's story had to do with her, but because of his *please*, she waited.

''History, yes. History that has worked its way down through the generations. I grew up on that history. My grandfather inherited the bill of lading for the gold that had been boarded on that ship.''

''Your great-grandfather had the bill of lading? Then why didn't he simply show it to his neighbors?''

''He did. They thought it was a forgery, but his son, my grandfather, never thought it was, and neither did I.''

Over his shoulder, she saw Ron answering another phone call, and she prayed it wasn't Jimmy Vega with yet another problem. Jimmy was the best tool pusher in the business, and she'd chosen him to supervise the entire operation. In turn, he had put together the best crew of roughnecks there was. Still, everything about this particular operation had been hard so far. They hadn't even been drilling a week, yet time and again, the axiom that what can go wrong will go wrong had been proven true. ''Again, Nick, it's all very interesting, but—''

''I've found the shipwreck and the gold.''

Ron came striding onto the terrace, carrying the portable phone, mouthing Jimmy Vega's name. Damn. She really did need to talk with Jimmy. But there was Nick, sitting across from her, and there was no way she would be able to focus on Jimmy as long as Nick's amber eyes were trained so intently on her. She motioned Ron away. A look of surprise crossed his face, but he turned back to the house. ''I'm sorry, Nick. What were you saying?''

''I said I've found the gold and I'm ready to start excavating it.''

''Well, congratulations.'' She tried to infuse as much enthusiasm as possible into her congratulations, but she couldn't say it with any strength or volume. Even though the percussion section in her head had quieted, the rest of the band was still playing.

''Congratulations aren't in order yet. I've got a serious problem.''

She exhaled a long breath. "Look, Nick, I could match you problem for problem and more than likely have a stack of problems left over. I've listened to your story, as I said I would, but now I need to get back to work."

"I'm not through."

"I'm sorry, but you are. At least with me." At any other time, she would gladly have lingered over her coffee and listened to Nick. He had the ability to touch and affect her in a way no other man ever had. But there was nothing normal or right about her current circumstances, and there wouldn't be for months to come. She started to push her chair away from the table.

"The *Águila* and the gold are not far from your drilling site, which is why I'm here."

She stilled.

"It's perched atop a scarp. You're drilling in a highly overpressurized zone. It will take only one catastrophe to send the *Águila* sliding off that salt ridge and into the abyss, where it will be buried so deep, it will more than likely be lost forever. Hell, even a series of minor catastrophes would do it."

There was only one thing she could say. "You're right."

He nodded, apparently satisfied that she understood. "I need time to shore up the ship, to brace it in such a way that it will be protected from whatever happens on your rig."

She rubbed her aching forehead, trying to focus. "I don't see how you can really do that."

"It'll be hard, but I can try to make sure it will be safeguarded as much as possible, and then I can pray like hell. Besides, with the crew you've got, plus modern technology, the possibility of a full catastrophe such as a blowout is considerably lessened. But there are other things. There are fault lines down there that would easily channel vibrations of any sort from your rig over to the *Águila.*'' Pausing, he looked at her in an assessing way. ''That's why I'm here to ask you to stop drilling for at least three months.''

''At *least?*'' If she hadn't been sitting, she might have fallen. As it was, the percussion section of the band in her head returned. He had no idea what he was asking of her. ''Nick, there's no way I could stop for even a week's time.''

His body tensed. She didn't see it; she felt it in the air between them.

''What's the matter, Ms. Baron? Aren't you rich enough yet?''

The question hit her like a slap. ''No, as a matter of fact I'm not, Mr. Trejo.''

Nick didn't move, not a muscle, not an eyelash. ''Funny, you didn't strike me as the greedy type.''

''Do you honestly think you have the right to call me greedy? You're asking me to give up three valuable months of an operation that will bring in millions so that you can have three months to ensure you can safely harvest a crop of gold worth millions.''

Cold amber eyes stared at her.

Ron walked out again, the phone in his hand, an anxious expression on his face. ''Vega insists on talking to you.''

She reached for the phone just as Nick rose. ''Hang on a minute, Jimmy.'' She covered the mouthpiece and looked at Nick.

''I won't take up any more of your time this morning.'' He glanced at his watch. ''I'll pick you up this evening at seven.''

''Excuse me?''

He was already walking away from her. ''Seven,'' he called as he disappeared from the terrace.

Seven? Had he just asked her for a date? A *date?* It was

hard for her to imagine Nick doing something as mundane as asking a woman for a date. He must want more time to try to change her mind, and there was no rule that said she had to go. Still…

"Tess? *Tess?*"

She glanced at the phone, then lifted it to her ear. "Sorry, Jimmy. What's happened now?"

Nick pulled his car onto the road that would take him to the little house he was renting. Tess Baron was every bit as smart and tough as he'd thought she would be. He'd known she wouldn't be an easy sale. Hell, why should she be? What he was asking of her required an enormous sacrifice on her part.

But he'd really thought that on some deep level she would understand and comply. He *still* had hope that she would.

His hand tightened on the steering wheel. Damn it. Why couldn't he just have kept his hands off her last night? Why couldn't he have kept his mind on business? It would have made things between them so much easier.

But now his personal feelings were in the mix, infusing every word, every gesture, with the possibility of volatility. How else could he explain his need to stand up from that table, circle it and pull her into his arms for a long, deep kiss, despite the fact that she'd told him no?

He exhaled a long breath. Obviously he was going to have to get his fast-growing appetite for her under control. He was also going to have to present what he was asking of her in an entirely different way. In effect, he was going to have to set a trap.

He had a little over nine hours to set things in motion, and there would be no margin for error. After this evening, he wouldn't get another chance to change Tess's mind.

Abruptly he took a turn and headed in a different direction.

Six forty-five. It had taken a while, but Tess could now see the face of her watch quite clearly. Nick was supposed to arrive in fifteen minutes, and she had no idea where they were going, or even if this was to be another business meeting or a genuine date.

If Nick planned to spend their time together attempting to convince her to cease her drilling, it would make for a very long and difficult evening for her. But today, as she'd thought about the coming evening, she'd been alarmed to discover that, even if that were his plan, she still wanted to go with him. Which was exactly why she needed to find out up front what he had in mind.

She had all the risk she could handle in her professional life, which was the reason she'd never allowed any risk to enter her personal life. Then last night Nick had appeared, and she hadn't had to look twice to know that, in one way or another, he would be a risk for a woman, a danger for a woman's heart.

Tonight was a prime example. She had no idea where he planned to take her, or why. She only knew she wanted to go. However, she had no intention of allowing that to happen unless he told her it would be a social evening.

She'd chosen an outfit that was suitable for a date. It was a red, sleeveless, A-line knit dress, with a matching cashmere sweater casually tied around the neckline. Her open-toed shoes with a midsize heel were also red. Last but not least, she'd wound her hair into a loose French twist.

If it turned out that Nick planned on talking business, she would politely turn him down, then treat herself to dinner and maybe even a movie. She just wished she knew what he had in mind.

As the day progressed, the pain in her head had lessened and her stomach had calmed. The party guests who stayed over had all left, and the house had quieted. Still, the day hadn't exactly gone great.

There had been all kinds of problems on the rig, from broken drill bits to machinery failure to tangled lines. Sometimes she thought the operation was jinxed—but she couldn't afford to think like that.

If anyone could handle the problems and bring in the oil, it was Jimmy. *If* there was oil to find.

She shook her head, then bent her head to rub her brow. That was something else she couldn't afford to think about. Every one of the tests had looked great, but they were just that—tests. Despite the sophistication of today's testing, in the end, drilling for oil was still very much a wildcatting venture. There were so many variables. To compete in the market, you had to have money, nerves of steel, a large portion of luck, perfect timing and, last but not least, a great instinct for oil.

So far, her wells were bringing in money in amounts that would make anyone deliriously happy. Anyone, that is, except her father.

She glanced at her watch again and noticed that her heart was beating just a little harder as the time drew closer to Nick's arrival. She drew a deep breath of the sea air to compose herself. Tomorrow she was scheduled to fly out to the rig for an inspection, plus an up-to-date cost-and-time report from Jimmy. But for tonight, well, she'd see.

"You look lovely."

She turned, and there he was, all darkness and brilliance, outlined against the sun. Her heart jumped into high gear.

"Thank you. Since I didn't know where we were going, I wasn't certain what to wear." Lord, she sounded like a flustered schoolgirl about to go out on her first date.

His gaze slowly raked her, his lips curved upward. "You chose perfectly."

Which told her exactly nothing. "Then where are we going?"

He held his hand out to her, and before she could stop herself, she took it.

"We're going a place that I love, and by the time we leave, I'm hoping you're going to feel the same way." He began to draw her toward his car, parked at the side of the house.

Abruptly she stopped and pulled her hand from his. "I don't like guessing games, Nick. You and I have been there and done that—last night, as a matter of fact. So what's this all about? Is this going to be a social evening? Or are you going to spend it trying to get me to change my mind about your request? Because if that's the case, you should know right now that it won't work. There's no way I can put off production for three months, and quite frankly, I don't want to spend an evening arguing with you about it."

He stared at her for several moments. Surprisingly his gaze didn't sear as it had the evening before, but rather caressed.

She felt his gaze as a gentle touch all over her body, and as she did, she discovered that gentleness from Nick was a powerful thing. It liquefied her bones. It made her want things for which she had neither the time nor the inclination. Even more remarkable, he wasn't even touching her.

"You've made your position abundantly clear," he said softly. "And as to the question of whether or not this will be a social evening, it's my hope that it will be."

He was saying all the right words, yet she wasn't sure she believed him. Then again, why shouldn't she? To her knowledge, he hadn't lied to her. Last night and this morning, he'd been completely up-front about what he wanted.

She'd told him no, and now he was telling her that he hoped their evening would be a social one. Her hopes matched his exactly.

She couldn't remember the last real date she'd been on, probably because it had been years. And Nick Trejo was the most intriguing man she'd ever met. Chances were their paths wouldn't cross again, yet tonight would be an opportunity for her to spend an interesting evening with an extremely interesting man.

And if his gaze burned or liquefied, and if his touch raised emotions that made her remember for the first time in a long time that she was a woman with normal wants and desires, so be it. Being with him made her forget, if only for a little while, the pressure that was her life.

With a smile, she reached for his hand.

"The airport? Nick, what are we doing at the airport?"

As he steered his car toward one of the outlying hangars, he glanced at her. "I've borrowed a friend's plane to take us to dinner."

Panic rose in her throat, yet there was no real reason. "Look, it's very nice of you to go to all this trouble for our dinner, but it's not necessary."

"I wanted to."

She shook her head, still fighting the mysterious panic. "I've had a rough day, and I'd just as soon stay in town."

He pulled the car into a parking space and switched it off. Turning toward her, he angled his arm along the top of her seat. "This isn't going to require any effort for you, Tess. I promise. All you have to do is sit beside me and relax."

Sit beside him and relax. *That* was the problem. Relaxing while she was sitting beside him in the close confines of a car had turned out to be harder than she had thought it would be. She'd been much too aware of him. She'd found herself mesmerized as she'd watched the confident way his hands had held the wheel and the quick, instinctive way he'd responded to every bump and curve in the road. Around his wrist he wore a slim, stainless steel watch that subtly spoke of masculinity as well as competency.

"If it's your safety you're concerned about, don't be. I'm an excellent pilot. As for the plane, it's the newest in Cessna's fleet and is serviced regularly after every flight. If those two things weren't true, I wouldn't have considered this trip."

"It's not that."

His tone lightened. "Well, it can't be that I'm the first man to ask you to fly to a special place for dinner."

She let out a pent-up breath. "No, you're not the first."

"When you were asked, did you go?"

"Yes."

"Then what's the problem?"

"No problem." She rubbed her forehead. There was no pain, but she felt a growing tension in her scalp, and Nick was the cause. In the short time she'd known him, he'd surprised her, but he hadn't made one move or said one thing to hurt her. Why, then, was her scalp tightening? And why did her instincts tell her to remain on guard? "Mostly I've gone with groups of friends."

"And not one particular man?"

"Once or twice. Look—"

"Please, Tess. This is important to me, and I've already made special arrangements."

Damn it, he'd said *please* again. Plus, she really did want to spend this evening with him. Most likely it would be the only one she'd ever get. Their objectives were so diametrically opposed that she could see no future for them. But for tonight, she really wanted to forget their differences and see if she could find any similarities. If she could find even one, she would consider the evening a success.

"Tess?"

She nodded. "Let's go."

Minutes later, she was buckling herself into the passenger seat beside him. And she couldn't help but notice as they took off that they were flying directly into the sun.

Three

"Uvalde? This restaurant that you love so much is in Uvalde, Texas?"

The plane glided to a stop. Then and only then did Nick look at her. "Trust me. You're going to love dinner."

She mentally shrugged. He'd engaged her in pleasant small talk for most of the trip, and she'd actually enjoyed the flight. He had a quick mind that she appreciated, and not once had he mentioned anything about the *Águila* or her drilling.

But as soon as they'd touched down, her original uneasiness had returned. Stupid, really. He certainly hadn't dragged her here, kicking and screaming. She'd wanted to come. Still…

As she came down the stairs of the plane, he offered her a steadying hand. An unnecessary gesture, but definitely a nice one, and after she reached the ground, he continued to hold her hand. "I'm really hoping you'll like what I've planned."

His suddenly serious expression took her aback. "I'm sure I will."

"Good." He stared at her as if he were searching for something in her, or maybe even in himself, but in the end he shook his head.

"Nick? Is there something wrong?"

"Not a thing." He lightly tugged her hand. "Come on. The car is just around the corner."

The car he guided her to was a spotlessly clean, beautifully preserved 1975 Cadillac.

"Is this car a rental?" she asked.

"No. It belongs to my family."

"Your family?"

"My grandparents."

"Oh. So they live in Uvalde?"

"That's right."

Everything was beginning to make sense. "I wondered how a restaurant in Uvalde could have become such a special place to you. You were raised here, right?"

For some reason her remark drew a smile from him, and her heart gave a hard thud. She returned his smile. "Let me guess. This place serves great Tex-Mex, right?"

"On occasion, but not tonight. Hope you're not too disappointed."

She shook her head. "I can get my fill of Tex-Mex in Corpus."

"Good." His smile warmed her inside and out, and she realized that whatever wariness she'd been feeling had disappeared. For the first time since she'd looked across the terrace and seen him, she was totally at ease with him.

He turned onto a highway, then gunned the car so that it zoomed ahead. Given Nick's special affinity with the sun, she wasn't surprised to see that they were still heading west. But given the time of evening, the sun had disappeared, leaving behind only trails of muted reds and oranges on the horizon as a reminder of its existence.

"You said you're a professor at the university?"

"That's right."

"So then you have a home in Austin?"

"Yes. Do you know Austin?"

"I went to school there. It was a requirement for me and my two sisters."

"Requirement?"

She smiled dryly. "Oh, yeah. It had to be the University of Texas or it would be nothing."

"Sounds as if your father had very definite ideas."

"That's one way of putting it." Dictatorial was another.

"One thing about it—no one can make a mistake by going there. What was your degree in?"

"Petroleum engineering." Such a shame, she thought. She'd never had a professor who looked even remotely like Nick. She could only imagine the clamor of the young, attractive women lining up, trying to get into his classes. In fact, if he'd been a professor there when she'd attended, she would have been clamoring right along with the others. She smiled to herself at the thought. "Austin's a really great city."

"It's also a wonderful place to live and relatively easy-going."

"Not like Dallas, huh?"

His head swung around. "You don't like living in Dallas?"

Even she had heard the wistfulness in her voice, so she wasn't surprised that he had. "Oh, I love it. There's always something happening there, and it's a great base for international dealings." It was the truth. Only the word *easy-*

going had caused her wistfulness, though she wasn't sure why. Her life was made up of discipline, drive and ambition. She'd never known any other way.

"In this day and time of faxes and modems, I imagine you could work anywhere and still maintain international ties without any problems."

"I'm not sure that's entirely true. For the type of business I do, it's almost imperative to have an international airport close by, and Dallas does."

He turned off the highway onto a two-lane country road. "DFW is a short flight away from Austin."

"Uh-huh." His Chamber of Commerce-like promotion of Austin was interesting, but it didn't affect her one way or another. Her home was in Dallas because her uncle and her father had decided the offices of Baron International should be there. And as soon as she'd graduated from college at the age of twenty, she'd dived headfirst into the deep end of the high-tech, high-stress world of the oil business. She loved it. She thrived on it. She was good at it. She'd never minded the long hours or the pressure of risking huge amounts of money on what, in the end, came down to her instincts.

Only her father's ability to reach beyond the grave and affect her life, along with those of her sisters, had sucked the fun out of her work. And the last couple of years, that same ability had accelerated her stress to warp speed.

Suddenly she glanced around her, gazed out the back window, then looked at Nick. "I may have my directions wrong, but isn't town that way?" She pointed a window to the east.

He eased his foot off the gas pedal. "Yes, but our dinner is this way."

"Oh." Once again she looked around her. "But this is all country. There's nothing out here."

"Not quite nothing." They topped a hill, then Nick took a left onto a dirt road. "We're almost there."

She sat back and watched as the road unfolded before her—around a bend, along a line of broken fence, up a slight hill with buffalo grass growing on either side. Then ahead a house gradually appeared, starkly outlined against the dusky sky.

The house was two stories, with gingerbread trim that outlined its porch. Cream-colored paint peeled off its wooden exterior. Two chimneys, one at either end of the house jutted out of the shingled roof. A weather vane perched between the chimneys, along with several lightning rods. It looked abandoned. "This isn't where we're going to eat dinner, is it?"

"Yes." He pulled the car to a stop in front of the house, then got out, walked around to open her door and offered his hand.

She took it and slid out. There wasn't another car in sight, nor could she see any lights in the house. "But it doesn't look as if there's anyone here but us."

"There's not. This is going to be a very exclusive dinner."

"But—"

With one of his slight smiles that made her skin tingle, he lightly squeezed her hand. "Come on. This has always been my favorite place to eat, and I'm anxious to share it with you."

"Ooo-kay." No sense backing out now. She'd known that an evening with Nick would be out of the ordinary. She just hadn't known *how* out of the ordinary.

She climbed the front steps, looking around her as she went. Then Nick pushed open the unlocked front door, and she walked into a darkened hall. Almost immediately, a heavenly smell wafted toward her.

He flipped on a light switch. Completely mystified, she saw faded wallpaper and a scarred wooden floor.

"Whatever that smell is, it's *wonderful.*"

For the first time he fully smiled at her. "I can assure you that the food will be as wonderful as it smells. Would you like to wash up?"

"Yes, thank you."

He pointed toward another hall at a right angle to the one they were in. "First door on your right." He pointed down the main hallway to an open doorway. "Come in there when you're finished."

"If that's where the heavenly smells are originating from, I'll be right in."

She found the bathroom and shut the door after her. Out-of-date fixtures greeted her, along with towels and washcloths that, though faded, looked freshly washed. The wallpaper was peeling in spots. The linoleum had holes worn into it, yet the smell of a recently used lemon-scented cleaner hung in the air.

She shook her head in wonder. This place certainly wasn't a restaurant, yet the smells coming out of the kitchen were making her salivate. She'd never once entertained the notion that there was anything simple about Nick. Now, she realized, she was about to learn just how complicated he was.

And if in the end she discovered that he'd planned this evening as a way to convince her to stop her drilling, she wouldn't be surprised. But she *would* be deeply, deeply disappointed.

Damn the man, anyway. Why hadn't he just taken Ron's no for an answer when Ron had told him he couldn't see her? Why did he have to crash her birthday party and bring more complications into her life at a time when she could barely handle the ones she already had?

She sighed. Because he was Nick Trejo, that was why.

Minutes later, she walked into a dimly lit kitchen. Small lamps were lit at either end of an aged sideboard. A square table graced the middle of the room. Covered by a blue tablecloth, set for two with blue and white plates and lit by a short, round blue candle whose base was surrounded by field daisies, the table looked as if it had just come off the pages of *Country Homes*. In fact, the whole kitchen did.

On the counter, a freshly baked loaf of bread rested on a cutting board with a bottle of wine beside it. Beef stew simmered in a large pot on the stove. Nick stood at the table, forking a crisp salad into two small bowls that matched the plates.

She eyed him wryly. "This is a set, isn't it? And everything here is a prop, right?" But even as she said it, she knew she was wrong. Whatever was happening, she hadn't figured it out yet.

"A set?" He took the salad bowl to the counter. "You mean like for a TV show?"

She shook her head. "Never mind."

"Take a seat and I'll pour you some wine."

She settled into one of the chairs and watched him as he poured the wine into two glasses, then carried the glasses to the table. He'd taken off his jacket and rolled up his sleeves, and she was suddenly struck by how comfortable and at home he seemed.

"Okay, Nick, I think now is a good time to tell me what exactly is going on. No one lives in this house, do they?"

"In one way, yes, but in another way, no."

"I'm not interested in playing guessing games, Nick. Exactly whose house is this?"

"My grandparents'. They live in town now."

"So no one lives here."

"They live here, too."

"But you just said..." She waved her hand in front of her as if she were erasing her words. "Forget it. Let me try another question. Where did the food come from?"

"My sister, Kathie." He brought the bread to the table and sliced off several pieces, then angled the knife he'd used across the cutting board. "She's married to a pharmacist, and they live in town with their two daughters. But my grandmother taught her to cook, and everything we're going to eat tonight is from my grandmother's recipe file. Believe me, our dinner is guaranteed to be delicious."

She only had to inhale to know he was right. She sipped her wine as she tried to understand the rest of what he'd said. "So let me get this straight. Your sister came out here, cooked all this and then left right before we arrived?"

Deftly he ladled stew into two bowls. "She knew our schedule, so it was fairly easy for her to have everything ready, and she didn't mind at all."

"That's very nice of her. She must have done this same sort of thing for you before."

He paused and looked at her. "No."

"You mean you've never brought other women out here to this same sort of setup?"

"No, I haven't."

"Really." Disbelief flattened her tone.

He left his task and moved to her, his broad-shouldered, leanly muscled frame radiating a barely contained electric tension that seemed, with his next breath, to have the potential to turn to danger.

How could she have forgotten that when she'd first seen him last night, her instincts had told her he was a man who should be treated with caution? With her next breath came the answer. Obviously his kiss the evening before had knocked all sense from her head. Then, this evening, he'd been a charming host, lulling her into a false sense of security. But still, she should have remembered.

He braced his hands on the table and leaned toward her, his amber eyes bright against his dark skin. "This is the very first time I've ever asked Kathie to do something like this, and when I told her who my guest would be, she was more than willing to cook our dinner."

"You told her who I was." The light dawned. "I see. So it all comes back to my drilling site, doesn't it?"

He lapsed into silence as he returned to the stove for the two bowls of stew. He took his time, making sure everything was on the table that needed to be. Was he trying to think of an answer she might find acceptable? Or was he simply going to ignore her question?

"There was no need for this elaborate ruse, Nick." Her tone held deliberate and cutting derision. "I could have told you no back home as well as I can tell you no here. As a matter of fact, I did."

He settled into the chair across from her and leveled a piercing gaze on her. "I won't lie to you, Tess. Part of this trip does involve me trying to get you to change your mind and stop your drilling for three months."

"Then you haven't been *listening* to me. I've already told you—"

He held up his hand. "But at the same time, I meant it when I said that I hoped this evening would be a social one." Without dropping his gaze from her, he ran his fingers up and down the stem of his wineglass. "The truth is, Tess, I want to get to know you better."

His amber eyes glittered like stars in a dark, stormy night sky. If there was some way to look at his face without having to see his eyes, she reflected wryly, she would be a lot better off.

"You see," he said quite casually, "I want you. I have since the first moment I laid eyes on you."

The breath caught in her throat. "You—"

"I want you much more than I know how to tell you." He paused, his gaze never leaving hers. "I didn't count on that happening. Last night, when I went to your party, I went strictly for business reasons. But then I saw you, and felt you against me as we danced—" his gaze dropped to her lips "—and I kissed you. And I left wanting much more."

She tried to swallow but found her throat constricted. She took a gulp of wine, tried to swallow again and this time was successful. "You are either very direct or you're lying for your own ends."

"I wouldn't lie to you, Tess. Not about this."

"And how am I supposed to know that?" She heard the hint of desperation in her voice, but there was nothing she could do about it. "I just met you last night. Then tonight, under the guise of having dinner, you flew me out here to this isolated house."

"We *are* about to have dinner, so that was no lie. And I'm not lying to you about wanting you. Deep down, you must know that."

She did know it, which was why she was feeling so desperate. He'd declared desire, not love, which was good. She wouldn't have believed him if he'd said he loved her. But either way, he was bringing emotions into their relationship that she wasn't prepared to deal with. In reality, she simply didn't know how.

"I hope you feel the same way I do."

Damn. That was one of the problems. She did. But she'd never been any good at this sort of thing. It was why she had friends instead of lovers. Give her a tough negotiation to handle, or a complicated drilling site to tackle, and she was in her element. But Nick, with his commanding presence and his heated stare, threw her. She had no practice with womanly wiles.

Her sister Jill would know exactly how to handle Nick. Jill was an expert at luring men into her sophisticated web, then, more often than not, she would walk away and leave them hanging. Even Kit would know. Kit would simply give a toss of her red hair and laugh, and within minutes she would have a man wrapped around her little finger. Then she, too, would walk away.

But Tess didn't know how to play games with men. All she knew how to do was to tell the truth, and in this case, she really, really didn't want to do that. The truth would make her vulnerable, something she couldn't afford to be with this man. The truth would also make it almost impossible for her to walk away, even though that was exactly what she would have to do.

"Do you, Tess? Do you want me even a fraction as much as I want you?"

She turned her face away and briefly closed her eyes. She could lie to him, but she was so terrible at it, he would know. There was really only one thing she could tell him. "I wouldn't be here if I didn't."

It was as if a two-ton elephant had just lumbered into the room and sat down at the table with them. They couldn't ignore it. They couldn't make it disappear. It was here, and now they were going to have to figure out what to do with it.

"There's one last thing you should know, Tess, because in some ways it takes us beyond the realm of the feelings that are between the two of us. There are things I hope you will learn while we're here."

"Things?" Her wariness was back, and she didn't even attempt to hide it.

"Things about my family."

She didn't want to do this. She wanted to snap her fingers and be back at the house in Corpus Christi. Alone. And with another snap of her fingers she wanted to make Nick disappear from her life. He came with too many demands, too many complications. But as hard as she'd studied in school, she'd never learned to snap her fingers and make things happen. "Isn't learning about your family the same thing as learning about you?"

"In some ways, I suppose so."

She didn't understand why he would try to separate the two. She didn't even want to understand. She rubbed her brow. "Whether we like it or not, our family dynamics play a huge part in shaping who we are."

His slow smile was warm. "I'm glad you understand that."

She understood it more than he knew. Her own family dynamics were worthy of the fictional Ewings of *Dallas*.

She needed time to regain her balance, so she began to eat the stew, which turned out to be mouthwatering, and was extremely grateful when Nick did the same. For now she was more than happy to pretend she didn't see the elephant.

She knew she was awkward when it came to relationships with men. And when it came to Nick, her awkwardness was multiplied by a thousand. Given the same chance she had, any other woman on the planet would already have cleared the dishes with one sweep of her arm and started making love to Nick right atop his grandmother's kitchen table.

But she couldn't—*wouldn't* do such a thing. She wasn't up to delving any deeper into their mutually declared desire. Not now, with him so close.

At this point, all she wanted was to get home. In the

solitude and safety of her bedroom, she hoped she could get a better perspective on everything that had happened and been said this evening. Because when she faced the desire they felt for each other, she would also have to face the fact that at least part of Nick's desire for her involved what he wanted from her. And that would be extremely hard on her.

Realistically, she knew there were different kinds of seduction, and two kinds were involved here. There was seduction for the purpose of getting someone to have sex with you. And there was seduction for the purpose of getting someone to agree with you.

Nick wanted both, and she didn't think she could handle letting him have either. She didn't have enough experience to be able to tell one type of seduction from the other, so, knowing her, she would concentrate on the desire he made her feel, which from her side would be pure. And in the end, when he walked away from her because she couldn't give him what he wanted, she would be hurt. Badly.

So she deliberately led the conversation down the most innocuous paths she could think of. They talked about the food and she coaxed Nick into telling her anecdotes about his nieces.

She badly needed the time their dinner gave her. The evening wasn't close to being over, yet it had already turned out to be one stunning surprise after another. She needed to catch her breath so she could be ready for the next surprise. Because if there was one thing she was learning, it was that, with Nick, there would be a next surprise.

And that elephant was still sitting there, waiting for them to resolve, one way or another, the issue of their desire for one another.

* * *

Nick cleared the dinner dishes from the table, while Tess lingered over her coffee and a bowl of peach cobbler. "Please remember to tell your sister how much I've enjoyed the dinner."

"I will. She's accustomed to getting compliments on her cooking, but it still makes her day when she receives another."

She took her last bite of cobbler, then pushed the bowl away. In keeping with her plan of maintaining a stream of conversation until they could leave, she asked, "So, tell me about this house. If your grandparents live in town, why is it still fully furnished?"

After he'd stacked the dishes in the sink and squirted them with soap, he turned on the water. "My grandfather has a severe heart problem that needs to be closely monitored. My grandmother's health is better, though at her age, anything could happen. They needed to be in town so they could be closer to their doctor and the hospital. They knew it as well as Kathie and I did."

The water rose higher and higher in the sink until it covered the dishes, then he turned it off. "Still, when it came to the move, they dug in their heels. The only way they would agree was for Kathie and me to promise that this house would still be here for them, just as it always has been. We keep all the utilities on and have the place cleaned once a month. And every once in a while, they drive out here and have lunch and stay an hour or two. It makes them happy and, at the same time, they're safe, which are the two things that count the most." He turned and leaned against the counter.

She smiled. "You know what I think?"

"What?"

"I think they're very lucky to have you and your sister as grandchildren."

"Kathie and I are the lucky ones. They raised us."

She blinked. "How did that come about?"

"Our parents were killed in an airplane crash."

"How awful."

He nodded. "Yes. I was eight, and Kathie was seven. But our grandparents were there for us, so now it's our turn to be there for them."

"That's wonderful," she said seriously.

"What we're doing for them is very little compared to what they did for us."

Damn the man. She couldn't find a thing she didn't like about him. Nevertheless, a single fact remained true. They had opposing interests. She couldn't agree to the postponement of her drilling schedule, and as soon as he realized she couldn't be swayed, she would never see him again.

"You know what I find remarkable? The fact that your parents were killed in an airplane crash, yet here you are, a pilot."

He grinned, and she was momentarily stunned. It was the first time he'd grinned at her, and she was charmed by the hint of the boy behind the man.

"I'm a pilot *because* my parents died in a crash. The crash gave me a strong fear of flying. The only way I could overcome it was to learn all I could about planes and flying."

"And that's the reason you made a point of assuring me how safe our flight would be."

He shrugged. "I worked and studied until I felt that I was the very best pilot I could be. And I won't fly a plane unless I can see its service record and then go over the plane myself. I believe in stacking the odds in my favor."

He believed in stacking the odds in his favor. From what she knew of him, his statement made perfect sense, and she wasn't thinking about the way he'd overcome his fear of flying. She pushed herself up from the table and carried the cobbler bowl and her coffee cup to the counter.

"Is that the reason you brought me out here? Do you think that bringing me to your grandparents' house and feeding me your sister's cooking will somehow stack the odds in your favor and I'll just give in?"

"It's part of the reason, but I've already told you that."

For a while during dinner, as she'd listened to him talking about his nieces, she'd done her best to push from her mind his ultimate objective and had tentatively tested the waters of what it was like simply to be a woman on a date with a man to whom she was strongly attracted.

But the harder she'd tried, the harder she'd hit that wall of knowledge that nothing serious could ever develop between them. And instinctively she knew that, emotionally, she would never be able to handle a casual affair, not with any man, but especially not with Nick.

Nick wanted her and would probably be more than satisfied with a casual affair, but she would bet her last dime that, if given the choice, he would forget the affair and choose to have her halt her drilling.

"I can't stop the drilling, Nick. That answer will never change, no matter what you do or say. And I'd like to fly back to Corpus as soon as possible, so let me help you with these dishes. The sooner we get everything put away, the sooner we can leave. Switch places with me. Since you know where things go, I'll wash and you dry." She stepped around him to the sink and plunged her hands into the water.

Watching her, he picked up a dishcloth. "Why are you so anxious to leave? Didn't the dinner live up to my billing?"

"Absolutely. The food was delicious, and the place was

unique." She flashed a quick smile at him. "Thank you for inviting me."

"You're welcome. But you didn't tell me why you're so anxious to leave."

"I have a busy day tomorrow, and I need to do some preparatory work tonight before I go to sleep." She handed him a plate to dry.

"You keep a grueling schedule. Haven't you ever wanted to just take off somewhere for a day or two?"

"Only occasionally. The reality is I love my work." She rinsed off another plate and handed it to him.

Drying the plate, he glanced at her. He couldn't begin to guess what she was thinking, but one thing he knew. She was anxious to leave because she was anxious to get away from him, and under the circumstances, her attitude wasn't entirely unexpected. "As dates go, I suppose ours hasn't been a huge success."

"I wouldn't exactly say that. The whole evening has been a very unique experience."

"Good. I'm glad you think that, because I'd like you to meet my grandparents."

She handed him a wineglass to dry, with another one quickly following. "I'd like that, too. Perhaps another time."

Her answer was automatic, her tone vague. Obviously her mind was already back in Corpus and on what she needed to do there.

God, how he wished the two of them really were on an uncomplicated, getting-to-know-you first date. But more importantly, he would give practically everything he owned if he didn't have to carry through with his plan to snare her in the trap he'd conceived.

Women had come and gone in his life. Sometimes the woman would decide to leave; other times it was his decision. It had never bothered him that he hadn't found the one who would make him forget all others. He was like Tess—his work was all-encompassing to him. His life ranged from the interesting, challenging world of academics to the risky, exciting business of diving for treasure.

But now he'd met Tess, and it had been evident to him from the first that she was different from every other woman he had ever met. And he wasn't only talking about his attraction to her, though there was certainly that. Standing as close to her as he was, he only had to breathe to smell the perfume of her skin. He only had to look over to see how her ivory skin gleamed in the dim lamplight and the way her breasts curved enticingly beneath the red dress. He hadn't yet held her breasts, hadn't yet drawn her nipples into his mouth. And the fact was, he probably never would.

He threw the kitchen towel onto the counter, grabbed her upper arms and pulled her against him. A quiver ran through her body; he felt it beneath his hands as his mouth came down on hers and his tongue plunged deep into her mouth. Heat surged to his loins, and instantly he was hard.

Her wet hands fluttered in the air, then settled on his shoulders. She was giving in to his kiss, accepting it. But more than that, she *wanted* his kiss. He could feel it in the way her body had instantly softened against his, in the urgent way she wound her arms around his neck and clung to him.

Their sudden, mutual need for each other had seemingly sprang from nowhere, but that meant it had been running beneath their skin and through their blood all along.

The knowledge gave him a savage gratification unlike anything he'd ever felt before. She wanted him, and God knew, he wanted her. But if he took her before she agreed to what he wanted... Damn it, he didn't care. He wanted her *now*.

He slid his hands along either side of her jaw, then pressed his lips harder against hers, and she responded by opening her mouth wider. He tilted her head back, then, with a rough sound, once again took deep and full possession of her mouth. Their tongues tangled in a sweet, compelling dance that increased his need with a force that nearly knocked him off his feet.

She tasted of coffee, peaches and honey. No doubt now what she tasted like. The honey had to be her natural taste. And the feel of her—the soft curves of her breast and the smooth skin of her throat—he was fast reaching the point where he was going to have to have her or die from the wanting, so fast that he was nearly dizzy with the need. It was in his bone marrow; it was in his blood.

She moaned, the sound of her satisfaction going deep into his mouth. He swallowed the sound and experienced the combined tastes of her passion and his own. That was it. He'd reached the end of his control. He had to have her. He reached behind her for the zipper of her dress.

Suddenly she pushed herself away from him, catching him so off guard that he had to throw his hand out to grip the counter to steady himself.

"Please...please take me home now." She turned away from him and kept her eyes downcast, as if she couldn't meet his gaze.

He struggled to regain control of his feelings, but it was well-nigh damned impossible. Another minute of her kisses and he would have had her on the kitchen floor, making love to her. Afterward he wouldn't have been sorry, but it wasn't his reaction he would have been concerned about.

"What just happened, Tess?" He asked the question even though he was afraid he knew the answer.

He didn't think for a minute that if they made love, she would change her mind and give him the time he needed.

But *she* might. No matter how many times he could tell her otherwise, she might still think his ultimate purpose in making love to her was to get her to agree to give him the three months he needed to secure the ship and the gold. She would be wrong, but after they'd made love, it wouldn't matter. He would never be able to convince her otherwise, and the damage would be done.

This time he'd almost let his desire overrule his good sense. Damn it, he was still suffering from the lapse. He felt pain in every part of his body. He couldn't afford to lose control like that again. From now on, he had to keep his mind trained on his goal.

Silently he cursed. Logic told him that he should be grateful she had put a halt to what had nearly been fast, hot, hard sex. Even now, powerful feelings were urging him to pull her into his arms and kiss her until they were both mindless with desire and tearing each other's clothes off.

"Nick? I said I'd like to go home now."

He let out a long, shaky breath. "Is that all you've got to say? Don't you think we should talk about what just happened?"

Slowly she turned to face him, her arms wrapped around herself, her face pale. "I don't think there's too much to say about it, except that it shouldn't have happened and we both know why. Now, *please,* I'd like to go home as soon as possible."

This was the moment he'd been dreading since he'd picked her up at her house earlier this evening, the moment that would positively rule out any chance of personal involvement between the two of them ever. "I'm sorry, Tess, but I'm not taking you home tonight."

Four

"Excuse me? What did you just say?"

He folded his arms across his chest and leaned against the counter. He still needed its stability. "We're going to spend the night here so that in the morning we can drive into town and you can meet my grandparents."

"Tell me you're kidding."

"I'm not kidding."

"I don't have a clue what you think you're doing, Nick, but one way or another, I'm going back home tonight."

He appeared unmoved. "You're the head of Baron's oil division. That means you can take time off whenever you like. What's the problem?"

"The problem is, now is *not* a time I like. In fact, I don't like it even a little bit. You've been told more than once that my schedule is packed. *Believe* it."

He nodded. "Oh, I do. But one more day is not going to make any difference."

Her anger erupted, and her voice rose to a volume few had ever heard from her, though she wasn't screaming. Not yet. "How in the hell do you know that? And just who do you think you are to make this kind of decision for me?" She punched her finger against his chest. "I'll tell you who you are. You're just someone who crashed my party last night. I haven't even known you twenty-four hours, and you think I'm going to let you rule my life? No way!"

"It's very important to me for you to meet my grand-parents, so we'll be staying here for the night."

His tone was calm, his expression composed, and she wanted to kill him. "Like hell we will. You can do what you want, but I'm going home."

"You can't."

"Watch me." She wanted to scream and was determined not to, but she couldn't stop her voice from shaking. "I'll simply charter another plane and fly home."

"There is no charter service available here."

"But there are private planes at the airport. I saw them when we flew in. When I get to the airport, I'll simply ask for the name of one of the owners, call him or her up, and charter their plane."

"It's late. Here, people go to bed early because they get up early. They're not going to want to climb out of bed to fly some stranger to Corpus Christi."

"How do you know what they'll want to do? Contrary to what you obviously think, you can't tell what people will or won't do, and you sure as hell can't keep me here against my will."

Still perfectly composed, he shrugged. "Even if you can get someone to agree, which I doubt, how are you going to get to the airport? I'm not taking you."

"I'll call a cab."

"No cab will come this far out, especially this late."

"For enough money—"

He shook his head. "I hate to disillusion you, Tess, but you just may be in the one place on earth where your money won't help you."

"This is unconscionable."

"You're absolutely right. It's also desperation. I want you to meet my grandparents so that you'll understand why the *Águila* and its contents are so important to me."

"And by holding me here against my will, you honestly think that I'll view your request more favorably?"

"It's my only shot, and I've got to take it."

"I've got a news flash for you, Nick. Holding me here will flat out guarantee you won't get even the smallest thing that you want from me."

She thought she saw darkness flash in the depth of his eyes, but he blinked, and then it was gone.

"Like I said, I have to try."

"And so do I." She glanced around the kitchen. "Where's the phone and a phone book? And don't tell me you don't have one. You'd have to have a phone out here in case one of your grandparents got sick while they were visiting."

Silently he pointed to the side of a cabinet where the phone hung. Then he opened a drawer, pulled out the phone book, and handed it to her.

For the next fifteen minutes she called everyone she thought could help her, from cab companies to the airport. She even called the police department, but once they heard her name and who was holding her against her will, they turned less than helpful. As a last-ditch effort, she tried to hire an ambulance, but when she had to admit she wasn't ill, they refused. Finally she tried to get in touch with Ron, but she ended up having to leave a message on the answering machine in his office. She glanced at her watch.

He was probably still out with that new girlfriend he'd met since they'd been in Corpus. It would be just her bad luck if he decided to spend the night at the woman's apartment.

"Not home?" he asked when she hung up.

She sat down at the table and shot him a killing look. "You heard."

While she'd been making her calls, he'd finished cleaning the kitchen, and now he hung the dish towel on a hook. "Frankly, I'm surprised your assistant has a life outside work. I would have figured you'd have him at his desk twenty-four hours a day."

Drumming her fingers on the table, she glanced sightlessly around the room. It wouldn't do her any good to call one or both of her sisters. Instead of offering help, they would laugh themselves silly at the situation she'd gotten herself into.

Nick's deep voice broke into her thoughts. "If you're looking for something to throw at me, please don't go for anything that could break. My grandmother would be very upset."

She glared at him. "And tell me again why I should care? She should have taught you better manners than to kidnap someone."

"May I remind you that you came of your own free will?"

"Because you lied to me."

"I didn't lie to you. I simply didn't tell you the whole truth."

"A lie of omission is still a lie, and you know it."

"I couldn't have gotten you on the plane any other way."

"Oh, sure you could." Her tone was laced with sarcasm. "You had any number of alternatives at your disposal. You could have drugged me, or hit me and knocked me out cold.''

He frowned. ''Do you honestly think I would physically harm you?''

She spread her hands. ''How would I know? I would never have thought you'd kidnap me and keep me here against my will, but I was wrong, wasn't I? You're just full of surprises.'' She began to pace around the kitchen. She always paced when she was agitated and needed to think.

She couldn't call Uncle William for help, because she wouldn't want him upset. And she had no idea how to get hold of Des. His office would know, but his office was closed. As for his home phone, she'd called it so few times that it wasn't a number she had committed to memory, and she knew it would be unlisted. Colin Wynne would come to get her if she called, but she really didn't want her friends to know how easily Nick had duped her.

''Come on, Tess. Don't make such a big deal out of this. We had a nice trip out here, and by your own admission, the dinner was wonderful. Now all I'm asking is that you spend the night in a perfectly nice bedroom with clean sheets on the bed, and I'll have you back in Corpus by lunchtime tomorrow.''

She whirled on him. ''Oh, *that* was good. Just the right touch of sincerity and with a dash of entreaty. And don't forget the kiss. That kiss was quite something. But it was just another weapon in your arsenal, wasn't it? Much like that damn *please* of yours.''

His brow furrowed. ''My please? What are you talking about?''

''Nothing. Absolutely nothing.'' She folded her hands. ''Okay, Nick, I'm going to ask you once again. Will you please take me home?''

He stared at her. Her face was flushed with color. The

pulse at the base of her neck was pounding. He wanted nothing more than to scoop her into his arms, take her into his bedroom, strip her naked and make love to her until they were both satiated. But that was no longer an option. And if he were honest with himself, it never had been.

"I'll show you to your room. It was my sister's room, and there are still a few things of hers left. She laid out something for you to sleep in, plus she left fresh towels and a new toothbrush and toothpaste for you. They're in the bathroom."

"How very kind of her. And thoughtful, definitely thoughtful. You know, I didn't think about it before, but it's obvious now that your sister is in on this crime with you."

"Crime?"

"Quite obviously you're going to find this hard to believe, Nick, but holding someone against their will is a crime. I tried to explain that to the chief of police of this fine town, but he seemed more amused than concerned."

"Uh, yeah. He and I went to school together. And, anticipating how you might react to, uh, staying the night, I gave him a call earlier today and explained the situation."

"Perfect. Just perfect." Her words were cold and sharp as an ice pick.

He levered himself away from the counter and started toward the hall. "Follow me and I'll show you to your room. And if you can't find what you need, just ask."

Tess couldn't sleep.

She was too angry at Nick. He'd quieted her unease at the idea of flying out of Corpus for the evening by telling her he'd made special arrangements for this evening, and she couldn't fault him there. He'd definitely made special arrangements.

But she was just as angry at herself. She should have paid more attention to her initial panic when he'd told her they were going to fly to some undisclosed place for dinner. How could she have been so stupid and naive? She'd trusted him, and he'd betrayed her.

Pulling the pillow over her face, she groaned. Truthfully, trust had only been a small part of the reason she'd gotten on that plane with him. Her attraction to him had been the main reason. She threw the pillow across the room.

Thinking about it, she decided the word *attraction* was way too mild to describe what he made her feel. He hadn't needed knockout drugs or violence to get her on the plane. He'd simply smiled at her and said please and charmed her right into the seat beside his.

But as angry as she was, at him and at herself, it wasn't enough to keep her awake. She was also worried. Bringing in this well on schedule was so vitally important to her that she often spent sleepless nights worrying.

True, it was too early to expect to see oil, but still, she couldn't stop worrying. She was so afraid that somewhere along the line she'd miscalculated, and either they wouldn't strike oil, or they would strike oil but the well wouldn't come in as big as her instincts were telling her it would.

It wasn't an overstatement to say that a major portion of her life would be lost if either of those things happened.

She rolled onto her side. The house was quiet and still. No doubt Nick had fallen asleep with no problem at all. But then, what did he have to worry about? With a stratagem worthy of a battlefield general, he had maneuvered her into a trap and now had her exactly where he wanted her.

Angrily she kicked the covers aside and got out of bed. Nick's sister had left a soft cotton nightshirt on the bed for her to sleep in. It covered her nearly to her knees, and since

Nick was asleep and she had no wish to dig through someone else's closet, she decided she didn't need a robe.

As quietly as possible, she wandered out of the bedroom,
down the hall and into what she presumed was the living
room. Carefully, trying not to make a sound, she closed the
door. Then, feeling her way around, she turned on the first
lamp she came to.

An overstuffed sofa and two comfortable-looking reclin-
ers met her gaze. A padded rocker and a table were positioned by a window. Outdated magazines lay on a wooden
coffee table. Crocheted doilies covered the arms of the sofa
and chairs. A crocheted afghan in green, orange and gold
lay over the back of the couch, the hues telling her the
afghan had been made some time in the sixties or seventies.

And then there were the pictures, many of them, on the
tables, on the mantel and on the walls.

She started with the wall closest to her and worked her-
way around the room, turning lamps on and off as she went.
A picture of a young bride and groom in sepia tones caught
her attention. From the age of the picture and the style of
the clothes, she realized it was probably a picture of Nick's
grandparents on their wedding day. The young man in the
picture looked as if he were about to burst with pride. The
young woman's face was full of joy.

Farther on, Tess found another picture of the young
woman, only this time she held a baby boy in her arms.
The baby had to be Nick's father. As the years passed in
pictures, she saw the baby grow into a young man, go off
to war and return. His marriage to a lovely young woman
was celebrated on another wall. Next, the picture of another
baby boy appeared—Nick, she guessed—and, soon after,
another baby, a girl, Kathie.

There were no more pictures of Nick's parents, but on
another wall she found yearly school pictures of both Nick

and Kathie. A smile touched her lips as she went from picture to picture, witnessing Nick turn into the man he was when he graduated from college.

At his college graduation, his proud grandparents stood on either side of him. Kathie must have been taking the picture, she reflected, studying it. Since that picture, Nick had filled out; the lines of his face and body had matured, hardened. But on the day of his graduation, his amber eyes were filled with nothing but happiness and dreams.

She lingered over that picture the longest, wondering about the years between his graduation and now. Since she'd met him, she'd seen him express many emotions, but none of them had been the pure happiness that had been on his face the day of his graduation. As for his dreams, she supposed excavating the *Águila* was his dream. Had that also been his dream back then? Did he have other dreams? And, if so, what were they?

There were other pictures, of course—Kathie's wedding, her two darling little girls, growing up in each succeeding photo.

Now she understood why Nick's grandparents wouldn't let go of this house. Their entire life was right here in this room.

"A lot of pictures, right?"

She stilled, then slowly turned to face Nick. One look at him jolted her to the present. He was wearing only a pair of faded jeans. Everything else—his broad chest, his sinewy arms, his flat abdomen—was bare.

And his jeans left very little to the imagination. The soft-looking denim closely followed the muscled length of his hips, thighs and calves and intimately cupped the large bulge at his crotch.

The sight made her mouth go dry. "Pictures? Yes, there are quite a few."

As he leisurely made his way toward her, shadows from the lamp's light shifted over his face and body, creating mysterious markings and contouring. She should turn her back to him and return her focus to the pictures she'd been studying. That was exactly what she should do. But she couldn't.

As was his way, Nick held her complete attention.

"Kathie and I offered to take down all the pictures and put them up in their new home, but they wouldn't hear of it."

He reached her side, and she could smell soap and heated bare skin. He was too close. She should move, but the intensity of his gaze, such a contrast to the gentleness of his voice, held her where she was.

"My grandmother said if we took the pictures down, they would leave faded spots on the wall. We offered to put up new wallpaper, but they said no. They love this wallpaper. They put it up after my dad came home from the war, and they don't want it taken down. They said the pictures belong in this room, on this wallpaper."

A sleep shirt and a pair of panties didn't constitute a lot of clothes, but at least she was more covered than he was. Why, then, did she feel practically naked? "I think they're right."

In the quiet and darkness of the house, they were both speaking softly, as if the room required a reverence. Plus, she knew—and more than likely Nick did, too—that all he had to do was say one wrong word and she would be ready to argue with him again. But she didn't want that to happen, and she sensed he didn't, either, not here, not in this room with its generations of love, laughter and remembrances.

She glanced at him and saw a new heat glinting in his amber eyes. Damn. She could feel the heat on her skin and in her blood. It was clogging her lungs and fogging her mind.

Then he dropped his gaze to her breasts. "I don't remember that shirt looking as good on Kathie as it does on you."

His husky voice grated along her nerve endings, bringing even more heat. Automatically she looked. Her nipples were hard, their rigid tips clearly visible against the T-shirt. Color rushed to her cheeks.

Awkwardly she crossed her arms over her breasts so that her hands were on her upper arms. "Uh, did I miss some pictures? I didn't see any of your great-grandfather."

"There aren't any." He reached for her hands and pulled them away from her breasts. "Don't cover yourself."

If she stayed, something was going to happen that she didn't want to happen. She could feel it in her bones. The situation was too ripe for seduction, something she wasn't emotionally equipped to handle right now. Anger tangled with the heat, stress with the excitement of his nearness.

"You know, I think I can sleep now." Her heart was beating so hard, so loud, she could barely hear her own words.

"Liar," he whispered. "You could no more go to sleep now than I could."

"You're wrong. I could."

"I'm right. Besides, don't you want to hear more about the pictures?"

She hesitated. The insanity of it was that she *didn't* want to leave. "As long as we stay on the subject of the pictures."

He slowly smiled at her. "Okay. According to my grandfather, his father would never allow any pictures to be taken of himself."

"What about pictures of his wife and of your grandfather as a boy?"

He reached out for several strands of her hair and wound them around his fingers. "I like your hair loose and free."

She tried to move away, but his hold on her hair kept her close. "You're off the subject." Apparently the heat—in him, in her—had absorbed all the air in the room. She could barely breathe.

"So I am, and I'm sorry. But…" He rubbed the strands of hair between this thumb and fingers, as if fascinated by their texture.

She reached up and, as best she could, untangled her hair from his fingers. "The pictures?"

"The first picture ever made of my grandfather was on his wedding day. He was twenty-two years old."

"That's very sad."

"Yes, it is. In some ways, my grandfather led a very sad life, even a dark life, until the day he met my grandmother. Unfortunately, though, not even she could banish all the sadness of his childhood. It has stayed with him his entire life."

"That's a shame." She knew all about how a parent could color a child's existence. In fact, she knew more than she wanted to know. "Still, this room is a testament to a full life that was well lived. It must make them both feel good."

Deliberately she moved away from him. Heat, desire and passion permeated the air that surrounded him. Under the circumstances, she shouldn't be anywhere near him. But as she strolled to another part of the room, she could feel his gaze on her—that damn ability of his to touch her even when the length of a room separated them. It was an amazing skill, a dangerous skill.

"No matter what my grandparents have had to go

through in life, they've always had their love. To this day, they are as in love as they were on their wedding day. And you're right, theirs has been a life well lived. Unfortunately, according to the doctors, my grandmother will soon be alone. At this point, the doctors are not even sure what's keeping my grandfather alive."

He paused. As she sensed he wanted her to, she looked at him. Then and only then did he go on. "But Kathie and I know what it is. So does my grandmother. He's waiting for something to happen. He has a great will, my grandfather does." He shook his head in admiration. "He's said he'll know when the end is near. And when the time comes, he wants us to bring him back out here so he can die in this place where he was born, and where his son was born, and where he raised Kathie and me."

Tears filled her eyes, but she hastily blinked them away. "I suppose a person couldn't ask for much more than to die in a place they love, surrounded by people who love them."

"No, I don't suppose they could."

She made her way to an old Victrola. A stack of records sat atop the lid, and she pulled off a few to read the labels. Except she couldn't really see the song titles. She was too overcome by the powerful emotions that this room and the people who had lived here had evoked in her. Damn it! She didn't even know them.

Obviously sadness had been a large part of Nick's grandparents' lives. For one thing, they'd lost their only son and daughter-in-law. But their pain hadn't stopped them from taking two small, hurting children into their home and life and spinning happiness and love around them until they felt safe and cared for. No matter what else, Nick's grandparents had a full grasp of what a family should be. It was something she'd never been taught.

By preserving this house, this room, Nick and his sister were returning their grandparents' love. And though Nick hadn't said so, she would bet this house would be kept just as it was now long after his grandparents had left this world.

In her family, love expressed or shown had always been in short supply. She'd been almost four when her mother had died. Jill had been just three, and Kit had been two. Their mother's early death had left the three of them to be raised solely by their father, a man who, if he had possessed any emotions, kept them to himself.

Sometimes, when she tried real hard, she could conjure up a memory of her mother tucking her into bed at night with a kiss and a hug. But she couldn't be sure if the memory was a true one or simply one she desperately wanted to be true.

Briefly she wondered if her life would have turned out differently if, after her mother's death, she'd been raised by people like Nick's grandparents. It was hard to say, and ultimately it didn't matter, anyway. If she'd learned nothing else from her father, she'd learned the uselessness of crying over spilt milk. She glanced at Nick who was leaning against the fireplace mantel, watching her.

"Why couldn't you sleep?" he asked, his voice carrying that same huskiness it had when she'd been standing beside him. "Is it because you're still angry at me?"

She replaced the records. "That and other things." It was all she was willing to say on the subject. Her anger and worry were justified, but anger didn't belong in this room, and her worries were none of Nick's concern. "I'm sorry if I woke you. I tried to be quiet when I came in here."

"I wasn't asleep, and I didn't hear you. I couldn't sleep, either."

"Why couldn't you sleep?" she asked softly, unable to resist the jab. "Guilt?"

The corners of his mouth turned upward in a rueful smile. "Maybe."

In the half darkness, in the silence, neither his face nor his body language gave her a clue as to what he was thinking. But if she'd had to guess, she would have said he was probably thinking of new ways to win her agreement to what he wanted of her.

She supposed she couldn't blame him. This room had given her a glimpse into what was driving him to recover the *Águila*'s treasure. It was family. Ironically, it was the same thing that was driving her to strike a Class-A oil field, and it was as vitally important to her as the air she breathed.

He broke the silence. "It's a long-standing habit of mine to come in here when I can't sleep. Even as a kid growing up, I'd come in here when I was having a restless night. Often I'd stay in here so long, I'd fall asleep right there on the couch. Then, sometime in the night, my grandmother would come in and cover me with one of her afghans. I'd wake up warm and rested."

And loved, she silently added. "I can understand why this room would have a soothing effect on you."

"Can you?"

Suddenly she remembered that she was wearing only a T-shirt. The fact that she'd forgotten in the last few minutes spoke volumes about how Nick and the room had affected her. Another few minutes and she would completely lose touch with reality. "I'm going back to my room now."

"Don't."

She looked at him in surprise. "Why?"

He made a vague gesture with his hand. "I could make us some hot chocolate, and we could talk some more."

Hot chocolate and conversation with Nick. Amazingly,

it was a much harder offer to turn down than it should have been, but she couldn't afford to hear any more about this room or Nick's family. She had to keep her mind on what was important to her rather than on what was important to Nick. Again, something surprisingly hard to do.

"No."

She didn't see him move, but suddenly he was in front of her. "Then how about this for a reason? Because I don't want to let you go just yet."

She tensed, ready to resist when he pulled her into his arms, but he surprised her yet again. He didn't. Instead he merely took a step and closed the distance between them.

"I should know better than this," he whispered, slowly lowering his mouth toward hers. "I should have learned after what happened between us in the kitchen." She could feel the breath of his words on her lips. "But you...there's you, and I don't know what to do about the way you make me feel."

She had plenty of time to move away or say no. But she did neither. She waited, listening, understanding. One moment the wanting wasn't there. The next it was. Inside her, full blown and impossible to ignore. And when finally his lips touched hers, she almost sighed with relief.

This kiss was unlike any other that he'd given her. It was unhurried and so gentle that she couldn't find any reason to resist. Their bodies were touching, but his hands weren't on her. And the pressure of his lips continued to be delicate, undemanding. Yet somehow, as he moved his mouth back and forth over hers, he still managed to find and awaken every nerve ending in her lips until heated sensations seeped through her, spreading, expanding.

She'd never experienced anything like it. He was only kissing her, yet she'd never been more aroused in her life. Her breasts began to ache. If only he would touch them.

Heat pooled between her legs until the area throbbed. If only he would put his hand there and stroke her, fill her....

She was in agony, but he continued at his own slow pace. His kisses remained gentle, as if he were memorizing every aspect of her lips—their shape, their softness. At that moment she actually felt as if she could die of need for him. Stifling a groan, she parted her lips. She had a fierce need to have him thrust his tongue deep into her mouth, but instead, he lightly nipped at the edges.

She swayed toward him. Her breasts with their rigid tips touched his bare chest, and she almost cried out at the pleasure that shot through her. It was a new kind of torture, and she could feel herself coming undone. Winding her arms around his neck, she stood on her tiptoes and pressed herself against him. Her body badly needed the contact. He was the source of incredible pleasure, and her body was craving it, him.

"Nick," she whispered, almost in pain, and threaded her fingers through his hair.

"Tell me," he whispered.

If her life had depended on it, she couldn't have expressed a clear thought. A low sound came out of her, saturated with frustration and need. Then his hand closed around her breast, and his thumb flicked her nipple. Fire scorched through her. Moaning, she closed her eyes and writhed against him.

Time became suspended as he backed her up until she felt the wall behind her; then he lifted her. Instinctively, she wrapped her legs around his hips and held on to him with all her might. His kisses turned harder, and at last his tongue delved deep and strong into her mouth. His hand slid beneath the T-shirt and this time closed around her bare breast. It was what she'd been wanting, needing, but she couldn't even enjoy it, because by this point she wanted more, so much more.

Feelings were rapidly closing down all thought, but some distant part of her brain was still working. Her body was vibrating with a crucial need for satisfaction, and in another few moments Nick would give it to her, but…

She felt him lift her bottom, adjust his stance, then he was pressing harder against her at the juncture of her thighs. Denim rubbed back and forth against silk panties. His hips rotated and thrust against her sensitive, pulsing flesh beneath the silk.

Oh, she wanted this. She *needed* this. And she could have it. Just another minute, less. But…what would be the cost to her? Her fingers tightened in his hair. "Stop." The word wasn't a whisper, more an amalgamation of feelings and sounds. She didn't even know what part of her it had come from, and in the next moment, she wished for it back.

Nick halted all movement. A hard shudder violently racked his body. "Did you say stop?" His voice was broken, hoarse, pain-filled.

"No. No. Oh, Nick. I want you so badly…. But…please help me."

An agonized noise rumbled from his chest. Slowly, with tremors shaking his whole body, he eased both of them away from the wall. At first she wasn't certain she had the willpower or the strength to let him go. She waited. Finally she managed to unwrap her legs from around him.

He dropped his hands away until the only thing holding her to him was her arms around his neck, but once again, she had trouble letting him go, yet she knew she had to. Doing her best not to meet his eyes, she loosened her hold, and her arms fell to her side.

Breathing in great gulps of air, Nick stepped away from her and turned his back to her.

She felt sick to her stomach. Her body was on fire, but there would be no satisfaction for her throbbing body. Worse, she had no idea what to say, and she was embarrassed beyond words.

"Nick... "

"Don't say anything. Not now." He held up his hand. "I'm sorry, Tess. I let it go too far."

"Only because I wanted you to. At the very least, fifty percent of the blame goes to me."

Shakily she started for the door, then thought of something. "Will I be able to hear the phone if it rings?" After what had just happened between them, she felt ludicrous asking the question. Or, for that matter, even thinking of it. Maybe it was her mind's way of trying to protect her, taking her thoughts away from her hurting body and putting them on business. If so, it wasn't working.

Without turning to face her, he nodded. "There's a phone in the hall. Unless you're a very heavy sleeper, you'll be able to hear it."

She stared at his back, searching her mind for something to say that would make the past fifteen minutes go away. But there were no words adequate enough to accomplish that feat.

From the start, the deck had been stacked against them. They'd both been half-dressed, in a half-lit room, with too much bare skin, too many raw emotions and too much sexual attraction.

She wrapped her arms around her waist, trying to stop herself from shaking. She didn't know why it was so important to her for him to turn around and look at her, but it was. So she asked him another question, a question that should have been left unasked. "And you haven't switched off the phone?"

"Check it yourself," he snapped, a man on the edge "It's on."

"Okay. " She hesitated, then reached for the doorknob "Good night."

"Tess?"

Her heart jumped. She looked to find that he'd finally turned to face her. "Yes?"

"I wish things could be different."

She knew exactly what he meant. His treasure. Her oi well. It was a stalemate.

Without answering, she opened the door to the hall, ther quietly closed it behind her. Back in her room, back in the bed, she stared at the ceiling. Nick would never know how much she'd wanted to stay with him or how hard it had been for her to walk out. But staying would have been too dangerous.

Whether they were angry at each other or talking abou something as innocuous as family pictures, they struck sparks off each other. And sparks, if not controlled, led to fire. She only had to look at him to want him. And wher he kissed her, she came apart in his arms.

Somewhere in the house she heard water come on. She didn't have to think twice to know Nick was taking a colc shower. She wished for one for herself.

God, if she could just get home tomorrow, whole and without a broken heart, she would consider herself incred ibly lucky.

Five

Tess slowly awoke to the warmth of sunshine on her face and the delicious aroma of coffee. A glance out the window told her it was going to be a beautiful day.

Amazingly, considering the events of the previous night, she'd slept remarkably well. Then again, maybe it wasn't so amazing. In that dimly lit room with Nick, her emotions had run the gamut from anger to passion, emotions so powerful they'd rocked her world and left her spent. By the time she'd crawled into bed, she'd felt as if she'd been put through a meat grinder.

And she had only herself to blame. She'd been incredibly stupid for accepting a date with Nick, even though deep down she'd known the real reason he'd asked her out. And she'd been stupid for getting on a plane with him even though she'd felt uneasy about it. But most of all, she'd been stupid for wanting him as much as she had last night.

Soon, though, it would be over. She just had to get past

meeting Nick's grandparents, and then she would be on her way home to her usual life. Then maybe, just maybe, this strange mixture of dread and uneasiness in her stomach would go away.

The phone rang. *Ron.* She leaped out of bed and ran toward the hall phone, but before she could reach it, it stopped ringing. She hurried into the kitchen to find Nick with the receiver to his ear, listening.

"Is it for me?" she asked.

Shaking his head, he continued to listen to whoever had called.

She watched him, wondering what or who had him looking so serious. He wasn't wearing a shirt; his hair was wet and tousled, and she could see droplets of water clinging to the fine black hair that covered his chest. He must have just showered.

She would love to lick him dry.

The thought came from nowhere and nearly knocked her to her knees. She swallowed hard. She couldn't allow those kinds of thoughts. Last night, that room, what had happened there between them…it had all been a piece of time away from the real world, away from reality. It wouldn't happen again. It couldn't.

Her gaze continued down his body to his hip-hugging jeans. They weren't the same jeans he'd worn last night, but…they were zipped, but not yet buttoned.

Oh, God… She felt her blood begin to warm. Before Nick had arrived in her life, she would never have thought she could be capable of such thoughts and feelings. She walked over to the counter and poured herself a cup of coffee.

To the uninformed, she speculated, they could easily be mistaken for lovers who had awakened together after a night of passion. She was in the same T-shirt she'd slept in.

And if it *were* true, if they had indeed slept together after a night of lovemaking, she knew without thinking twice that she would be feeling completely satisfied this morning. In fact, she probably wouldn't have a nerve left in her body.

Her hand flew to her forehead. She had to stop thinking about things like that, things that would never happen, could never happen.

"How bad is it?" she heard him ask and forced her attention to his end of the call. "And the doctor is sure?" He paused, then smiled. "That sounds like him. So okay, then—" he glanced at her "—that's what we'll do if at all possible. Be sure and call if anything changes." He nodded. "Right, I'll let you know. Give the girls a kiss and a hug for me and save a couple for yourself. Bye, honey."

He hung up the phone, then leveled his amber gaze on her. "That was Kathie. Our grandfather had a bad spell this morning."

"I'm sorry to hear that." It was the truth, she realized, sipping her coffee. Because of the pictures she'd seen last night, she felt as if she already knew him. "But now that our visit is obviously off, I'll get ready and we can head back to Corpus as soon as possible."

"My grandfather wants to meet you very badly, Tess. He's requested that we come later on this afternoon, when he thinks he'll be feeling better."

"I hope he is, but I can't afford to waste any more time."

Muscle by muscle, he tensed. It was something she sensed, but if she'd had her hands on his body, she couldn't have felt it any better. And the amber of his eyes darkened to an intensity and a sharpness that could have cut a dia-

mond. "Is that what this has been to you? Truly? Just a
big waste of time?"

She couldn't truthfully say that. She'd wanted to learn
more about him, and she had. But perhaps more importantly, she'd also learned something about herself that she'd
never known. Last night, looking at the pictures in the living room, she'd realized that she badly wanted a close,
loving family, something she'd never had and probably
never would have.

"This morning starts a new day," she said carefully,
averting her eyes to her coffee cup, "and it's a day I badly
need to spend back in Corpus." She paused and looked at
him. "I'm sorry, but I just can't wait around all day to see
your grandfather."

He ran an agitated hand through his hair. "Look, I know
that all you have to do is pick up the phone and call your
assistant. He'll be in the office by now, and he could have
a plane chartered, arrange for a car on this end and have
you home by noon, but—"

"Calling him is exactly what I intend to do. Last night
he must have slept over at his girlfriend's, so he didn't get
my message. But by now, he'll be at work."

And as soon as she got back to Corpus, she planned to
tell him that from now on, no matter where he spent the
night, he was to call the office and check his messages.

"Please, Tess, just listen to me for a minute."

"Don't say please to me ever again." She slammed her
cup on the counter with enough force that coffee sloshed
everywhere. It was a wonder the cup hadn't broken.

"I'll get down on my knees and beg you if it would
help. Tess, my grandfather is dying, and meeting you is
important to him."

She could feel herself beginning to weaken. *Damn it.*
Giving in to his requests was how she'd gotten herself into

this mess in the first place. "Why, Nick? Does he, or do you, actually think hearing the story from a dying man will change my mind? It can't. Don't you understand? *It can't.*"

"No, Tess. I don't understand. I'm only asking for a postponement of a few months. At the end of that time, the oil will still be there. It's not going anywhere."

She sighed. So after all that had transpired last night, they were right back to the basics. He wanted something from her, and she couldn't give it to him. "There are reasons I can't stop the drilling."

"Tell me."

He'd said *tell me* last night when, in the heat of passion, she had moaned his name. But then he hadn't really needed her to tell him what she'd wanted. He'd known. "My reasons are private."

Tense silence charged the air. Praying for composure, she went about cleaning up the spill, then poured herself more coffee.

"Okay, Tess," he said, his tone gruff. "Forget about what I want. Think about my grandfather, instead. He's going to be very disappointed if he doesn't get to meet you." She opened her mouth to speak, but he rushed on. "And not only because you have the power to stop the drilling. He's heard me talk about you and—"

"What do you mean, he's heard you talk about me? We only met two nights ago."

"I did a little research on you before we met."

"So you said before."

"The library and years of microfiche clued me in to a few things, but basically, family-owned businesses such as ours are very secretive. But you...your name and picture came up quite a few times, both in the business section of the paper and the society section."

"And what does that have to do with your grandfather?"

He slowly exhaled. "Even before you and I met, he told me that my tone of voice changed when I was talking about you. And after we met, he said that even though I've mentioned quite a few women to him over the years, he's never heard this particular tone in my voice before. He says it's clear that I'm attracted to you. He's lived to see Kathie happily married and settled, and he has just about decided that…that you will be the one I'll marry."

Her heart jumped into her throat. "He must have a spectacularly vivid imagination."

His eyes thoughtfully narrowed on her. "I suppose so. But you have to remember that he's dying. From his viewpoint, he's afraid he won't live to see me married. So now he's decided that the next best thing is to meet the woman he thinks has won my heart. As I said, he's very excited about your visit this afternoon."

She stared at him, her mind busy absorbing the newest surprise he'd pulled out of his hat for her. "But that's ridiculous."

"Not to him," he said, his tone very firm. "So you see, this visit involves much more than the *Águila* and its safety. You would be doing me a great favor if you would wait until after you've visited with him to leave."

"You don't fight fair."

"I never said I did."

She put a hand to her forehead, where she could feel pressure beginning to build. "I have to think about this." With her coffee cup, she turned to go to her bedroom.

"Would you like some breakfast? I can make just about anything."

She didn't even glance back at him. "No, thank you."

Tess showered, soaping her body and shampooing her hair. Then she simply stood beneath the water and let it rain down over her. It was wonderful.

She forced herself to concentrate only on the water and to think about nothing else. Too many things had happened too fast. Her mind needed a rest. And her body... Unfortunately, it needed much more.

But it didn't matter. Telling Nick to stop last night had been the best thing she could have done. It really had been, she assured herself. She was already more involved with him than she should be.

Physically, she'd gone way too far with him. Emotionally, she was all tangled up in him *and* his family, whom she had yet to meet. Figure that one out, she told herself ruefully, as she leaned against the tiles and allowed the water to sluice over her. She couldn't.

She climbed out, dried off and dressed in her red sleeveless dress. Her hair was wet, but she hadn't been able to find a hair dryer, so she decided to let it dry naturally.

In order to avoid Nick, she went out the front door.

The day was warm, with only a slight breeze. She could see the wonderful scenery she'd missed last night. The hills were white with caliche. Thickets of mesquite and wild grasses tangled in the eroded ravines. Yellow and red blooms on the prickly pears clumped in the bar ditch, indicating a recent rain. And the vine that everyone called Grandpa's beard wrapped itself around the fences and telephone poles, each petal a silvery white.

Nick's grandparents might not own that many acres, but what they did own was beautiful. She made her way around the house and saw cattle grazing in a distant meadow. Closer to the house, she spied a swing hung in a gazebo. On three sides, the junipers grew thick around it and would filter the air.

Nice. She imagined that Nick's grandparents had probably spent many evenings right there, discussing the events of the day and their grandchildren. And the fact that she had even thought of that worried her.

She settled into the swing and lifted her face for the cooling breeze. What was she going to do? Nick didn't have a clue what she was up against, and even if he did, he would never agree that what she had to accomplish was more important than the dreams of his dying grandfather.

She couldn't blame him for that. But… She closed her eyes and shook her head in bemusement at the decision she was about to make.

But she supposed that since she was already here, the least she could do was to stay and meet Nick's grandfather. He believed Nick was in love with her, and even though nothing could be further from the truth, she couldn't find it in herself to disillusion him. She sighed. She hadn't even met the man, but here she was, trying to make him happy.

Making a dying man happy was a big responsibility. It was also an unfair responsibility, imposed on her by Nick. But because of the pictures, she would stay and do her best.

"May I join you?"

Her eyes flew open. Outlined against the blue sky, surrounded by brilliant sunshine, dressed in a gold knit polo shirt, Nick appeared every bit the sun god she'd first thought him to be.

In the incredibly short time she'd known him, he'd turned her life completely upside down. She'd gazed into his amber eyes and, like a lamb, had followed him wherever he had led her. She'd made not only bad decisions, she was now making bewildering decisions.

And at that moment, looking at him, all the hunger and need she'd felt for him last night came flooding back. Damn it. Somehow, in some way, she had to make those feelings go away for good. The sooner she was in her office, dealing with problems that she knew how to handle, the better off she would be.

"Actually, yes. I have a question for you." He started to sit beside her, but she quickly held up her hand. "I'd prefer it if you didn't sit here."

He stared at her for several moments. "Okay." His slid one hand into his jeans pocket and, with the other, gripped the swing's chain.

Briefly she considered the very real possibility that she'd made a mistake in telling him not to sit beside her. As it was, her eyes were even with the waistband of his jeans. Thankfully he'd buttoned them, but with very little effort, she knew her gaze could wander downward and her imagination could take flight with thoughts of what was behind that fly. Truthfully, it wouldn't take a lot of imagination. She'd felt it last night as he'd moved against her....

Her mouth went suddenly dry. "The night we met, you said that somehow you thought you had a chance at convincing me to give you the needed time. Why?"

"I thought you'd understand about a man who'd had one dream his whole life."

"I assume you're talking about your grandfather, but why would you think I would understand his dream?"

"I've already told you that I'd done a bit of homework on you. In the course of my reading, I found several articles on the Dream Foundation that you've established for underprivileged children."

She nodded. "I've always thought that just because a child comes from a poor background doesn't mean that they shouldn't have a way to follow their dreams. And in my foundation, the words *underprivileged* and *poor* can mean many things. Maybe a child comes from a family who has money, but they belittle the child's dream, or give that child no emotional support. My foundation tries to reach those children, too."

"Exactly. My thought was that if you had the ability to understand that children need help in making their dreams come true, you would also understand that some adults have the same need."

He'd cornered her by using her own beliefs against her. Very neat. Very sharp. "I *can* understand that, but in this case…" She cleared her throat. "In this case, it isn't possible to grant any part of what you're asking."

"Why?"

"You've already asked that question, and I've already told you the reason is private." By unspoken agreement, no one in their family ever talked to any outsider about its dynamics, and she wasn't going to be the first. "Just because I have autonomy over my section of Baron International doesn't mean I don't have pressures and responsibilities that involve the family. You have to understand from our initial surveys and core samplings, it looks as if this particular well has the potential to bring in millions per year."

"So will my gold, though of course not for years. But I'm not doing this for the money. Even though my family has proof that we legally own that gold, the State of Texas will still get its slice, the backers will get their slices, and I'll donate most of the antiquities to the university." He shrugged. "Then, after the Internal Revenue Service takes its bite, there'll be something left over for my grandparents, if they're still alive. If not, it will be divided between Kathie and me. But the money isn't the point and never has been."

He released the swing's chain and squatted in front of her, his forearms resting on his thighs, his hands clasped, two fingers held together in a point. "Look, Tess, I'm not saying my problems are more important than your problems. I'm just saying that I've got a time crunch. And right now will be my *only* chance."

"Why? As you said about my oil, your treasure isn't going anywhere. What happens at my well may disturb your treasure, but you'll still know its general area."

"*Now* is when I have to act. After years of trying to make it happen, now is when everything has come together. I have my backers lined up, and believe me, getting backers for such a speculative venture was not easy. I've also got the people lined up who will be working with me to harvest the gold, along with the machinery. But if my backers get a whiff of any delay or difficulty, they may very well withdraw their money. Then I'd have to start all over again from the beginning, and that could take years."

"Your backers don't know about my drilling site?"

He shook his head. "And, if possible, I've got to keep it that way. I can't afford for them to start getting nervous. It took me years to get some of these people to commit, and at that time I knew nothing about your plans. So now what I'm doing is lying to them by omission. And as you pointed out last night, a lie of omission is still a lie. You may not believe it, but I rarely lie. I don't feel exactly great about keeping my backers in the dark, but that's how desperate I am to keep them committed to my project. And that's how immediate my need is. You've got to stop drilling *now,* Tess. Because if you continue drilling, and if something happens to send the *Águila* over that salt ridge, it will be buried so deeply, it may very well be lost for all time, or at least for my generation."

Once again, that now familiar pressure band was beginning to squeeze her head. There was really nothing she could say to Nick. He could never understand what she was up against or how every day was a struggle for her. Nor would he understand how and why her every waking minute was spent trying to fulfill her deceased father's goals for her, and there was no reason he should. There was also no reason she should try to make him understand. Soon he would be gone from her life.

The phone rang in the house. Nick took off at a slow jog to answer it. With a sigh, she stood and rubbed her temples, then remembered she'd forgotten to call Ron.

Nick met her at the back door. "It's for you. He said to tell you it's Des."

Des? *Oh, God. Uncle William.* She raced to the phone. "Des? What's wrong? Is it Uncle William?"

"No," he answered, his voice deep and even. "He's fine. I'm calling about you."

"Me?" she asked, astonished. It was a rare day when Des called her. "What about me?"

"Your disappearance. Tell me right now—are you in trouble? Are you being held against your will?"

She glanced at Nick, who was listening intently. "No."

"Okay, good. What happened was this. Ron didn't sleep at your house last night, but when he showed up for work this morning, he found your message on the machine. It said you needed help and to please call you back as soon as possible. But you didn't leave him a number."

"I didn't?" She pressed the heel of her hand to her forehead. Had she forgotten to give Ron the number because she'd been so agitated? Or was the reason more basic? A Freudian slip? "I can't believe I did that. But there's always my cell phone."

"Which he found on your bed, when he searched the house."

"Right." She remembered tossing it there right before she walked out the door. Damn.

"So Ron questioned the staff, and they all said you had

left last night on a date and hadn't returned. Ron became alarmed, and rightly so. So he called me.''

''I see. But how on earth were you able to track me down?''

''I had a little luck on my side. First of all, Guadalupe described your date, and from the description, Ron was able to identify him as Nick Trejo. Still, if Trejo had stayed in town, I probably wouldn't have been able to track you down. Same thing if he'd chosen to drive you to Uvalde. But because he chose to fly, it was a little easier. I called the airport and made inquiries until I found someone who had recognized you getting on a private plane. Then all I had to do was track down the flight plan and call Uvalde information.''

''You went to a lot of trouble, Des. I'm sorry.''

''If you had left a number for Ron and he had called you back last night, what help would you have asked him for?''

''I would have asked him to charter a plane and come and get me.''

''Did you know when you left the house yesterday evening that you were going to Uvalde and wouldn't be home last night?''

She glanced at Nick, who was regarding her solemnly. ''No, I didn't. It was a...surprise.''

''And obviously not a welcome one, since you wanted to leave so badly.''

''Right.''

''In other words, you were kidnapped.''

''You could say that, yes, but—''

''I'll come get you. Give me the address where you are.''

She hesitated. If she'd tried, she couldn't have planned a better way to trick Des into spending time with her. He was actually offering to come to her rescue. If she agreed, it would give her at least a couple of hours alone with him, which was exactly what she'd yearned for the night before last. But today… "That won't be necessary, Des. I'm staying until this afternoon to meet Nick's grandparents."

"Of your own free will?"

"Yes. And afterward, Nick will fly me home."

"Are you sure you don't want me to come get you now?"

She closed her eyes, having a hard time believing she was going to turn him down. "Yes, I'm sure."

"And if he decides to keep you there another night?"

Her eyes opened and she looked at Nick. She couldn't tell what he was thinking. "He won't, but if he tries, I'll call you. Wait a minute. Give me the number where you are." She pantomimed a pencil and paper to Nick, and he quickly produced them. "Okay, Des, what's the number?" She wrote it down. "Thanks. I promise I'll call if I need you."

"Just to be safe, call me this evening when you get home."

She was nearly stunned into speechlessness. He sounded as if he cared about her. Not romantically, but in a way that made it seem as if she mattered to him. "Are you sure? I mean, Ron could contact you again if I don't get home. And if you don't hear from him, then you'll know I'm home. That would be less trouble for you."

"I don't mind this kind of trouble. If you're in trouble, Tess, never hesitate to call. You're family."

For a moment she thought she'd misunderstood him. He'd never said anything remotely like that before. More often than not, Des seemed to go to great lengths to avoid her and her sisters. "Thank you. I appreciate this more than I can say."

"No problem. Talk to you this evening."

"Right." She hung up.

"Who is this Des, and why does he think you need rescuing?"

She turned to face Nick. "Oh, I don't know, Nick. Probably because I did need rescuing."

"Did?"

"Last night. If you'll remember, I *did* want to leave."

"You were never in danger."

No, she reflected. Not the type of physical danger he
meant. "There's no point in arguing about it now. I'll be
home by this evening."

"You didn't answer part of my question. Who is Des?"

"He's the son of my aunt May from her first marriage.
When she and my father's brother, Uncle William, married,
Uncle William adopted Des. Uncle William and Aunt May
never had any other children."

"So the night of your birthday party, why were your two
sisters so anxious for him to be there?"

"Just a game we play."

"A game?"

She shook her head. "It's complicated."

"And you don't think I'm smart enough to grasp the
complexities?"

"Let's just drop it, okay? I don't want to talk about it."

"Okay." He studied her. "Is Des satisfied now that
you're in no danger?"

"You heard me tell him that you would fly me home
this evening."

He crossed his arms over his chest. "And do you believe
that I will?"

"Yes."

"And what if I don't?"

"I'll call Des, and he'll come get me."

"And what if I ask you to stay?"

She paused for a moment to insure that her tone of voice

was as casual as she could manage. She wanted him to
believe she saw his question as involving his grandfather
or the *Águila*. She didn't want him to bring up the personal
or know that her mind had gone straight to the image of
him holding her against the wall, with her legs wrapped
around him, wanting him with every molecule of her being.
"Why would you do that? I've agreed to stay and meet
your grandparents. After that, you will have accomplished
what you set out to do by bringing me here."

A volatile silence filled the room; she had the feeling
that if she lit a match, the whole place would explode into
flames.

Finally he spoke. "So that's the way you want to play
it? As if, last night, nothing at all unusual happened between us?"

She clasped her suddenly shaking hands together and
looked down at them. "I think that's best. I mean, it happened, but it was a product of the night and the place."

"That's pure *bull* and you know it."

"Then let me put it this way. There's nothing that could
come from it. You want something I can't give you, Nick.
That's the beginning, middle and end of our relationship.
The fact that I can't agree to what you want will taint anything else."

"Damn it, Tess. Last night, right here in this kitchen, I
told you I wanted you. And then later—"

"Later we almost made a terrible mistake. I stopped it
because there is no future for you and me."

"And there's no trust, right?"

She looked at him. "Trust?"

"Let's put the cards on the table. If we made love, you
would think I was trying to seduce you into doing what I
want. And me? Maybe I'd think you were trying to get my

focus off the *Águila,* to make me want you so badly that I'd forget any and everything but you.''

She felt herself pale. The first part was true. She had thought that. As for the second part—there was no way she could ever believe that, by having sex with him, she could make him forget anything.

''But,'' he said, his voice soft, ''knowing all that doesn't make the wanting go away, does it, Tess?''

No, damn it, it didn't. She felt as if she was frantically juggling, trying to keep all her various balls in the air—the tenuous hold she had on her emotions when it came to Nick, her work and its time crunch, not to mention her future, her rivalry with her sisters, Des and, strangely enough, the compassion she felt for Nick's grandfather. And she was convinced that if she let just one ball drop, they would all drop, and she would lose everything.

Waiting for her in Corpus was a long list of things that only she could make decisions on. The well being drilled in the Gulf of Mexico, while vitally important to her, was by no means her only concern. The rest of her business continued. Her piece of the Baron pie, while being only one-sixth, was enormous, which, in turn, brought enormous responsibilities.

More immediate was the upcoming visit with Nick's grandparents. She didn't think for a minute that it would be easy.

And Des. He had called her out of the blue, worried about her, offering to rescue her like a knight on a white horse. It would have been a perfect opportunity for her to blindside her sisters and attempt to get him to look at her not just as family but as a desirable woman. But she'd let it pass. Even more bizarre was the fact that she didn't even want to think about why she'd turned him down. Not now, at any rate.

She was much too busy trying to keep some sort of emotional balance with Nick. But later, she told herself, she would think about her reason. Later, when she got home and felt on safer ground, she would think about it. Later...

And last, but certainly not least, she had Nick telling her he wanted her, then laying out the reasons they both knew should keep them from making love. But as he'd said, the reasons didn't make the wanting go away.

At the moment, it was just one ball too many for her. "I need to get back to Corpus Christi this evening, Nick. And if you won't take me, I'll find another way."

"That won't be necessary. I'll take you."

Six

Frail arms warmly enfolded Tess in a hug; then Nick's grandmother stepped back and beamed at her. "How lovely to meet you, my dear."

"Thank you, Mrs. Trejo. It's nice to meet you, too."

"Oh, please, call me Alma. We don't stand on formalities around here."

"Alma, then."

Alma was a tiny lady, wearing navy polyester pants with a neatly ironed pink flowered blouse. Her gray hair was cut short in a soft, flattering style, and her skin had its share of wrinkles, both from age and, Tess guessed, the Texas sun. Alma's wedding picture flashed into Tess's head. It had shown a pretty but shy young woman, shining with happiness and hope. Today Alma no longer seemed shy, but the happiness was still with her, along with the hope.

Amazing, she reflected. Alma had suffered a hard life and had known the pain of losing a son. Now she had to

cope with the knowledge that her husband might not be
with her much longer. In addition, she had health problems
herself. Yet she hadn't lost the capability of feeling happiness and hope.

Remarkable.

Alma's brown eyes sparkled with pleasure. "Now come
over here and meet Ben. He's been waiting all day for
this."

"Damn right," a breathy voice said. "Come over here
Tess, and let me get a look at you."

She followed the voice to a hospital bed set up in an
alcove where a big bay window offered a view of flowers
trees and a sky so blue it looked as if it had been painted
On the window ledge there was a picture. In the center of
it, Nick's grandfather was sitting in a chair. Nick and Alma
stood on one side of him, Kathie and her husband on the
other, and two little girls sat on the grass at their great
grandfather's feet. Another important picture to add to the
legacy of their family.

"Mr. Trejo?" She held out her hand to the wizened old
man, who was breathing with the aid of oxygen.

He shook her hand with surprising strength. "Ben
Name's Ben. Nick, pull her up a chair so I can talk to this
pretty young lady."

Without a word, Nick did as his grandfather asked and
motioned to Tess to sit down.

"I'll be right back with some iced tea for all of us,"
Alma said, still beaming.

Tess started to say she didn't want anything, but Alma
had already disappeared. She returned her attention to Ben
"How are you feeling? I understand you had something of
a bad spell this morning."

Ben waved a dismissive hand. "It was nothin'. No matter
what the doc says, I'm not ready to go yet."

"That's good to hear." She'd started off with pleasant-ries, but from here on out, she decided, it would be best to let him lead the conversation.

"Nick, come rearrange my pillows so I can sit up straighter."

"You're at the angle your doctor wants you to be, Grandpa."

"Damn it, Nick." Ben looked at Tess. "You know you're old when your pup of a grandson won't do what you say."

Nick grinned. "Your pup of a grandson is only trying to keep you alive for as long as possible."

Ben made a disgruntled sound. "Go off someplace and leave us alone. Tess, you and I need to have a nice long visit."

She smiled. It was easy to envision this old man whose life was drawing to an end as a virile, vital young man. She only had to look at Nick to see the likeness. "I'd like that."

For the very first time she was happy she'd given in to Nick and stayed long enough to meet Alma and Ben. She saw now that Nick hadn't been exaggerating when he'd said they wanted to meet her. There was no doubt they would have been very disappointed if she hadn't come. But she also had the odd feeling that somehow her life would have been diminished if she'd missed meeting them. Funny thing to feel, but true.

Despite his grandfather's order to leave, Nick, she no-ticed, had drawn up a chair at the other side of the bed and settled into it.

Ben's fingers absently moved on the sheet. His hands and arms were dry and wrinkled. At the bend of his elbow were purple and yellow bruises, probably from myriad nee-dle pricks. "Nick's told you about his find, hasn't he?"

"If you mean that he's found your father's gold, yes, he has."

Tears moistened Ben's milky eyes. "I never thought it would happen. In fact, I didn't think it was possible." Silently Nick rose and handed his grandfather his handkerchief, but the old man didn't bother to use it. "I can't tell you how much I wish Papa was alive today. It would mean the world to him."

"Yes, I'm sure it would." She tried to keep her response as neutral as possible and avoided looking at Nick. Nevertheless, she could feel his gaze trained on her, and she sensed he was ready to pounce if she said anything to upset Ben.

The old man shook his head. "No one knows. No one knows." He blinked the moisture from his eyes. "After the ship sank with the gold, Papa's life just went to hell. He'd dreamed of a ranch the size of the Briscoe or even the King. Instead he had to settle for a few measly acres and a lifetime of ridicule."

"Ridicule?" She hadn't meant to ask him anything that would encourage him to continue with something that obviously upset him, but the word just popped out.

"No one would believe Papa when he told them how he'd mined a fortune of gold but lost it in a hurricane. They ridiculed him, and Papa…well, he was a proud man, way too proud, Mama always said. But knowing that people felt he was nothin' but a joke sliced him up all inside." He paused and wiped his eyes.

"Don't overdo, Grandpa." Nick's soft voice revealed concern.

Ben didn't appear to hear him. "Somehow Mama was able to get through to him and show him what real kindness and love were all about. And at least he had the good sense to marry her. Of course, her parents were mad as hornets about it, but Mama was every bit as determined as Papa was proud, and she got her way. Still, as the years went on, he just got worse and worse, all locked up inside himself.''

''Grandpa, take it easy. Getting upset is not going to do you any good.''

Ben waved him away. ''Didn't I tell you to go someplace?''

Nick settled into his chair as Alma walked in carrying two glasses of tea. She handed one to Tess and the other to Nick. ''The mint came from my own garden, Tess.''

Alma waited expectantly while Tess took a sip. ''It's delicious. Thank you.''

Alma's smile lit up her face.

''Where's mine?'' Ben asked hoarsely.

''I only have two hands, now, don't I? I'll be bringing yours next.''

Ben looked at Tess, and she was surprised to see a twinkle in his eyes. ''Another way you know you're old is when you have to drink decaffeinated tea without much sugar.''

''Don't listen to him, honey,'' Alma said. ''He only knows it's decaffeinated with just a pinch of sugar because I told him. The truth is, the way I fix it, he can't tell the difference.''

''So she says.'' When Alma left the room, Ben winked at Tess. ''I let her think I can't, but the truth is, I really can.''

Tess couldn't help but smile. ''How long have you two been married?''

''Nearly sixty years.''

''That's wonderful,'' she said sincerely. What was especially wonderful to her was the obvious and deep love they still had for each other. She'd never before had the chance to witness that type of durable love that had lasted through good times and bad.

"Now, let's see, where was I?"

"You were telling me about your father."

"Oh, yes, Papa." Ben's gaze drifted toward the window, as if it were a movie screen and he was seeing scenes from long ago. "Well, you know how it is, Tess. Kids can be so cruel. They'd hear their papas talking about mine, and they'd say the same things to me. They'd throw stuff at me, rocks and such. To them, we were both crazy, but when it came down to fightin', I gave 'bout as good as I got. Still, they made it so that I could never belong. They had a baseball team that I really wanted to play on, but..."

With a shrug, he focused on her. "A lot of those kids are still alive today, and now that Nick has found the ship and the gold, I swear I'm going to live long enough for him to bring up a sizable amount. I want him to stack the bullion in the middle of town, so those men who used to throw rocks at me can see it and know how wrong they were. I want them to know that my papa didn't lie and that I didn't deserve the way they treated me."

The tears that sprang into her eyes surprised her. She quickly brushed them away. "I'm so sorry."

"Well, now, there's nothing for you to be sorry about." He gazed at her for several seconds. "Nick tells me you might stop your drilling for us."

For the first time, she looked at Nick, but his expression remained impassive. "Mm, yes, I'm considering it." What else could she say?

Ben nodded. "I'm very grateful to you for that. I know I don't have long to live. I also know I don't understand the ins and outs of the world anymore or what you young people have to face in your business lives. But if you could e your way clear to do this for us, it would mean the arth to both Alma and me."

Frantically she searched her mind for a noncommittal ply. A glance at Nick told her that he wasn't going to elp her out. But Alma saved her by appearing with Ben's ea. "Here you are, sweetheart. Just how you like it."

"Thank you, honey. Now sit down and get acquainted ith Tess. She's not only pretty as a picture, she's an awful ice girl."

Alma laughed. "I never doubted that for a minute. After l, Nick's taken quite a fancy to her, and we both know hat good taste he has."

Tess glanced at Nick, but he wasn't giving anything way.

Alma looked at her husband and apparently didn't like hat she saw. "I've got an idea. Tess, why don't you come ut to the garden with me? We'll pick some flowers so that can send you home with a lovely bouquet."

Ben's brows rose slightly. "Don't overdo it, Alma."

Nick stood. "I'll take Tess."

Alma waved her hand. "Sit down, Nick, and, Ben, relax. m taking her out to the garden, and that's that." She rned toward her. "Come on, sweetheart."

With a grin, Nick sat down. "You might as well go, ess. No one can change my grandmother's mind once she ets an idea."

Tess rose and followed Alma.

"I hope you don't mind that we came out here," Alma id as soon as she shut the door of the house behind her. I could tell Ben was overdoing it and needed a little rest."

"I don't mind at all." She remembered that Ben had ld his wife not to overdo. What would it be like, she ondered, to have a husband who loved you so much that e worried about your well-being even after sixty years?

She could think of no one who worried about her well
being in that way, though Des had been ready to come ge
her when he thought she was in danger. *Des*. Somethin
was bothering her about her decision to turn down his offe
an offer that only a few days ago she would have move
heaven and earth to get. Later, she reminded herself. Late
she would think about it.

"I had a much larger garden out at our home," Alm
said as they walked toward the relatively small but never
theless pretty beds of blooming perennials and annuals.

"I stayed at your home last night. It's a wonderfu
place."

Once again Alma beamed. "We've always thought so.
also had a large vegetable garden there, but I just can'
seem to work like I used to. Kathie does most of the wor
for me here."

"I don't see why you should have to work hard at thi
stage of your life," Tess said, instinctively responding t
the touch of sadness she heard in the older woman's voice
"After all, your retirement years are to enjoy."

Alma abruptly stopped and looked at her. "But you see
it's never been work for me. Taking care of my family an
making gardens for them to both appreciate and to eat fror
has always been a joy for me. Someday, when you hav
your own family, you'll understand."

Tess couldn't think of a thing to say. She couldn't eve
begin to imagine herself with a family such as Alma wa
talking about, much less a garden to tend.

"Start with those roses there." Alma handed a pair o
garden scissors to her. "You're a very sweet girl, Tess, bu
the truth is, Ben and I are past retirement. We're at the en
of our lives, and we know it."

It was all the pictures, she supposed. She'd seen Alm
and Ben from the beginning of their life together until now

which was nearly the end. But she found she really cared for this woman and her husband. Once again, she rushed to reassure her. "You don't know that for sure. None of us knows what's going to happen tomorrow." She bent to cut several white roses, then straightened to place them in the basket Alma carried.

This time Alma didn't bother correcting her. "I'm so glad we've had this opportunity to meet you, Tess. I always knew it would take an extraordinary girl to make Nick give up his wandering ways, and I can tell right off that you are that girl."

She shook her head, unwilling in this instance to let Alma get her hopes raised. "You may be reading too much into our, uh, relationship. Nick and I have really only just met." Then again, time, in the normal sense, didn't seem to apply to them.

"Nonsense. I know my Nick." She pointed to a grouping of irises. "Take some of those. Particularly the purple ones. They're very special. I brought cuttings of them from our home. They're from the original bunch that my mother-in-law started years ago."

"Really? I saw them this morning, and they're still beautiful."

Alma nodded. "It's a good feeling to know that they've survived through the generations. Kathie has them at her house, too. And before you leave, I'm going to have Nick shovel you a start of them. It will make me feel good to know that they'll be passing into your hands, so that your children and your grandchildren will be able to enjoy them as much as the previous generations."

"Thank you. That's very kind of you." A multitude of emotions nearly overwhelmed Tess. To her surprise, she was close to breaking into tears. But she couldn't allow herself to show any of what she was feeling. She didn't want to distress Alma in any way.

Obviously Alma thought she and Nick would be getting married and establishing their own home, and Tess couldn't find it in her heart to tell her that she was wrong. More than likely she would find out soon enough.

"Over there." Once again Alma pointed, this time to a grouping of creamy yellow flowers. "Those are spring bells. They'll look nice in your bouquet."

Nodding compliantly, Tess cut several stalks of the delicate-looking flower.

"Have you had a chance yet to see much of the land around our home?"

"Only a little."

"When you go back, look around if you can. When Nick was a little boy, he learned every inch of those cliffs, hills and arroyos. And not just ours. He'd explore our neighbors' land as well. Fences of any kind never much bothered him. Cut yourself a few snapdragons, too."

"Okay, but this is the last. Your basket is full, and what I've already cut will give me a beautiful bouquet."

Even though Alma was looking right at her, Tess wasn't sure she'd heard what she'd said.

"It seems to me that Nick has been searching for something his entire life. He's always been a restless, serious boy. When he was young, he'd go off on his own for hours at a time. By late afternoon, I'd always start to worry about him, but along about sundown, here he'd come, his pockets and hands filled with the treasure he'd found." Alma smiled. "Rocks, mostly, but he'd stick them in his pockets because he thought they were pretty, or shiny, or had a nice shape. I had big baskets of his rocks everywhere, but I never dared throw one of them out. Eventually I got the idea of placing them in prominent places in my garden which made him happy. And I can't tell you how many arrow heads he found, plus agates of Apache tears, tiger's eyes and snowflakes. He had boxes of each of them.''

Lost in reverie, Alma smiled. "Then, as he grew older, his interests changed, but he was as restless and solemn as he'd been as a boy. Sports and girls became important to him, but they didn't satisfy him. Every chance he got, he'd go out walking, still searching for something, still looking for treasure, I suppose. Our son never cared one way or the other about the *Águila* or its treasure, but Nick...that boy was born with his grandpa's dreams in his soul.''

"Then he should be happy now, because he's found the treasure.''

Slowly Alma focused on her. "Yes, he's found the *Águila*'s treasure, but he's more restless than I've ever seen him—oh, not on the outside, but on the inside. He tries to hide it from us, but I know him too well. Before Ben dies, Nick wants more than anything in the world to be able to give his grandpa his life's dream. He wants to stack that gold in the middle of town so that everyone will know how wrong they were about his grandpa and his great-grandpa. In a way, it's a passion he shares with Ben, except with Ben, the passion goes deeper. He's the one who had to watch helplessly as his papa was constantly humiliated and eventually became a broken man. And Ben's the one who was made to suffer so by other kids. I firmly believe that showing people the proof of that gold is what's keeping Ben alive.''

Alma took Tess's breath away. She'd never met any woman like her. "And do you think if Nick is able to do that for his grandfather that Nick will at last be satisfied and his restlessness will finally go away?''

"I think the answer to your question lies in you.''

"Me?'' she asked, surprised.

"Nick is in love with you, child. Nothing could be plainer to me. But what's not plain is whether you love him in return. I hope you do. Nick's trying so hard to please his grandpa, but I don't want *his* dreams to get lost in the process."

"His dreams?"

"Why, child, ultimately what everyone wants is a deep and abiding love, now isn't it?"

She was at a loss for words. Alma's life was so different than hers. The way in which she'd been brought up had left little time for dreaming.

Alma glanced around her garden. "We should go inside now. I'll wrap the flowers for you so they'll stay nice and fresh until you can get them in water."

"Thank you." What else could she say? She couldn't reassure Alma about any of the things that were concerning her. She couldn't tell her that she would stop drilling. She couldn't tell her love was going to smooth the rocky path she and Nick were on, because there was no love. And for them, at the end, there would be no happily-ever-after love story. Nick had a restless soul that more than likely could never be soothed by love. As for her, she had never even been taught *how* to love.

While Nick straightened the house in preparation for leaving, Tess placed a call to Ron and asked that he meet her at the airport with an overnight bag and a briefcase filled with work. She also asked that he charter a plane and have it ready to go when she landed.

The flight to Corpus Christi was relatively silent. As soon as the plane taxied to a stop, Tess was out of her seat and heading toward the cabin door.

"Wait, Tess."

"I'll wait by the bottom of the stairs."

She opened the door, then reached for her bouquet of owers and the brown paper bag that held her start of irises. t the bottom of the stairs, she found Ron. "Were you able) do everything I asked?"

Ron nodded. "The plane's close. Everything you re- uested is already on board, including the pilot."

"Excellent. Thank you."

"No problem. Listen, Tess. I'm so sorry I didn't get your essage last night. I was—"

"Never mind. It's over, and I'm sure I'll never find my- elf in that situation again. But just in case, make sure that e next time you spend the night away from home, you all in for messages."

"Don't worry. I've learned my lesson."

"Good. Will you please take these flowers to the house nd put them in a vase for me?" She thought for a second. Then put them in my bedroom. I'll be back tomorrow." he handed the flowers and the paper bag to him. "Put the ises in the pantry for now. We'll plant them in a pot >morrow."

"Sure. Oh, there's just one thing he said to tell you."

"What's that?"

"He said he may not be able to stay awake until you get ere."

She nodded. "I understand."

Nick came down the stairs. He saw Ron, then cut his aze to her. "Why is he here?"

"Ron, can you give me a minute?"

"Certainly. I'll be waiting by the terminal door."

Tess waited until her assistant was out of earshot. "Ron here because I asked him to be." She paused, trying to ecide what she wanted to say. In many ways she felt as isoriented as if she'd just returned from another planet here warm, loving families were the norm. On her planet, the only thing that counted was lots of big, healthy numbers that represented millions and millions of dollars.

She tilted her head and looked at him. "Why did you tell your grandparents that I might stop the drilling?"

"Because under the circumstances they wouldn't have understood a flat no. This way, if you say no, they'll think you did your best."

"Would the truth be so hard for them to understand?" Even as she asked the question, she knew the answer because she'd met them, seen their life through pictures, seen Alma's garden and been given a start of her cherished irises. "You know, Nick, it all basically boils down to one thing. You're asking me to give up millions so that you can make millions. What's so hard to understand about that?" Once again, she knew the answer. The *Águila's* gold didn't represent money to Ben and Alma. It represented vindication.

He regarded her calmly. "You sound upset."

She laughed. "Yeah, as a matter of fact I am. By introducing me to your grandparents, you once again attempted to stack the deck in your favor."

"Did it work?"

She closed her eyes for a moment. Without knowing it he'd put her in an untenable position. If she did what was best for him and his grandparents, it would put her in a far more desperate position than she was in now. In fact, it would end a large part of her life that was as vital to her as air.

On the other hand, if she did what was best for her, it would be the end of the light and hope in Nick's grandfather's eyes, which for Nick, would be unforgivable. Not only that, it would crush him, his grandfather and his grandmother, and no doubt bring an early death to his grandfather. Plus, she would never see Nick again.

She opened her eyes. "I'll try."

"What does that mean?"

"It means I'm going to try to see if there's a way I can stop drilling for the period of time you want, but at this moment I can't give you any promises."

Frustration etched lines into his face. "But whether to drill or not is up to you, right?"

"Ultimately, yes. Whether I proceed or not will be my decision. But...I need additional information, and there's only one person who can give it to me. Then and only then will I be able to give you an answer that might be different than the one I've already given you."

He shook his head. "I still don't understand."

"How could you?" She smiled slightly. "Whichever way my decision goes, I'll call you when I get back tomorrow."

He caught her arm before she could walk away. "What do you mean, when you get back? Where are you going?"

"I told you. There's someone I need to talk to, and to do that, the best way is to go to him."

"Then I'll go, too."

"No way, no how. I have to go alone."

He stared at her, no doubt trying to read her, but in this part of the game of life, she'd been schooled by the best.

"Why?" he finally asked.

She smiled, in complete sympathy with his inability to understand. "Just because you successfully kidnapped me for almost twenty-four hours doesn't mean you now have the right to butt into my life and know all my comings and goings."

Slowly he released her arm. "No, I guess I don't. You said you'd call me, right?"

She nodded. "As soon as I get back into town."

He exhaled a long breath. "And would it be too much to ask when you think that will be?"

"Sometime tomorrow afternoon or evening."

"Okay, then, I'll be waiting."

Seven

The sun was rising, streaking the sky with corals and pinks. Wrapped in a blanket and sipping a cup of coffee, Tess rocked in one of the many rocking chairs that had lined Uncle William's front porch since her earliest remembrance. The house where she and her sisters had been raised sat less than a mile from Uncle William's, but Kit was the only one who lived there now.

When her father and his brother, William, had first come to this land west of Dallas and Fort Worth that would become the Double B Ranch, they'd each built a home. Uncle William's was a large, rambling two-story house with a long, wide front porch and rooms that no one had ever used.

Her father had built an equally large two-story house, but there was nothing rambling about it. Its lines were clean and precise, with no wasted space and a definite purpose for each room. Besides his bedroom, he'd built exactly three extra bedrooms, rooms he'd expected her mother to fill with his sons. Instead she'd presented him with three daughters in as many years, and then had had the bad luck to die in a car accident on the way back from a shopping trip to Dallas.

Tess took another sip of coffee and pondered the ways of her family. If she'd chosen, she could have spent the night in the house and in the bedroom she'd grown up in. She might even have had a chance to visit with Kit. But the bedroom held no fond memories for her, and to visit with Kit, she would have to catch her first. Kit was perpetual motion.

In the end, she'd had the ranch hand who had picked her up last night from the landing strip bring her here to Uncle William's. After all, he was the one she was here to see, and as soon as she did, she had to fly to Corpus. As for the pilot, he had been taken to the comfortable guest house built to look like the equally comfortable bunkhouses where the ranch hands lived. His close proximity insured there would be no delay when she was ready to leave.

Ellie stuck her lined face around the screen door. "There you are, child. I'd thought you might want to sleep in a bit, but I should've known better. None of you girls ever slept past sunup."

Tess smiled dryly. "That's because our father wouldn't let us."

"Well, his lesson took real good." Ellie closed the screen door behind her, ambled to the rocking chair beside hers and settled her large, big-boned frame into it. "Many's the dawn I look out my bedroom window and see that sister of yours streaking past the house on that big devil of a stallion she rides, that red hair of hers streaming out behind her like a flag."

Tess nodded. "No one else can ride him but Kit."

"You mean no one *wants* to ride him but her. Oowee, hat devil scares me."

Tess grinned with affection. "Well, if that's the case, ie's the only thing I've ever known you to be afraid of."

Back in the forties, Ellie had come to the Double B as , young girl, ready and willing to tackle anything, including he duties of a ranch hand. But Uncle William, a bachelor hen, hadn't thought riding fences and herding cattle was it work for a young girl, so much to Ellie's disappointment, ie'd made her his housekeeper. But not even he had able o keep Ellie inside all the time.

Uncle William had always said he'd never known a voman who could come up with as many excuses for being utside as she could. And so slowly the sun and the years iad changed her appearance. Her skin was wrinkled and eathery, her hair gray, her shoulders stooped, but her trength, will and commonsense approach to life remained he same.

Ellie had outlived Tess's father and mother, along with Jncle William's wife. Now it looked as if Ellie would out-ive Uncle William, too.

"You sure know how to make good coffee, Miss Tess, ut you're 'bout the only one of your family who does. Miss Kit can't be bothered, and Miss Jill prefers tea. Now vhere do you suppose she got that from?"

Tess laughed. "I don't have a clue." When she and her isters were born, Ellie had affixed the Miss to their name, ind, despite their protests as they'd grown older, she'd nade it clear that she considered Miss to be a part of their names. "We didn't have too much time to talk last night. How is Uncle William doing?"

"'Bout the same. Like all of us, he has his good days ind his bad. I'll tell you one thing, he sure was sorry to niss your party."

"If he wasn't feeling well, he did the right thing by staying home."

Ellie shook her head. "He don't like to hear this, but just between me, you and the fence post, I think his travelin' days are over."

"I don't like to hear that, either. In fact, I don't even want to think about what that means." Uncle William was the glue that held her family, such as it was, together. As independent as she and her sisters were, they each, in their own way, relied on him. She glanced at her watch. "When does he usually get up?"

"It all depends on the kind of night he has, but soon now he'll be wakin' up, and Wilbur will be wanderin' over. Directly, I'll be goin' in and startin' breakfast. Wilbur'll get your uncle up, washed and dressed. Then he'll be ready to see you."

"Good." Wilbur was about a decade younger than her uncle, but he'd worked on the Double B from the beginning and was one of the two men in the world her uncle would allow to help him. Des was the other.

"Why don't you come on in with me and you can catch me up on your news, especially that party of yours. I saw Miss Kit on her way to the airstrip wearing nothin' but jeans and a T-shirt. I told her she needed to wear somethin' a bit nicer, but she just laughed and went on her way with Rodney, that new hand of ours."

Tess nodded. "Kit doesn't worry about the rules, written or otherwise—we all know that."

Ellie rolled her eyes. "Lord, yes, we *do* know that."

"But Kit looked fine, and I think she and Rodney had a good time."

The older woman snorted with disdain. "That Rodney is another one of those boys caught up in what he thinks is the glamour of being a cowboy. Me 'n' Wilbur got a be

ping. He thinks the boy'll last another month, mainly
cause he fancies Miss Kit so much. Me, I don't think he'll
make it another week." Ellie grinned. "You come on in
now, you hear?"

"In a few minutes, when I finish my coffee."

As soon as she was alone again, Tess returned her gaze
to the horizon. The sun had risen above it, a brilliant,
golden ball full of promise for a new day. And staring at
the sun, she knew without a doubt that Nick was also
awake.

"Morning, Tess," Wilbur said, wheeling her uncle into
the big front room where the morning sun flooded.

Several years ago, when Uncle William had realized he
was losing his mobility, he'd moved back to the ranch from
Dallas and ordered his large desk to be relocated to this
room. He'd also had large picture windows installed along
each wall to bring as much of the ranch as was possible
indoors. Here he could continue overseeing his businesses
and, at the same time, have the best possible views of his
beloved ranch.

"Good morning, Wilbur. Good morning, Uncle William."

Wilbur wheeled her uncle to his desk. Then, with a nod
and a smile to Tess, he left.

"I'm so happy to see you, Tess. When I couldn't make
your party, I was afraid it would be a while before I'd be
able to see you again."

Tess circled the desk to kiss her uncle. "I missed you,
but I completely understood why you couldn't come."

"Well, then, you're one up on me," he grumbled, "because I didn't understand it at all. It was that damn doctor
of mine. If I didn't have such a good time arguing with
him, I'd get another doctor." He paused while Ellie came

in with a saucer full of prescription medicine and vitamin along with a large glass of orange juice. When she left, h drank a little of the orange juice and pointedly ignored th contents of the saucer. "I don't suppose that son of min showed up, either, did he?" Des had been a young bo when his mother had married Uncle William, and from th beginning, Uncle William had never called him anythin but son.

"No, no, he didn't." Tess pulled a chair to the side o the desk. "How are you?" she asked, searching his fac for signs of decline that hadn't been there the last tim she'd seen him. Happily, she found none.

"I'm fine, I'm fine, and don't you believe otherwise. I'r going to outlive that doctor of mine just so I can prove hi prognostications of doom and gloom wrong."

She laughed with delight. In that moment, she truly be lieved her uncle would live forever. In that moment, h seemed the same as he'd always been, a big man with booming voice, enormous strength and a brilliant mind. He father had been born with the very same characteristics Together, the two of them had carved a great ranch out o a hostile land and built a multimillion-dollar corporatio that today was respected all over the world. Unfortunately though, unlike her uncle, there had been no place in he father for affection, laughter and humor. "You just don' know how happy that makes me."

He reached over and took her hand. His skin felt dry but the strength she'd always known remained. "You, you sisters and Des are what keep me going. You still need me and as long as that continues, I'll be here for you."

Tess blinked back tears. "Thank you, but you shoul know, there'll never come a day when we won't nee you."

He laughed. "That's music to an old man's ears, even i

know it's not the truth. But at any rate, let's get down to he reason you're here. Is it something to do with your vell? Or is it something to do with the man Des told me ad kidnapped you off to Uvalde?''

She grimaced. She wished Des hadn't put it quite that vay, no matter how accurate he'd been. ''It's about both, ctually. And also about my father's will.''

He released her hand and sat back in his wheelchair. 'Tell me about it.''

She did. She told him about the well, how she felt it had he potential to be the greatest moneymaker of all her sites et that there was no way she could know that for certain intil the drill actually hit oil and they began pumping. Then he told him about Nick, his family and its history, and bout the hope of his grandfather to use the treasure for vindication.

She saved the conflict between Nick and herself for last. She reported the precarious position of the ship and how ne slight miscalculation on her rig could send the ship and ts treasure over the scarp where it would lie buried for ears, maybe for all time. Last, she explained about Ben's nealth and Nick's plea that she halt the drilling for at least hree months.

When she fell silent, her uncle let out a long breath. 'Well, I can certainly see your problem. I also see some-hing else. You're in love with this Nick Trejo.''

She opened her mouth to tell him he was wrong, then losed it. Unbidden, images and emotions flashed through ler head and heart, one after the other—the way he could nake her go weak at the knees with just a smile, the way le'd made her want him last night in the living room of he farmhouse, the way she'd turned down Des's help, when just twenty-four hours earlier, she would have gone o any lengths to gain his attention.

God, why hadn't she seen it before? The knowledge had been right there in front of her the whole time, but she'd kept pushing it to the back of her mind. Now, though, she had no choice but to face it. She *did* love Nick.

Slowly she nodded. "Yes, I'm afraid I do. But unless can figure out a way to give him what he wants, he'll never love me in return."

Uncle William's gray eyebrows shot straight up. "If his love is dependent on your granting him what he wants, then his love isn't worth having."

She knew he was right. She also regretted stating it the way she had. "Perhaps it would be more accurate to say that no matter which way things go, I doubt if he'll ever love me."

"Okay, then, in that case it sounds as if he's going after you for two reasons. Because you're a smart, beautiful woman and he just plain wants you, and because—"

"I never said—"

"You didn't have to. He wants you physically, and he wants you to cease drilling for a spell. But then you already know those two things. What do you want from me?" Her uncle was nothing if not earthy and direct.

"I want to talk to you about my father's will and the clause that states that unless I've earned *his* idea of a fortune within ten years of his death, I'll lose my portion of the company." She folded her arms across her waist, comforting herself, in a way. "And you know as well as I do that for most people the figure our father gave me and my sisters would be impossible to attain."

"But from what you've said, this well is going to put you over the top, though with very little time to spare."

She nodded. "Uncle William, I'm betting everything I've got on just that. Still, it'll take months before I know for sure."

Uncle William regarded her gravely. "And you only have a little under ten months left to do it."

"Right, but it's doable." She sat forward, the excitement she felt for the new well seeping into her voice and expression. "If I'm lucky, we'll hit oil in two more months, give or take a couple of weeks. Then I'll have eight months to pump enough oil to give me the figures I need. But that's if I have no major holdups or breakdowns and, at the same time, drill twenty-four hours a day, seven days a week. The problem is, I understand and sympathize with what Nick is trying to do. I'd love to be able to shut down and give him whatever time he needs."

She rose and began to pace. "So what I'm hoping for from you is a way to interpret my father's will in a different manner, but that would still keep it within its legal boundaries. For instance, if I strike oil but the well hasn't yet produced enough, could I slip under my father's guidelines on the grounds that there is the potential for the amount named?"

He sighed. "I wish I could tell you yes, honey, but your father's will couldn't have been more clear. He saw to that. We made up our wills together, you know, and when he told me about that clause, I counseled him against it. I just didn't feel he was being fair to you girls, but your father was insistent. He saw it as a way to make the three of you prove you were worthy of inheriting your shares of the company."

Tess dropped her head, trying to hide the tears she couldn't seem to keep back. "To prove we were *worthy*. For any other man, love of his children would be enough." She walked to one of the windows and blindly gazed out. "He controlled us in life, and now he's controlling us in death. Most children look forward to their birthdays, but all they meant to us was more responsibilities, more challenges, more goals to be met. He kept raising the proverbial bar.''

''Yeah, I know.'' Regret laced her uncle's voice. ''I've never known a man who wanted sons as badly as he did. But when you girls came along instead, he decided it was his job to make you tough.''

''And don't forget the competitive part. Today, Kit, Jill and I will go to practically any lengths to one up each other.''

''I know, honey.''

''And while he was alive, we'd work until we were exhausted, trying to please him, yet when we accomplished what he asked of us, he barely acknowledged our achievement. It was almost like he wanted us to fail.'' She looked at her uncle. ''Did he?''

Reluctance shaded his tone. ''Maybe in some twisted way he wanted to prove that he was right in thinking sons would have been superior to daughters.''

''I don't know about Kit and Jill, but I've worked my entire life to prove him wrong.''

He sighed heavily. ''I can't count the number of times he and I fought over the way he treated the three of you. I called him every name in the book, but when it came to you girls, he ignored me.''

She walked slowly to the desk. ''More than once I've actually wondered if Mother's death was an accident.''

His head shot up, and his eyes sharpened. ''What do you mean?''

''Knowing Father, I can only imagine the hell he made her life because he'd expected her to produce sons and instead she'd given him daughters. Maybe she decided.. Who knows.''

He didn't say a thing. He didn't have to. She walked around his desk and sat down. ''Tell me something, Uncle

William. You knew him better than anyone else in the world. Do you honestly think he ever loved us?''

He took several moments to ponder her question. ''It's hard to say for certain, but in his own way, yes, I think so. If he didn't, he would have left you alone and wouldn't have cared what you did.''

''What an awful way to love.'' She wiped the tears from her eyes. ''Jill's already proved herself worthy of her one-sixth of the company. She's already hit the mark and made even more, despite the fact that she has another year, because she's a year younger than I am. Kit has two more years.''

''Jill has already reached her mark because real estate is a booming market.'' He watched her for a moment. ''I wish I could help you with this, but, again, the will is very clear. You have to make the money yourself. No gifts.''

''I know.''

''So what are you going to do?''

Her lips firmed. ''I don't have a choice.''

''That's not entirely true, you know. Even if you lost your one-sixth of the company, you'd still be able to run your division.''

''Right,'' she said flatly. ''And I'd be nothing more than a hired employee. Besides you and Des, I'd have to answer to Jill and Kit. They'd have the right to examine every decision I made, and to say yes or no to any undertaking I might want to pursue. And that would be completely intolerable to me.'' Not only that, she reflected with pain. If she couldn't make the money by her deadline, her father would win. That was also intolerable to her. She shook her head. ''No, thanks to Father, I really have only one way to go. My part of Baron International is *my* legacy, *my* right. It would destroy me to lose my part of the family business, and I'm going to do whatever I have to do to keep it.''

Eight

Tess wandered to the open French doors that led from her bedroom to the terrace. Against a black sky, dark gray clouds piled up over the Gulf, one atop the other.

Lightning streaked the horizon. Thunder rolled in the distance. The wind strengthened by the minute. A storm was brewing, and the turbulent atmosphere suited her dark, restless mood.

Nick. Where was he tonight? She hoped he had been able to secure the *Águila* as much as was possible. But more than that, she prayed he was safely on land. According to reports, the major portion of the storm looked as if it would stay far out at sea, and Corpus and its surrounding areas would only get grazed by its edge. Still, it would be foolish not to take precautions.

If she had called Nick, as she'd promised she would when she returned from the Double B, she might know where he was. But she was a bona fide, freely admitted coward and was trying to put off as long as possible the moment when she would have to say no to him for the final time.

Sipping at a glass of burgundy wine, she leaned against the door and lifted her face to the mist-filled wind. Even though she'd worked at her usual frenetic pace all afternoon, her mind had been on the conversation she'd had with Uncle William and the irrefutable fact that, as they talked, had hit her squarely between her eyes.

She loved Nick.

The idea astounded her. She didn't even know *how* to love, perhaps because, to her knowledge, she'd never been truly loved. Yet there was no doubt. She was definitely in love with Nick.

Right from the first, the signs had been there, all of them in big, bright, red neon letters. How could she have missed them?

There was the way he'd mesmerized her on the night of her birthday and the way her body had melted against his when they'd danced. There was the way she'd so easily acquiesced to the idea of flying to some unknown destination for dinner and the stunning fact that she'd turned down Des's offer for help.

But in her defense, she'd never been in love before. She'd never even experienced what she would consider normal love—the love of a child for a parent or vice versa, or even the love of one sister for another. No wonder she hadn't recognized the signs.

Drops of rain began to fall, splattering the terrace. The lightweight ivory caftan she'd changed into after work was getting wet. She didn't care.

The rain was cool. Her skin was hot. She wanted Nick. She wanted to see him, to touch him, to make love to him as they almost had the night before last. And she wanted him to hold her and kiss her until they both forgot that their lives were going in two different directions and that they could never have a future together.

She might not know anything about love, but she was learning fast. Love hurt, and there wasn't a thing she could do about it.

She couldn't pursue Nick, nor could she tell him of her love. But for the rest of her life he would remain in her heart, a heart that was already breaking. Somehow, in some way, she was going to have to learn how to bear it.

The agony of it was that Nick had come along at literally the most critical time of her life. If things had been different in their lives, if they'd met under any other circumstances, where neither of them wanted anything from the other except truth and trust, they might have had a chance.

Damn her father!

She let out a long breath. She should have called Nick this afternoon, as she'd promised. She was only prolonging the inevitable. This afternoon, this evening, tomorrow, a month from now, her answer would still have to be the same. She should get it over with, but she couldn't make herself. She needed this time, this respite, when she could tell herself that Nick didn't hate her. Not yet, at any rate.

The rain was coming down heavier, and still she wasn't ready to go in. She was hurting too much, wanting too much. Lightning split the sky. A boom of thunder shook the windowpanes of the door she leaned against. Lightning again charged the air with electricity.

Nick walked out of the dark rain. Water streamed off his hair, his face, his forearms. His clothing was soaked and plastered to his hard body. He stopped several feet from her, his hands balled into fists at his sides, his stance wide and firm. Anger and heat filled his gaze as it raked her from the top of her head right down to her bare feet. At that instant he seemed a part of the storm—fierce, elemental, dangerous.

"You didn't call."

Unable to take her gaze off him, she slowly shook her head. "It was a hectic day and I... " There wasn't a single thing she could say that would assuage his wrath.

"Damn you, Tess." His deep voice rolled over her like thunder. "You *had* to know I was waiting."

"I'm so sorry—"

"Your answer is no, isn't it? *Isn't* it? And *that's* why you didn't call."

"Nick, I tried—"

"Damn you." Slowly he started toward her. "Damn me. *Damn* our situation." As he reached her, he extended his hand past her head to brace himself against the door. "And the worst part of it is that right now, I don't care."

She didn't either. Nothing mattered except the craving for him that involved every part of her. Tomorrow she would care. But not tonight.

He sank his body against hers until he had her pressed back against the door. Then he crushed his mouth on hers and thrust his tongue deep into her mouth.

This night, this lovemaking, was meant to be. The vague thought whispered loudly in her mind. Over the past few days, their sexual need for each other had gathered momentum until this moment when neither of them could do anything to stop it.

When he'd walked out of the storm, she'd taken one look at him and known it didn't matter whether or not he would try to use sex as a way of getting what he wanted. She wanted him, and this one night she would have him.

She let go of any restrictions, constraints or reserves and pushed away any and all doubts. She stood on tiptoes,

slipped her arms around his neck and returned his kiss with
all the enthusiasm and love she possessed.

It didn't matter that he didn't love her. She loved him,
and for tonight that would be enough.

The fury of the storm continued, the rain soaking her
hair and skin. But the fire inside her kept growing, astounding her, taking her over until she was all heat and need. He
kissed her lips, her face, her neck, seemingly drinking in
the rain and the taste of her, and she did the same to him,
licking his neck and face. She was starving for him.

His hand grasped her breast; then, leaning down, he drew
the nipple and the wet, transparent caftan that covered it
into his mouth and strongly sucked. Her head fell back, her
womb contracted, and softly she moaned. She was helpless
against the onslaught of heated sensations that followed one
after the other. And just when she thought she'd reached
the pinnacle of the amount of pleasure she could feel, he
showed her she was wrong by turning his attention to her
other breast, pulling that nipple into his mouth, briefly re-
leasing it, then tugging at it again and again until she was
almost crazed with desire.

Fire coiled through her to the point that she no longer
felt the cool rain against her skin. In fact, she felt so hot
that she was surprised the rain didn't dry as soon as it
landed on her skin.

"Nobody stops," she whispered, sliding her fingers
through his hair, then down to the buttons of his shirt. She
began to undo them.

He lifted his head from her breast and stared at her with
a brilliant heat. "Nobody stops," he muttered, then kissed
her once more with an urgency that matched hers.

He dropped his hands to the caftan at her thighs and
gathered the wet cloth. Wrenching his mouth from hers, he
pulled the caftan up and over her head and tossed it onto

he rain-drenched terrace. Then he crushed his mouth down
n hers with a desperation she felt to her bones.

She could no longer tell the loud beat of her heart from
he booming thunder. She could no longer tell whether the
vorld was spinning around her or whether Nick was mak-
ng her feel as if it was. She pushed the edges of his shirt
side and immediately closed her mouth over one of his
igid nipples.

With a loud groan he plowed his fingers through her hair
nd held her head against him. Fascinated, enthralled, she
ghtly bit and nibbled his nipple, then circled it with her
ongue, lapping up the rain and him. She'd never known a
ian's nipple could be so erotic.

Without warning, he knelt before her. His hands gripped
er bare buttocks, caressing them, and his tongue dipped
ito her navel, where again he drank from her. Then slowly,
otly, his mouth slid downward.

She was glad for the support of the door. Her legs felt
veak. Her breathing became labored. Her chest hurt. And
wonderful, unbearable ache built between her legs.

Acting on pure, inexplicable instinct, she shifted her
tance and parted her legs. She'd had sex a couple of
mes—infinitely forgettable sex. Still, she would have
iought she was prepared for anything regarding sex. She
asn't. Not at all.

His fingers opened the two folds that guarded that most
itimate part of her; then his tongue thrust against the ach-
igly sensitive nub. Like a bolt of lightning, pleasure
iocked through her, and she cried out. "Oh, Nick!"

The wind and rain absorbed her words as his tongue
roked and licked. Her fingers tightened in his hair. She
iimaxed—hard, fast and powerful.

Aftershocks shuddered through her as her body absorbed
ie sweet, hot ecstasy. But before she had a chance to catch

her breath, he straightened and lifted her. She wrapped her
legs around him and wound her arms around his neck. As
she had been at the farm house, she was open against the
denim of his jeans and his hard sex.

He walked with her into the bedroom. Impossibly, she
climaxed again. Crying out, she held on to him as if he
were life itself. And indeed, at that moment, he *was* her
entire life, her entire world.

On her bed, she could hardly bear the wait for him. Lying
on her back, she drew up her knees, agonizingly sensitized.
A bedside lamp illuminated the room, along with the occasional flash of lightning. She tried to concentrate on
breathing as she watched Nick strip out of his clothes, but
she wasn't certain she always breathed.

He was magnificent. Lean muscles shifted and rippled
beneath his bronze skin as he undressed. Scars appeared
that she hadn't had a chance to see before, but now she
longed to touch them. Fine black hair covered his chest and
arrowed down to his groin, where his sex throbbed with
power. He was a picture of pure, undiluted virile masculinity.

A new wave of desire quivered through her. As if he
could feel what she felt, his amber gaze cut to her and
scorched her skin.

She couldn't think of a thing to say. Besides, in the short
time they'd known each other, they'd already said so much.
For tonight, at least, maybe words weren't necessary. Tonight was the time to let their bodies speak, and what they
were speaking of was basic needs and elemental passion.
They were speaking *truths,* truths that the two of them
would never verbally speak of to each other.

He came to her and positioned himself over her. His
breathing was rough, his body taut, his face tight with intensity. She expected him to immediately enter her, wanted

eeded him to. Yet instead he stared at her. Feverishly, eetingly, she wondered what he was thinking, but she vanted him too badly to spend time asking him or trying o figure it out.

This night would never come again, and as surely as the un would rise tomorrow, discord would insert itself beween them. For now, for tonight, she wanted there to be nly pleasure between them—pure, white-hot, ecstatic pleaure.

Later, she supposed, she would be shocked at her attitude nd behavior. It was so radically different from who and hat she was normally. Or maybe, deep down, tonight, she *as* the person she was supposed to be, and she'd only eeded the right man to make her understand that.

Except Nick was the wrong man.

Determinedly she smiled up at him, slid her hands to his houlders, then to his back. They were both slick with rain. Nick," she whispered, pleading. "Please. Oh, *please.*"

With his jaw clenched, he drew back his hips and drove eeply into her, burying himself completely in her. A hard nudder racked his body, a shudder that she felt deep inside er and that nearly brought her to climax again. With a soft noan, she wrapped her arms and legs around him and held im to her as tightly as she could. She didn't think she'd ver felt anything as wonderful as having him inside her. was insanity. It was bone-deep rapture and satisfaction.

She was going to peak again soon. She could feel it. She as almost there. She wanted it to happen immediately, nd at the same time, she wanted to prolong as much as ossible the pleasure of having Nick inside her. But she asn't in charge.

He hammered in and out of her like a man out of control, nd mindlessly she matched his rhythm, lifting and undu-

lating her hips, attempting to take him deeper and deeper
into her.

Then it started again. Fire and passion built, filling her
taking her over. Her fingers clutched his shoulders. She
opened her eyes and looked at Nick. His face was strained
his neck muscles corded, the muscles of his back and shoul
ders bunched, but in his eyes she saw the sure knowledge
that he knew exactly what she was feeling and that he wa
with her.

He reached for one of her hands and tightly entwined
their fingers. As a harsh sound tore out of him, he drove
into her with short, quick strokes. They strained together
urgent, frantic, almost mad with the sweet agony of plea
sure. Then he thrust deeply into her, once, twice, three
times.

Then it happened. She arched her back as she climaxed
and a flaming ecstasy took her soaring up and over an un
known precipice. At the same time, Nick convulsed with
his own completion. And as he had promised her with hi
hot amber gaze, this time they soared together.

A soft rain fell on the terrace. The only other sound Tes
could hear was Nick's uneven breathing as he lay beside
her. Inches separated them, though it felt like miles.

He wasn't asleep. Though he lay perfectly still, she could
feel the energy and heat that radiated off his body. Some
how, though, she knew that this time the heat and energy
didn't come from sexual desire. She'd known that feeling
and this was different. This feeling came from anger. Anger
at her, no doubt, for telling him no. Anger at himself fo
giving in to his desire for a woman who wouldn't give him
what he wanted.

Sadness overwhelmed her. She shivered and reached
down to pull the sheet over her. Their passion had bee

spent. Now there was nothing between them, only a void that couldn't be filled.

She'd known this time would come, when Nick would feel nothing for her but disdain. But knowing it didn't make it any easier for her to deal with. She just wished he would say something. Anything would be better than this silence.

"I guess I should have closed the doors," she said softly. "The carpet must be soaked." She waited for some kind of response, and when it didn't come, she went on. "Not that it matters. If the damage is too bad, I'll have it replaced."

"Tell me something." His voice was equally soft, but the underlying hard tone she heard made her blood run cold. "When did you plan to give me the bad news?"

She looked at him. "Tomorrow. I was definitely going to call you tomorrow."

"You mean like you were definitely going to call me as soon as you returned from your mystery trip?"

There was nothing she could say to that. She'd already admitted to herself that she was being a coward when she'd made the decision to put off the call, though she had no intention of admitting it to him.

"No answer to that, Tess? Okay, then tell me something else."

She tensed. The sudden sharpness in his voice could have cut through steel. "What?"

"Did I ever have a chance?"

She quietly sighed. "I thought there might be a chance. I knew it was a long shot, but I checked it out anyway." She shook her head. "I tried, Nick. I really did."

He jammed a pillow behind his head. "Right."

"Look, there's no point in continuing to talk about this. I did try, but it didn't work out as I had hoped it might."

"What's to work out, Tess? It's easy. All you have to do is say stop."

"It's not that easy. It's much more involved than you'll ever know. In fact, nothing about any of this is easy."

He came up on one elbow and stared down at her. "Why not? You're the oil baron—or baroness, if you prefer—with money to burn. What's so difficult? You stop drilling for three months—hell, at this point I would take two. Then, after that time, you start up again. You can't be so cash poor that waiting a couple of months to bring up the oil will be that detrimental to your balance sheet."

She sat up, shoved the pillows into a pile behind her, then, taking the sheet with her, leaned against them. "You don't understand, Nick. You just don't."

He sat beside her, not bothering with the sheet. "Baby, have you ever got a way with understatement."

She shook her head—at his sarcasm, at the futility of this conversation, at her sadness. There was no way they would ever agree on this. In different ways, they were both hostages to the past. Neither could call the present their own.

"I'm waiting."

Her brow furrowed. "For what?"

"For an explanation."

"You and I have been over and over this subject, Nick. There's no point in continuing, because there's nothing more to be said. I'm not going to change my mind. I know that's hard for you to accept, but you're just going to have to."

"You're wrong. I *don't* have to accept it. Besides, maybe, just maybe, with enough talking and explaining, you and I can come to an agreement."

She would have smiled if she hadn't felt so much like crying. "You mean, you think with enough talking, I'll come around to your way of thinking."

"That's not what I said."

"No, but it's what you meant. Let's face it, Nick. No xplanation, no matter how compelling, will matter to you. 'o your way of thinking, nothing is more important than ,etting that gold stacked in the middle of downtown Uvalde efore your grandfather dies."

"You're right. You're absolutely right. But I'd just like o know, Tess. What reason do you have that could be more mportant than that?"

"Nothing that I could convince you of." The sheet was ngled across his groin, leaving everything else bare. Shad-ws from the lamplight fell across his flat stomach and ower. Memories of the ecstasy they'd just shared came looding back to her and her heart began to pound.

"Try." The word came out through bared teeth, and her nind snapped back to the subject at hand.

Her family had a tacit agreement that they never dis-ussed their business with outsiders. However, in this case, f she'd thought it would do any good, she wouldn't have esitated to tell him. But she knew it wouldn't help.

Nick would never be able to understand the deep-seated esire that had burned in her practically her whole life, the esire that went bone-marrow deep to prove to her father er worth. Using her father's own method of measurement, he desperately wanted to prove she was worthy of owning er part of his company. But most of all, she wanted to rove to him that she was worthy of his love and had been ll along.

Of course she knew he would never know if and when he fulfilled his requirements. After all, he was dead. But *he* would know, and it would make all the difference in he world to her.

Upset, restless, she held the sheet to her with one hand nd pleated its edges with the other. "As I said before, I

can't convince you that I have a more compelling reason
than you do. And to tell you the truth, you're probably right
in thinking your reason is more important than mine.''

"Then why—"

"Because I *can't* stop the drilling, Nick. I just *can't,* and
don't ask me again.'' She slipped off the bed, taking the
sheet with her. Wrapping it around herself toga style, she
crossed to the French doors. The moist air felt cool on her
warm skin. Absently she reached up and ran her fingers
through her hair in an attempt to put some order to it. Earlier, the rain had given it a thorough soaking, but during
their lovemaking it had dried and she couldn't imagine how
awful it must look. Not that it mattered. Nick would be
leaving soon anyway.

She braced herself for what he would say next, but she
heard nothing but the whisper of the gentle rain. She
glanced at him over her shoulder. He was lying where she'd
left him, obviously not at all self-conscious about his na-
kedness. Unfortunately she couldn't say the same. A look
was all it took for her body to begin to ache and her mouth
to water for just one more taste of him. Quickly she turned
away. "Aren't you going to say anything else?"

"No."

Curious, she glanced over her shoulder again. "Why?"

"You just told me to quit asking you to stop the drilling,
and that's exactly what I intend to do."

"Just like that?"

"Just like that."

She could hardly believe that he'd finally agreed to drop
the subject. In a way she felt lighter, knowing there would
be no more arguments. Except…without the conflict, there
would also be no more reason for him to seek her out.

Her gaze returned to the rain-drenched patio. "So what'

to become of the *Águila*? Do you think the storm did any damage to it?''

''I hope not. Despite all the fireworks, we really didn't get the brunt of the storm. I'll find out for sure tomorrow.''

She whirled. ''What do you mean? You're not going to dive again, are you?''

''Of course I am. I have to go where the ship is, and the ship is sitting on a scarp in relatively deep waters.''

Barely aware of what she was doing, she slowly walked toward him. ''But I've just told you I'm not going to stop drilling. That means it's way too dangerous for you or any of your men to continue to dive.''

''That's probably true.''

''Oh, it's definitely true. And knowing that, you're still going to do it?''

He fixed her with a level gaze. ''I don't have a choice, Tess. That gold is too important for Grandpa, and because of his health, I don't have a lot of time to waste.''

She sat on the edge of the bed. ''I know all that. You made sure I did. But as much as he wants it, would he want you to risk your life getting it?''

''Not if he knew.''

''But he must have some idea.''

''No, and that's the way it's going to stay.''

''Wait a minute. Remember, I met him. His mind is still sharp. If he really thinks about it for a minute, he'll figure it out.''

Nick shook his head. ''When he's pressed me for specifics, I've glossed over them and put heavy emphasis on the manned submersible.''

Her hand flew to her forehead. ''Of course. How could I have been so stupid? I'd forgotten about submersibles and their robotics capabilities. At the depth you're working, you'll use one, won't you?''

"Part of the time. I've managed to procure the use of a secondhand one, and it will certainly be of great help in bringing up the gold."

He moved off the bed and slipped into his briefs, then his jeans. Her heart sank. He was getting ready to leave.

"Part of the time?"

"A great deal of the *Águila* was made out of wood. Some of the wood is already gone. But I want to try to preserve what's left of the ship as best I can. And that means the work on the ship itself is too delicate to be left to anything robotic."

"The gold is what's important to you and your family. Why bother trying to preserve the ship?"

He gave her a half smile, but there was no humor in it. "I told you the other morning when we had breakfast out there." He nodded to the terrace. "I'm a professor of archaeology. Granted, the ship is not as old as some of the ships they've found and excavated on the east coast, but nevertheless, every nail and plank of the *Águila* is important to me."

"Nick, from what little I know about it, the current submersibles are very sophisticated. I've heard that robotics can give doctors the capability to operate on someone who's in a hospital miles away."

His eyebrows rose. "Does that sound like something you'd like done to you?"

"We're talking about a ship here, Nick. Not a human body."

"Everyone has to do things the way they feel is best." He sat on the bed and pulled on his socks and shoes.

She felt sick to her stomach. "It never occurred to me that you'd continue to dive."

"It's simple, Tess. We all do what we have to do. Just as you have to continue drilling, I have to continue diving."

He rose and made his way into the bathroom. He shut the door, but she could still hear water running and the flushing of the toilet.

When he came out, he looked freshly washed and much more dressed than she. She envied him both those things. He walked to the nightstand, where his watch lay. When had he taken it off?

She shifted on the bed so she could watch him. "Look, I know little or nothing about diving in the depths that you're talking about, but I do know that it's much more complicated and dangerous than scuba diving. I know you can't breathe simple oxygen. It's a mixture of something. And if the mixture is one little bit off, you're in trouble. Plus, if you come up too fast—"

His nod cut her off. "That's true." Casually he walked to the French doors, where she'd been minutes before.

"And I've heard of something called rapture—rapture of the deep."

"Nitrogen narcosis."

"Whatever. But I hear you get this feeling of great well-being, like being on really good drugs. Except you die, because it's almost certain you'll do something stupid, not to mention that the nitrogen pumping into your system is poisoning you."

He leaned an arm against the doorjamb. "Yeah, there's that."

"Damn it, Nick, are you *hearing* what I'm saying?"

Collected and composed, he turned to look at her. "Every single word."

She came off the bed. "And you know the dangers that can come from my rig. That's why you came to me in the first place."

His brows arched. "Your point?"

"My point, damn you, is that you've got no right to risk your life like that."

"It almost sounds as if you care."

She had to force herself to wait several beats before she answered. An instant reply would guarantee that she would give away her feelings for him. "Of course I care. I'd have the same concern for anyone I know."

He stood there, staring at her for what seemed an eternity. She could feel her pulse throb at the base of her neck and in the vein of her forehead. Had he guessed that she loved him?

"I'm sorry, Tess."

The anger and roughness in his voice had disappeared. Without warning, he had switched gears. "Sorry?"

He gestured to the bed. "I never meant for it to happen. I..." He rolled his shoulders.

She'd never seen him awkward, not in gesture or in word. But she was seeing it now.

He shook his head. "I tried my damnedest to resist you. Two nights ago, at the house, we almost—"

"I know." If she lived to be a hundred, she would probably never forget that moment when she'd made herself pull away from him.

"Just in case you have any doubts, stopping was one of the hardest things I've ever had to do in my life. And doing it took every ounce of control I had."

She shook her head. "It was hard for me, too, but I—"

"I know what you were thinking. You were afraid that I was using sex to get you to agree with what I wanted."

"I was thinking a lot of things."

"It's not true, Tess. It wasn't then, and it's not now."

"It doesn't matter what the reason was or is," she said almost wearily. "Let's face it, Nick. There have been too many emotions running between us. Sooner or later it was going to happen. And whether it happened two nights ago or tonight, it won't change my mind about the drilling.''

"I know that. I've known that all along.'' He ran an unsteady hand through his sun-streaked dark hair. "The thing is, Tess, from the first, I wanted you almost too much. I still want you...way too much.''

She could feel herself begin to tremble. "Is there such a thing as too much?''

"In our case, yeah, I think there just might be. Because if you take away the sex and leave only the subject of whether or not you'll stop drilling, there's no way both of us can win. Hell, we can't even compromise.''

"I know.'' She looked at her hands. "But if it helps, I feel the same way...about wanting you too much.''

"Yeah,'' he said softly, his eyes darkening with heat. "It helps.''

Slowly he crossed to her. Automatically, naturally, she held out her arms to him. And as he took her back to bed, the sheet slowly slipped from her body.

When she awoke the next morning, she was alone.

Nine

Ron stuck his head around the door to her office. "Jill's on line two."

Tess almost groaned. She was already in a bad mood. She didn't need a call from her sister to make it worse. She swore if Jill murmured one patronizing or gloating word about the fact that she'd already met the will's requirements, she would hire a hit man to go after her. "Thanks Ron." She picked up the phone.

"Good morning, Jill. To what do I owe this unexpected pleasure?" Her pleasant words didn't come close to matching her tone.

"I heard you were in danger."

Her mind went blank. "Danger?" She'd been too busy thinking about Nick and the night they'd spent together to consider much else.

"Oh, come on," Jill said impatiently. "Don't pla

dumb. You got yourself kidnapped so that Des would feel like he needed to go rescue you.''

''Oh, yeah, that. Well, it wasn't exactly a kidnapping.''

''I heard it was.''

''I went willingly, but once I was there, I was kept there until the next day.'' She swiveled her chair so she could look out the window at the Gulf. Nick was probably deep beneath the sea. She sent up a silent prayer that he was safe. On the other hand, she didn't exactly wish him well, either. Damn him. At the very least, he could have left her a note. ''It was one of those things that you kind of had to be there to understand.''

''Uh-huh. Well, *this* is what I understand. You got yourself into a situation that made Des feel he needed to step in and help you.''

She slowly smiled. ''You sound upset. What's the matter? Jealous that you didn't come up with the idea first?''

''Frankly, yes.''

Tess chuckled. ''Well, you don't have to worry. I turned down Des's offer of help.''

''So I heard. And I've got just one question. *Why?*''

''Because I was in no danger. And because I knew that, one way or another, I could get home by that afternoon.''

''Still, Tess. You passed up a golden opportunity to get Des all to yourself, and I don't understand why, unless it was somehow part of your scheme.''

''I can't explain it to you, Jill, but know this. I have no scheme to get Des, not yesterday, not today.''

For a couple of moments there was silence. Then, ''It was that guy at your birthday party, wasn't it? The one you danced with?''

''That's the one.''

''He was interesting, all right, but, Tess...*Des.*''

She had no intention of telling Jill the truth, that she'd

fallen so madly in love with Nick that now she could never marry another man, not even if that man did come with fifty percent of Baron International attached to him. But to lighten her mood, if only temporarily, she decided to give Jill a hard time. "Hey, did you ever think I might be using the old hard-to-get ruse on Des?"

"Are you?"

"Sorry. My methods are top secret. But I will say that Des was *very* worried about me. In fact, he told me some things that he's never said to me before. Things about the way he feels about me. Really *lovely* things." It was all true, though not in the ways she was implying. It was also guaranteed to put Jill into a tailspin.

"Bitch."

She nearly laughed out loud. "Why, Jill—such *language*."

"Never mind my language. You've got worse problems. Since it doesn't look as if you're going to be able to meet the will's conditions by your deadline, you're obviously pinning all your hopes on Des. But let me tell you something. I wouldn't do that, if I were you. The game is far from over."

"What can I say, Jill?" she asked, infusing her tone with brightness. "You're absolutely right. Now, you have a really great day. Goodbye."

She hung up the phone and dropped her face into her hands. The elation over getting the best of Jill had vanished even more quickly than she'd expected it to, and regret had rushed in to replace it. She shouldn't have baited her sister like she had, but it was a habit of a lifetime, a habit encouraged by their father.

What would it be like to be as close to her sisters as Nick was to Kathie? After all, Jill and Kit were the only two people in the world who really understood the pres sures under which they'd been raised—the pressure to measure up to their father's standards, the pressure to constantly compete and best one another. Sharing their emotions and feelings with one another might lighten some of the load the three of them carried on their individual shoulders.

But would that even be possible? She tried to envision a situation that would allow harmony to exist among them, and couldn't. Perhaps a few years down the road, if she and Kit were able to meét their father's goal for them and were able to join Jill in an equal partnership in the company, they could forget about their stupid competition. But for that to happen, Des would have to marry someone other than Jill or Kit or Tess. And the three of them would have to let go of a lot of old habits, along with years of hurtful words and deeds.

Even then, she couldn't envision them ever being as close as Kathie and Nick were. But would it be possible, she wondered, for them to find their way to at least some sort of amicable relationship?

It would be tough, no question about it. However, she'd once heard the longest journey began with one step. She swiveled her chair to her desk and placed her hand on the phone. If she called Jill back and apologized for baiting her, it might be a good first step.

The phone rang beneath her hand and she jumped.

"It's Vega," Ron called from the next room.

She let out a long, steadying breath, then picked up the phone. "Good morning, Jimmy. Give me some good news."

"As a matter of fact, I can do just that. The storm didn't touch us."

"Great."

"We got some of the fireworks and a little of the wind, but in the end, it was nothing to speak of."

"That *is* good news. That also means the ocean floor wouldn't have been disturbed, right?"

"If it was, it was minimal. Why?"

"An acquaintance of mine has a diving site nearby."

"Oh, yeah, I've seen the support ship as I've flown back and forth. What's he diving for?"

"There's a shipwreck down there that he's interested in, and it's in a precarious position on a scarp. If anything happens on our rig that might affect the ship, let me know, will you?"

"Sure. I keep you informed anyway."

"I know, and thanks."

Tess spent the rest of the day in her typical high-speed mode, doing what she did every day, making decisions, reading reports, solving problems. Her business interests ranged the world. She had to constantly monitor not only the condition and output of the wells themselves, but she had to make sure her working relationships with the countries and the politicians she did business with remained good.

But no matter how busy she stayed, or how hard she tried, she couldn't forget Nick or the night they'd spent together. From the start, their combined chemistry had been volatile. Last night it had finally exploded. And the explosion had been beyond her wildest imagination.

There had been times she couldn't breathe because the ecstasy was so strong. Then, just when she didn't think she could go any farther or reach any higher, he had proved her wrong and showed her there was yet another level of rapture to reach.

She'd infused every moment they'd spent together, every movement, every touch, every kiss, with her love. But just because she'd fallen in love with Nick didn't mean she'

completely lost her ability to think. When it came to sex,
he was a master, a magician, but he didn't love her.

He seemed to have finally accepted that she wasn't going
to change her mind about the drilling, but even if he hadn't,
it didn't matter. It wouldn't change one thing that had happened last night.

To him, it had been sex. To her, it had been love. But
both of them had experienced the same deep, immeasur-
able, intense fulfillment and satisfaction. Those kinds of
emotions couldn't be faked.

And then, while she'd slept, he had left, without a word
or a note, or any sign that he would ever return.

As the day drew to a close, she let Ron leave work early
for a date with his new girlfriend, but she continued to work
until her eyes blurred and her shoulders ached and she had
no choice but to stop.

Once in her bedroom, she slowly undressed, then sank
into a tub of hot, scented water, leaned her head back and
closed her eyes. She was tired, but she was used to being
tired. She hurt, and to a certain extent she was used to
hurting. But she'd never known what pain was until she'd
awakened this morning, alone. And she didn't know how
to make the pain go away.

The perfumed scent of bathwater drew Nick through the
bedroom and into the bathroom. At the sight of Tess, his
breath caught in his throat and he came to a standstill. She
lay in the tub, her eyes closed, her arms floating on the
fragrant oiled water, her legs stretched out. She looked relaxed, but not completely.

He'd seen her face at the moment of climax, when she'd
let go of everything except him. But now, though any other
person might not be able to detect it, he could see the tiny
lines of tension on her face. They bothered him. Yet the

memory of last night, the sight of her now, had him hardening.

Her skin glowed sleekly with a faint rose color. Her blond hair was pinned atop her head, but at the back of her neck, tendrils had escaped, and the moisture had tightened them into small, beguiling curls. Her breasts rose halfway out of the water, her nipples so soft he could almost taste their sweetness.

He had to fight the urge to kneel beside the tub, lean over and pull her nipples into his mouth one at a time. With one suck he knew he could have them tight and her breasts throbbing for more. He wasn't bragging. It was fact. After last night, he knew her body inside and out.

He hadn't meant to return to her tonight.

That first night he'd met her, he'd tried his best to resist her, but somewhere inside him, he'd known that before he would be satisfied, he was going to have to have her. Still, he'd tried to fight his growing need for her.

She'd admitted that she thought his pursuit of her was to coerce her into doing what he wanted. But she gave him way too much credit.

Truthfully, there wasn't much he wouldn't do to make his grandpa's dream come true. He'd crisscrossed the country many times to get the needed backing. He'd worked for years, pushing himself mentally and physically, to get to where he was now, shoring up the ship so the true excavation could begin. But he would never, ever willingly hurt Tess.

Yet that was just what he was doing.

She'd made it too easy for him. She was entirely too desirable. She'd unconsciously molded herself against him when they'd danced. She'd responded to his kisses with the fire of someone who had never been truly kissed before.

And when they'd made love, she'd gone up in flames and taken him with her.

Still, in no way was it her fault. His original plan had been simply to get one-on-one time with her so he could tell her his story. But when he'd seen her, complicated needs and desires had clouded his intent.

He'd wanted to hold her, so he'd asked her to dance. He'd wanted to taste her and feel her soft lips, so he'd kissed her. He'd wanted to have her, so last night he'd finally taken her to bed. And still it wasn't enough for him. He wanted more.

He couldn't explain what he was feeling to himself. How could he explain it to her? Besides, under the circumstances, anything he told her would be suspect.

Tess opened her eyes and looked up at him. Immediately her expression turned wary. "I didn't think you'd be coming back."

"To be honest, I wasn't sure myself. But it turned out...I had to."

She hesitated, expression after expression chasing across her face too quickly for him to read them. Then, slowly, she lifted her arms to him. "Join me."

He began tearing at his clothes, unable to get them off fast enough. He knew that soon the day would come when he would pay for his greediness, but right now all he could think of was his all-consuming need for her. He slipped into the scented water, then into her.

The next morning, Ron answered the phone, then called out, "It's Kit."

She smiled. Chances were, the news about Des offering to rescue her had finally reached her younger sister. Remembering her thoughts of yesterday about trying to be close with her sisters, she decided to try something new—

being nice. Kit wasn't as hard-boiled as Jill. Instead she was wild as the land she governed and rebellious as a west Texas storm. Tess never knew which way she would jump.

She reached for the phone. "Good morning, Kit. How are you today?"

"Cut out the Mary Sunshine crap. I'm not interested."

Tess looked at the ceiling, searching for divine guidance. She found none.

"I heard about the ruse you tried to pull on Des."

"It wasn't a ruse, Kit. Besides, you don't have to worry. I didn't take him up on his offer."

"But you made him *think* about you, which, as we know, is half the battle with him."

"I—" Automatically she started to defend herself, but Kit sounded as unhappy as she'd ever heard her. "Kit, what's the matter?"

"Oh, gee, Tess, I don't know. What could be wrong? I've got the best job in the world, running this ranch, and I simply couldn't be happier."

"Then why do you sound so *un*happy? Are you worried about making the will's goal? You've got two more years, you know."

"That stupid will is the last thing I'd worry about."

"Okay." Obviously Kit had gotten up on the wrong side of the bed this morning. "Anything else I can do for you today?"

"Yeah. Lay off Des."

"Okay."

There was stunned silence on the other end. Then, "Did you just agree to stop running after Des?"

"I've never run after Des, Kit, but yes, basically that's what I agreed to."

"Why?"

There was no point in bringing Nick into the explanation

Nick had walked into her life as suddenly as he would one day walk out of it. And, as usual, she would be left to deal with her pain alone. "I've decided that if I can meet the will's demands, I'll be perfectly satisfied to have my one-sixth of the company."

"You're kidding, right?"

"No, Kit, I'm honestly not. As it is, I'm going to have enough of a battle to meet Father's conditions. But even though I may be going right down to the wire with it, I believe I can. After that, I don't want to wage any more battles. I'll be happy."

"If you're serious, that's the most amazing thing I've ever heard."

"I couldn't be more serious. Anything else?"

"No. I guess that's it. But, Tess?"

"Yes?"

"Good luck."

She smiled. Admittedly, Kit's tone when she'd wished her luck had been somewhat reluctant, but it didn't change the fact that she had said the word. She would take it. "Thank you. Talk to you later."

"Yeah, sure. Bye."

Tess hung up the phone, still smiling.

The phone rang again. This time it was Jimmy Vega. "Hi, Jimmy."

"Hi. Just called to report that things are finally settling down and going our way. No broken drill bits or equipment. The last few days have been smooth as silk."

"Great. That's music to my ears. Now if we can just hit the oil on schedule…"

"It'll be a couple more months, but I've got my money on your instincts. There's a lot of oil down there, and we're heading right for it."

"Thanks for the confidence, Jimmy. Talk to you later."

After hanging up, Tess leaned back in her chair. She ticked off the good things that had happened so far this morning. Kit had done the previously unheard of thing of actually wishing her good luck. Jimmy had called to report good news. And then there had been last night.

Nick had showed up and made love to her with an intensity that had been even stronger than the night before. But once again, when she awoke this morning, he was gone.

That night became a routine that was repeated over and over.

Just when she was certain Nick wouldn't show up, he did, hungry for her. Without words, they would fall on the bed and make love until they were both exhausted.

Even after their lovemaking, they never said much to each other. She didn't ask how his work was going, and he didn't question her about her drilling. But their tacit agreement to focus on lovemaking and forget about any other subject encompassed far more than their respective jobs. Anything personal was also strictly off-limits.

Tess knew why *she* remained silent. She was afraid that her words would in some way reveal to him how very much she loved him. She was convinced that if he were to find out, he would disappear even faster than he eventually would anyway. As to why he remained silent, it was no doubt as simple as her reason was. He didn't want to say anything that she might misconstrue as a commitment.

And so it continued, days of work, nights of passion. During the day, when rational thought was possible, she tried to warn herself to remain more objective about what was happening between Nick and her. But during the nights, when he held her in his arms, she would realize that she was already so deeply in love with him, and so deperate with wanting him, that when he left, she probably wouldn't survive.

The night was bright, with a full moon. Its light illuminated the terrace with a silver brilliance and streamed through the French doors into Tess's bedroom, providing light for the two entwined lovers as they lay on the bed, facing each other, recovering from an exhausting bout of lovemaking. Only the waves of the Gulf breaking onto the shore, along with their ragged breathing, interrupted the silence of the night.

Nick held Tess to him with a possessiveness that surprised even him. But then, right from the first, nothing about his feelings for Tess had been normal. He was still inside her and he didn't want to pull out. As long as he remained inside her, he could pretend she was his. And as long as she remained content to be held, he planned not to break the connection.

Slowly, gently, so as not to startle her, he lifted a hand and pushed her damp hair away from her face. "Are you sleepy?"

"I'm tired," she replied softly, "but not ready to go to sleep yet."

"You work long hours." He was very aware that he'd just crossed a line that had been drawn by both of them, though it hadn't been intentional. Thinking only of her, he had been trying to find out if he should leave her alone and let her go to sleep.

"Yes." Her answer was short and simple.

His hand lightly followed the smooth curves of her waist and hips. "I've been wondering about something."

She moved, breaking the sexual connection that he'd wanted to maintain as long as possible. "What's that?" she asked, rolling over on her back and stretching like a cat.

Desire stirred in his loins, but he did his best to ignore it, something that with Tess was almost impossible. Still, he tried. "The first night we met—it was your birthday party."

She looked at him, a faint smile on her lips. "I remember."

"From a couple of remarks I overheard, I gather it's an annual event, with only the party's location changing from year to year."

"Right. The change of location keeps it fresh and fun."

"I also gathered that you're the one who throws the party."

"Uh-huh." She raised an arm and rested it on the pillow above her head. The movement lifted her breast.

He had to consciously make himself stare into her eyes. "Why?"

"Why what?"

"Why do you have to throw your own birthday party? What about your family? Or your friends?"

Her brow puckered, and she didn't answer him right away. The silence stretched out so long, he wasn't sure she was going to answer him.

Finally, though, she spoke. "I suppose either Kathie or your grandmother throws you a party every year?"

He grinned. "Yeah, they do. Even though I'd just as soon not make a big deal out of it, it's important to them."

"Did you have a party every year when you were growing up?"

The question surprised him. "Of course. Doesn't every kid?"

"Yes," she said in a tone that made him think she was answering the question with extra care. "Were your parties fun?"

"Yeah. Sure."

"With cake and ice cream and gifts?"

"That's what a birthday party is, isn't it?"

She swallowed. "Back to your original question, I enjoy throwing my own parties. It's the only way I can insure that everything is just as I like it."

"So what you're basically admitting is that you're a control freak." He'd meant the comment to be funny, but she didn't smile.

"I suppose so. Anyway, why all the questions about my birthday parties?"

"I just thought it was odd that you throw your own parties, that's all."

"Not everyone was raised the way you and Kathie were raised, Nick."

"What do you mean?"

She shook her head. "Never mind."

"Are you saying you weren't given birthday parties when you were growing up?"

"The lady who has worked for my uncle for years always baked me a cake. She did the same for my sisters. And that's the last thing I'd like to say on that particular subject. I think I'm sleepy now."

"Hey," he said softly. "I didn't mean to dredge up any bad memories."

"Don't worry. You didn't."

But he had, he thought. He would give money to know the true story, but he would probably never hear it. One of these nights, when he walked into her bedroom, she was going to tell him to leave. It might be after they struck oil in the rig and she was getting ready to return to her Dallas office. Or it might even be sooner. Quite simply, she could grow tired of him arriving every night and expecting her to welcome him with open arms.

With their objectives so diametrically opposed, it was a

wonder she even let him through the door. But she reveled in their lovemaking as much as he did. Pure and simple, they pleasured each other, though pleasure was too tame a word for the passion they ignited in each other night after night.

But he wasn't kidding himself. Soon she would either leave Corpus or grow tired of him. Or both. She had a whole other life in Dallas. As for him, if he got lucky, and nothing happened on her rig to disturb the *Águila*'s site, he would be in Corpus for the next few years. After that, he would return to Austin and his teaching.

He couldn't see a future for the two of them, but his need for her continued to grow. Consequently, each night when he drove into her, he could feel himself becoming more and more desperate.

If only there was some way to make her need him as much as he needed her. If only there was some way to make her his permanently. But there was nothing he had that she wanted. Besides, she was too independent. If nothing else, the fact that she threw her own birthday parties told him that.

Their worlds were completely different, except when they were in bed. Here they could shut out the world. The problem was, he knew he couldn't count on this relative peace to continue for much longer.

Ten

Tess stood at her office window, staring at the Gulf, wondering what Nick was doing at that exact moment. It was a familiar position for her. Every minute of every day, she worried about him. Each night, when he came to her, it took all her willpower to resist begging him to give up the deep-water diving.

But how could she expect him to give up trying to attain his goal when she wasn't willing to give up trying to reach hers?

She hadn't done any research on the subject, yet common sense told her that the use of submersibles was the safest way to go. True, something from the ship could fall on the submersible and trap both it and the person inside it. But the danger of that happening was minuscule compared to the inherent dangers of the diving Nick was doing.

She'd flown out to the rig yesterday, and the helicopter had passed over Nick's support ship. The divers' flag had

been up. When he'd come to her last night, it had taken
every last ounce of willpower she possessed to keep from
begging him to stop diving. She hadn't done it, but she
hadn't been able to stop herself from clinging to him a little
harder.

She heard the phone ring on Ron's desk and returned to
her chair just as Ron called to her. "It's Vega."

She picked up the phone. "Hi, Jimmy. Everything going
okay?"

"It is now, but, Tess, a little while ago we came as close
to a blowout as I've ever been or want to be again."

She could feel the blood drain from her face. "Oh, my
God. What happened?"

"We drilled into an unexpected high pressure pocket,
and if I hadn't been there watching the instruments, it could
have been disaster."

"Thank God you caught it in time."

"Yeah."

She shut her eyes. "Jimmy…"

"I know. Believe me, I know."

She couldn't think of any words adequate enough, but
then, with Jimmy she didn't have to. He knew the ramifi-
cations as well as she did, probably even better.

If a blowout had occurred, it would have been a disaster
too horrible to contemplate. Any pipes or equipment in the
bore hole would have come shooting out with enough pressure to cause a catastrophe of massive proportions. In addition, any fuel or gas in the bore hole would have been
propelled to the surface and ignited into an instant fire that
would have created an explosion big enough to kill everyone on the rig.

And if Nick had been diving, he would also have been
killed. His death would have been caused by the percussion
of the explosion or by the ocean floor earthquake or b

flying pipes and equipment that, if they had enough force behind them, could have reached him. Any one of the three things would have been enough to kill him, and it very well could have been all three.

The earthquake alone would have sent both him and the *Águila* plunging over the side of the scarp into the abyss. And when the *Águila* finally came to rest, Nick's body would have been buried, his lifeline cut.

Jimmy kept talking, but her mind was on Nick.

When she hung up, she was shaking. She quickly filled Ron in, then asked him to hold all her calls. She went to the terrace and stared at the point on the horizon where she knew Nick's crew and ship were. God, if it hadn't been for Jimmy's fast action, Nick would almost certainly have been killed today.

She started to pace, her mind locked on the horror of what had almost happened. With today's modern technology, blowouts were very rare. Unfortunately, though, the very genuine possibility still existed.

They'd already known they were drilling in an overpressurized zone, and they'd been prepared. But they'd also known that the conditions the drill encountered could change within a few meters and they could hit a pocket that contained an even higher amount of pressure than was the norm for their site, which was exactly what had happened today. It was why everyone on the rig had to stay on their toes at all times. It was also why she'd hired Jimmy Vega as her supervisor. He was the best.

She lost track of how many times she paced the length of the terrace and back. She had no idea what time it was. Fear had her in a viselike grip. Her mind was spinning, racing, but always it returned to the same subject. If Nick had been killed today...

Suddenly she whirled and returned to her office. Without

a word to Ron, she placed a call to Jimmy. When he answered, she didn't hesitate. "I want the drilling stopped now, Jimmy. *Now.*"

"What?"

"I want it stopped for at least two months."

"Tess, are you crazy? We had a close call today, but—"

"Listen to me, Jimmy. Stop the drilling now. Keep all personnel on the payroll. Make up a schedule so that you have a maintenance crew working on the rig at all times, but rotate them so that everyone will have a chance for a paid vacation."

"Tess, what in the hell is going on? I thought—"

"And you thought right, but this is just something I have to do for now, and I won't explain it. Two months, Jimmy. Then, at the end of that time, we'll start back up again at full speed. So make sure the rig is ready to go at that time."

"Sure. Okay, but...?"

He sounded bewildered, and she couldn't blame him. "You did a great job today, Jimmy. Arrange it so that you can get in some vacation time, too. In the meantime, I'll be in contact, and I'll definitely be back in two months." She hung up the phone and stared at it. She'd just cut her own throat.

"Tess?"

She glanced up. Ron was standing in the doorway of her office, looking thunderstruck. "You heard?"

He nodded. "Do you know what you're doing?"

She flashed him a rueful smile. "Unfortunately, I do. Pack up. I want to be ready to leave here in an hour."

"Where are we going?"

"Dallas, to start with."

Nick climbed the steps to the terrace. It had been a bruta' day, and all he could think of was getting to Tess. He coulc think of nothing he would like better than to soak in a nice hot bath with her, then make slow, hot love until steam was coming off the water. He smiled in anticipation.

The lights were off in Tess's bedroom, he noticed, but that wasn't unusual. Maybe she was already in the tub, waiting for him, with candles lit. But her French doors were closed. That *was* unusual.

He turned the handle, and the door opened. "Tess?" He looked around for a light switch and found it. The room was quiet, and Tess was no where to be seen. "Tess?"

He walked into the bathroom. The tub was empty. The area on the marble counter where she kept her makeup and perfume was bare. A chill crawled down his spine. An investigation of her closet revealed that almost three-fourths of her clothes were missing. Had a sudden business trip come up? He'd given her the phone number on his support ship. Why hadn't she called him to tell him where she was going?

Then he saw it. An envelope was propped up on one of the pillows on the bed. He tore it open and read. *I've ordered the drilling stopped for two months. I hope that will give you the time you need.*

Stupefied, he stared at the paper. She hadn't even bothered signing it.

"*Guadalupe!*" he bellowed, striding angrily out of the bedroom and through the house. "Guadalupe!"

"Yes, sir?" An apprehensive Guadalupe appeared.

"Where did Miss Baron go?"

"I don't know."

"She didn't tell any of the staff?"

"No, sir."

"Then did she say when she would return?"

She nodded. "In two months."

Nick let out a string of oaths that had Guadalupe backing

up. As soon as he saw her reaction, he stopped. "I'm sorry, Guadalupe. I apologize." He let out a long, shaky breath. "Do you have any other information about her? Did she say anything, perhaps even something small, that might help me know where she went?"

"No." Despite his apology, Guadalupe continued to eye him cautiously.

"Okay. Thank you."

Guadalupe turned to leave.

"Wait. Please, could you get me a pen and piece of paper? I want to give you a number so that if you hear anything from Ms. Baron, anything at all, you can call and tell me. Okay?"

She nodded and went off to get the pen and paper.

Now that the rig had stopped drilling, Nick could do what he had to do with the assurance that, if anything went wrong, it wouldn't come from outside forces. It was up to him to continue to make sure his operation ran safely. But keeping his mind on his work was much harder than he would have expected.

The days were difficult, but the nights were impossible. He ached, he missed Tess so much, and he spent a lot of time taking cold showers that did absolutely no good.

At first he tried to track her down. He called her Dallas office and spoke to the now all-too familiar Ron, but according to Ron, she wasn't there. When Nick pushed, the assistant finally told him that Tess was making an inspection tour of all her business sites. When he asked for her itinerary, Ron informed him that Tess had specifically asked that it not be given to him.

He attempted to reach her two sisters. At first he was rebuffed, but after telling each of their assistants that he was calling about Tess, he was put through. Jill took the

ews of Tess's abrupt departure strangely. She muttered
omething about Tess crying wolf one too many times, and
hat this time, she was going to call Des herself and tell
im not to bother. Then she'd hung up. Kit's response had
een one he could better understand. She'd simply in-
ormed him that if Ron had said Tess had gone off on a
usiness trip, then that was where she'd gone, but that no,
he didn't have a clue where she would be.

Those short conversations had left Nick frustrated. He
ouldn't believe that Tess's trip had been a planned one. If
t had been, then why hadn't she told him? What had hap-
ened to cause her to bolt?

Had he done something wrong? Said something that hurt
er? He searched his mind for some sort of clue but could
ind nothing. His memory of their last night together was
trong. As usual, their time in each other's arms had con-
isted of sheer, unadulterated pleasure, and they'd both
een left sated and drowsy.

Afterward, she had fallen asleep in his arms. He remem-
ered he'd watched her for a while, listening to her breathe,
omething he'd done before. It was such a simple pleasure
nd one he'd never bothered to analyze.

After their lovemaking, when all the energy had been
rained from her, she slept with the peace of a child. It was
he only time he ever saw her truly relaxed. He didn't need
o think twice to know she was under pressure she never
alked about.

He'd always understood that by asking her to stop the
rilling, he was asking her to give up an enormous amount
f money that would have a long, long line of zeros in it.
And he'd known that if she agreed, it would be a sacrifice
hat would show up on her profit-and-loss statement at the
nd of the year. But he'd also known it wouldn't come near
o breaking her financially.

Plus, although he could be wrong, he'd never received the impression that it was financial greed that kept her drilling. He'd taunted her with that at the beginning, but after he'd gotten to know her, he'd come to the conclusion that there was something else at the core of it all. But no matter how he'd poked and prodded at her, trying to figure out why she wouldn't give an inch on the matter, he hadn't been able to get any closer to an answer he could understand.

The night after he'd contacted Tess's two sisters, he went to her house. Guadalupe let him in.

"Thank you." He made a point of smiling at her. "I'm not going to stay long."

She nodded, her demeanor formal. "Is there anything can get you while you are here?"

"No." Then he hastened to add, "Thank you, anyway."

With another nod, she disappeared.

He slowly walked through the big main living room with its walls of windows that overlooked the terrace, the sloping green lawn and the Gulf beyond. But it wasn't the view he was there for. In fact, he wasn't entirely sure why he was there. He just wanted to be where Tess had been and where the two of them had been together.

But there was an empty feel about the whole house. By rights, it shouldn't feel so deserted, because he knew the staff was there, and all the rooms looked just as they had when Tess had been there, giving the impression that she would walk in at any minute. But the house still felt empty.

In her bedroom, he sat on the end of the bed and looked around. God, he would give anything, do anything, to have her back with him here. Physically, he craved her in the worst possible way, his body felt tormented with need for her. But surprisingly, his desire for her went beyond the physical. Emotionally, he realized, he needed simply to cradle her in his arms and hold her with no sex in mind.

He loved her.

There it was, out in the open at last. He'd finally let himself admit what his heart and soul must have secretly known for a long while. He was in love with Tess.

In all probability his heart had been lost the moment he first laid eyes on her. Then he'd possessed her and found that he couldn't get enough of her. Even when he'd been mad as hell at her, he'd still wanted her. But he'd never let himself think beyond that point.

Things had settled into something of a routine with them. Each night he'd showed up here and she'd opened her arms to welcome him. He'd known that it wouldn't last. He'd also known he wanted to find a way to keep her with him, but he hadn't thought of being in love with her. For some reason, it just never occurred to him. He lived in the present with her. He lived for the nights they spent together.

Then she'd disappeared from his life, and in the process of trying to figure out what had happened, he hadn't had any choice but to face the truth, and when he did, he wondered why it had taken him so long to figure it out. He loved her. He wanted to spend the rest of his life with her, each day, each night. He *had* to have her back.

If only he could find something that would help him make sense of why she'd left in the first place. And, maybe more importantly, he needed to understand why she had finally decided to stop drilling.

The last time they'd talked about it had been the night of the storm. She'd told him then in no uncertain terms that he couldn't stop. Yet now she had.

Why? He shoved himself off the bed and began to pace. Could it conceivably be that she'd made the decision because she'd fallen in love with him? That thought stopped him in his tracks. But if that had been the reason, why in the hell had she left?

No, she couldn't possibly be in love him. She'd never shared any of herself with him other than the physical. She was too independent. She'd left too abruptly. She didn't, couldn't love him.

But facts were definitely missing.

As much as he'd told her and showed her about himself and his reasons for wanting to preserve the *Águila* and harvest the gold, she'd never once hinted at the reason she couldn't stop the drilling. There had to be something more at stake than money. Except now she'd given the decision to stop. Had that something, whatever it was, simply gone away or ceased to be vital?

He shook his head. No matter which route he took with his thoughts, there wasn't one damn thing about any of this that made sense.

He moved around the bed and grabbed the phone. After punching in his credit card number, he dialed the number of an old college friend who worked as a journalist for the *Dallas Morning News*. Without preamble, he asked him for a favor.

The next morning he was at work at the *Águila*. For whatever reason, Tess had given him this gift of two months. He didn't plan to waste a minute of it. Besides, the one thing he was positive of was that in less than two months she would return.

It was good to be back, Tess reflected, as she unpacked her suitcases. If nothing else, returning to the house in Corpus Christi and settling in meant that she could finally stay in one place for longer than three days. And she was way past ready for that. She'd had enough of hotels and airplanes.

She'd already been in contact with Jimmy Vega and given the order to resume drilling first thing in the morning. Though she didn't know whether she'd given Nick enough time to finish shoring up the ship, she'd given him most of the time he'd asked for, and that was all she could do.

Now she would have to sweat out the next few months and pray like hell that they would strike oil. After that, she wasn't sure what would be possible in regards to meeting the will's condition. She just knew one thing. Giving up was not in her genes.

"Hello, Tess."

She whirled. "Nick." She was stunned. "How did you know I was back?"

"I didn't know for sure." He walked slowly through the open French doors, his gaze fixed firmly on her. "But during the last few days there's been increased activity out at your rig. I've checked here each night since."

"How did you know about the increased activity? You can't see the rig from your site."

"Helicopter flights increased, plus I would drive the runabout out a bit so I could use binoculars."

"Oh." She turned to her unpacking, trying not to think too hard about how her heart had jumped when she'd seen him or how fast it was pounding. She forced herself to take a deep, calming breath.

During the last two months she'd spent long, lonely, sleepless nights, trying to push all thoughts of Nick from her mind. It had been useless. Her body had constantly ached for him, and her mind had retained perfect recall of every moment she'd spent with him. But most of all, her heart had hurt because of her love for him that would never be returned.

Now he was here, standing in front of her, dressed at his most casual in jeans and a dark teal T-shirt. With the dark color so close to his face, the already vivid color of his amber eyes was more pronounced, their strength more piercing.

"Your grandparents—are they both okay?"

"Yes."

"How's the *Águila*? Have you been able to shore it up sufficiently?"

"It's as good as it's going to get. Why did you leave, Tess?"

She could feel the waves of his anger surging toward her. It was almost like the night of the storm, when they'd first made love. Then it had been waves of lust and passion that had overwhelmed her. Now it was anger, and she had very few weapons against it. The only thing she could do to protect herself was try to keep her guard up.

She hadn't gone through two months of hell only to once again be caught up in a maelstrom of passion. She still loved him, maybe even more than when she'd left. But over the past two months, she'd attempted to scrape together every last ounce of objectivity she could manage about him. The result was that she'd come to an important conclusion. If she let her guard down and once again accepted him as her lover, there would be nothing left of her heart or of her but pieces when he walked out her door for the final time.

He didn't love her, and one day soon he would grow tired of her. If not tonight, then perhaps six weeks from now. If not six weeks, then perhaps six months. But when it came right down to it, it really didn't matter when it happened. She had to remain strong, stop any passion before it started and convince him that she wasn't interested in resuming where they'd left off.

She pulled a couple of dresses from her suitcase and hung them in the closet. "Once I gave the order to stop the drilling, there was no reason for me to stay here. I made the decision that my time would be better spent elsewhere.''

"And you didn't think I'd be even mildly interested in that decision?''

She'd known that sooner or later this confrontation would come. She'd hoped she could have a chance to settle in and catch her breath first. She glanced at him, then away. She reached into the suitcase and pulled out a pant suit. "I thought you'd be happy. I made the decision you wanted. I also left you the note, telling you so. After that…'' She gave a nonchalant shrug.

He placed his hands on his hips, and his amber eyes flashed dark fire. "Okay, Tess, let's cut right through the crap. I'll concede the fact that your business is far-flung and that you felt, since you'd stopped the drilling here, that your time could be better spent elsewhere. That makes perfect business sense.''

She tensed for the next volley she knew would come and it came fast.

"But damn it, Tess—what about *us?*''

She bent to reach for a sweater, paused for a fraction of a second, then lifted it out of the case and straightened, certain he hadn't noticed her pause. "I don't like good-byes.''

He exhaled a long breath, then walked to the dresser where, before he'd arrived, she'd absently tossed a camisole, meaning to put it in the drawer later. He picked it up and rubbed the silk and lace material between his thumb and fingers.

"Okay,'' he said, continuing to finger the camisole, "let's go another way. I lost count of the times you told me no. So what happened to make you change your mind?''

The sight of him fingering the camisole, an intimate undergarment that had been against her skin, unnerved her. She walked over and carefully took it from him. "I'm not sure what you want me to say, Nick. You worked long and hard to get me to make the decision you wanted. So I made it. But now it's not enough for you? Remember that, thanks to you, I met your grandparents. They touched me. I liked them a great deal. And I just kept thinking about them." She shrugged again, as if, in the end, her decision had been easy. "Finally I decided it was the right thing to do."

Nodding, he leaned against the dresser and crossed his arms over his chest. Watching him, she saw something that made her pause. There was an ever-so-slight change in him that she might have missed if she hadn't been keeping such a careful eye on him. Still, she couldn't identify what was different about him. It could very well be her imagination.

"I have something I need to tell you, Tess. I called up an old friend about a week after you left. He was one of my roommates in college, but now he's an investigative reporter for the *Dallas Morning News.*"

Tension and dread gripped her as she anticipated what he would say next.

"He has more resources at his command than I do, so I asked him as a favor to dig around and see what he could find out about your family, its background, the company and…you."

Anger rushed through her, extinguishing the dread. Depending on what he'd learned, the knowledge could leave her completely vulnerable to him—something she couldn't afford. "Just what in the hell gave you the right to do such a thing? I had *done* what you asked. Why couldn't you simply let it be?"

"Because it didn't make sense to me and I needed it to. I—" He gestured vaguely. "Obviously the reason you made the decision was for me and my family. Except righ from the first, you'd been so adamant that you *couldn't*. I needed to find out what had changed.''

She pointed at him, her anger so great she was almost shaking. ''If I'd known you were going to invade my privacy, not to mention my family's, I would *never* have stopped the drilling, and you and the *Águila* be damned.''

''Believe me,'' he said, his expression grave, ''I knew when I made the request of Jerry that you wouldn't like it.'' He paused, as if giving careful consideration to what he would say next. ''But at the time, I just thought I'd get an explanation that would satisfy me, and that would be that.''

She pointed again, this time to the open French doors. ''Get out.''

He shook his head. ''I'll go, but not yet. First I want to tell you what I found out, because there's still something I don't understand.''

''And you think I care?'' Her hands clenched and unclenched at her side. ''God, Nick. You got the drilling stopped. You even had me for a while. Why wasn't that enough for you?''

With Nick, her emotions had always run high, but she'd never expected anger. Now, though, she was practically choking with it. The thing she feared the most was to have her feelings for him laid bare. That would leave her absolutely defenseless. And she had this awful feeling that that was exactly what was about to happen.

He moved his hand in a pacifying gesture, and once again she thought she caught a glimpse of something different about him. Her curiosity was just enough to stop her from going over and bodily pushing him out the door.

''I found out that when you ordered the drilling stopped, you made a far greater sacrifice than I ever could have imagined. In fact, I'm staggered by it.''

He'd found out about the clause in the will. After that, it wouldn't have taken a rocket scientist to figure out why she'd given the order. She waited for what he would say next, dreading the sound of pity that would fill his voice.

But instead of saying anything, he slipped his hands into the pockets of his jeans, then brought them out again, glanced toward the terrace for several moments, then at her, a frown on his face.

That was when she realized what was different about him. He was *uncertain* about something. She'd never seen him hesitate about anything. He'd always been completely assured, even when he'd maneuvered her into the position of having to spend the night at his grandparents' house.

He glanced at his feet, then looked at her. "Why, Tess? Why would you make such a huge sacrifice for me?" He gestured, and this time she thought she saw his hand tremble. He stared at her, his brow furrowed. "As I understand it, because of your decision, it's now almost one hundred percent certain that you'll lose your part of your family's company. You *needed* that time you gave me. God, Tess, why didn't you tell me? If I'd known..."

Her knees suddenly weak, she sank onto her bed. If he had figured out that she loved him, her decision would make sense to him. Yet he was still saying he didn't understand, which meant she still had a shot at keeping her feelings to herself. "Believe it or not, Nick, I have a heart." She made her tone very matter-of-fact. "The day I made the decision, we came close to having a blowout on the rig. I decided I didn't want anyone's death on my conscience. Not your men, or you, or my crew. So I stopped all operations so that a complete maintenance check could be conducted." It wasn't a complete lie, and he just might buy it.

His shoulders slumped, once again something she wouldn't have noticed if she hadn't been watching him so carefully. Then, slowly, he walked around the bed and went down on bent knee in front of her.

He gazed up at her. "When you just left without saying goodbye, I felt like I'd been hit with a battering ram. I went a little crazy. Ron, as usual, was no help. I even called your sisters, trying to find out where you were, but they gave me the impression they couldn't have cared less." He reached for her hand and looked at it. "It's probably a good thing I didn't know where you were, because if I'd known, I would have gone after you instead of staying here and taking care of business."

He laced his fingers through hers. By doing that, it would make it harder for her to pull her hand from his, though she couldn't be sure if that was why he'd done it. She couldn't read him, not at all.

"Finally I calmed down," he said, his gaze searching her face, "and I realized I had no other alternative but to wait two months until you returned. That was when I started thinking. During the day I'd been focusing on the *Águila*, and at night I'd been coming here and focusing on you."

She could feel herself holding her breath. She had no idea what he was leading up to, but she could hear an uncertainty in his voice that matched the way he was acting.

"But when you disappeared, I had no choice but to stop and think about it. That's when I realized how vitally important you had become to me. And I figured out something should have known from the beginning. I figured out I love you, Tess."

She was stunned. It was the last thing she'd expected to hear him say. Her fears had been unfounded. *He* was the one who was setting aside his pride and laying bare his heart, and she knew exactly how hard it was for him, because she knew exactly how hard it would be for her.

He hadn't guessed she loved him, she realized. How could he? From his point of view, she'd walked away from him without a backward glance. She hadn't even given him the courtesy of a phone call. She'd told Ron not to give him her itinerary. Now she understood his uncertainty.

He was opening himself up, telling her that he loved her without any reassurance that his love would be returned. It obviously hadn't occurred to him that the only reason she could have made such a decision was because she loved him.

In effect, she'd given up her part of the company for him, but he'd given up his pride for her. To her way of thinking, it was an even trade.

"Tess?"

Tears of pure bliss appeared unbidden in her eyes. She smiled unsteadily and squeezed his hand. "I can't begin to tell you how happy you've just made me, Nick. In fact, I'm overjoyed." She blinked away the tears. "I love you more than I can ever tell you."

"You…" He slowly shook his head, and a trace of wonderment entered his expression. "You're not just saying that, are you? Because if you are—"

"I wouldn't say something like that if it weren't true." She pulled her hand from his and tenderly framed his face. "Nick, I stopped the drilling because I couldn't bear the idea that I was putting you in even more danger than you already were. And I left because I badly needed some breathing space from you. I needed to find some objectivity because I was afraid that if I stayed, I would eventually be so crushed when you left that I would never recover."

His expression solemn, he closed his fingers over her wrists and pulled her hands down to hold them. "God Tess. I love you. I will never leave you. *Ever.* Please believe that."

She nodded, her eyes tearing once again with happiness. "I do."

He laughed, and to her surprise his eyes glistened with tears that matched her own. "You love me. I can hardly believe it. But..." He shook his head, and the tears disappeared. "Tess, the sacrifice you made. I don't completely understand all the whys and wherefores, but the part I do understand is that you've probably lost your portion of Baron International."

"It could very well turn out that way, though if I wanted, I could keep the job. But I'm not going to give up yet. While I've been away, I've had some time to think about that, too, and I may have a plan. I don't know if it will work or not, but—"

"What is it? I'll help you. I'll do anything you want."

She laughed lightly. "Then make love to me, right here, right now."

"But your plan—I want to help."

"I'll tell you about it later. Right now I need you more than I can say."

With a groan, he stood, and with one sweep of his arm, he cleared the bed. The suitcase fell off the end and the remaining clothes in it scattered, but neither of them noticed. She reached for him and pulled him onto the bed with her.

She kicked off her shoes, thinking that at last she knew what true happiness was. She felt exhilarated, and, at the same time, she felt completely at peace.

He shifted so they lay side by side. "I hope you realize that now that I know you love me, I'm never going to let you get away from me." His voice was husky, and his touch was tender as he traced the lines of her face and jaw. "I want to marry you and have babies with you and live the rest of my life with you. I want to grow old with you."

"We'll be a family," she said with soft elation. One day she would tell him how important that was to her, but not now. She slipped her hands under his T-shirt to feel the familiar warmth and smoothness of his back, and joy bubbled up in her and filled her voice. "And we'll spend part of every summer at your grandparents' farmhouse so that our children can run free and discover their own treasure. And we'll start our own wall of pictures, and we'll continue the tradition of growing your great-grandmother's irises, lots and lots of them that we'll pass on to our children for their homes."

His amber eyes shone bright as the sun. "By the way, even though you haven't said it, you will marry me."

She laughed, because it had been a statement, not a question. His uncertainty was gone and his self-assurance had returned. "Yes, Nick," she whispered, as she drew his head down to kiss him, "I will marry you."

Epilogue

Seven months later

In her uncle's office on the Double B Ranch, Tess stood and handed one of the Baron International lawyers a check. "There it is—every penny required by my father's will, and four days early, I might add."

Uncle William smiled broadly from behind his desk. "Congratulations, Tess. I knew you'd do it."

She laughed. "Then you knew more than I did." She glanced at Nick, who was sitting to the left of her in one of the big easy chairs positioned in front of her uncle's desk. The pride beaming from his amber eyes and the rock-solid certainty that he loved her gave her a sense of security she'd never known before.

The rest of the family was there, as well. Des's chair was to her right. Jill sat on the other side of him. Kit was restlessly roaming the area behind the desk.

To her gratification, Des stood and reached over to give her a light, brief hug. "Let me add my congratulations to Dad's."

"Thank you."

Jill glanced pointedly at Nick. "I'm glad for you, Tess. It's just too bad you were put into a position where you had to sign away your rights to millions of dollars."

"Quit glaring at Nick," Tess said mildly. "If it's anyone's fault, it's Father's for making up that stupid clause in the first place. Besides, in the end I got exactly what was most important to me—my portion of the company *and* Nick."

Kit stopped her pacing, cocked a hip and frowned at Nick, then at Tess. "Still, you did give up an awful lot. And you were just plain lucky that Becca's husband works for one of the biggest oil companies in the world and was ready and willing to make you a deal. You could easily have lost it all."

"It was more than luck," Des said in quiet rebuke. "She chose Mel's company because he's a friend of hers, but any of the other big oil companies would have jumped at the chance."

Kit glared at Des, so Tess tried to divert her. "Turned out Mel and his company believed in me and my abilities more than my own father ever did. They're making the leap of faith that the well will pump enough oil over the years to make the money they paid me worthwhile."

Des rested his hand on Tess's shoulder. "You made an excellent deal, too. They not only paid you up front what you needed to satisfy the will, but they're also going to pay you a percentage of future royalties after they make back the advance."

"I suppose it's as good a deal as she could expect to make," Jill said, glaring at Des and at his hand on Tess' shoulder. "But she had to sign over the rights of something that had come about because of her own instincts and hard work."

Tess smiled at her sister. "Uh, was that by any chance a compliment?"

Jill's brow creased. "You know it's true, Tess. You're just like Kit and me. We never let go of anything that we've developed. Father taught us that. We keep what's ours, develop it as we see fit, then sit back and collect the money for the rest of the project's life. But because of your lost time, you had to give up the well, and in the end, you won't make nearly the money you would have if you'd been able to keep it."

"She's right," Kit said. "Have you calculated the money you're going to be losing?"

"Yes. But I've also calculated what I'll be gaining. I now have what should have been mine in the first place. Plus, I have something else that's far more valuable to me."

She reached for Nick's hand, and he stood. "We'd like to invite all of you to our wedding in two weeks. It's going to be a small ceremony, just for family, held in the little Uvalde church where Nick's grandparents, parents and his sister were married. Afterward we're going to throw a big party for all our friends, plus a great many people from the town."

"The party will be on the grounds of my grandparents' farm," Nick said, speaking for the first time. "We've arranged for it to be held beneath a giant tent, so we won't have to worry about the weather."

"And we're going to have a fantastic band," Tess said, continuing where Nick had left off. "There'll also be lots of fabulous food and drinks."

"And in the center of the tent," Nick said, "there'll be

a large, very impressive stack of gold with a sign below it saying there's much more to come.''

Tess slipped her arm around his waist. He slid his arm around her shoulders. ''And the best part of it will be that Nick's grandparents will be able to attend. And you, too, Uncle William.''

He nodded. ''I'll be there, even if I have to bring my doctor to do it. You can count on me, honey.''

''Good, because I think you're really going to enjoy meeting Nick's grandparents, especially his grandfather. I think you two will have a lot in common. And he'll need special medical arrangements, too.''

''I'll look forward to meeting him.''

Des smiled at her and Nick. ''Sounds like a wonderful occasion. I wouldn't miss it.''

''And I'll be there, too,'' Jill said quickly as soon as she heard Des's acceptance.

With a look of irritation at Jill, Kit shifted her stance. ''I suppose I will be, too.''

''That's great,'' Tess said brightly, ''because I want you two to be my bridesmaids.''

''Excuse me?'' Jill asked, clearly astonished.

''You're my sisters, and I can't think of any one else I would want more than you two to be by my side on the happiest day of my life.''

''You're kidding, right?'' Kit asked.

''Not one bit. So will you?''

Jill looked distinctly shell-shocked. ''I—I don't know.''

''Oh, sure you will,'' Des said with a smile at her. ''I know you wouldn't want to disappoint your sister, would you?''

''Uh, no, I guess not.''

Kit's expression was distrustful. ''Don't think for on

minute I'm going to wear one of those silly, odd-colored dresses with all the frills and ruffles.''

Tess laughed. ''I would never do that to you. We'll go shopping together, and you can pick out whatever you like.''

''Shopping together?'' Kit glanced at Jill, who still looked shell-shocked.

''In fact, we'll take Jill with us,'' Tess said, thoroughly enjoying herself. She knew this was only one step in getting closer to her sisters, but she was so happy, she was overflowing with optimism. ''Jill has excellent taste. We'll all buy our dresses at the same time.''

''I wouldn't miss this for the world,'' Des murmured.

Uncle William held out his hand to Nick. ''Congratulations, young man. You're getting a wonderful girl.''

Nick shook his hand. ''Thank you, sir.'' Then he looked at Tess, tenderness and love etched in his expression and glowing in his eyes. In fact, all the sunshine and brightness that flooded through the windows and into the room seemed concentrated on him, and because he was holding her against him, on her, too. ''All my life I've been looking for treasure, and now, at last, I've found it.''

*   *   *   *   *

Look out for The Barons of Texas: Jill
in July 2002 in a 2-in-1 volume called
His Kind of Woman.

▼™ SILHOUETTE®
DESIRE™

AVAILABLE FROM 21ST JUNE 2002

HIS KIND OF WOMAN

THE TEXAN'S TINY SECRET Peggy Moreland
Suzy Crane's and state governor Gil Riley's passion was explosive—
and so was their news of a baby-on-the-way! Suzy refused to become
a wife only to prevent scandal. But was that all sexy Gil had in mind?

THE BARONS OF TEXAS: JILL Fayrene Preston
All tycoon and friend Colin Wynne was asked to do was teach Jill how
to win the man of her dreams. But Colin's 'lessons' were all about
making Jill fall in love with *him*!

UP CLOSE AND PASSIONATE

LAST VIRGIN IN CALIFORNIA Maureen Child
Bachelor Battalion
Lilah Forrest would *never* marry a military man—not even sexy soldier
Sergeant Kevin Rogan. But this determined virgin just couldn't resist
the drill instructor's tender touch. Suddenly she agreed to meet
him—at the altar!

UNDERCOVER SULTAN Alexandra Sellers
The Sultans
Sheikh Haroun al Muntazir was honour-bound to recover a
priceless family jewel…but what was lovely operative Mariel's
mission? Until her motives were known, he would do *anything* to
keep her by his side…

AND BABY MAKES THREE

HAVING HIS CHILD Amy J Fetzer
One night of passion left Angela Justice pregnant and overjoyed! But
despite her overwhelming desire for Dr Lucas Ryder, she wouldn't
accept his proposal until she was certain of his true, eternal love!

MIXING BUSINESS…WITH BABY Diana Whitney
Successful bachelor Rick Blaine wanted to know everything about
employee Catrina Mitchell—*except* that she had a baby daughter. But
now single mum Catrina was in his blood…could he give up his
bachelor ways for fatherhood?

AVAILABLE FROM 21ST JUNE 2002

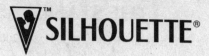

Sensation™

Passionate, dramatic, thrilling romances

FUGITIVE HEARTS Ingrid Weaver
THE SEDUCTION OF GOODY TWO-SHOES Kathleen Creighton
THE SHERIFF'S SURRENDER Marilyn Pappano
BORN A HERO Paula Detmer Riggs
PROTECTOR WITH A PAST Harper Allen
MOONGLOW, TEXAS Mary McBride

Special Edition™

Vivid, satisfying romances full of family, life and love

DADDY IN DEMAND Muriel Jensen
THE STRANGER IN ROOM 205 Gina Wilkins
WHEN I SEE YOUR FACE Laurie Paige
STORMING WHITEHORN Christine Scott
STARTING WITH A KISS Barbara McMahon
STRANGER IN A SMALL TOWN Ann Roth

Superromance™

*Enjoy the drama, explore the emotions,
experience the relationship*

WHITE PICKET FENCES Tara Taylor Quinn
THE NEGOTIATOR Kay David
A SELF-MADE MAN Kathleen O'Brien
SNOW BABY Brenda Novak

Intrigue™

Danger, deception and suspense

NIGHT-TIME GUARDIAN Amanda Stevens
TO PROTECT THEIR CHILD Sheryl Lynn
SOMEONE TO PROTECT HER Patricia Rosemoor
THE ARMS OF THE LAW Jenna Ryan

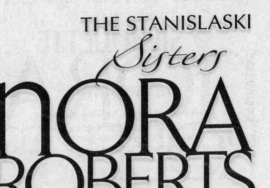

MARIE FERRARELLA
BEVERLY BARTON
LINDSAY McKENNA
DANGEROUS TO LOVE
3 SENSATIONAL, SEXY ROMANCES!
On sale 21st June 2002
0702/81/SH32

Welcome back to the Fortune dynasty

The drama and mystery of Fortune's
Children continues with a new
12-part book continuity series.

Fortune's Children: THE GROOMS
and
Fortune's Children: THE LOST HEIRS

The drama, glamour and mystery
begins with Fortune's Grooms,
five strong, sexy men surrounded
by intrigue, but destined for love
and marriage!

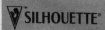

Fortune's Children
THE GROOMS

March	Bride of Fortune
April	Mail-Order Cinderella Fortune's Secret Child
May	Husband-or-Enemy Groom of Fortune

Fortune's Children
THE LOST HEIRS

June	A Most Desirable MD The Pregnant Heiress
July	Baby of Fortune Fortune's Secret Daughter
August	Her Boss's Baby Did You Say Twins?!
December	Special Christmas Anthology Gift of Fortune

SILHOUETTE® DESIRE™

is proud to present

Maureen Child's

BACHELOR BATTALION

Defending their country is their duty;
love and marriage are their rewards!

PRINCE CHARMING IN DRESS BLUES
(*in* Special Delivery)

HIS BABY!
(*in* Secret Child)

LAST VIRGIN IN CALIFORNIA
(*in* Up Close and Passionate)

0502/SH/LC31

FREE
1 BOOK
AND A SURPRISE GIFT!

We would like to take this opportunity to thank you for reading this Silhouette® book by offering you the chance to take another specially selected title from the Desire™ series absolutely FREE! We're also making this offer to introduce you to the benefits of the Reader Service™ —

- ★ FREE home delivery
- ★ FREE monthly Newsletter
- ★ FREE gifts and competitions
- ★ Exclusive Reader Service discount
- ★ Books available before they're in the shops

Accepting this FREE book and gift places you under no obligation to buy; you may cancel at any time, even after receiving your free shipment. Simply complete your details below and return the entire page to the address below. **You don't even need a stamp!**

YES! Please send me 1 free Desire book and a surprise gift. I understand that unless you hear from me, I will receive 2 superb new titles every month for just £4.99 each, postage and packing free. I am under no obligation to purchase any books and may cancel my subscription at any time. The free book and gift will be mine to keep in any case.

D2ZEC

Ms/Mrs/Miss/Mr ....Initials..........................
BLOCK CAPITALS PLEASE

Surname...

Address...

....

....Postcode ....

Send this whole page to:
UK: FREEPOST CN81, Croydon, CR9 3WZ
EIRE: PO Box 4546, Kilcock, County Kildare (stamp required)